CW01429538

Circled By Thousands

by J Lacey Brooke

RCH (1956-2006)

AVE ATQUE VALE

For Margaret + Charles
with love

1

Acknowledgements:

I owe several debts of thanks for this, my second novel. To Susannah Evans, for expert advice in matters pathological and toxicological; to Moira Macfarlane, who advised on matters concerning Italian bureaucracy; to Frazer Pearce for some invaluable insider information on the world of film-making; to Ciaran Logan who suggested Mr Partridge's London location; to violinist Liz Graham for putting me wise about Julian Blyth's professional injury; and to Vanessa Hall-Smith, Michael Coates, Annie Meredith Peacock, Gabrielle Blond and Georgia de Chamberet at Bookblast for reading the first chapters which such enthusiasm.

I am also indebted to the inhabitants, indigenous and otherwise, of Ortigia, Sicily, the place which inspired this new adventure. The real adventure was undertaken with my beautiful Rupert, to whose memory this novel is dedicated.

Any resemblance to locations, organizations and persons living or dead is probably entirely deliberate...

CIRCLED BY THE SANDS, by J Lacey Brooke

PART ONE: POISONED CHALICE

i: Anonymity

"Do you know who sent these?" Veronica asked, shivering slightly on the doorstep in her dressing-gown and clogs, taking the young woman's clip-board.

"Nope – sorry, love. Just this order for this address. Dearborn. Number 42A, Maxwell Road. S'right, innit?"

"Yes…thank you…" She scrawled an illegible signature.

"Spect it says in the little card inside."

"Oh – of course… Where?"

"Here – little flap tucked inside the wrapping. Here we are!"

"Oh, yes. Oh! No name. How strange…Er, thank you," she said again, frowning.

"P'raps an anonymous admirer, eh? Lucky you!" The girl – a female version of the Artful Dodger, a freckled snub-nosed face under a leather cap – winked.

"Yes…they're lovely…very…"

It was a spring arrangement of white freesias, yellow jonquils and little scrolled purple irises amid the inevitable florists' ferns, and she carried their powerful scent indoors, cut away the cellophane and placed them on top of her desk, where they joined various cards of congratulation, all duly signed and accounted for. Lovely, indeed. She would have to get used to her house smelling like a florist's. But who…? She examined the card again. Just 'Well Done!' in a shop-girl hand.

Todd? No, not possibly Todd. A miserable year, a dwindling hope of some word, some sign, that his extraordinarily sudden cancelling of their beginnings of a life together was a mistake, a regret, something he wanted to undo… Now that she knew that Todd was dead, this half-expectation crazily persisted. The tilt of a head on the tube, a profile in shadow in a queue, black-clad shoulders on an escalator… and her heart would skip a beat, her hand clutch the rail, her mouth go dry. Madness, of course, but they say this sort of madness is 'normal', whatever that really means. Her emotions not so much see-sawed as cart-wheeled. Bitter anger with him, for such an abrupt ending of something that had seemed to promise such joy; frustration, for so many questions that could now only remain forever unanswered; anger with herself, for allowing herself to *believe*. The shaking self-doubt, that she could have been so completely mistaken, that her deepest instincts were *wrong*; and simple unalloyed grief – she missed him still, passionately – and, of course, one could not ignore the *hurt*… These things went round and round in an acrid fiery circle in her brain, polluting her sleep, her few moments of forgetful tranquillity. For it was only by very deliberate intention that she could will herself not to think about it, to concentrate on something else. The cart-wheel required vigilance. The only remedy for misery, as she had long discovered, was work. She had concentrated on the proofs of her book solidly through February and March. Now, she did not even have that.

For the book was out, launched, the first encouraging comments beginning to appear in the Sundays and the periodicals – more encouraging, indeed, than she had dared to hope. Hence the cards of enthusiastic congratulation – all of them, Veronica thought wryly, prompted because the work had come as a bit of a surprise in the circumstances. She should have been at least a little satisfied – even proud of herself – but all she felt was taunted by the accolades, taunted by the fear that she could not repeat this success, and – bathetically – at a loss for something to do. 'The next book, of course,' Lydia had said. But the thought almost terrified her.

Weird about these flowers. Anonymous gifts – indeed anonymous anything – rattled her. She was fifty-three, for God's sake – well past the age when such things were exciting, in the girlish way that Valentines might be exciting if one is say, twenty-three, and surrounded by any number of possible admirers – and besides, in her time she had been the recipient of a great many unpleasant unsigned things in the post. Whoever had sent this doubtless well-intentioned gift in this way had seriously misjudged her reaction. But who? Not, presumably, anyone who wished her anything but well. And someone who knew about the book, obviously. Of course. Idiot! The florists' shop would have credit card details, presumably. Or be able to route her to the Interflora office that had taken the order. That was the sensible thing to do. Deal with it. Erase the question-mark She snatched up the florists' card and glared at the pretty blooms as she lifted the telephone.

She promptly put it down again as the ring-tone sounded on her mobile.

Her agent's assistant, Lydia Medley. "Hi, Lydia…"

"Veronica, hi! Sorry if I'm interrupting anything. Are you at home?" Lydia had a bright and businesslike voice. It was no surprise that she was working on a Saturday.

"Yup – no, not busy especially. Tell me…"

"Sorry! I'd have emailed, but I wanted to run something by you straight away, do you mind? Okay, well, first, I'm *really* sorry about the short notice, but would you be available to do an interview for the *Observer* on Monday or Tuesday latest? Marina Lavender's just been in touch and wants to know this morning…"

"Oh God…" Veronica felt her spirits sink. "What do you advise?"

"Well, it's got to be early next week, if it's going to get into the following Sunday's edit…and I really think you should do it. Marina's very nice…and she'd come to your house, provided you agree…in the afternoon, maybe, or early evening – she can be flexible. Or you could meet in a café or a pub or something, whatever suits. But I really need to let her know…"

6

"Okay…Yes, okay, Lydia. Oh God, I so hate interviews! The ones after *Cry* were ghastly. Sorry. My problem. Okay, you can tell her yes. Here, I suppose. The Fulham flat. Sure, give her my number. Monday evening…or say Tuesday before lunch? Yup, okay…Sorry. I really will try and be a bit enthusiastic and not – um – let the side down, all that." Veronica sighed. "I'll try and be a bit tidy, too…"

"Don't worry, Veronica. I'm sure it will all be just fine. There won't be anything other than the stock photos, no 'at home' pics. Give her a glass of wine, talk about your research methods, all that. And introduce her to gorgeous Greymalkin. She's a cat-lover, by all accounts…"

"Sure…Look, I don't want to talk about *Cry* much…or at all. Lydia, I – I'd be grateful if you'd warn her in advance. I'm so hoping….well, that *Henry Cuffe* has released me from all that…a bit…"

"Yes, okay, no problem. I'll tell her. Listen… Veronica…?" For the first time in the conversation, Lydia sounded hesitant. Even embarrassed. "Um… there's something else as well…"

"Oh?"

"Yes…look, this might be a bit inconvenient, but could you possibly come in and see Marcus early Monday morning? He needs to talk to you…if you're not too busy, of course. I gather it's a bit urgent…"

"Oh…Okay. What's up?"

"I think Marcus wants to tell you himself, the details, you know…I mean I don't know for certain exactly what the deal is, but…." Lydia was blathering. Bad sign.

"Lydia…what deal?"

"Something to do with a new publishing contract…all a bit complicated, I gather…" Lydia had pulled herself together. "Too complicated for the phone, you know…papers to look at, et cetera, and he can explain far better than me…"

"Oh, okay. Well, I can come in on Monday if you like. Perhaps we'd better make Marina Lavender's thing on Tuesday, then…"

When Lydia rang off, however, Veronica was left with a distinct impression that there was something she was not being told. This, together with the prospect of the Lavender interview, left her feeling jumpy and uncomfortable for the rest of the weekend. As for the anonymous flowers, it turned out that they had been paid for in cash at a West End branch of Interflora by someone nobody could recall.

"Oh no, Marcus, *no!*"

"All I'm asking is that you just consider it…mull it over, you know. I could negotiate a very decent deal."
Marcus Frayle, mid-forties, good-looking in an untroubling and unremarkable way, and possessed of one of those flat, unaccentuated voices that seldom either rose or fell, rarely bothered with charm. He left that to Lydia, but Lydia was out,

lunching a client. Marcus's forte was acumen, pure and simple. That and the ability to face out publishers and up the ante on the table with a dogged unblenching quality that had earned him a considerable reputation. Great man to have one's side. He was unswayed by titles, unswayed by femininity, and unswayed by literature, as such, since he could never consider a book without also considering markets and trends. Now he looked at the Honourable Veronica Dearborn dispassionately and mentally rolled up his sleeves.

"I told you ages ago I'd never in a million years consider a film. Now it seems you've simply gone behind my back. That was frankly dirty, Marcus."

"Not at all. In fact Flix contacted us. Through your publisher, as a matter of fact, but it amounts to the same thing." This was true. On the other hand, as far as Frayle was concerned, Veronica's only asset was that highly bankable autobiography that had caused such a stir a couple of years ago. The fact that she had followed it with this slender history book concerning government machinations in the court of Queen Elizabeth I – which was admittedly receiving some not unfavourable reviews in the highbrow press – was a matter of little interest to him, a diversion in course that he had counselled against. The publisher had been keen to take it – at *her* prompting, blast her, and despite his best advice to follow *To Big To Cry* through with some gritty fiction – but she had been unmoveable, the stubborn bint, and had refused. He represented her; and so he had, reluctantly, backed her. The name alone would carry the sales, and it kept her in the public eye…and he had been happy to leave dealing with her to Lydia, who 'understood' her, apparently. This Flix offer or something like it had been bound to happen sooner or later without his overt prompting. He was damned if he would simply let it go, just because she had come over queasy. It seemed he could not appeal to her pocket, damn it, but he could apply his own version of persuasion.

"The thing is, it would only need to be *based* on your book. Different title, all the characters significantly altered…and of course anonymous, from your point of view, I mean. Simply the storyline, the aristo junkie in prison and all the childhood flashbacks, the 70s London scene. Once they owned the rights, they could give it any twist they cared to…"

"I don't understand. They want to buy *my* book to make into a film…that's what you've just said. How can they alter it?"

"It doesn't work like that exactly. Look…they want to buy the *rights* to your book to make a film. It's not even that, precisely. They'd be buying an option for a year, while they raise the backing. It's a gamble for them, if you like. If they don't get the backing they forfeit the rights and somebody else can put in a bid. You would always have control over the book, *qua* book. That belongs to you."

"Oh…"

10

"But once they buy the film rights… *if* – all right, yes, of course, *if* … It's up to you. But they would then own them outright. To make a film. After that, they could change anything they like."

"Or not."

"Say again?" Her rather fierce tawny-green eyes interrogated him across the table. She had guts, this female, but he rather hated her all the same. Who was she to get picky?

"Or not. It's the Dearborn name that made it, for better or worse. I'd have thought the chief selling point of a film would be just that. And they could change everybody's names, but everyone would *know*…it would be completely pointless otherwise, surely. Besides, so many people have read it."

"Well, yes…precisely, Veronica." Damn it all – didn't she *realise*? "We need to – to follow it through, therefore…"

"No we *don't*. *I* don't. I'm sorry, Marcus. I know how much you want me to agree and sign it over, but I'm really not going to. Please, just accept that. I've exposed my family enough."

Frayle shuffled some papers on his desk. "Don't you think," he said, not looking up, "that it's a little late for – well – finer feelings, if I can put it like that? Anyone can pick it up and read it, as you've just pointed out. And it's not as if…I mean, your mother. It can't – well – actually hurt her now, can it?"

"I'll thank you to leave my mother out of this, Marcus. I've said no. That's all there is to it. Please just stop."

11

Frayle realised he was getting nowhere. He tried a new tack. "Veronica. Listen. I can negotiate a deal whereby we not only sell the film rights, but where you would continue to receive a small percentage. This isn't the norm, I may say – when rights are sold, they're sold. But if – and at this stage I can only say *if* – I could negotiate a contract whereby instead of a percentage *per se* you retained some control over the content – again, this would be highly unusual, but Flix is a young and flexible company. I think they'd agree to anything you suggest, within reason." He actually smiled, using facial muscles unaccustomed to the effort. "We could even discuss your being taken onto the staff of the film. Script editor. Co-writer, if you like. That way you could take a pre-agreed share of the profits. They'd probably be delighted. I could get you an answer to that one right away, if you want." His hand hovered above the desk telephone.

"No, Marcus."

"It would be worthwhile…"

"You mean lucrative."

"Well, of course." Blast her. She could afford 'finer feelings'. "Why ever else are we in the game? Sorry, joke. But I really mean I think it might be – er – prudent – for you, I mean, to consider this offer very seriously. As your agent this is what I strongly advise…" He examined his unattractively bitten nails. "You see – or perhaps you don't. The story itself is in the public domain anyway. It's not your brainchild, as such. It isn't fiction. The words in your book are yours, but most of the story is newspaper reportage. Come on, you're an intelligent woman, Veronica." He smiled again.

"Yes. You're saying I can't stop them whatever I say. Oh, God..." Veronica was feeling slightly sick.

"*No*, Veronica! I'm saying that if you agree to a deal now, you personally could retain control over the content. If you refuse, then – theoretically – anyone, any film company at all – could look at it as a commercial venture, take a notorious story from the public press and do all the things you don't want to happen, and they'd be within the law if they did..."

"So why doesn't this film outfit just go ahead without my permission? Publish and be damned, as the man said!" She heard her voice rising and made herself take a breath. "If that's truly the way it is. I'll check with my lawyer, but the answer is still no. I can never put my name to this. I'm sorry."

"Veronica, I think I really do know how you feel. By all means consult your lawyer. I advise it in fact. But I think you'll find any lawyer will tell you the same thing." Frayle's reptilian smile remained, and he became what passed for silky. "Veronica, if you agree, you can keep control. If you don't, well..."

"Why does that sound like a threat?"

"A threat?" Frayle pretended to be stung. "Veronica. I am on *your* side. *Of course* you want to know exactly what you'd be agreeing to, signing. See your lawyer, and then have him look over the contract. I just want you to sleep on this one."

"I've slept. And had nightmares," she added under her breath. "Please," she said. "Marcus. I've explained it all to Lydia. I really don't see why I have to go through it all again. It's not fair to keep hammering at me like this. No *means* no." She rose, and Frayle decided that there was no point in continuing. He gave up.

"Well, I'm glad you don't have to worry about the next gas-bill, love, that's all," he said, at which point Veronica Dearborn marched out of his office without another word.

When his junior colleague returned from her lunch, he was in a cold, tight-lipped temper, impervious to Lydia's attempts at soothing.

"She could just decide to leave us, Marcus," Lydia said.

"Let her!" He was more obviously put out than Lydia had ever seen him in three years. "I hope Marina Lavender makes mincemeat of the stupid stubborn cow," he said. "In fact – let's get hold of her shall we?" He was dialling before Lydia could answer.

"Anything you say, Marcus," said Lydia with a sigh. It would be she who would have to pour oil on troubled waters, as usual.

Friday, and Marcus Frayle was working late. Lydia had long since gone home where – presumably – someone awaited her. He knew next to nothing about Lydia's private life. His own

14

private life might as well not exist. Evening in London. Early afternoon in New York. He was expecting the call.

"Frayle." The deadpan voice into the receiver.

"Marcus? Russell Roper. How's the boy? How's the *lady*?" An urbane voice, British, with transatlantic overtones. Matthew Lucodin's sidekick and legal henchman.

"The same. Obstinate cow. I'm working on it. You'll have to wait."

"Well? Do we have a deal or don't we?"

"Not yet." Frayle had decided not to hedge. No point. He heard a mild curse.

"But you're still applying the pressure, huh?"

"As much as I can. She says she won't play, Roper. She doesn't want to do it. And she doesn't need the cash." Despite Frayle's own interests in the matter, he rather enjoyed stymieing Lucodin, the neurotic pony-tailed prick. He was supposed to be the powerhouse. Let *him* do some persuading for a change. "I can't think of another inducement. Can you?"

Another curse. "You told her she could have a say?"

"I told her. But I'm telling you, she's not interested. I wouldn't hold out much hope."

"You know we would be happy for her to write the screenplay herself...at least with some editorial safeguards...maybe with a 'co'. You need to present that idea to her as a positive way of keeping control of her own work...Oh...I see. You have."

15

"*Yes.* You're not listening, Roper. She's adamant. Doesn't want to play. End of."

"Hell! Luco'll go apeshit…"

"Well that's Lucodin's problem," said Marcus Frayle. "And yours, presumably."

"You don't understand, Marcus…If Flix can't produce something that will pay off its last backers, it's down the tubes time. I'm serious. And this affects you…as I understand."

Marcus Frayle grunted. He had small but significant shares in Lucodin Publicity, an independent Anglo-American PR company that was having a brush with the recession. Flix was a subsidiary, and its last effort had been an elegant, expensive box-office flop.

"Win some, lose some. Short of pulling her teeth out on a rack, what do you suggest?"

"I was hoping – Luco was hoping – that you could *suggest* something, Marcus. You know the lady. She can't be that rich."

"Perhaps it's not merely money. It isn't for everyone."

"Shit."

Marcus Frayle was not one of the world's deep thinkers, but it was occurring to him that someone in Veronica Dearborn's position – that is, someone comfortably set up and prepared to live modestly without, say, a yachts-and-diamonds lifestyle – was someone in a very strong position indeed. Veronica could afford to say 'no', and to mean it. Pity she wasn't still addicted.

That would have got her... Of course it pained him deeply that his investment would suffer – he stood to lose it altogether if Lucodin actually went under – but Roper's implication that he was being personally obstructive rankled. Roper, Frayle decided, was either thick or being disingenuous.

"All I can suggest, *Russell*, is that the usual way round these things is you write a treatment yourselves, you make a movie from the available public material and you deal with the lawsuits afterwards. If any. Disguise it a bit, change the names, don't lift word for word, claim ignorance, coincidence, and do a lot of word-of-mouth. Better still, get a name to write it, give him a bare-bones scenario and let him worry about plagiarism. If she sues, she'll be on a sticky wicket anyway, and the notoriety alone will ensure the sales. Don't know why I have to tell you your business – you're the lawyer. And you didn't hear me suggest anything of the kind. She's my client..."

"It's not quite as simple as that, Marcus, truly."

"Balls," said Frayle unpleasantly. "Most of it's in the public domain anyway as you perfectly know. And if I've got her number, she probably won't sue...More bad publicity, the way she'd see it, petrol on the fire."

"What about the family? There's His Nibs...and that brother-in-law in the Shadow Cabinet."

"Ditto...I think they'd do anything to avoid the circus. You've worked this out. What's the real problem?"

A deep sigh on the line. "The insurers, who wouldn't accept liability for claims of anyone portrayed, including her. They read contracts six times over, Marcus. And if the insurance isn't there, then no backers. No one in their right mind would finance a film on such a risk. That's the obstacle. If she or anyone else wins even half the right to halt filming, a fractional risk of that, even – well, that doesn't bear thinking about. Time's money in film-making. You know that. And infringement of copyright's a big crime both sides of the Atlantic, and so is defamation. It's not straightforward, Marcus. And you don't have to tell me my business. Thank you."

Frayle grunted. It passed for an apology.

"Look, Marcus, I know you've done – are doing – what you can. I'm thinking perhaps I should try and see her myself. Go through the options point by point. Make her see this really is the best way to go forward..."

"An offer she can't refuse? Good luck to you. She's no pushover. When are you next over?"

"I'm here already. I'm in the Soho office. Got in yesterday..."

"Oh!" For the first time, Frayle felt wrong-footed. For some reason, it was disquieting to discover that his conversation was relayed across a mere mile or so, instead of thousands of miles to a Manhattan office. "Good luck," he said again, sourly. "Keep me posted."

18

"Matt...please. Just listen! *He* might be bullshitting, but I'm not, okay? Actually, I don't think he is either..." This time the call was relayed across many thousands of miles, and there was an unpleasant echo in Roper's ear. "What's that? Okay...Fine. I'll set it up. But it's previous, Matt. We need time....yeah, I know. I know. Listen, we *won't* lose Potter. He's in. His wife's having a baby in London. He wants to work in the UK...what was that?"

Lucodin's heavy sigh shivered down the wire. "I said, I've spoken to that slimeball Feltz at Cinéast. They want it for themsel-elves. And we'll lose Logan-an if we can't have Potter-otter! Shit, this *fucking* line-ine!"

"It's appalling. Try Skype next time. Okay, week after next. Yeah, sure, I'll set up a meet..." He scribbled a rapid note. "Potter, Logan, and her ladyship. Got that! On the case, Matt."

"Just get *her* in-in!

But the Hon. Veronica Dearborn was out. "Hello," said a recorded voice, contralto, patrician, pleasantly husky, but businesslike, not remotely sexy. "I can't speak to you at the moment. Please leave a message after the tone." Russell Roper left a message and his number with dwindling hope. It was his fourth attempt, and he gave up for the weekend.

ii. Versatility

Sixteen months, sixteen days, and about nine dragging hours. Sundays were the worst. She only occasionally reached out in her semi-sleep. She had long since stopped expecting him by her side. Her lonely bed was strewn with newsprint, books, crosswords and pens as in pre-Todd days. The lonely old routine. Birdsong in the courtyard. A London spring. Tranquillity. Then, from above, came a dull thudding of bass speakers. Blast Rory! Still in pyjamas and propped up in bed with a cup of strong coffee, a cigarette, a heap of newsprint and her large and amiable grey tom-cat purring on her toes, Veronica tried to read the front pages, but – and feeling slightly sick – she opened the Arts section of the *Observer* instead.

If 'write about what you know' is the mantra of creative writing courses everywhere, then, according to Veronica Dearborn, she's done it, and she doesn't wish to do it again. One can see why. 'It' of course, is Too Big To Cry: *the story of her wild, unhappy, overweight drug and drink-fuelled youth culminating in a prison sentence in her mid-thirties. Lest we forget: it was a story that made headlines upon headlines, first because of its appeal to the gossip gobblers, avid for the opportunity to peer under the lid at the peerage in all its unloveliness. Add the tragic death of a young viscount, a sobbing fiancée (Dearborn's half-sister, the twenty-four year old*

20

Lucinda Callington, now the ultra-respectable wife of the Rt Hon

Peter Penrose) and a court-case in which one notorious family

battled another grimly under its Ascot hats, and a still young and

frightened woman convicted and sent down for dealing death,

and inevitably you have a best-seller. You don't necessarily have

a writer. When Cry *won the small but prestigious Victor Punter*

prize for memoir writing, however, Dearborn's undoubted talent

was confirmed, a talent now endorsed by a new book which is

about as different from the first as it could possible be.

Dearborn could have proceeded to write endless turgid

fiction on the same themes, but she resisted. "I'm not

particularly imaginative in that way. I don't think I have it in me

to write proper fiction," she says. "So one does something else.

One goes and finds out. Like the Mongoose, you know? And then

one writes about that..."

"Oh, shit," murmured Veronica.

And she did write about 'that' – that being the life of

Henry Cuffe, the 16th Century Machiavellian secretary and

henchman of the Earl of Essex and sometime spy for Elizabeth's

aide Robert Cecil. The result is a short, well-researched and

scholarly document, written with flair but with remarkably few

concessions to dramatic imagination, certainly; a book in which

she clearly resisted all temptation to pad out the gaps in

available source material with fictional dialogue and

motivations. Because of this rigorous sticking to facts, Henry

Cuffe, a Life *is hardly pitched at the sensation market, although*

21

it has to be said that Cuffe lived on a knife edge for most of his career – and Dearborn captures the atmosphere of political favour, disfavour and espionage in the court of Elizabeth with admirable immediacy. The book has received some well-deserved attention from the scholarly fraternity, a notably closed world, hard to penetrate without published articles and a full flush of university degrees. (Dearborn was sent down from Cambridge in the 80s, and can only boast a "bad A-Level in Eng.Lit." from Duddingdale, the private school in Sussex from which she narrowly escaped being ejected.) Undoubtedly, the book deserves praise: it is well-written, informative and – despite its lack of overt drama – full of a well-imagined flavour of 'low instincts in high places', to quote Aelred Swanson in the London Review.

Even so, it is inevitable to conjecture that Dearborn's notoriety has propelled this inevitably slender work into the public view. "I can't deny that, obviously," she says. "If people see my name on the jacket and expect something very different, then good luck to them. At least some people seem to have taken it on its own merits." Does she see herself now as a scholar, an historian? "No," she replies, after a pause. "Not really at all. Scholar is far too big a word. It's more like being a detective...a detective in a library...I enjoyed doing 'Henry', but I am aware of my limitations. Mostly, Henry Cuffe had always fascinated me. He was an oddball. I did some research. One thing led to another. It wasn't anything particularly special." Yet it seems that Dearborn's undoubted talent, as a writer and as an historian, is a thing as yet untapped. Another piece of Elizabethan research in the offing?

Now, insistent drum-rhythms impinged as Veronica paused, accompanied by loud singing and feminine giggles. Damn and blast Rory! She stumped out of bed and shut the sash window which reduced the noise to a dull thump. There was a whole empty storey between her and the racket. She had imagined he would not disturb her. She would have to speak to him. As if I haven't had enough of confrontations lately, she thought angrily.

Dearborn is cagey about her next project, however. There have been suggestions that she is researching Sir Hugh Dearborn, her father's namesake and a direct ancestor of hers, a martyr of the Counter-Reformation cause. But she is hesitant. "He's an interesting subject. It's an interesting story...a rather touching one...he hid a recusant friend out of loyalty rather than idealism, and he was executed for treason..." So back to the family, then, I suggest. "Well, I suppose. At a four hundred year remove. That's if I do it. It's a big project. Huge. Probably beyond my scope. I haven't made up my mind..." She can of course pick and choose now.

I have been warned in advance that she will not welcome questions about Too Big To Cry, *but now there are serious rumours of a film. Any truth in the rumour? "Over my dead body," she responds, cheerfully enough, not quite answering my*

*question. I have clearly touched a nerve. Does she regret having
written it? The fall-out was fairly devastating, and it is
understood that she has been ostracised by her family ever since.
I get the impression of an intensely private person who has
probably suffered from her own self-exposure.*

"Bugger," Veronica murmured. "Bugger, bugger…" .

*But Dearborn is prepared for this one. "How can I
regret it? I did it quite deliberately. I take full responsibility. But
it's over. Done. A film based on* Cry *would be over-kill." And
identify her with it forever? Perhaps. "It would just be utterly
beside the point, redundant," she says firmly. She describes
Henry as a 'malcontent'. Does this in some way describe her?
"Not really…I've been pretty pissed off – read the book, if you
see what I mean – but malcontented in the Henry Cuffe sense,
no. In his world, one had to work unseen, and all the plaudits
went to the patron. That isn't the case for me, obviously…"*

*Dearborn pours glasses of good white wine, offers cheese
nibbles, smokes Lambert & Butler cheapies and declines my
offer of a Marlboro. We joke about smoking, fellow travellers.
Very tall and far more slender and elegant than her 'Too Big'
reputation rendered her, we briefly talk 'clothes', a subject
apparently close to Dearborn's heart: "I can't bear to be
uncomfortable. I like Wall, Sahara, Nicole Fahri…Mostly I just
go for Marks & Sparks…Lands' End…Nothing special…Labels
are just, well, labels, aren't they? I just go for things in fabrics I
like and designers who know how to dress larger women…I*

24

never was easy to dress, you know." She has a rather infectious,
low-pitched chuckle.

This is a woman who has re-invented herself very
thoroughly, I suggest. "No," *she replies.* "I've merely moved
on..." Into? "Into writing. I've moved on into writing. Writing is
what I do. Now. One needs to find a metier, hone one's talents
and stick to a routine. It's so much more 'do' than 'am'..."

"Oh, Christ...did I really say that...?"

I have had plenty of warning that she can scathe for
England. Yet this interview is the opposite of rebarbative. She is
friendly and mostly relaxed, and seems to parry what might be
unwelcome probing with robust good humour. I admire her cat,
a blue-grey Russian beauty with thick fur she assures me is pure
moggie with pretensions of grandeur: unlike Dearborn, who is
an aristocrat to her long square fingertips with apparently no
pretensions at all.

Dearborn now is the antithesis of an ex-wild-child, and
there is no vestige of the plump, ungainly little girl whose
shallow, chic, socialite mother told her that she was 'too big to
cry' when she was bullied, Mr Murdstone-fashion, by a hated
step-father. A poised, bespectacled woman of fifty-odd with
greying sandy hair piled into a clip and dressed in dark orange
which suits her colouring, she has acquired a vaguely bohemian,
college-professor cool, belied by the odd betrayal of nerves .
Very hard now to imagine her overweight dyed-black gothic

incarnation, injecting her tied-up arm with heroin; very hard to imagine her in prison uniform...

So back to books. Is she daunted by the challenge of this late-blossoming career? She hesitates before answering: "Only a bit...I'm not even sure it really is a career..." She must be very pleased with Henry Cuffe's *success. "Chuffed to bits," she agrees disarmingly. "Frankly, I think I threw myself to the lions... Oh, there were a lot of raised eyebrows, you know, people waiting to see if the dirt-dishing deb could hack it..." Nerve-wracking? "Of course. But one gets to a point when it really doesn't matter. I did my best. I enjoyed it. I'm glad that it's not been a total turkey, if you like..."*

I have a feeling that Dearborn's next book might be worth waiting for, whatever it is. Really no fiction? Ever? "I played with short stories when I was young – and they all featured a girl very like me, or at least some alter-ego I could imbue with my thoughts, my take on the world. That's the sort of fiction I dread producing, and rather hate reading. The better stuff takes real invention, and I'm not inventive enough."

Dearborn's basement flat in Fulham is full of books, and she tells me she turns to Bleak House *or* Jane Austen *if ever she gets the flu. A handsome 18th C walnut writing desk – on which stand a number of cards and a large bouquet of spring flowers, which I guess rightly are messages of congratulation following the recent launch – shows every evidence of work recently paused, the lap-top screen-saver swirling on hold, a wodge of papers, pens, a notebook, an unemptied ashtray. The desk chair looks recently sat in, and I have the impression that as soon as I leave, she will resume her usual place. Dearborn is difficult to pin down, intensely protective of her privacy, perhaps understandably, given that she turned her youth literally into an open book. She will not be drawn into any personal revelations.*

That took some doing, damn her, thought Veronica. Thump, thump, thump. Fucking shut *up*, Rory!

There is something inescapably cheering about a writing talent emerging in later life. "Don't hold your breath." She smiles ironically, and perhaps a fraction less amiably, but over a second glass of wine, she shows me her courtyard, a carefully tended oasis of greenery, Italian terracotta, promising roses, wisteria, and something she tells me is a species of climbing hydrangea. There is a wrought-iron table and chairs beneath a pergola. Even on a coldish day in early April, it looks inviting. She began it for fun when she took the house on ten years ago, she says. "And then it sort of grew..."

Dearborn has undoubtedly 'sort of grown', and demonstrated in just two books written in middle age an extraordinary versatility, and I for one am holding my breath, just a little.

Veronica, holding her breath no longer, and damned if she was going to actually go up there in her dressing-gown, rang Rory's mobile. There was no answer, and the noise persisted. PLS CLD U CAN THE NOISE??? VX she texted.

27

*

Veronica Dearborn sat drinking coffee in an Italian coffee house in Soho with Lydia Medley, a young woman who gleamed with health and an energy that Veronica would have envied had it not made her feel more tired and depressed than ever.

"I know, I know…you thought I came across as negative. It was a bit wince-making. I felt sort of on the ropes…"

"No…not *negative*…not at all. And she was positive – it's a great piece! I mean, she obviously *liked* you, found you a sympathetic subject…"

"I don't think she did. She thought I was being obstinately unforthcoming. Said so, in so many words. But she would keep pushing and prompting about making a bloody film of *Cry* – more than got into print, thank God. I had to tell her I'd make a public denial, and she obviously took the hint. She's pretty thick-skinned, isn't she?"

"She's notorious for that. Forget it. I thought it was – well, fine. More than fine, really. Everything fairly vague, but intriguing…and a sympathetic portrait of you, nice things about *Henry*, nice, up-beat finish. It's a great bit of publicity. Look at it like that."

"I'll try. I was still feeling on the defensive after seeing Marcus. I suppose he's still furious…"

"Of course, but only because he can't bear to be turned down. Big male ego, all that, and he's feeling the recession a bit, like we all are. This movie deal would have been quite a *coup*."

28

"Hmph. Making me feel guilty isn't going to work either, Lydia."

"Sorry. I truly don't want to be pushy. Look, Veronica – I know why you've got an issue with this, but this would be a rather fantastic project, if you *were* to agree…"

Veronica rather detested the fashion for the word 'issue' to mean 'objection'. Annoyed, she said: "Well I won't, ever, so please – as a favour – just both of you back off. Oh God, sorry, but I do so hate all this… I should never have written the fucking thing. Marina Lavender wanted me to admit that, and I didn't, but it's true." This sounded incredibly lame. She *had* written it and with a sort of furious glee. At the time, she had been concerned mostly with revenge and had enjoyed it; and if it had been simply a cathartic exercise, a sort of spiritual puking out of all the poison, it would have remained unpublished and in her own possession. Unfortunately, perhaps, Veronica could write, and the combination of a decent talent for prose and a notorious *cause célèbre* had sealed its fate: Marcus Frayle had leapt at it, and it had been a stunning success.

"So, now! Let's talk about what next." Lydia was one of those people, Veronica decided, whose cheerful, up-beat way of looking at the world was actually natural. One could tell. This was a girl who probably took baths with scented candles before bed after cooking a nutritious supper for herself or someone special, chatted with a friend on the telephone, joked with her lover at breakfast time, and whizzed off to her office in a good

29

mood, perhaps took in the gym on her way home… "Have some more coffee…and what about one of those fruit tarts – they look so-o tempting! Or perhaps you'd like a brandy in the coffee? *Caffè corretto*?"

"I truly don't know, Lydia…I mean what next. Yes, a brandy would be nice. Better skip the bun. Trying to keep the weight down. I'm a bit stuck…"

"Well," said Lydia adroitly, "I *really* like your Sir Hugh idea. More history, with the angle that he was one of your ancestors. It would make a great sequel, too – I mean to *Henry Cuffe*. If I've got my dates right, your old Sir Hugh might have known Henry Cuffe personally."

"Cuffe probably helped to have him murdered, you mean! Oh, God. I liked the idea too, up to a point. But such a hellish amount of research if it's going to amount to something original. There's masses of stuff on recusant families already anyway – I mean proper academic stuff. I'm not an academic, Lydia…"

"Maybe not, but you seem to be earning a respectable reputation in the academic fraternity. Look, I know you're not going to like this much, but why don't you write the Hugh Dearborn story *as* a story? That way you wouldn't need to be too careful about all the dates and things."

Veronica sighed under her breath. "A bodice-ripper?"

"No – much more Philippa Gregory, Antonia Fraser even, something like that. It's quite exciting – the family hiding the fugitive, the danger…just, you know, present it dramatically, all the servants who must have known. Being paid to tell, or to shut up. I think it'd be such fun! It's only a suggestion..."

Veronica could almost *see* Lydia treading carefully, hear the words 'obstinate', 'difficult', 'pain in the arse'... "Whose suggestion? Marcus's?"

"No. Mine. But he is concerned with the marketing side of things, obviously. We have to keep you in the public eye with – well, something the public will go for. Something with impact, and something which will follow on from *Henry Cuffe* logically. The right thing could mean a film deal that you'd feel happy with. Or you could simply write a film treatment – go straight for film drama. Look at Kate Masterson's thing on Queen Anne and Sarah Churchill... it was brilliant!"

Veronica shuddered. "That's posh lesbian bodice-ripping, and not even very original...or necessarily at all authentic. Just a sexed-up take on that *Viceroy Sarah* thing from the Thirties. Oh God! Look, I really don't want to embark on fiction, Lydia. I told Marina Lavender that much. Sorry. I know I'm not being very helpful. All this stuff about a film of *Cry*...I honestly just feel rather stupid I didn't see it coming. I don't exactly blame Marcus for being so angry. I must have been rather trying. I know I owe him a lot. Both of you..."

Veronica's bolstered coffee arrived with a strawberry shortcake for Lydia. "You're depressed, Veronica. Look, I think I might have a small tonic for you." Lydia had bright brown

31

eyes that actually smiled. In the hard-nosed world of literary marketing she was a bit of a rarity, Veronica thought.

"A tonic?"

"Yes. A sort of stop-gap while you're mulling ideas over. Ever heard of Flora Forde – with an 'e'?"

"I don't think so. Why?"

"Almost nobody has, but they're about to. She was a very minor novelist between the wars. She wrote a couple of goodish mystery romances in the Thirties, both about pretty but penniless secretaries getting involved in crimes and then getting rescued by the detective. One of them became a stage play…She's all but disappeared…."

"Eugh! I'm not surprised…"

"Wait…the thing is that Vixen Press is digging out all this old mystery stuff and doing a big reprint, complete with critical introductions by well-known writers. Emphasis on women's stuff, but not exclusively. Marcus and I had a meeting with Penny Crewe of Vixen last week, and we wondered if you'd be interested in taking on Flora. Penny Crewe would be very keen."

"Are you advising me to?"

"Well – I think this would be a shoo-in. You do need to keep in the public eye, Veronica. This wouldn't be much home-work – she only wrote three."

"I thought you just said two."

"No – this is the intriguing bit. She wrote a third that was considered far too lurid and which never got past the first imprint. Then she went off the air. No one really knows anything about her... Fancy having a go? Vixen will send you everything, of course, and we'll do the contract. It might just keep things, you know – ticking over. This can't hurt."

"Okay," said Veronica, resigned. "I suppose not. Okay, Lydia. I'll give it a go. Send me the stuff." She owed Lydia that much. Working with Marcus couldn't be any picnic.

iii. Coincidences

The next day found Veronica in a large branch of Waterstone's, scouring the 'Crime & Mystery' section. As she crouched awkwardly at a bottom shelf, someone touched her shoulder and she rose hastily.

"Why, it *is* Veronica! Darling! Fancy bumping into you!"

"Freddy?" From her private fog, it took Veronica a few moments to recognise her old friend. It had been at least a year. More like two. "Gosh!"

"Don't worry – I've changed my hair." Freddy was greyer, otherwise completely unchanged: tall, slender, dressed with a certain nattiness that was his trademark. "I was only thinking of you the other day...*Henry Cuffe*...so sweet of you, *and* a little deddy in the flyleaf. I was just about to write and thank you. How absolutely amazing!"

"Oh – oh, thanks. I mean, yes it is. How are you, Freddy?"

The aisles were narrow between shelves and islands, and a woman with a small child in a pushchair barged into them without apologising. "We seem to be in the way here. Have you got time for coffee? Or are you too busy, sweetie?"

"No...it would be lovely to have coffee, Freddy. How nice. But can I meet you in about fifteen minutes? There's a coffee place downstairs. I want to order a book if I can't find it…here we are, Follett…Foulds, Furnival…no Forde with an 'e'…"

"I'll stick with you like a limpet. What's all this? Lonely bed-time reading? Whodunnits for the respectably vicarious spinster?"

"Bastard! You haven't changed in the least, Freddy. If you're going to be spiteful, I shan't speak to you for another two years. No, it's work, believe it or not. I'm trying to find something that may be out of print."

"Then the internet's your only man!"

"I've tried Amazon, if that's what you mean," Veronica said.

"Amazon, shmamazon! I'll reveal all. Trust me. Oooh, look! Dorothy Sayers – love her. Fell wildly in love with Peter Wimsey in my errant youth, got horribly jealous of Harriet Thingy…but, see! Here's a Millicent Fox – *Sermons in Stones* – that was good, as I recall. Unbelievably camp…lovely stuff. All about this very sweet piano-tuner who solves the mystery of the missing poor-box at the Cathedral or some such, and finds a murdered curate. The fair Millicent was a distant aunt of mine, did you know? I'm really frightfully well-connected for a pleb…"

But Veronica's mind was on Flora Forde with an 'e', and Freddy followed her to the sales desk. "I'm sorry, it seems to be out of print," said the assistant, after looking up the title on her screen.

"Oh…no point in ordering it, then, I suppose."

"You could certainly place an order, if you'd like to leave your details, madam. We do have an out-of-print service…"

"Okay. Would it be quick?"

"Well, obviously we can't guarantee anything…"

"Come on, Vee. There are ways and means. Trust your Uncle Freddy. Come on, old love. I'll tell you all about it over real blinis in this fabby little Russian place down the road."

"Now these are excellent," said Freddy Partridge, biting into a thickly filled smoked salmon and sour cream pancake. "Almost lunch. I reviewed them last year, and for once I was telling the truth."

Freddy always seemed to live a life of infinite and enviable leisure. He seemed to pluck his weekly column for *The Bystander* out of the air, and if this was something of an illusion, since he was careful with his prose and his word-limit and his editor held him in high regard for this alone, his boast that he made his living from lunching and dining was a literal fact. His personal life, however, seemed to take place at breathtaking speed and be endlessly ramified, and for this reason among others of her own, Veronica and Freddy had lost touch of late.

"Scrummy," agreed Veronica, beginning to relax. "Though this will be lunch for me. Possibly dinner too. I don't know how you do it, Freddy. You ought to have a girth like a gasometer." Freddy was pencil-slim, slightly tanned and

36

inclined, very slightly, to smirk. Veronica was very fond of him. She patted his hand. "How very nice to see you after all this time."

"An utterly delightful coincidence! I was just thinking of you, too, what with seeing your fair face under La Lavender's by-line in the papers at the weekend. I almost rang you. You're never out of the news, Vee, these days. That thing in the *Observer* wasn't too bad, was it? But I can't *bear* that woman, I'm afraid. All silvery-blonde fragility on the surface and *the* most predatory intentions. She tried to *convert* me once. Can you believe that? She made *the* most frightful lunge at me at some literary party and I nearly climbed up the curtains... Darling, don't laugh! It was almost not funny, if you see what I mean. I fear I had to be rather rude."

"Blimey! You're too dishy, that's your problem, Freddy. You don't look nearly queer enough. She was quite civilized to me, really. Perhaps a bit disappointed I wasn't in full gothic get-up or wearing a tiara. I gather she's frightfully chippy underneath all the hob-nobbing. It was okay. We talked about clothes and she liked the cat. I suppose it was all right...but I hated it. I hate interviews anyway. It was all a bit depressing. She kept trying to dragoon me into saying what I'm working on next, and I fobbed her off with the Dearborn ancestor...anything rather than talk about *Cry*...she virtually accused me of hypocrisy....and all that 'versatile' stuff was just another way of saying 'aging overprivileged amateur lacking direction'. I can do subtexts as well as anybody. She's a subtle bitch. I mean that literally."

"Poor love! Eat your blini. So what is the next *oeuvre*? Something to do with Thirties detection, obviously..."

"Oh, that – that's just a sop to stop my agent going spare while I make up my mind about my next project. Vixen Press wants me to do a critical intro for the reprints of the most obscure mystery writer in the world. That's why I need the books as soon as poss. Homework. It won't take long. She only wrote three, and the last was a turkey, by all accounts. Never got past the first imprint. I have to say I'm a bit intrigued about that – it was considered too lurid for post-war sensibilities."

"Ooh-er! But this Vixen Press outfit will send you all the stuff, presumably."

"Yes, but I'd like to get it sooner. I want something I can buy and scribble notes on. You said something about a website...."

"Yep, there's a couple...now, then," said Freddy, whipping out a notebook and a biro. "Here we are...try these. You thought I was just a useless old queen, didn't you?"

"Never, Freddy, never useless. But tell me about you..."

"Nothing to tell. Eat food, write about it. Drink wine, ditto. I have become that wretched 'Epicure' column, but I don't care. I'm off to Italy for a month by the sea in a couple of days. Fish....and fishing..." Freddy winked slyly.

"Nice. Good at this time of year, too. I rather miss Italy, but the house near Siena is let permanently these days. Are you on a commission?"

"Nope. Doing a spot of freelance. You know, 'Mr Partridge is on holiday'. Business, pleasure…and a spot of familial duty on the side. I have to visit the Old Responsibility in Monte Farfalla. Jane usually does it, but she's going to be away. He's this old boy I was telling you about that married Millicent Fox. Most boring man on the planet, but Jane and I, we sort of keep an eye on the old sweetie. Like all the filthy rich, he pleads poverty endlessly, but I do get to visit one of the loveliest places in Italy…"

"Sounds like a fun investment…"

"Tsk! Cynical! But you haven't met Uncle Cadwallader. Blow by blow accounts of his very boring trattoria menus with the alimentary canal journey thrown in…eugh! He was a children's book illustrator in his salad days, and he still paints professionally – not too badly, after a fashion. He also collects silk cravats which I'm *seriously* determined to inherit…"

"Ah…."

"Why don't you join me for a few days? Meet old Cad and talk about Aunt Milly."

"God…I'd love so much to get away somewhere! But if I don't accept this wretched thing from Vixen, I'll be the one-hit wonder the Lavender woman thinks I am. And I'm afraid Millicent Fox is rather straying from the point. I'm not doing her, alas. Alison Truce is, I think. I think the only reason they've given Flora Forde with an 'e' to me is that nobody's ever heard of her."

"That was a big sigh. You do sound depressed, darling. And you're a two-hit wonder, whatever else you are. Let's have a vodka shot, shall we? Send the choccy-coffee down in the right direction…Felix!"

"You ought to come with a health-warning, Freddy."

"That's better. A smile. Now then, dear thing, what's up? I detect writer's block. Ah, here we are. Na Zda Rovy-ay!"

"Well, quite."

"That's 'cheers' in Russian. Courtesy of Sergey. A smattering of the language was one of the nicer things he left me with. And he turned me on to this place. Isn't it utterly darling? Tell me about this nasty blockage. No, don't sip. You have to just toss it down, like this…"

She laughed, threw the drink down her throat, blenched, coughed and told him. "You see, it's not so much a block. It's resisting reality. Very depressing. I've sort of got to get on with something real very soon. And now someone's approached my agents about making *Cry* into a film as you've probably gathered, and I've made myself very unpopular by refusing point blank. I can't really think about anything else."

"Ah. All those dark hints in La Lavender's piece. How ghastly! Poor you. Yes, I do see…"

"Do you? Do you seriously? Everyone thinks I'm being stupid or difficult or both. An ungrateful bitch, my agent says in so many words, especially as it would probably help to fund his retirement. And I know it's hypocritical in a way. But it really is impossible, you must see that…"

"Of course it is! I mean, who on earth would they get to play your late mamma, for a start? They'd need a sort of cross between Helen Mirren in *The Queen* and Sarah Miles. Remember her in *Ryan's Daughter*?"

"Dear Freddy…"

"With a bit of Joan Collins thrown in…"

"Too brash. Mummy was subtle. I've alienated my agency over all this. As it is, I've almost walked out. Marcus Frayle's furious, and everybody else is pussy-footing, hoping I'll change my mind…but I shan't, Freddy. I'm adamant."

"Kristin Scott-Thomas?"

"Closer…be *serious*, Freddy! I saw my lawyer just after I'd told Marcus to go to hell, and it's not at all straightforward. If this film outfit wants to use all the press stuff and go ahead, it can. It would be very difficult to bring a claim against them. It's not fiction, you see. It's a real story which in itself belongs to me about as much as to the average *Sun* reader."

"Dearie me…" Freddy shuddered delicately. "But there must be a reason why this Marcus is being so pushy."

"Yes. Apparently the main problem would be getting finance for the film, because the insurers would probably exclude

41

liability for claims on the part of anyone portrayed. They normally want written permissions. Without that insurance, no one is likely to risk financing it."

"Round to you then, sweetie."

"Yes – but it's by no means guaranteed. Someone might feel it's worth it – sort of venture capital thing. My lawyer says not agreeing was no safeguard at all really, and seems to be at one with Marcus on the script control thing if I do…Oh, God, Freddy…I actually do feel a bit scared."

"Sounds as if you're a bit stuck, duckie…but at least if you don't agree, there's a good chance it won't run, and if it does, well…"

"Well, all I can do is fall out fatally with Lucie and Jamie and claim the moral high ground, which is beginning to feel bloody draughty. James and Lucinda will want my guts *again*, and I had rather hoped…Brrr! Oh dear. Can I have another of these?"

"Certainly, Ma'am. Felix! Still, never mind. Cover your cards and concentrate on this lady writer…big butch person with a moustache who keeps slithering her sylph-like heroines into silk stockings, I bet, this Flora Forde with an 'e'.."

"Don't be so prurient. Was Aunt Milly butch?"

"Not a bit. She was rather feminine, and a complete pet as I recall. Frightfully old by the time I met her, but fun. And a thousand times more intelligent than Uncle Cadwallader, who is a dignified sort of gigolo. She entailed him her literary estate for his lifetime as a fellow artist, but she loved him apparently. I'm an heir…with Jane, of course. Great stuff for us if she's going to get reprinted, unless old Cad spends it all. He ran through all that ITV dramatisation royalty in no time flat."

"Nobody knows anything about Flora," said Veronica, pursuing her own thoughts. "That's the difficulty. There's just her titles on Wikipedia, even less in the *DNB*, and a big hint that 'Flora Forde' is a pen-name, but no identity. Apart from a very slender body of probably not very exciting work, she hardly exists. I'm just going to have to just read the books and produce some padded lit.crit…"

"You should try Jane. She collects all that stuff, or used to. Allingham, Sayers, and all the more obscure ones, all those nice green-and-cream Penguins. Partly because of Aunt Milly, I suppose. Ah, here we are. Djen-koo-yeh, Felix."

The waiter, very young and very blond with small, deep-set ice-blue eyes in a rubicund face, grinned and flushed before darting back to his post behind the counter. The place was evidently popular.

"Is that Russian for 'thank you'?"

"Polish. Felix comes from Warsaw. Perfect little sweetie, isn't he? Old fashioned bottoms up, dear heart. Do you ever hear from Jane?" Jane Hardcastle was Freddy's sister.

"Not for ages. I've – I've rather lost touch with everyone this last year or so, I'm afraid. Is Jane okay? She wrote to me when *Henry Cuffe* came out, and I don't think I ever replied properly. Oh dear..."

"Jane's fine. She's going out to Sydney, supervising grandchild number one. Little Hattie's all grown up and having a baby. That makes me a great-uncle. I can't bear it! I'm just longing for some sun, sea, swimming and sex to remind myself I'm still only a youthful fifty-four..."

"Lovely. I wish I had your energy, Freddy."

He looked at her. "There's something else, isn't there? Come on, Vee. I detect man-trouble, and what I don't know about *that* wouldn't waste a stamp. How's he maltreating you, this undeserving bruiser? Tell Uncle Freddy about the nasty man."

"Ex-man. Late man, actually. He died..."

"Oh, Vee! I'm *so* sorry. God! How?" Freddy Partridge was jolted into a seriousness of which he was perfectly capable when the need arose.

"He committed suicide, or overdosed or something...it was never very clear. Look, Freddy, I don't – can't..." Her eyes had filled suddenly. "Sorry. Shouldn't have had this extra voddy."

"Veronica Dearborn. Don't say another word. The moment I'm back from Italy, you are coming with me to the opera, something lush and disgustingly melodramatic, Verdi perhaps, or Puccini, followed by 'Il Tesoro' in Covent Garden in all your finery and I will choose us a supper that will knock your

44

cotton socks off, and wines that will make you glad to be alive!"
He meant it as sincerely as he meant all his well-intentioned
invitations.

"Thank you, Freddy dear," said Veronica, never quite
believing him. "I say...Freddy, you didn't send me flowers a
week or two back, did you? Someone sent me some anonymous
freesias..."

"How intriguing! No...I wish I'd thought of it, my sweet,
but no..."

iv: Facts & Fictions

Flora Forde's first books duly arrived, and Veronica got down to the task of reading and making notes, at first without much enthusiasm. The Press had promised the third to follow, warning her that this might take a little time, but it was one of Freddy's website recommendations that actually produced two copies with American stamps and a large sum to pay in import duty, and she wrote an email to thank him, telling him that indeed her spinsterish bed was much enriched. 'At least," she added, 'your great-nephew's gurglings and infant cries will be indulged by his grandmother. My nephew – Lucinda's eldest, Rory, still an infant at twenty-one – is living upstairs and creating either a sound-studio or a night-club. Whatever, it's a hell of a sodding din, despite two flights…Give my love to Jane. Busy, busy…'

Flora Forde's first two books were very light and rather juvenile *genre* novels – 'train-reads' once; 'beach-reads' now, doubtless, before the fixation with sex and shopping, of course, and aimed at a more or less exclusively female market… proto chick-lit. But they were real 'mysteries', stylishly written, and the author had addressed the question of plotting and balance with some skill. Veronica had been pleasantly surprised. 'Promising', is how she would have assessed them if she had been Flora's agent: two slender works that ought to have been the beginning of a career...

46

So whatever had happened to Flora Forde, with an 'e'? And who was she? Where had she come from? Write about what you know... While it was almost certain that 'Flora Forde' was a fiction in herself, there was something in the atmosphere of all three novels which smacked of a well-known reality. It is, Veronica thought, only possible to convey in detail and with authority that which is actually known: the very thing that deterred her from embarking on fiction herself. Flora's fictional world was conveyed with a certain *plausibility* which rang true. Therefore, she reasoned, 'Flora Forde', whoever the writer actually was or had been, was someone who had known the routines of office life, servitude and relative poverty very well. 'Flora' might have been anything, anyone – 'she' could even have been a 'he', after all – but whoever it was had seen life from certain perspectives.

Veronica began a draft:

Flora Forde is an enigma, but her heroines might provide a clue of sorts. Marianne in The Mystery of Darling & Co, *and Margaret in* Pearls of Wisdom – *the closest she came to success in a very brief career – are both young women of restricted means who work as secretaries: Marianne for the stern and old-fashioned boss of Darling & Co, a Midlands manufacturer of ladies' underclothing; Margaret for the eccentric Lady Wisdom. Both of these heroines are themselves suspected of the crime – theft in both cases – and there is a considerable sense in both books that class loyalty has fixed the crimes on the lowlier girl.*

47

In Darling & Co, *Marianne is accused of embezzlement actually perpetrated by the senior Darling's son, embroiled in a potentially scandalous mess with a 'fast' young woman. Marianne is eventually exculpated by the almost Dickensian Inspector Carter, who recognizes Marianne as one of his own – it is made clear that Marianne is the daughter of a country blacksmith – and the criminal is brought to book in shame, and Marianne exonerated. Margaret, the factotum-cum-ladies' maid to Lady Wisdom, has access to her ladyship's jewellery, including the marvellous 'Wisdom Pearls', which go missing. Margaret is accused of the theft, in a typical 'country house' mystery in which only the inmates can be implicated. This crime proves an elaborate hoax on the part of Lady Wisdom's beloved nephew, Albert, and his secret fiancée, Eleanor, of whom Lady W disapproves. Their scheme is that Eleanor will 'find' the hidden jewels and thus curry favour with Aunt Wisdom, but the old lady, reluctant to suspect her nephew, at first accuses Margaret. The hoax is later discovered by the piano-tuner, a war-wounded hero called Victor Dane, who falls in love with Margaret when he hears her singing as she dusts the china. The missing pearls are discovered in the belly of the Bechstein, and all is well, and Margaret takes the hand of her piano-tuning saviour...*

Veronica made use of the internet and visited the Library and made notes. Despite herself, she began to take a serious interest.

Both these light comic mysteries caused little stir and were reviewed at first with subdued enthusiasm. Pearls of W, *however, with its elements of farce, lent itself to dramatic treatment and was adapted for the popular stage by Eliah Vayne, who took the credit and doubtless the royalties too; and it was as a stage-play, re-titled simply* Lady Wisdom's Pearls, *that Flora's story enjoyed some brief success both in London and in New York in the mid Thirties. The original book was reprinted and sold rather better, benefitting, one hopes, its original author. Both books are well-plotted, and written with a light and ironic hand, but if* Darling & Co *is a lightsome take on Mrs Gaskell, then so is* Pearls *an attempt at sub-P.G.Wodehouse with a bit of Oscar Wilde thrown in. Quite good fun, in other words, but derivative – ' nothing worth writing home about' as Belle Forrest wrote of* Pearls *in the* New Yorker *in 1938.*

Clearly, meatier stuff was required. If Flora had next turned her hand to 'murder' in the Thirties idiom – in other words, had she treated murder as a detective puzzle-story – she would have been up against some very stiff competition. Compared with Dorothy L Sayers, Margery Allingham and the hugely prolific and popular Agatha Christie, it is hard to imagine this writer of slight crime comedy cutting the mustard. It is as if Flora – perhaps still quite young enough as an artist to be experimental, or perhaps frustrated by Vayne's success with her work – decided to try a new tack. In terms of commercial enterprise, this was a bad move – clearly she should have sat

49

tight and negotiated a better deal with Eliah Vayne – but from a literary point of view, Flora's change of direction is highly interesting.

For it is only when we come to Flora's third novel that we can begin to see a hitherto undisclosed originality. The Well-Trodden Stair *is altogether different fare. Laughably tame now, maybe, when it first came out in 1941 it was received with raised eyebrows and moral disgust, so much so that Gollancz decided not to reprint. It was not so much that it treated its subject – very much a murder this time – with a much grittier realism than the previous two, but that the heroine, Madeleine, turns out to be the murderess and – crucially – appears to get away with the crime. It is as if Flora had decided to shock.*

Doubtless, to the light reading sensibilities of wartime Britain, TWTS *represented an unacceptable reversal of moral expectations of such literature. Heroines, however beautiful and talented, who are unrepentant – even when the victim is a blackmailer and as thoroughly unappetising as Miss Eustace – would have made for uncomfortable reading, and in* TWTS, *not only is the criminal not caught and punished, but the novel appears to condone adultery and prostitution. 'Far Too French!' was the verdict of Godfrey Winn in the* Express, *where he had previously praised* Pearls *with characteristic fulsomeness. However, the novel evinces an emotional maturity the previous two had lacked, and has a realistic immediacy that saves it, however lurid the tale, from mere melodrama. It is also an*

experiment in narrative form – Madeleine's first-person
narration, in the epistolic form of a diary and her letters to a
friend and to her mother, interweaves with the third person, the
result a deliberately teasing, 'unreliable' narrative which keeps
the reader guessing. But only up to a point. The main reason, I
suspect, for TWTS's *commercial failure is that this novel is not*
a puzzle-story. This is not a 'whodunnit', for who 'did it' is made
obvious more or less from the first and is in any case beside the
point... TWTS *is a (presumably young) writer's attempt at a*
'serious' novel, and by any standards an interesting one. Flora
Forde's slender reputation, however, had been based on two
light comedy mystery stories. This third, awkward-to-place book
effectively disappeared, and so, instead of returning to the tried
and true (or at least promising), did its author...

Veronica, tongue between her teeth, deleted 'prostitution'
and hunted for the right word. Then the telephone rang. Damn!
"Hello?"

"Vee?" Unmistakably, her half-sister Lucinda. Instantly,
Veronica scented trouble.

"Lucie! How nice ...er, how are you?"

"Oh, I'm fine, more or less. You?" Tone brisk, as if it
were *she* who had been interrupted.

"Fine...busy...you know..."

"I hope I'm not disturbing anything *important*..."
Always, that certain note of sarcasm. 'Important' meant either
being a good political wife by her husband's side at the hustings,

51

or an excellent, jam-making mother who went to church and sat on committees. 'Writing' was a hobby. Lucinda was still in her forties. How in the world had she managed to become so *old*?

"No, not really – er, Rory seems to have settled in…"

There was always an awkwardness between the sisters, but at least they were on speaking terms these days. For a long time, after the publication of *Too Big To Cry*, they had not been on speaks at all. There was a pause.

"Good. It was very kind of you to have him…"

"Not kindness. He pays his rent…Um, is there anything special, Lucie?"

"Well, yes, there is. We read the *Observer* piece, obviously, Peter and I…"

"Obviously…" Veronica sighed inaudibly and lit a cigarette. She knew what was coming.

"Well, we need to know if it's true!"

"If what is true, Lucie?" She was being deliberately obtuse. Nothing could annoy her more than Lucinda's tone on occasions.

"All this about a film, for God's *sakes*! We need to know, Veronica. I'm not going to have the family dragged through the mud again. That woman calling poor Mummy vain and shallow…And there's Peter's *career* to consider, and although I know you don't give a flying *damn* about Peter or me for that matter, I…"

Veronica held the telephone several inches away from her ear. When Lucinda had apparently paused for breath, she said, "You said you'd read the piece in the *Observer*...is that so?"

"Of *course* we did! Haven't I just *said*? And we both think this is absolutely *outrageous*, Veronica! Peter's going ballistic!"

"Oh dear..." Veronica could not help smiling at the thought of the Rt.Hon. Peter Penrose MP going 'ballistic'. A premature old buffer, rotund of body and rubicund of face, he put Veronica irresistibly in mind of a bursting balloon.

Lucinda's voice had risen. "This is completely *unacceptable*, Veronica! Do you hear me? Completely and *utterly* unacceptable. You can't *do* this! You can't – and if you try, Peter's going to block you...he's very powerful these days, and he says – "

"Lucie – "

"And another thing! If you drag my son into this, I'll never speak to you again, do you hear me? Ever! This is the absolute *depths*, and I..."

"Lucie...please, Lucie – a word in edgeways?" When Veronica was angry, she could almost feel her temperature drop with the tone of her voice. Her fury was made of ice, not fire. With her sister, however, there was always a certain sheer exasperation. Lucinda never *listened*.

"Well? *Well?* I want to know, Veronica! You can't do this to us. You always have, but this is the finish, the last time, do you hear me?"

"Loud and clear, Lucinda dear. *Please* let me explain…and open the *Observer* at the appropriate page while you're at it."

"I've seen the bloody thing already! How can you! Oh, how *can* you? After that book literally *killed* Mummy…"
Sounds of tears.

"Lucie…please, Lucie, calm down. You can't have read the *Observer* thing properly, or you'd know. For God's sake, if you're going to shout the house down at least make sure there's a proper reason!"

"You'll give poor Peter a heart-attack! It's just *so* unfair!" Lucinda sobbed.

"You bet it's unfair," said Veronica, finally losing her temper. "Read the damn thing again, can't you? It's there in black and white. No film. No way. Okay? Repeat, NO FILM! When you can bear to be half civil, we'll speak again. Good night, Lucie." She put the receiver down with a slam, and frowned furiously at her text. "Oh, damn and *damn*…"

'Concubinage'…that was the word. But now Veronica felt too put out to continue. "Damn!" she said again.

Over the next days, Veronica scribbled notes, added to her 'Flora' text, and tried not to think about ringing Lucinda, who had not rung her… Another weekend, Saturday evening – the loneliest night of the week, someone had said. Not for Rory, evidently. All day she had been cursing the row from upstairs as she had tried to read and write, and cursed herself even more for not marching upstairs and telling him, despising herself for avoiding another confrontation. Now that she felt calm enough to do the thing with reasonably good grace, the noise had stopped. Rory had probably gone out.

She saw that there was an arrival in her in-box, and opened it: Freddy.

One hears from someone about four times in two years; then suddenly, for no apparent reason at all, one is in urgent and regular correspondence. The Partridge family – that is, Freddy and his sister Jane – had been friends for years, indeed childhood neighbours of the young Dearborns, for whom the Partridges had been considered 'acceptable' playmates, and whose respective nannies had struck up a gossipy friendship; but as they grew up, their paths had inevitably diverged. Freddy had his very outré private life alongside his regular public one; Jane had trained as a midwife, married a country GP and was now a grandmother; Veronica had become a celebrity ex-convict who made Sunday supplement reading… She was musing on this as she read Freddy's rushed and garbled message. *Guess what! Your FlorawithanE was best buddies with Aunt M, believe it or*

believe it! Fab here. Sun, sea views, fair fishers, and oysters,
darling, oysters…Come out if you can. GBH, Fxx

'GBH' stood for 'great big hugs' and she chuckled. Dear
Freddy!

She was aware of a soft tapping at the door.

It was Rory, looking sheepish, his fair curly hair still wet
from (she surmised) a recent shower. Pity he hadn't thought to
shave. Rory's pathetic little stubbly beard annoyed her intensely.
Behind Rory stood a small, slim girl with smooth dark hair cut in
a bob with a long fringe almost to her nose, and wearing a lot of
eye-liner. Both had jackets over their arms, and Rory clutched a
wrapped bottle. "Er – hello, Vee," said Rory. "We're just off out,
but could we come in for a moment? We brought you
something…it's a peace-offering for all the noise we've been
making. Er – this is Miranda, Miranda Hooper. Minx, this is Vee
– Veronica Dearborn. She's my aunt…and my landlady…" The
girl smirked politely and proffered a hand. The two young people
hesitated on the doorstep.

"Oh, hullo, Rory. I suppose you'd better come in," said
Veronica without taking the hand. "I've been meaning to have a
word."

"Ooh," said Miranda. "You've got a *cat*. Isn't she
gorgeous? Puss, puss! What's her name?"

"Greymalkin…and it's he, although he hasn't got all his
bits. Oh, please – shut the door before he runs upstairs…Oh shit,

56

too late! Grim! Grimbles!" The cat's thick grey tail was disappearing round the bend on the staircase. "Oh hell!"

"Don't worry, Vee, it's okay. Our door's closed."

"It's the street door that bothers me…this road. He hides and then dashes, blast him." She had noted the 'our'. "He'll be back if I rattle his food…come in, for heaven's sakes, do. Oh – well, thank you, Rory." She took the wine and unwrapped it. Sainsbury's, but quite a good bottle for a student budget. Lucinda and Peter meted out Rory's allowance with a stern hand. She took it through to her small kitchen. "Sit down, do." She indicated the sofa, and went back to the door with a bag of cat-biscuits. "Grim…Grimbles…" The cat reappeared and trotted in after her. "Come on, silly. Sorry – the silly beast will try to explore…"

"You mean the poor baby can't go *outside*?" said the girl Miranda, and Veronica instantly hated her.

"He's got the courtyard. He's just naturally curious. Cats are. Now please, do sit down. I suppose you'd like a drink. I've got white in the fridge, or I suppose we could open this…" It was six o'clock. She was restricting herself, but as she was planning to give the pair a thorough talking to, it seemed only civilized to offer refreshment to soften the blow. Rory and Miranda perched on the sofa, Rory looking embarrassed and Miranda stroking the cat, making cooing noises.

"We're fine with white, thanks, Vee, aren't we, Minx? Save the red for a dinner party, eh?"

Veronica poured Waitrose Frascati into glasses and as an after-thought, emptied some rather stale peanuts into a dish. She handed them round, and sat in her desk chair with a sigh, feeling old, crotchety and ill at ease. "Let's get this over with, Rory. I can't bear any more of the row you're making. You're disturbing me. I work at home. This – " she indicated her desk – "is my office. I really can't be doing with constant thump, thump all the time. Please, I really hate having to do the heavy bit, but please realise that noise travels, even despite a whole floor between us. I think it's your bass speaker or something. Er, cheers, I suppose…"

"Cheers. Oh God, look, we're truly very sorry, Veronica. Really. We've been a bit, well, ebullient…" Rory looked down at his trainers and blushed. The child was in love! It occurred to Veronica that some of the electronic noise had been intended to mask the more human noises of their love-making. And it warmed her that Rory could use a word like 'ebullient'…
"Yes, we're really sorry we've disturbed you. We'll keep it down, we promise…" Miranda, a good-looking girl with a round, wide-mouthed face, reminded her of a new conker: glossy brown hair, shiny brown boots, shiny brown eyes…which her big wide lip-glossed smile did not quite reach. Probably nerves. Veronica, very aware of her age and superiority, decided to be kind, but these second-person pronouns continued to bother her. "We?" she said, aware that she was playing headmistress.

Rory spoke. "Yes...That's...that is, um...we wanted to ask you, we came to ask..."

"Yes?"

"Miranda is my girlfriend. We wondered if she could – that is, do you mind – can she stay here with me for a while? Her place has gone a bit pear-shaped and..." Rory's face, despite the stubble, was incredibly juvenile, and reminded her very much of his mother, her half-sister Lucinda. It occurred to Veronica that Lucie would not approve, and she decided she did not care a whit.

"The upstairs flat is your home, Rory," she said. "It's none of my business whom you have to stay. All I care about is the racket...and the rent, of course." She twinkled deliberately, a benign headmistress now.

"You mean you really don't mind?"

"Of course not. Why should I?"

"I *told* you she's fabulous," said Rory to Miranda. "I just wondered about – well, you know, Mum..."

"My arrangement was with you, Rory, and not with your mother." She was aware of Miranda's rather calculating eyes summing her up. "Now then, if that's settled, let's have another glass and drink to it. You two pipe down with the noise, and you're very welcome, Miranda." Veronica poured more wine. "I take it you're at university with Rory. "

"Yes...and thank you." The smile became more genuine. "We'll be quiet as mice..."

59

"Miranda's a trainee journalist," said Rory proudly.

"Oh. What fun!" Journalists were not Veronica's favourite people. "Interesting, too, I should think."

"Oh, it *is*," said Miranda, seriously. "Last term I did some work experience with *The Mercury*. I want to go into television, but newsprint's an *experience*. I was assigned to the Labour conference…I was there for the whole three days. This is lovely, Veronica…I hope I can call you that?" She was gazing round the room. "What gorgeous flowers…"

"They were…they're going off a bit now." She regarded their faces. Entirely innocent. *Not* the anonymous donors, she decided. "Er – the Labour conference. Do you get sent out on your own or do you have a tutor with you?"

"Oh no – on something like the Conference we have a mentor, you know, a proper professional who acts as a sort of guide…" They talked trainee journalism for some moments. Then Miranda coughed. "We – we do have a number of special assignments we have to do by ourselves. I hope you don't mind my asking, but I was wondering if…well, if I could interview you sometime…" Miranda's smile dazzled. "It's for the course. We have to interview someone significant. I'm a terrific fan, and I just thought as you're here, and by amazing coincidence Rory's aunt…He said you mightn't mind…"

"Ah…" Veronica glared at her nephew.

"Being asked I mean. You could always say no. I know you've just done that thing for the *Observer,* but…"

"Minx…"

"It was just a thought. I'd be so thrilled. I read *Too Big To Cry* and I was just knocked out, you know? *I* cried…And it's still so *significant*. I think it would make a fabulous film…"

"*Minx…*" Rory kicked Miranda's booted ankle.

"But we needn't talk about that if you didn't want to…"

"I see. You want to interview me about what exactly?"

"Well – um - anything really. How you work, your typical working day, that sort of thing. What you do about research. You know, *Henry Cuffe* and all that, and how you went about it, the sources you consulted. That would be fascinating…" She was aware that Veronica was still frowning. "Or we could talk about your next project if you'd prefer – I mean if it's not still under wraps. I do realise you're very busy…"

"Miranda. My next book is very much under wraps. And I almost never give interviews, even to *The Observer,* and especially not ahead of publication." She knew how lofty she was sounding, and said, "After the *Observer* piece, I frankly feel a bit interviewed-out, if you see what I mean…" She forced herself to smile.

"Oh yes. Of *course*. This would only be for the journo course, you understand, not for publication as such, only in the course mag and my portfolio. I'd be so thrilled. I thought *Henry Cuffe* was brilliant and so did Rory."

"Yes…um, absolutely! It's just great!"

"Really?" She was losing the battle with austerity. Hard to be austere when your best-known book concerns your serious heroin habit and your imprisonment...and she sometimes forgot that *Cry* had been 'significant', and not only for the aristo-bashers. And perhaps they *had* read *Henry Cuffe.* "I'd been beginning to fear that only history students would find it of any interest..."

"Well, I thought it was absolutely amazing! Totally readable and so informative, so detailed..."

"Well, how nice of you to say so, Miranda...thanks."

Rory said, "And exciting. All those Elizabethan spies, wow. Really makes you think..."

"What, Rory? What did it make you think?"

"I thought...well, I thought it was amazing that there was this sort of Elizabethan MI5, you know, like a proto police-state...so modern in a way. Wasn't it?" Rory *was* a history student, of sorts: twentieth-century economics and politics.

"Yes. Although in order to have a police-state, Rory, one first has to invent a police force. Neither Henry the Eighth nor Elizabeth had quite done that, as I think I pointed out."

"Well, I meant enforcers. And the spy-network...several, really, I suppose, with everyone spying on everyone else..." Veronica tried not to feel dismayed that Rory would probably end up with a career in politics like his father.

"Oh, *yes,*" Miranda agreed. "And the – er – the machinery of justice all in the hands of potential criminals, at least, well, all potentially corrupt…" Miranda trailed off. A bright enough girl, Veronica decided, with her head rather too full of sound-bites imperfectly gleaned from reviews.

"Yes, all very nasty indeed," said Veronica lightly. "The world scarcely changes at heart, does it? Only the technology."

"Dead right there," agreed Rory. "Although I guess that each technological breakthrough produces a sociological change…like cheap air-travel, for instance. Everyone more or less able to get to places that were only myths before, or the province of the rich…"

"And the telegraph," put in Miranda. "Then the phone. All those instant communications that could get into print the next day. Proto email. But I know what Veronica means. The moral world is much the same as it was for the Elizabethans – or the Ancient Romans come to that. Just as nasty if twice as fast."

"A hundred times, I'd guess. I wonder if it would be fun to do a proper calculation…."

"Rory's got this thing about getting things into figures, haven't you, Rorykins? I'd say that if Shakespeare time-travelled to now, he would be gobsmacked by all the technological advances but not fazed at all by the political corruption – don't you agree, Veronica? I mean, that's very much a conclusion you can't help drawing from your book…"

"Oh! Is it? Well, perhaps. I'm not sure I drew any wider conclusions as such... I say, I don't want to be unsociable, but did you two say you're off out somewhere this evening?" She was rather anxious for the subject of the proposed interview not to crop up again.

Rory leapt on it rather gratefully. "Yes – we're off to Town – there's a Stunt Drivers gig at the South Bank. The drummer was at school with me. In fact, Minx, we'd better get our skates on…"

"Sounds fun. Well, you two, sorry to be a bore, but I'm going to go back to work…"

As they were leaving, Miranda said, "If you *did* agree about this interview, I'd of course let you have a sort of advance précis, the questions I'd like to address…you'd dictate the terms…if you agreed, I mean…"

"I see. Well, I'll think about it, Miranda, but I can't promise anything. And I'd certainly want to see the questions beforehand. That's only fair, isn't it?"

"Of *course!* Oh, it would be *fabulous* of you if you'd agree. I was going to try for Boris Johnson with his historian hat on, you know, but you'd be *so* much better…"

"Really? How quaint! But I really won't promise anything, Miranda. I need to think about it…and see the outline."

"Oh, that's just wonderful – really, *really* kind of you…"

"I've not been kind yet," said Veronica equably.

Rory tugged Miranda's sleeve. "We'd best be off, Minx. Vee, this has been great! Really kind. It's brilliant of you to not mind about Minx – Miranda – staying." Rory had a firm grip on his girlfriend's elbow. "We'll promise to keep the noise down, won't we, Minx?"

"Of course we will, Veronica! This has been amazing to meet you. Oh dear…I've overstepped the mark, I can tell. I'm sorry." Miranda looked downcast.

She's just a girl, Veronica reminded herself. Just a kid. She was almost fond of Rory, and she wanted to help. "Send me the précis and I'll think about it, Miranda. You journalists have to get used to being pariahs, I'm afraid…it's a tough world. Thanks for the wine."

"No, no – not at all. Thank you…thank *you*! Ooh, here he is, poor old pussikins, you do so want to be free, don't you, baby…"

Kid be damned! She was an embryonic journo with an already well-developed granite nose. The aptly-named Minx would almost certainly break Rory's soft heart. She even wondered, cynically, if Rory's relationship to herself was part of his attraction. And there was something distinctly unsettling about a journalist – however embryonic – on the premises. When the young had left, closing the outer street door with exaggerated caution, she poured herself another glass and logged on to her email.

'Freddy!' she wrote. 'Do you mean it about joining you for a few days? Suddenly rather desperate for oysters, more gen on Flora…and to get away! Let me know. GBH, V x'

Before she went to bed, Veronica threw the shrivelling anonymous bouquet of spring flowers into the bin.

Veronica booked a flight to Rome, and then did some homework. On the internet, she found a list of the books illustrated by J Cadwallader Jones, and managed to borrow *The Butterfly Garden*, *David's Country Holiday*, and *Agnes and Mr Bozo*, about a little girl who befriends a circus dog, from the local library. She also bought two or three Millicent Fox paperbacks and re-read *The Well-Trodden Stair* by Flora Forde.

The children's stories, all by one S.N. Doughty and written in the 40s and 50s, were a delight – mostly for the illustrations, which had been drawn with meticulous and loving attention to detail. At least she would be able to talk to Freddy's uncle about his work as well as that of his late wife. The Millicent Fox stuff was fun: an engaging musician-turned-detective hero with a well-rounded personality who solved intricately-plotted mysteries in unlikely settings. 'Aunt Milly' had had an observant ear for dialogue and wrote with a deft hand; she had researched police-procedure thoroughly, but resisted too much boring forensic detail; and the formulaic 'whodunnit' aspect was cleverly executed. She looked up as much biographical material on Millicent Fox as she could find. As for *The Well-Trodden Stair,* Veronica underlined various passages and chewed the top of her pencil, deep in thought…

Prompted by a pressing need for supplies, Veronica went out to catch the local mini-market before it closed at six, and returned to find an envelope wedged under her door.

'Dear Veronica,' she read. 'Enclosed is a draft of the questions I should like to put to you if you would be willing and had the time to see me and do this interview thing. I'd be VERY grateful. I do stress this is just a draft, and if you were willing to do it at all, I should be happy to leave the questions entirely up to you. Hoping to hear from you fairly soon, because I have a deadline. With very best wishes, Miranda Hooper.'

Polite, well-spelt, tactful, slightly gauche, determined but not overly pushy… She glanced through the questions with a sigh. Suddenly, she made up her mind.

'Dear Miranda,' she wrote. 'I'm off to Italy very soon for a few days. If you'd like to come down one evening this week, I should be happy to talk about my next project, the introduction to a new publication of Flora Forde's mystery stories for Vixen Press. I must stress I do NOT want to talk about either *Too Big To Cry* or about my next major undertaking. I can talk a bit about my researches for *Henry Cuffe*, if you wish, and you would need to show me your final draft before it goes into your course magazine. The price for this is glancing at this book and looking after Greymalkin and watering my plants whilst I am away. Let me know if we've got a deal…Best, V.D.' She put the note, together with the spare copy of *The Well-Trodden Stair*, into the top flat's mailbox by the front door and resumed her musings.

"This has been absolutely fantastic, Veronica," said Miranda, putting away a professional-looking blackberry. "I'm incredibly grateful…" Empty wine-glasses, crumbs of cheese and biscuits.

"I don't think I've actually given you very much, Miranda. But thank you, too. It's been rather fun to have someone to bounce ideas with, actually. I'm glad you see why I'm rather intrigued by it. For some reason, this book seems to be intended as a slap in the face. Do you see what I mean? Sorry – I'm not really sure myself."

"I think I see totally. This ought to have been a pathos thing, right? Talented girl has to give up music to support widowed mother and sick sister, and ends up in brain-deadening job she hates and isn't very good at anyway. Lots of noble wartime sentiments and self-sacrifice. Finds a couple of rich sugar-daddies and basically goes on the game, but falls in love with impoverished wounded war-hero, no money, and has to pretend to nice-minded man she's supplementing her income with piano pupils. Then enter the blackmailer…and at this point, she should have – what? Paid up? Confessed everything to nice man who forgives her, I suppose …"

"Or doesn't. Go on."

"Okay, doesn't. He finds out, and is horrified that his angelic girl has been selling her body. Busted illusions. So she commits suicide, or something, and everybody is morally clean as whistles, but it's a trag-ed-ee…"

"Quite. Instead of which we have a pragmatic-minded girl determined not to sacrifice her dreams, realistic enough to know that she can never tell hero boyfriend her secret, and who deliberately murders unlovely blackmailer over a cosy supper of curried aconite, and divulges the truth only to her own diary…It's interesting, don't you think, how the narrative – first person, mostly – teases the reader? But actually leaves no doubt. In the end, the fair Madeleine is as guilty as hell by her own admission, with a horribly simple but effective and clever murder that is virtually undetectable…"

"…And gets away with the crime, a place at the Guildhall, and decides the boyf is just too much of a priggish arse for words and urges him to marry the curate's daughter anyway.…It's great! Brilliant!"

"Yes, but you can see why this wouldn't ever have made the lists. Her 40s audience would never have cheered that she got away with it. Heroines were allowed to lapse and be penitent, but not to revel in capital crime. Tsk, tsk. I'm just wondering why on earth she wrote it. Or why her publisher let her. In effect, it wrecked Flora's career."

"Hmm. Wow, I wish we knew who she was! Can I say in my piece that you're approaching this with a sort of historian's thoroughness?"

"Well, yes…okay…but don't over-egg that one, maybe…I mean, my job as I understand it is simply to provide a bit of commentary on her novels. There's a school of literary thought that thinks 'who' is very unimportant compared to 'what'…"

"Yes, okay…but you playing detective on someone who wrote detective stories is rather a neat angle. I wonder – I mean as 'Flora Forde' is almost certainly a pen-name – perhaps she became someone else…Yeah! Look that's possible, isn't it? She writes this total commercial flop and a disaster for the Flora Forde name. She's disappointed, of course, but she isn't put off completely. She's young, and she's a talented writer. Isn't it just possible she began writing again but using a different name?" Miranda's bright chestnut eyes were shining.

"Well, yes. That is possible, isn't it? I'm off shortly to meet someone who knew her. I might get another clue or two…at least I might get a real name out of him, and a bit of background…"

"Will you keep me posted?"

"Yes – why not? You might even get a sequel for your piece."

"That would be brilliant, Veronica. A scoop!"

"Well, hardly that, I'd have thought. I mean, does anybody care? Nobody's heard of her. I hadn't. She's hardly P.D.James or someone…"

"No, no – but, hey, supposing she *became* P.D.James? I mean, not literally, but someone well-known...it's possible, surely...."

"Nice thought, but my guess is that it was all rather tame. Flora was probably as young and pretty as her heroines. Her last book was an experiment which didn't sell, and she gave up. I rather expect to learn that in real life she got married and had babies..." Veronica suddenly wanted to end the conversation.

Miranda said brightly: "Pity if so. Rather knocks this feminist angle on the head...but you will let me know?"

"Of course, Miranda. Promise. Now, I've shown you the burglar alarm and the back keys. Keep the kitchen light on at night...You *will* remember to be really careful not to let old Grimbles out onto the road, won't you? I know it's silly, but it really is important, Miranda. I care far more about him than the plants..." Silly, but there it was. Veronica *loved* her cat. A silly, lonely, middle-aged woman who loved her cat...

"Of course, Veronica. Truly, I do understand...he'll be safe as houses, won't you, darling? *Loads* of cuddles. Rory and I will take great care of you, won't we, sweetie?" Greymalkin snuggled up to Miranda's denimed legs and purred loudly.

"Traitor!" said Veronica to the cat when Miranda had gone. She turned back to her notes. Something was nagging at her brain, something as yet nebulous which she had not discussed with Miranda.

The telephone rang.

71

"Vee, darling? Freddy…sorry – rotten line. Listen, dear heart, I've booked you into the Albergo Del Mare. Let me know when you arrive, and I'll come and pick you up. Once you're off the superstrada from San Gregorio, you just head into town to the centre…Albergo Del Mare is in the main Piazza Umberto…you can't miss it…You've got my Italian number, haven't you?"

"Yes, I have…Thanks, Freddy, dear…I'm really looking forward to it…"

"Everybody's so looking forward to you coming…"

"Everybody? Who's…?" But the line fizzed and blanked.

Finding she could no longer concentrate on Flora Forde (with an 'e'), she looked up Monte Farfalla. Height above sea-level, miles from Rome, miles from Naples, adjacent airports…some very attractive pictures of narrow baroque streets, more of a splendid fortress with a magnificent view of the sea, a Medici gateway…links to several write-ups which she opened at random. Someone called "Hilarity" had written for *The Bystander*'s 'A Bit Off The Map' column the previous year: *'Head northwest from San Gregorio, let your passengers enjoy the jaw-dropping magnificence of the views as you avoid the charging killer buses along the switchback route, hang a precarious left just after the sign for Il Molino, and wind slowly down towards the vista of the sea, and you come to Monte Farfalla, a semi-isolated idyll with a 12th century castle, a network of Franciscan catacombs with an interesting WWII history, a grand Medici gateway, baroque architecture, and a* *blissfully calm and swimmable bay which hides some dangerous rocks (not for nothing known as the 'Denti Dei Cani')... This blond, sunny, rather grand little town, home to the local fishing, pottery-making and lemon-growing community as well as a Signorelli Madonna in the Lady Chapel of the Chiesa San Giovanni Decollato, is fast becoming a magnet for discerning boat-owners and the second-home property trade. Two or three B&Bs in town provide good old-fashioned accommodation, restaurants along the Marina will serve the best of the day's catch at local prices, and La Taverna Il Castello by the famous jug-handle fortress probably deserves a mention for the view alone. Alas, the one proper hotel in the historic Piazza Umberto is best avoided, unless you want Fawlty-esque hospitality, a Rome-size bill, scruffy accommodation and dodgy plumbing, but...'*

Oh, God, murmured Veronica to herself. I bet that's where I'm booked to stay...

v: Emissary

"I ought to be there with you," said Faye wanly from the bed. She looked a little better today despite the bandages on her head and her still lividly bruised face. There were stitches beneath her right eye: Faye had been lucky. Julian Blyth, who found hospitals profoundly unsettling places, especially since his own recent brush with A&E, was guiltily glad that this was to be his last visit for some time. "You don't speak Italian or anything. It's my responsibility. I wish I could be there…"

A nurse popped her head round the door of the private room. "Everything okay, Mrs Blyth? Oh, you've got a visitor. How nice! Good evening."

"Yes, thank you…my brother-in-law…" Faye tried to smile.

"That's nice," said the nurse again. "Supper trolley in a moment…" The nurse went away.

Julian put away the papers into his briefcase, closing it awkwardly with one hand. "No you don't, Faye. Not really. Not even if you were well enough. That's what this power-of-attorney thing is all about. You don't have to worry any more, Faye."

"All right…I'll try. Everybody's being so kind. You know Angela came…last week. So sweet of her. You are wonderful to do this…"

74

"Nonsense. It's not as if I've had to cancel anything…" Julian's 'default mode' was a slightly sour pragmatism.

"No. Poor Julian. How long before you can play again?"

"Quack says another three weeks. That's before I can even begin practising…it's basically something called repetitive strain injury. One mustn't repeat it…"

"God, what a bore for you. I'm so sorry."

It was more than a bore. It was almost terrifying. Without his routines, his two-hour morning practice, his afternoon rehearsals, the constant concert bookings, Julian felt lost to the point of paralysis. He could not possibly confide to Faye just how much this errand of mercy – if that is what it was – meant to him. It gave him something to do, rather than pace about his London flat feeling useless. He was forbidding himself to even consider that he might not be able to play professionally ever again.

"Well," he said wryly, "this gives me an enforced vacation…sorry. I didn't mean…"

"I know what you mean…and you're right. I couldn't bear to go back there. Even so, to think of you there…and him…" Her eyes began to fill. She was still horribly weak. "You will put some flowers…tidy it up a bit…I tried before I left…"

"Of course, my dear…" With luck, by the time he returned from Italy, Faye would be back in her little flat in Bath and things might be more normal, or whatever passed for normal. "You just concentrate on getting well, Faye." In his way, he was

75

fond of his sister-in-law. She was, whatever else, his last real link
with Hilary.

"I'll try…" He was unfolding his tall thin frame from the
chair, careful not to put pressure on his injured wrist.

"God, what a pair we make," she said. "Julian...?"

"Faye?"

"Julian – don't forget, will you?" Her eyes were urgent
beneath the bandages; far too bright. "See them. See what I
mean. They know what really happened and they're all covering
up, telling lies. I know you think I'm raving, and so does Angela,
but I'm not. Truly. I'm not making it up. Let them talk to you
and they'll give themselves away. They'll be utterly charming,
but they're not – not like they seem. They're bastards and they
made him die, Julian. And I wasn't there… He might have
lived…"

He made a sympathetic noise and longed to leave. He
crossed to the bed. "Faye…don't cry. Please, Faye. Just try to get
well…please don't make things worse. Um – read. I thought you
might like this history thing – it's by that woman who wrote that
thing about being in jail, but this is a life – you know, a
biography – about some nasty Elizabethan secretary
orchestrating a rebellion for the Earl of Essex. It's fun, your sort
of thing. I took it on that trip to Toulouse. Watch telly…you
know, try to take your mind off things…" He was babbling. Faye
was wiping her tears under the bandage.

76

"Sorry…so sorry, Julian. It – it – just comes over me. And I'm on enough tranks to subdue a wild horse. I dream of him. He's going to walk in here any moment, tell them all to go to hell and take me h-home…Oh, Julian! I still can't believe… Oh, God…it's been almost a whole fucking year, and I still can't believe it…"

"No, my dear," Julian said sadly. "Neither can I. A year's quite – well, short…" He took her hand briefly with his uninjured one. He was bad at emotions. Notoriously, according to his ex-wife. Faye gulped and took a fragile grip on herself, releasing his hand. He changed the subject. "Is Clarrie coming?" Clarrie was Faye's sister. Julian was anxious to avoid her.

"Later. This weekend, she said. She's been so good to me, Julian. She wants me to stay with her when I come out, and she's trying to get me onto a 'programme', whatever that is. I suppose it's what I need. I mean middle-aged female drunks aren't very elegant, are they, especially when they fall through glass conservatories…"

"Not very…" Faye's sense of humour was beginning to return, in patches. He twitched a smile. "Just get well, Faye. I say, my dear, I'd better be off. I have to meet Phoebe…" He was glad of the excuse.

"Dear little Phoebe…always so bright. Give her my love."

"Not so little now. She's twenty-one. Get well soon. I'll –
um – I'll keep you posted. Promise." Briefly he kissed the top of
her bandaged head, and left.

Julian's daughter, Phoebe, met him by the lifts in the
foyer downstairs. "Okay, Dad? How is she?"

"Not too bad…I suppose…" He sighed. She kissed his
cheek.

"How's the wrist?"

"Bloody nuisance. The doctors say 'sore' when they
really mean it'll hurt like hell…I can't drive, I'm afraid. Can't
change gear. It'll have to be a bus or a taxi if we're going into
town."

"I thought of that. I borrowed Mum's van. It's in car park
'C'…" Phoebe was home for the half term and staying with her
mother, and apparently enjoying parties rather than 'reading'.
Julian did not pretend to understand students. He supposed he
should be grateful his daughter had found time to meet him. She
carried his briefcase.

"I'm hungry," she said as they got into Angela's little
white Citroen van with the 'Willow Flower' logo painted on the
side. "I thought we'd go to the 'Wife of Bath'. It won't be too
busy, and we can park under Waitrose for a fiver…"

"Whatever you say, miss…as long as it's not too, well…"

"Booming. No, it isn't. I chose it rather carefully, in fact."

Paused at traffic lights, Julian studied his daughter's face in profile, realising how little he knew this pretty, slender, self-possessed young woman who drove with competent concentration. She wore a long sleeveless cardigan thing over a white linen shirt over tight denim jeans. Her hair, longish, was faded blonde and wavy, like his own, and he was secretly glad that she hadn't obviously coloured it. Her mouth was firm, almost to grimness, like Angela's, and she had inherited Angela's small neat nose. She wore bracelets which jangled when she changed gear, and a gold pendant he remembered giving her on her sixteenth birthday...a tiny fish for her birth-sign, Pisces... He wondered if she had a boyfriend, wondered if he would ever know anything about her grown-up life, wondered if the boyfriend would be his son-in-law, wondered if he would ever be introduced. So much he might ask and dared not.

"So how will you manage in Italy? About driving?"

"Easy. You change gear with the right hand."

"Clever old Dad!"

"Or I'll rent an automatic..."

'The Wife of Bath', which occupied the basement and ground floor of an elegant eighteenth-century terrace in Quiet Street, emphasised its vegetarian and vegan menus, served interesting bistro starters, main-course salads, and decent wine. The décor was a quaintly old-fashioned muddle – chintz chairs, glass lamps and deliberately mismatched tableware, and there were photographs of celebrity patrons on the walls, including one of Freddy Partridge, the food-writer, next to his glowing report for *The Bystander*. The inevitable background music was muted jazz – not at all unpleasant, really – and it did not 'boom' as Phoebe had promised, and conversation was possible. This being early on a Thursday evening, the little restaurant was not busy. Julian ordered the grouse patè with a damson sauce, and his daughter ordered toasted brie and rocket…

He felt jollier suddenly. "This seems very nice, Feebs. Something for both of us…You're still vegetarian?"

"Dad…"

"Sorry. It was an honest question, darling."

"Yes, Dad. I am vegetarian. There's no 'still' about it."

"Sorry."

Julian chose a bottle of chablis. He poured – a full glass for him, a mere splash for her, which she tasted and then added water from the jug. "Sorry. Driving. It's very nice."

"Cheers," he said.

"Cheers…" She smiled at him as she lifted her glass. *"Cin-cin…"*

"Chin-chin?"

"It's what they say in Italy, Dad…"

"Oh…of course. Sorry. I'll have to remember that, I suppose…"

"Last of the great travellers! I hope you've packed a phrase-book, Dad. You won't be in an orchestra-capsule this time." Phoebe Blyth gazed at her father's stubborn, good-looking face with a mixture of exasperation and affection that more or less summed up her feelings for him.

"This lawyer bloke speaks English."

"Just as well."

The first courses arrived, and Phoebe watched her father take a mouthful. "This is rather good, Feebs…"

"Mm. I hoped you'd like it."

"Delicious…Have you heard from Guy?"

"He texted yesterday. He sounds fine. Learning Cantonese."

"Good God! And er – how is – er – Mum?"

"Okay. She – er – she said to say hello."

"Ah…nice of her. She's – er – well? Is she?" Communication with his ex-wife was sporadic, and confined mostly to practicalities concerning their offspring. Phoebe's brother Guy was on a post graduate gap-year, teaching English in Southern China.

"Seems fine. Very busy with the shop. She's started a catering thing now. With Zoe. They do people's parties and stuff."

"Ah. Yes, of course, the shop." Angela made quiches and scones, and sold tea, coffee and home-made soups, jams and relishes from a tiny premises with two tables and a kitchen recess in a picturesque Bath alley. Zoe was her partner. "I hope they do all right. Not such a good time for small businesses at the moment."

"They seem to be doing – you know, okay. Word's spreading."

"Good." He wanted to ask Phoebe if she minded about Zoe, and knew he never could. As for his own feelings on the matter, he had buried those a long time ago.

"They've just done a big local wedding do – Mum got into *Tatler,* or at least 'Willow Flower' did. And now that Western TV gardening programme with Gordon Tregorran wants them to do the June Garden Party. Lots of great publicity. You must have heard of it."

"No. Sorry. Away too much to watch TV, and gardens aren't exactly my bag these days. But, well, that's good, isn't it? Good for Angela?"

"Mmm. Very."

They finished their plates in silence. He broke it. "Now then, shall we look at the menu again? If you're still hungry?"

"Don't need to. Nut roast with salad and battered zucchini flowers – they're delicious. You've got to try some. By the way, I really won't be totally horrified if you want veal or something, Dad. They're supposed to be good here. Organic, not raised in crates." She was grinning a little. Julian was examining the list.

"No – I'm going to go for this avocado and bacon salad thing. I'm not really up to cutting veal with this wrist. Perhaps I will try these battered flowers…" He thought unaccountably of Faye as he had just seen her. They ordered, and the place began to fill up.

More food arrived. "Now, this looks very good..." He ate a forkful of avocado and bacon and murmured appreciatively. Julian Blyth enjoyed his food "More wine, darling?"

"A smidge...Dad?"

"Yes, love?"

"Dad? Can I ask you something?"

"Of course. Not that I shall necessarily answer you...I can't always."

"I know that. Oh, Dad...Look, it's Uncle Hilly. And Faye. I want to know what happened to them. Mum says...well, Mum says that Faye's completely lost it and hit the bottle. She also said – well, she implied – that this accident wasn't. An accident, I mean. That Faye jumped rather than fell. Is it true?" She frowned. "Did poor Faye really try to kill herself?"

"Phoebe...darling...I'm not at all sure. I don't think anybody's sure, not even Faye. She had certainly drunk a great deal too much at the time...the balcony gave way, or something..."

"Balconies don't just give way, Dad."

"Feebs, I really don't think..."

"And is it true she thinks Hilly's death was caused deliberately? Mum went last week to see her. She was raving, according to Mum. Something about those people they knew out in Italy who were really responsible... It all seems a bit garbled, and people do say terrible things when they're grieving, and want to blame someone, but suppose it's true?"

83

"Feebs …"

"Mum dismissed it, but Mum would. I'd like to go and see Faye. Do you think she's up to it? Mum doesn't seem too keen."

"I see…"

"Do you? Mind?"

"I don't see why not. You could ring her. Or text. She's got her mobile. Ask her. Seeing you might cheer her up. But she'll be out soon. Look, darling, perhaps it's better not to – well – *delve*. Faye's going to get well. Poor Hilary drowned. There's no question about it. The reports are perfectly clear – and, well, he's dead and we can't bring him back, you know."

"I know… Sorry, Dad. You must miss him so much. I – I really miss him too." She forked salad round her plate, concentrating on it. "I just adored him as a kid. I thought he was marvellous. His funny voices and the pop he made in his cheek when he uncorked a bottle…like this." Phoebe demonstrated, and some Dutch tourists at a nearby table looked up and laughed. "Oops! Sorry! Remember? He sort of made a party wherever he was."

Julian remembered and laughed sadly. "Yup…That was Hil. He was just always – well, a bit rackety…up one minute, down the next. He could be so…*sunny*…until he did one of his nosedives…poor old Hil. I'm – um – glad you remember him so well…" The wine was getting to him.

"Remember that party you and Mum had in the garden after we moved to Cornwick? Faye was my favourite teacher – I was about twelve, remember? And all of a sudden I had to get my head round the fact that she was my uncle's girlfriend, and dressed in lace and smoking! Talk about weird! Remember that song routine on the piano? Cole Porter or Gershwin or something. She could really sing, too. It's so weird hearing your teacher sing! He could really play, too, couldn't he? Improvise jazz, all that. Looking back, I think I was witnessing a serious grown up love affair for the first time..."

"Yes...I think perhaps so..." Julian, too, remembered the evening vividly: himself and Angela, perfect hosts to the house-warming guests in a new home they should never have bought, with Angela's wonderful food inviting such murmurs of appreciation, and the congratulations, the brightness, the compliments, and him knowing the whole thing to be a sham, teetering on the verge of a fatal distance that no stones and mortar could really shore up... And Phoebe and Guy, children still, unaware (but were they, really?) enjoying the party, playing rounders on the lawn with their young friends, and gathering as the evening deepened into the large and pretty sitting room where Hilary was playing a rousing music-hall medley on the piano and the whole party, becoming uproarious, breaking into a rousing chorus of 'The Tavern in The Town', and someone starting 'The Barley Mow', the song petering out as people forgot the words, and his own hesitation as Hilary yelled, "Come

85

on, Jools, what about a spot of fiddle!" and he had gone to get it, but when he returned with his violin, Hilary had changed the subject, playing blue notes and summoning the lovely red-headed woman to his side, who began to sing 'Summer Time'…and he had put in violin harmonies, tentatively, and Faye, shy at first, had grinned at him, and softly touched his brother's shoulder at the piano, and he knew that the two of them had done this routine before. He had grinned at Angela – the mood was powerful, sexy, even, and the joy of the two at the piano was infectious – but Angela had merely given him a look of sad resignation and disappeared to the kitchen…

"What was he like? When he was young? When you both were young? You must have both been budding musicians…"

"Yes…" Unaccountably, Julian felt suddenly near to tears, and helped himself to more wine. "Hilary. He was – he was very different from me. I was the studious one. Did the dots, you know…well, perhaps you don't." Phoebe had taken after her mother: not really a musical bone in her body. All those piano lessons coming to nothing. He had made a point of never forcing it. "I was rigorous. Practiced every day. Passed exams. That was Grandpa – do you remember Grandpa Blyth, Feebs?"

"Of course. Very well. He scared me when I was little."

"He scared me when I was little too, but I sort of stayed scared, I suppose. Hmph! We were twins, did you know that? Hilary and I? Twins…"

"Of *course*. But only fraternal ones. Different eggs. Different zygotes. You'd have had a different gene pattern."

"That would explain it, I suppose. I mean, why we were so different. Hilary wasn't really afraid of anything, except maybe the dark. He didn't like winter, when the nights closed in. And – he was the real musician, you know. He could invent. I've never been able to do that. I treated music like – well, a bit like a scientist, I suppose. Funny thought, that."

"So you became a successful pro, and Uncle Hil just gave parties…"

"Something like that. I expect he had more fun…*was* more fun. Poor old Hil."

"There's got to be the scientists, too, Dad…I'm one." They had foregone pudding and ordered coffee.

"Well, now…I suppose you are at that. What are you going to do? Do you know yet?" He was very relieved the subject had come up naturally.

"Yes. I do. If I get a really decent grade, I'm going to apply to do post-grad child psychology. Early learning research, with a special interest in elementary physical sciences. If I screw up, or at least if I don't get a decent two-one, I'm going to do primary school teaching. Not reception class. Proper sciences for eight to ten-year-olds. At least for a bit. Then I might write it up anyway and re-apply for the research degree."

Julian gazed at his daughter. "Phoebe! How wonderful – I mean – that's very good, isn't it?"

"You mean," said the young psychologist, "that you'd imagined I didn't have a clue. Didn't you, Dad?" She was smiling at him broadly, her vivid blue eyes crinkling on the verge of laughter.

"Well…"

"Admit it!"

"I'm just – well, I suppose I'm a bit out of touch…" After his marriage broke up, and especially since Hilary's death, he had been virtually nomadic with tours, taking every opportunity he could to take himself off to travel and play: from Salzburg to Sydney, from Berlin to Buenos Aires, Karachi to Cape Town, Tokyo to Toronto, he had been living a life of airports, planes, hotels, and concert halls that had all begun to look alike. Perhaps it should not surprise him that his daughter should have grown into such a – a *person* in his absence. He had not seen her since December, when he was just passing through, depositing presents, refusing Angela's Christmas lunch, knowing that somehow his plea of an imminent plane was inadequate, however true…seeing the disappointment in Phoebe's face. And Guy's.

She kept the engine running as she dropped him off with his briefcase at the station.

"Say hello to your mother."

"Of course. You do know you could have stayed with us if you'd wanted."

"Hmmph. I need to get back to the flat." It was always 'the flat', never 'home'.

"All right, Dad. I know you couldn't. Good luck in Italy, Dad. Keep in touch..." She kissed his cheek briefly.

"I'm very proud of you, darling," he mumbled.

"Thank you." She waved as she turned the van. He waved back. He knew that she did not need his pride. She had learned to do without it.

vi: Herding Cats

"Grim! Grimbles...puss, puss, puss! Oh *God*...Rory!" She
yelled to an upstairs window from the street: "Rory! *Rory*! Please
come! Oh *no*!" The dark-haired young woman in the patterned
red silk Chinese robe and velvet slippers was seriously agitated,
as Russell Roper could see. He could also see that she was
wearing next to nothing under the robe, and this disconcerted
him quite considerably.

"Excuse me...you're not Miss Dearborn?" he asked,
feeling faintly foolish.

"No! Oh God, Grimbles has *gone*...I'm looking for a
cat..." The girl bit her lip in anguish. She was remarkably pretty.
"He's not mine – I'm looking after him for someone." She
looked this way and that about the street in agitated alarm. "Oh
God! If he gets run over! Grim! Pussy-boy!"

Russell Roper, a young man of sharp wits and possessed
of sharp eyes, said, "There he is – look – under that red
Fiesta...see? A big grey cat...that him?"

"Oh, *Grim*! Yes! Thank God! Oh shit – look, can you
stay and talk to him? I'll fetch his food..."

"Sure – okay..."

The young woman darted back into the front door of the
house. Russell Roper, feeling more foolish than ever, crouched

down in the road and made eye-contact with big unblinking feline ones. "Hey, boy…come on out, kitty…Come on, boy…"

The young woman returned rattling a bag of cat-biscuits. "Grimbles…?"

The cat sat under the car, and began to wash a paw.

"Oh God…what am I to do?" She took in the stranger for the first time. He was about thirty-two, slim, dark and good-looking, dressed in jeans and a light-coloured tweed jacket. "This is really kind…I only opened the door to someone with a parcel…and he just dashed out…Oh, God!"

"Perhaps if you leave his food in a bowl – you know, by your door, he'll come in of his own accord…"

"Worth a try, perhaps. I'm just so frightened of this road…he isn't mine…I'm looking after him and now he's escaped…Oh, Grimbles…" The young woman crouched, and realised too late that her robe was gaping. She stood up and clasped it round herself, glad to see that the stranger's rather vivid brown eyes were concentrated on the cat.

"Here, give me that food…".The young man took a handful of biscuits and held it out. The cat's nose twitched and it edged forward, sniffing. "That's right, boy…easy now…easy…" Russell Roper reached under the car, grabbed at a thick furry neck and pulled. "Got him! He's quite a weight! Ow!" The cat Greymalkin struggled violently and leapt from the man's arms, darting back into the house.

"Oh! Look, he's gone back indoors! Quick – come inside – I need to shut the door! Oh, thank you! Oh God – you're bleeding! And look at your jacket!" Russell Roper's hand was indeed bleeding, and his sleeve had acquired a long oily smear.

"Well – er – if it's not troubling you, I would be grateful to wash my hands a bit…"

The young woman led him inside, along a carpeted corridor beside a staircase. At the end of the passage, a door with a bunch of house-keys in the lock stood ajar. Beside it, there was a perspex covered bell, and a name, 'V Dearborn', written rather carelessly in blue biro. "Come in, quick. Let me shut the door. The kitchen's just through here – or better still, the bathroom – that's just through there on the left. Help yourself. Grimbles! Oh, you wicked, wicked boy!"

"You're such a naughty, naughty pussikins," the girl in the Chinese robe was cooing when Roper re-emerged. "Look at him now! Butter wouldn't melt!" The cat was munching biscuits from a bowl. "How's your poor hand?"

"Still a bit messy…you wouldn't have a band-aid or anything, would you?"

"I don't know. I'll go and have a look. Would you like some coffee?"

"Thanks," said the man. "That would be great. I'm Russell Roper. I'd shake hands, but…" Roper's right hand was still bleeding.

"Oh God, that looks deep – and painful! You *poor* thing! Look, run the cold tap on it some more and I'll find some Dettol…I'm Miranda Hooper. Hang on a sec!" The girl darted off through the main door.

Roper ran the tap, but finding some kitchen paper, he made a rudimentary bandage and sneaked a look round. Veronica Dearborn's kitchen – more a kitchenette – was divided from a comfortable sitting room by an arch with shelves, on which stood several potted plants and some cookery books. The sitting area – books, papers, sofas, a handsome old bureau-style desk, a couple of Victorian lamps – was a delightful clutter, a sort of invitation to one of those Sunday supplement 'room of my own' pieces. French-windows, curtained in heavy old lace, led out onto a pretty courtyard…

"Here we are! First-aid!" The girl had returned, silent on the velvet slippered feet. "Sit down, Mr – er – Roper? Here, at the kitchen table…" She began competently applying some antiseptic ointment to his wound and then a large sticking plaster. She still wore the robe, wrapped rather more tightly with its silk cord, and was so close to him he could smell her – good scent from (he guessed) the day before, overlaid with the almost irresistible aroma of a healthy young woman who had only recently left her bed…her skin was unblemished and creamy…

"Thank you. You're a marvellous nurse…Amanda?"

"Miranda…Hooper…and people call me Minx. Er, there you are. You won't bleed over your jacket now. No need for thanks. It's the very least I can do. Perhaps we can find some white vinegar or something for that oil on your sleeve…it should come out. You were an absolute star, helping with Grimbles like that! Thank you!"

"My pleasure – only too glad to help. He's a very fine cat," said Roper politely.

"Isn't he? Everybody calls him 'Grim' but he's really Greymalkin…from *Macbeth*. Oh dear, sorry. I got into a bit of a panic…" She was blushing. "I promised you coffee – I'll make some if I can find Veronica's coffee things. It's one of those old-fashioned Italian percolators. I hope that's okay…" She was clattering about, chattering, finding milk.

"Fine, Miranda…Just great…"

"I'm really sorry. God knows what you *think*…I'm not even dressed or anything…I just came down to feed him and then the bell went, and I left this door open, stupidly…and then you came…Thank God you did, Mr Roper!"

"Call me Russell, please, Miranda. I quite understand." Roper smiled. He was delighted. This was a completely unexpected twist on a morning he had imagined would be fraught with difficulty.

Miranda, for her part, was young enough, and confident enough, for *dishabille* before a handsome stranger not to worry her unduly. Moreover, for reasons that were not entirely clear to her, she was relieved that on her mission upstairs to fetch first-aid things she had not had to disturb the still soundly sleeping

94

Rory... The *caffetiera* bubbled. "Here we are, Russell – coffee. These contraptions are amazingly quick. I bet you'd like a proper American one with hot milk? It's fresh. Veronica only left yesterday... Here we are! You *are* American, aren't you?"

"Everybody says that. Actually I'm English – folks come from Surrey – but I've worked in the United States for so long, I've sort of gone native. No sugar, thanks..." He sipped. "Great coffee! And you're joining me. So – Miranda – Miss Dearborn's away and you're house-keeping, right?"

"Not exactly – I mean, sort of. I – that is we – live upstairs. Veronica's in – away – and we're taking care of the cat and everything...she's our landlady. My boyfriend – Rory – he's Veronica's nephew. We're students."

"Ah..." Shame about the live-in boyfriend. "I expect you're wondering why I'm here."

"Oh! All that panic about Grimble and your hand put everything out of my head..." He had a rather wonderful smile. "Oh no! Ohmigod! Are you a *journalist*, Russell? Because, if you are, you probably shouldn't be here at all..." But her conker-brown eyes shone with mischief. "Veronica's sort of allergic to them...and I can't in fairness tell you anything at all," she added importantly.

"Don't worry, Miranda. I'm not a journo." Roper sipped coffee. "I work for a film company."

"A film company? Wow! But why...? Oh! Hang *on* a minute..." When she frowned, she looked prettier than ever. "Is

95

this about *Too Big To Cry*? Her book?" Miranda's trainee-journalist nose was twitching.

"It might be. Look, I was really hoping to have a word with Miss Dearborn in person…an off-chance thing. But she's away, you say, Miranda… Minx…it suits you…"

"Thank you! Yes. She's – abroad. I'm afraid you'll have to get hold of her in person, Russell. You should have made an appointment instead of just turning up."

"I should have, yes…" Russell Roper's eyes were mock-solemn.

"But you didn't. You didn't, because you thought she'd never agree to see you. I get it. You were going to doorstep her, weren't you? And you got me instead! Poor you…"

"I can think of worse things…" The red robe was gaping again. "When's Miss Dearborn due back?"

"A week or so, maybe longer. You'll have to try ringing her or texting, and then she can decide for herself whether to see you or not."

"Would you be kind enough to let me know when she's home?"

"I don't know…I might. I'm not at all sure I should…"

"She can always say no…can't she?"

The front door down the passage rattled, and she hastily pulled the robe round herself. "Rory!"

A young man, tousle-haired and rubbing his chin, appeared in the doorway, dressed in a blue track suit and nothing on his feet.

"Hi, babes...what's up? I heard a noise. Oh..." He took in the stranger, blinked.

Miranda took charge of the situation with an alacrity that Russell Roper was forced to admire.

"Rory, this is a hero called Russell Roper. He's just helped me grab Greymalkin from the jaws of death in the road and got wounded in the process. I'm giving him some coffee to compensate, not to mention Dettol and plasters. Russell, this is Rory Penrose, my boyfriend." Russell stood up. "Don't try to shake hands. Russell's hand's out of action, Rorykins. Grimbles savaged him!"

"Oh, shit! Sorry. He's a lot less cuddly than he looks. He belongs to my aunt. I'm glad Miranda's – um – taken care of you."

"Wonderfully. Great to meet you, Rory," said Roper.

"Me too. I thought I heard a hullabaloo. So he went for the great escape, did he? He's a bit of a liability. I say, um, thanks a million. How amazing. Where is the cat, Minx? Is he okay?"

"Curled up on the sofa, cosy as pie. Oily smear on his back. Just look at him! I did *shout*, Rory, but you were still asleep! Russell was just passing and he came to the rescue..."

"That's really kind of you – and what luck for us! My aunt would have gone ballistic."

Roper got to his feet. "And now I'm probably in the way! I have to run – I have a business meeting. Thanks for the coffee! Great to meet you both…Not at all, so glad to be of help…Some cat, that!"

"I'm just so *grateful*…"

"Yeah, we both are…really kind of you. Cheers, Russell. Really lucky for us you happened to be there."

"I'll see you out, Russell," said Miranda. "There's some coffee left on the stove, Rory…" She shut the door of the Dearborn apartment firmly, and led Roper back down the corridor to the street door. "I'm so sorry about your poor hand…should you get antibiotics? See a doctor or something?"

"I'll risk it, Miranda. Thanks for the coffee and – er – everything."

"Oh, that was nothing! And – well, um, how nice to meet you…." They stood awkwardly, half in and half out of the doorway.

"Could I have your number? It would be fun – nice – to get in touch sometime…" His gaze held hers, two pairs of knowing brown eyes unable, quite, to look away.

"Yeah, okay. Why not? Here, let me." She took his notebook and wrote. "But if this is just about meeting Miss Dearborn, I'm not sure I can help. I really can't give you her private number or anything."

"It isn't…it's about meeting you…Minx," said Russell Roper, who in any case had Veronica's number already. He took

98

her by her silk-clad shoulder with his good hand, kissed her cheek, and left.

"This is pristine, Datchery....pristine." Matthew Lucodin put the treatment and the first five scenes of *Too Big To Cry* in his attaché case.

"Thanks, Luco. Usual deal?"

"Of course...still don't see why."

"Call it my whim. You know where to find me."

"Fair play, Datch. But if this wins a Best Screenplay Award, what do I do?"

"You collect it, Luco. You just collect it."

Matthew Lucodin faxed the treatment to Eddie Potter and another to his colleague in London, and then boarded his plane at JFK and followed it there.

Matthew

Great book, great treatment. Like it! Date?? No problem next Friday.

Best, E.P.

Lucodin read. "You spoke to him, you say?"

"Sure. He's keen. But he's got another offer, Matt. It's in the States, and he's hesitating because of this baby. Katie can't travel. But we have to give him something definite."

"Shit," said Lucodin. The air around him seemed to fizz and crackle with his pent up energy, and his appearance in the

Soho office had, as ever, created a mild maelstrom. His two travelling bags were on the floor, his leather jacket was half on and half off the back of his chair, and he chain-smoked as he read the screen, looking wild and travel-stained, and as if he had medicated himself out of jet-lag. He paced the floor. "We're going to lose him, Roper. We have to give him a date at the very least. Damn and fuck that *stupid* dame! You said you were going to see her…I take it your fatal charm failed."

"It didn't even get an airing, I'm afraid, at least not with La Dearborn. The lady's gone away. Short vacation in Italy. Pity. I saw the lodger and ended up rescuing the cat…got wounded in the fray. She might have weakened if she'd been there to see…the bloody animal ought to belong to a witch!"

"Rescuing a *cat*? For Chrissakes, Roper! Look, Roper, you spoke to Frayle after I did. He's pretty pissed with her. You say he's half suggesting we go ahead anyway."

"Quite so, fairly directly. Naughty Mr Frayle. If he were my agent, I'd tell him where to stick it, frankly."

"Fuck that. Her problem. We have a story. We have a writer. We have a private backer with an itchy cheque-book. Logan's in if Potter's in. Potter can get Frazer Pearce. A director and a camera for a dream-team. I'm onto the casting…I suppose we have to kow-tow to whatever Potter wants in the end…and we need him. He's the ace. Okay. Don't look at me like that. Tell me the worst." He sat down exhausted.

"Porter-Maine," said Roper succinctly. "Wensum Edgar will simply nix it."

"You've tried the others? Cottonflex? Chattaways?"

"Of course. Matt – it's going to be the same everywhere. No indemnity, no insurance. No insurance, no backers. Bottom line. Logan won't be enough by himself."

"So much for loyalty! So you're saying we're fucked. Okay. What the fuck are we going to do now? Frayle's being about as helpful as a band-aid on a broken leg. We *need* her, goddammit! We get Porter-Maine if we can get the indemnities, signed and sealed. Logan's in if Potter's in, but Potter *and* Logan will only sign if we can get a *Cry* company formed asap, on the table, and we can only do *that* if the contracts pass scrutiny, and they'll only pass if all the boxes are ticked. This dame could solve it with one flourish of her stupid fucking name, and she's got us by the balls. Potter will only play it by the book. Round in circles. Fucking Brits. Sorry. Nothing personal. I want some strong coffee. Where's that Mandy?"

"Mandy hasn't worked for us since *Rhapsody*, Matt…we do have a machine…" Russell Roper was in for a long morning.

"That cat's piss! Forget it. No. Don't forget it. Ring down to Cohen's and get them to send up something. Coffee and a club sandwich and a strudel. I need sugar. And get another Mandy asap! Someone who doesn't yap the whole time, and someone who can spell. Hell, you're not saying we have to wash the thing out? I've just bought half a script."

101

"No-o…not exactly. But I am saying that unless we get backers who are prepared to punt out uninsured we have a problem. Show me someone who'll be prepared to lose his wad on this, and we can go ahead, and say to hell with Porter-Maine and the rest. My guess is that we have to find another story. Something Potter will like, and something safe. There is other low-budget stuff about…"

"Shit…"

Russell Roper straddled a chair opposite his senior colleague, whose blue eyes seemed huge behind his wire-framed specs. "Matt… there's nobody in the world who's going to chance this one. Let's look at some other low-budget celebrity biog stuff and stop dreaming of flying pigs, okay?"

"Go and get some food and decent coffee."

While Roper was out on this necessary errand, Lucodin made a call.

vii: The Last Resort

Daubney's Bar was tucked into a side-street between Long Acre and Floral Street. It was old-fashioned seedy, the sort of place that had always been faintly seedy, catering as it always had for the down-market end of 'West End business' rather than 'City trading', and thus had retained a louche sort of theatricality, quaint like a stage-set uncannily preserved since before the First War. It still did old-fashioned meals, now over-priced and decidedly second-rate: the meat-pies gluey, the suet puddings sticky, stickier still with packet custard and ersatz cream, but it still kept a decent cellar, and some half-good malt whiskeys. Its darkly forlorn interior was a shabby studded leather and velvet curtained affair – curtains that must once have been crimson – with oak panelling adorned with fly-blown Hogarth prints, and framed Edwardian political cartoons at which no one had laughed for a very long time. Behind the bar hung a sepia portrait of Lillie Langtry, whose once sumptuous delineations were now blurred with the grime of nearly a century. The public part occupied just the one long, dingy room that almost never got the light and smelled of stale cigar-smoke (Daubney's was a private establishment – in theory, one had to be a member – and a smoking area at the end had been legitimately retained.) At the farther side of the bar counter, a door marked 'private' led to a scruffy, unpleasant office and the kitchens (which perhaps did not bear thinking about) while next to that, another door led to the old-fashioned tiled 'conveniences' which were kept surprisingly clean despite the ancient plumbing.

The original 'Daubney' was long since forgotten. Sometime in the nineteen-noughts he had opened a small hotel that had catered mainly for touring actors, but the rooms to let had closed in the late nineteen-forties, and the upstairs premises, being long since sold, now housed an advertising agency. Only the Bar remained, and Daubney's was now run by a sour-natured old woman called Mrs Elvira Lake, whose fat be-ringed fingers were rumoured to be in any number of pies, and who these days almost never put in a public appearance, her former habitual post at the wooden cash-kiosk at the entrance deserted but somehow expectant. The only visible staff were two ageing waiters who cordially loathed each other. 'Dolly'- nobody knew his real name - was a tall and soldierly old fellow who had actually worked for the Dorchester in his heyday, and considered himself a considerable cut above Frick, a small, balding, émigré Hungarian Jew who had simply worked for Daubney's time out of mind. Rumour had it that Frick was a lapsed actor who had played junior leads on the West End stage – unlikely, given his accent – and that, perhaps more probably, he had been the venerable Elvira's paramour when she was young and slender, but that was hearsay too, and the clientele, such as it was, usually had other things on its mind.

At any time between the hours of eleven in the morning and ten pm, you might find the sort of people who could no longer afford the Carlton or the Garrick; or those who could, but who for purposes of their own actually preferred the dubious murkiness of Daubney's. No actor would be seen dead in the place now, not even if he were out of work and up for rent; but the Bar was popular with collapsed hedge-fund dealers, sidelined bankers, displaced politicians, bankrupt businessmen, losing gamblers and drunks of the smarter sort. This was networking of a very old-fashioned and trusted kind. In some circles, Daubney's Bar was known as the Last Resort… Conversation was invariably hushed, if sometimes agitated, conducted in urgent whispers. Here, under-the-table deals were thrashed out and contracted in undertones; here, too, dubious cheques and sometimes hard cash changed hands, some of it finding its way into the pocket of 'Dolly', or, as it might be, Frick – as a little tip, for thanks, for silence. Often, someone divulged a real 'tip' – the three-thirty at Exeter on Foldaway, maybe – for which Frick was obsequiously grateful.

Now, in a corner of the smoking area, a handsome, overweight roué of uncertain age, a man with a flushed fair face and light blue, bloodshot eyes – a man who had once been very good-looking, but who had shaved badly, whose wavy greying hair needed the attentions of a barber, and whose once smart Savile Row gents' natty now badly needed a clean – was in deep and earnest conversation with a younger man, a stockily-built individual wearing wire specs with thick lenses and a leather jacket, and whose straggly grizzled black hair was tied back in a ponytail; a man who, despite his attire, looked sleekly successful as well as odd and arty, and who as such had caught the sharp attention of 'Dolly'. For one thing, the younger man was sober. He also spoke with an American accent (almost certainly New York – one acquired an ear for these things at the Dorchester) and 'Dolly' listened unashamedly, adjusting the table accoutrements, mats, salt and pepper...poured napkin-wrapped wine into the glasses... "Sir...sir..." A murmured undertone.

"This needs a bold touch, a bit of vision. If anyone's got it, you have, Gilbert," the American was saying. "You've done it before..."

"But the *risk*..." wailed the Englishman softly. "If Porter-Maine won't insure, nobody else will..."

"This isn't like you, Gil. These companies have to behave like milksops because the shareholders hold the whips, and their lawyers need to fund their golf subscriptions. You know this. Sure, I'm not kidding you. It's a risk! It's also a potential goldmine. Another *Four Weddings*..."

"It's hardly a bloody comedy, Luco, old boy. It's not even a tragedy. It's just a bloody mess..."

"All right, forget *Four Weddings*. But it's no mess. It's realistic drama about English upper-crust low-life – present company excepted, of course – and with a huge appeal potential in the US. You're a gambler, Gil! Take a punt!"

"Shhh…I know, Luco. Lissen…" The older man was obviously very drunk, but drunk in the way habitual drunks can remain virtually sober-seeming, or at least sit up straight. "I have gambled, right? Don't deny. Gambled. Sometimes I've won. Good eye. Good *nose*…but I've lost my nerve. Never trust a woman. Stupid t'truss a woman! I'm liquidating everything I've got." He helped himself to more wine, and Dolly was once more adroitly at his elbow, ensuring that most of the wine went into the glass. "Sh'wass going to see me right…in the end…"

"As I understand it, the estate was mostly all entailed anyway, Gil," said the American when the waiter had faded. "Your late wife couldn't have left it to you even if she'd wanted to… Now you have to re-nvest, and invest well, Gil. Way I see it, you need a way out. You can't afford cold feet." The American's voice was slow, patient; but the observant 'Dolly' saw that under the table the ponytailed man was cracking his knuckles.

"But we're talking about the last drop, Luco. Everything liquid I had went down the pan with Goldfarb. Everybody went broke. You lost yourself. Then that *Betty Luck* show flopped when that neurotic fart Blakemore went lame. Nervous 'b' bedamned. He just saw a turkey before I did. Fucking comedians. I – we – Annie and I – we had a holding of eighteen percent – *eighteen percent* – of what should've been a smash hit, Luco. I'd planned to recover everything….Anabel never knew, thank God. Now I'm selling the Dorking house, Cap Ferrat's gone, of course, and the pictures, the lot…the cars are up for

107

auction...and the market's dire...I'm down and out, Luco, old boy. Down and out...I live from hand to mouth...in squalor." The man's bloodshot eyes watered as if he were about to weep, but he paused, seeing 'Dolly' hovering with a tray. "It's all been so *fast*..."

"Cheer up. You need some sustenance, Gil, my friend."

The man called Gil lowered his voice to a messy whisper after the unappetising plates had been put in front of them and 'Dolly' had vanished. "I've been desperate, Luco. I'm being honest with you. Honest. I've been dipping into waters no sane man would go near if he weren't desperate. I've – I've trusted people I shouldn't, follow me? There was a – a burglary at Cap Ferrat. Lost some pictures. Can't say too much. The insurance paid up. But I'm not cut out for crime, Luco. Lost my bottle. I could be facing jail – and what for? It amounted to scarcely enough to eat...even this crap. Used t'be better, this place...Look, I need another risk like a hole in the head. I need something sound, kosher. You understand..."

"That's what I'm offering. Chrissakes, what is this? Tastes like boiled warthog. Now then, about this movie...pass the pepper, would you?"

"Oh God...You're asking me to gamble *again*! And on this, of all things!" Gilbert took a mouthful of grey gristle and became aware of overdue dental work. "I was always there for her, y'know? Right up t'the end...feel a bit of a traitor. This is

108

her family we're talking about. I'd rather anything but this. I used t'be half decent once."

"But – Gil – Anabel won't know about this, will she?"

"No. True enough, s'pose." He put down his fork with a grimace. "Poor Annie. She was always a sport, Annie…almost miss her, y'know…I *do* miss her! Gave her a good time. Loved the Silver Ghost, did Annie…rode around Menton with a veil and the top down, like Isadora Duncan…had a stroke, y'know. Brainstorm. One minute pouring us a gin and tonic on the veranda in Cap Ferrat, the next minute on the floor. I heard the glasses rattle and then an almighty crash… At least it was quick. It was that book that did the real damage. That fat junkie bitch practically killed her own mother!"

"And she can't be killed all over again, now can she? You have to be a bit practical, Gil."

"But she wouldn't have wanted them to hate me…and they'll sue. They'll all try to sue, and halt the filming. Gang up."

"Let 'em try! Look, they won't have a leg to stand on. Like I keep telling you, Gil, the story is there, for anyone to pick up and use. It's not *criminal*, for Chrissakes! We're not, repeat not, going to be breaking copyright. It's just lawyers rattling the bars, and that's only an 'if'. The point is, if we don't grab it, someone else will, and we'll have lost the whole shebang, including any say-so over content, and for what? Cinéast is interested, and they won't care that the rights aren't sold. We have to get in first. This is serious property, Gil."

109

"S'nobody's property but hers unless we own it."

"And I'm saying that it doesn't matter. Look at it as a payback for all your devotion. Think about it!"

"Hmm. You say Frayle's in?"

"Go ask him. He suggested this way forward himself. No kidding."

"Frayle's no fool, s'pose... James Dearborn's just disappeared, know that? Couldn't be fished to come to the funeral even. Somewhere in South Africa...but he'll be back. Bloody hippie. Bad as the sister. That fat bitch hates me. I helped her, you know. Helped her! When she came out of jail, I set her up. Little flat in Fulham. Practically Chelsea. Nice little place. Was she grateful? Was she hell! Insisted on paying rent so she wouldn't owe me or her mother a sou. Left as fast as she could and took some slum up the road and wrote that poisonous best seller...I did *try*, you know, Luco, with all of Annie's brood. Did my best. No children of my own, y'know..." The man Gil poured wine with a shaking arm, spilling an expensive red puddle onto the tablecloth.

Lucodin muttered: "Oh, Christ... Gil, *forget* James Nibs! *Forget* the fat junkie! Forget the indemnities. Gil! The poisonous best seller is about to sell again! You might as well get something out of it for yourself. For Chrissake's, man, hear me, will you? Holy fish! I've got enough in this myself, haven't I? So's Frayle. I'm no more a fool than you are, Gil. The ones who are too scared to come in are just going to lose and eat shit...

110

Hell, I can't eat any more of this…" He pushed his plate away. "We just have to act a bit fast if we're going to, Gil…this is no time for sentiment."

"The real problem's goin' to be whatsisface…the politico…married little Lucie…Rather loved little Lucie. Sweet kid…"

"Oh, shit…" murmured Lucodin.

"We'll have to watch out for him." Gilbert sounded suddenly more sober. "Really. He'll have more clout than the others. Funny. Heard something about him the other day…memory isn't what it was, but I know it made me laugh. Wonder what it was…Sorry?"

"I said we have to make a move, Gilbert."

"Can we really get Eddie Potter?"

"Potter.and Pearce for the cinematography. Same crew as before. Dream team. If Potter and Pearce are in, Logan's in. He'll punt on Potter, with or without indemnities. Word will get round if you and Logan back it…nobody will want to miss it. *Everybody* will want a slice, for Chrissakes! It's not as if we're talking big budget here."

"You mean it's cheap?" Gilbert's face fell comically.

"It's a steal. Potter swears we only need two real locations – a small stately home, some grounds, and a big London mansion we can pass off as Mayfair…the rest is bars, interiors and archives."

"And the prison? The courtroom?"

"Studio stuff. Sets, and some of it exists already. This is not, repeat not, an expensive movie."

"Hmph. I don't believe you. These things always cost. Closing down bits of the West End at five in the morning...And if it's too cheap, it'll be crap anyway..."

"I mean it's relatively cheap to *make*. No special effects, and no stunts, obviously, unless you count the flyer off of the balcony..." Lucodin was still hungry. "I'm going to chance a dessert...You? No, okay. Trust me, Gilbert. Look at it this way. We save on the options. We can start. Can you wear a cognac with the coffee? Waiter!"

'Dolly' appeared as if from out of the panelling – his white jacket to the sozzled eyes of Gilbert Wardley-Hill almost ghostly in the dingy light. "Sir?"

Matthew Lucodin ordered the cognacs and a custard trifle. He had scented triumph.

Gil was musing. "What about the lead role? She'll hefterbegood...*good*. Not a glamour-puss...an actress, proper actress to play that overweight hussy...Th'whole point'd be not to change the story, glamorise it..." Gilbert had been, in his time, amongst a great many other things, a theatre 'angel' with a reputation, whose backing had attracted other backers like mackerel to a sprat. When his brain wasn't addled, he knew what he was talking about. Listening to a load of horse-shit was all in Lucodin's day's work. And despite his protestations, Gilbert Wardley-Hill was still a seriously rich man, and his 'squalor' was furnished apartments in Albany. "And Annie," Gilbert was saying. "You'll need someone good fr' Annie...don't want her to come out too, y'know, savaged...need a propractress..."

"Of course, of course. You said. We'll find her. We've got good people, Gil. We'll use Catto for the casting. But, hey, we're being a bit previous, talking about actors..."

"Hmm? Whaty'say?"

"Gil...look, we can't begin casting yet, you know that. No agent will bite unless the project actually exists...can I take it you're in?"

Gilbert took a sip of cognac. "If I do it, and I'm only saying 'if', old man, it would still be better all round if we get her say-so, if only to muzzle Penrose. Sorry. I may be a bit the worse for wear these days – rather a lot on my mind, y'know... But I'm not a bloody fool..."

"Roper's onto it...Roper's a lawyer and he's English. He understands these people. I – er – take it you don't have any – er – personal influence there?"

"Good God, no! Wish I could remember about that Puffing Penrose...Loved little Lucie, I did. Best of the bunch." Gilbert was becoming maudlin again. Lucodin considered his companion, calculating shrewdly that for now everything useful had been done.

"Gilbert, I brought along some documents, but perhaps they might keep until later...like tomorrow, after you've had a rest...Take the copies home..."

113

A little later, after they had emerged blinking into the bright mid-afternoon in the alley between the theatres, and Lucodin had helped Gilbert, who was staggering only just a little, into a taxi in Long Acre, with arrangements, several times repeated, to meet over documents the next day, Lucodin called Eddie Potter.

PART TWO: NEST OF VIPERS

viii: Vacation

The tall fair-haired man beside Veronica at the edge of the baggage carousel at Rome Fiumicino had an injured left arm, bandaged and strapped inside his jacket. He made an awkward grab for his bag with his good limb and missed, swearing under his breath as it sailed slowly out of his reach. The polyglot crowd of holiday makers jostled and chattered and reached for their luggage, barging into him with their trolleys, putting him visibly out of temper. Veronica spied her own bag emerging. "Excuse me," she said. "*Posso? Per favore*?" But she was almost certain he was English. The man stepped a little to one side with a grunt as Veronica reached across to haul her small suitcase from the conveyor. The tall man saw his own re-emerge and stepped in front of her without apology. He made an inept grab as it levelled with them. "Damn and blast!"

"Here, let me," Veronica said, seizing the handles of an old-fashioned grip. "There! I hope it's the right one."

"Yes – yes it is. Bloody things! That was very kind. Sorry. One needs two hands…" He tried to smile. Veronica thought he must be in pain.

"How rotten for you. Well, goodbye. And um, have a good trip!"

Veronica was determined to have a holiday. She had booked a car, and felt a certain holiday freedom as she drove away from the pound. She left the autostrada when she emerged from the flat purlieus of Rome past Latino, and motored south down the coast road into the sparkling mid-morning. She enjoyed the whole process of driving: the feel of a powerful little car under her feet and hands, the sense of foreignness, driving on the right. She felt her spirits lift. In a scruffy resort she paused for a double-strength cappuccino in a seaside bar and checked her map. To reach her destination, she could continue along the coast which, now flat and scruffy, had begun to bore her, or she could ascend into the forested hills. A switchback road with sudden blissful vistas over vertiginous drops which took all her skill and concentration occupied the next hour, and she paused again for a light lunch in a tiny mountain village and allowed herself to simply sit for a while, breathe the air and stare at the view. She sent a text to Freddy.

It was balmy early evening when she found Monte Farfalla – as promised, a handsome medieval town perched on rocks above the sea – and she found the Piazza Umberto remarkably easily, parking the little Lancia in one of the marked spaces immediately outside the hotel. The Albergo Del Mare, an elegant baroque building festooned with flags, looked welcoming. She handed over her passport and checked in, asking about her car in careful Italian. But the girl behind the desk

116

spoke English. English, indeed, with an Estuarian twang. "That's okay, Mrs – er – Dearborn, isn't it? We've been expecting you. You can leave it in the street outside where it's marked, and I'll give you a residents' card you can put behind the windscreen. If you'd just fill out the details here for me…okay?   Just the one bag, is it, or would you like some help?"

"No, just the one, thanks…"

"Great – okay, I'll get Gianni to show you up. Here we are. If you just pop this in your car everything will be fine or Gianni can do it if you want to leave the keys. Here's your room key – I've put you in number four. I hope everything's all right for you. Number four's got a nice bathroom, and you'll find a kettle and everything. We serve breakfast between eight and ten, down here in the bar. I'm afraid there's no lunches or dinners, but there's lots of restaurants if you fancied a wander down to the sea. I can give you a little map…here we are."

"Thank you. I'm sure everything will be fine. Actually, a friend is meeting me here later. You must be English…"

"Half! Actually only a quarter. My Dad's English, from London, but my gran, my Mum's mum, she's Italian…"

"That explains it…."

"There's lots of English here …are you on holiday?"

"Yes…touring a bit, seeing friends."

"That's very nice. It's turned lovely and warm for us now, hasn't it? Gianni!"

"Oh, don't worry about the car – I can do it."

117

"It's no trouble! He'll show you up to your room – I can't leave the desk. *Numero quattro*, Gianni…"

Gianni, a swarthy unsmiling youth of about twenty-two, took the key and Veronica's case. "This way, please, madame," he said ushering her up a flight of narrow marble stairs.

The room, a single with a pleasant en-suite bathroom, had a view not of the bay but of the Albergo's small and rather pretty walled garden, which was already rich with wisteria and gelsomino, and Veronica spotted borders with bearded irises and budding roses. A little pergola gave onto a paved area set with wooden tables and chairs. "How pretty," Veronica remarked. *"Che bello – un carino giardino…"*

"Yes, madame. It is the spring." The straight-faced Gianni put Veronica's bag on a small platform. "Enjoy your stay." Veronica wondered if she should tip him, but he vanished, closing the door quietly behind him.

When Veronica descended the stairs after her shower, she found Freddy Partridge, dressed in loose linen and a silk cravat, waiting for her in the lobby.

"Vee! Darling! Welcome to Monte Farfalla!" He embraced her extravagantly.

"Wow! You look amazingly summery, Freddy…" Her own dark jacket and trousers seemed suddenly very British and probably too heavy for the weather.

"Ah – you've found your friend, Mrs Dearborn," said the girl, emerging from an inner office. "Oh, it's Freddy! Ciao, Freddy! Hi! Have a nice evening…"

"Thanks, Becky," said Freddy cheerfully. "Now then, dear thing – I think lobsters, don't you? You don't mind a little walk, do you? It isn't far…"

They dined on the gay little canopied terrace of a small trattoria, one of several along the sea-front. The pavement was still thronged with the *passeggiata:* mostly locals, strolling, chattering; middle aged women walking arm in arm; family parties with children, little ones running on ahead, smaller ones in pushchairs; one or two tourists gazing at menus; and the little bay was busy – fishing boats tying up after the day's work; others pushing out for an evening catch. There was a dusky iridescence on the water as the evening deepened, and across the water on the other side lights began to wink in the twilight. They bit into garlicky bruschetti and toasted each other with the local red wine. "You have to admit it is all rather sublime. *Al dente,*" he added to the hovering waiter, "*ma ti prego, caro, non troppo.*" Freddy was in the highest of spirits, and Veronica caught his mood.

"It is rather fabulous, Freddy. Terribly picturesque. I'm looking forward to seeing it properly in daylight. I can see why your uncle settled here. 'Farfalla'. Doesn't that mean butterfly?

"Clever girl. It does. Because of the shape of the bay, I think, rather than local fauna. But really it ought to be called 'Monte Fossili'...."

"Fossils?"

"In one, my dear! The place is just crawling with superannuated ex-pat Brits. Americans too. It would be absolute hell to live here, believe me."

"You know them at the Albergo, I gather...do you know everybody?"

"Everybody who's anybody. That's just the tip of the iceberg, dearie. You've not met Becky's parents yet? Silvana and Dennis Barker?"

"No – I only arrived a couple of hours ago..."

"Well, the Barkers are like the Fawltys but even less lovable. I've been coming here on and off since Uncle Cad decided to leave the comforts of Somerset and set up home. I'm a sort of tolerated infiltrator. Now then, I've got it all planned. I'll take you to 'Il Cacciatore' outside San Gregorio tomorrow for a mountain lunch. That will be rather splendid – they're basically a winery with a simple restaurant, but they're seriously good. I'm writing them up, and they'll treat us like the queens we are. Then we're having dinner, just you and I, with Uncle Cad tomorrow evening at his favourite haunt. He's insisting on paying, by the way, and he'll give you a serious dissertation on why it is enormously good value, from starters to gooey pudding via the house red. Corinna can't join us, which is probably just as well."

120

"Who's Corinna?"

"Cad's squeeze. Aging blonde bombshell. English. Ve-ry charming, local nursing angel, ex-wife of a local notary – famous long-sufferer, by all accounts, because hubby won't stump up the alimony – but between you and me a sort of *grande horizontale*. But brains under the hair-do. Thinks she's got her elegant manicured paws into Uncle Cad's pockets. She's part of the Crew. Look, dear heart, I've got a teeny confession to make…"

"Oh? What? Oh, this *does* look delicious…" The pasta had arrived, and Freddy beamed at the young waiter.

"Indeed! Let's dig in. Yummy, yummy. Listen, I'm afraid I've had to promise Daphne to bring you along on Saturday. She holds a sort of weekly salon affair where they're vampires for new blood. They're all just dying to meet you…."

"Ohmigod. Who's Daphne?"

"Daphne Allerton. Local queen bee. Octogenarian widow, rather grand, sort of English county but more cosmopolitan and very eccentric. Perfect sweetie, really…feisty. Still sails boats. Late hubby was an American oil squillionaire. Like I said, she's longing to meet you…"

"You said 'all'. And 'crew'. What have you said to them, Freddy?"

"Well not much, really…you know, friend down for a visit, writer, come to talk to Cad about a friend of Milly's. I say, this pasta really is quite good…just goes to show you don't have to pay a fortune for a decent supper if you know where to go…"

"Heavenly. Don't change the subject."

"I'm doing a special feature for 'Epicure' on small restaurant economics."

"Freddy…"

"You know, from fishing-boat to table with the market in between. These little chaps were in the sea this morning…"

"Freddy!"

"All right. Pax. They asked your name and I told them, I mean I couldn't *not* tell them, and old Cad was boasting. It was Cecilia Porter who put two and two together. She reads, which is more than you can say of most of them… Perfectly ghastly crowd, straight out of Somerset Maugham. Think of them as a sideshow. Or material if you ever decide to embark on fiction. Oops, sorry, *sorry!*"

"Freddy. You just said they were sweeties. Damn it, they read the news don't they? The British press?"

"Well – you know – I imagine they have a pretty consistent diet of Sky telly and the European Torygraph and the Speccy. You know it's outrageous how most of them don't bother to learn Italian! Cecilia Porter's an Italian and her English is next door to perfect!"

"You're hedging, Freddy. They know exactly who I am, don't they?"

Freddy pulled a little-boy-in-trouble face and said 'Oops' again.

"Oh, *damn!* Honestly, Freddy!"

122

"Vee, darling, please don't get cross. Here, have another forkful of this delicious *vongole al spaghetti*, and we'll have the delicious Donato bring on our lovely lobbies..."

"I am cross, Freddy. If I'd thought this was going to be an exposure-fest, I wouldn't ever have come. I wanted a break."

"Vee – come on, old thing. Be a sport. Get it over with. If it makes you feel any better, they're much less interested in your interesting past than your handle. They're the most fearful snobs..."

"Oh, better and *better*..." But the lobster when it arrived with a theatrical flourish was indeed delicious, the wine was excellent, and Veronica's annoyance partially evaporated. It's not as if, she thought rather meanly, I actually have to go at all... "Saturday," she said. "I might have to escape quite early. I'm taking in a visit to Siena before I go back. I need to talk to the house agency."

"Not until Monday, surely, sweetie?" Freddy said, his deceptively innocent eyes twinkling with mischief. "We can just put in an hour or so. *Please*, Veronikins? I'll take you to a really fabulous dinner afterwards if we can shed Uncle Cad. Michelin. The works."

Veronica sighed. "All right, Freddy. I ought to kill you, but I suppose it's the price I pay for daring to take time off. I'll square up."

"I always said you're a trouper!"

123

"Hmph!" But she couldn't help smiling. "No, honestly, darling, not another drop. I've been up since dawn and tomorrow sounds like a busy day…"

ix: Routines

Daphne Allerton lived a strictly regular life. That is, she had a Routine. Her great friend, Corinna de Benedetto, teased her that it was more of a Timetable, and she too was inclined to imagine a capital letter.

As ever rising almost before the sun was up, on Mondays Daphne walked as briskly as she was able with her increasingly arthritic hip along the steep cobbled pavement to the fresh-produce market outside the Medici Gate to buy fruit, fish, bread, prosciutto and cheese, and call in at the Post Office before lugging the small load – Corinna had recently persuaded her into acquiring one of those canvas shopping carts on wheels – back to the crumbling antique *palazzo* where she owned a small, cramped 'eyrie' apartment with a large roof-terrace and enviable views up a great many stone stairs, fortifying herself with a strong vodka and tonic and cheese biscuits as she reloaded her fridge. In the afternoon after a frugal lunch, she dozed and spoke to her son Jonjo in California on the telephone.

On Tuesdays, she shopped at her local mini-market for household goods, went to the bank, and called in at the Albergo Del Mare in the Piazza to have coffee with Silvana Barker. This used to take place on a Monday, and Daphne had taken some persuading that Silvana was far too busy with the laundry supervision during the season to take a long and chatty coffee break. For this reason, Daphne had recently altered the Routine, so that coffee with Silvana now occupied Tuesday mornings, and her weekly walk in the countryside with Hedley Porter took place on a Thursday instead. Hedley's failing eyesight had forced him to give up driving, and so Daphne drove them to one of several favoured spots in the hills in her tiny Fiat 500, often so precariously that Hedley had had cause to remark to his wife Cecilia that it was just as well he could scarcely see (although it was true he could *feel* the swerves and bumps well enough, and sometimes he had to stiffen his resolve on a Thursday morning with a small nip of brandy with his breakfast eggs.)

Friday mornings were devoted to Whim. In the old days she had been an enthusiastic sailor, and had regularly sailed the 'Patrick II' round the Bay with a friend or two and a liquid picnic. Now, to Daphne's resigned regret (old age was such a *bore*) the yacht was sold, and she had consoled herself with the sturdy little 'Serena', a traditional wooden fishing vessel with a diesel engine that she had bought from a retired fisherman, and now shared with Dennis Barker, who would sometimes accompany her for a chug round the coast. After her last fall, Dennis had persuaded her that she must not go out alone (and what a *bloody* bore to bruise so easily) but Dennis was busy with the hotel and with his tour-bus, and she was careful not to ask him too often. So on Friday mornings, an old friend or perhaps a new friend might be invited to elevenses drinks on Daphne's terrace or in her little conservatory if it was chilly. These newer arrivals, more recently enfolded in Daphne's circle, were, alas, inveterate landlubbers – Dorinda Daly did not own a pair of shoes without high heels, and poor Minette Marquis was seasick. Nevertheless, they had both rather compensated for the loss of her regular sea-going adventures, and with either one of these ladies she would stare out across the water with a first and then a second double-strength vodka and tonic, gossiping and reminiscing with increasingly wild abandon.

Saturday morning saw the preparation for Saturday evening, which was, as J. Cadwallader Jones was wont to remark to anyone prepared to listen, the Focus of the Week. For it was on Saturday evenings that this small circle of friends, old, new or simply picked up by the Marina (where could usually be found a number of coastal journey-makers tied up to temporary moorings, pausing to replenish stocks and glad of the offer of a sociable evening in civilized company among fellow English, Americans or Antipodeans) would gather for drinks and barbecued sausages on Daphne's terrace in the summer, or squeeze into her cramped and overcrowded sitting room when the weather turned, and where indifferent wine flowed and plates of nursery food – egg and rocket rolls, tuna pâté and tomato sandwiches – circulated along with cheese and crackers, which people ate from plastic plates perched on their knees and mopped their mouths with kitchen-roll napkins. This regular Saturday *soirée* had been a part of life – the ex-pat life, that is – in Monte Farfalla for more years than anyone could remember. Apart from the time a couple of years ago when Daphne had had to go into hospital with her knee, and on the infrequent occasions when she visited her son Jonjo in California, it never varied.

On the Sabbath, unless someone provided a luncheon, Daphne rested, read light novels and drank vodka cocktails over her vast collection of videos, often falling into a long doze over *Bleak House* or *The Good Life* in her chair. But this morning was Wednesday, and invariably, Wednesday morning was Corinna.

Corinna de Benedetto, a tall, blonde, elegant woman of sixty-two if she would admit it (and a very fit sixty-two, and perfectly groomed and turned out, one who could pass for fifty-two easily, everyone said so) dressed casually on a Wednesday morning in pearls, trousers and a linen shirt or a cashmere pullover and a puffa jacket, depending on the weather – would leave her smart apartment with its newly-acquired parquet flooring and bespoke kitchen in the baroque *palazzo* across the road and let herself into Daphne's condominium street-door with her own key on the dot of ten o'clock, and climb the three flights of stone courtyard stairs to Daphne's apartment where Daphne would have left the door open in readiness. This Wednesday morning – it was early May, and promising to be hot – Corinna arrived bearing a large creamy *caldo-freddo* cake in a flimsy cardboard box. Because she had forgotten to put it in her fridge on the night before, it was now far more *caldo* than it was designed to be, and she was hoping it would not begin to drip. She held it carefully away from her white trousers.

"Hello, m'darling!" she called, entering the open door. The mat said 'Welcome', and above the door a framed sampler proclaimed in old-fashioned New England *petit-point* 'Good Friends Gather Here'. Corinna scarcely noticed these things, being as they were familiar time out of mind.

"Ah, at last, darling! You're here!" Corinna was not in the least late, but Daphne had been waiting, and (as Corinna put it to herself) the elderly are inclined to feel time acutely. Daphne, a tiny, thin, vigorous woman of almost eighty with a weather-beaten face and a lot of springy grey curly hair, dressed in khaki shorts to her bony knees, gym shoes, a white polo shirt and a great many gold chains, greeted her wielding a kitchen-knife and a lemon. The two women kissed the air by each other's faces, Corinna bending to Daphne's tiny level. "Oh…you brought another of *those*," said Daphne, indicating the cake-box. "I don't like them. Take it to Cad, dear. He's got a terribly sweet tooth. I'm in the conservatory. Sit down."

"Don't blame me. It was a present from Minette. She left it for you before she went back to Scotland. I'd better put it in the fridge. It's going gooey."

"Oh. Nice of her, dear, but I can't think why. She knows I don't like them. Generous, but silly."

"The *pasticceria* next door to her lets her have the leftovers. God knows what they must *think*," murmured Corinna.

129

She opened the fridge and tutted. "This fridge needs doing again, Daph. There's no room for this thing and it's melting." She gave up, found a plate and left the collapsing confection on the crowded worktop.

"I'll decide when my fridge needs cleaning, thank you, dear. Now, here we are…Quoddy-voddy, as poor dear Hilary used to say." Daphne got busy with the knife, and there came the powerful aroma of cut lemon. She poured very large measures from the vodka bottle, put in jagged lemon slices and cubes of ice. "I forgot to get any new tonic…this is a bit flat, but never mind…" She handed a glass to Corinna, who sipped cautiously. They went through to the tiny conservatory, where Daphne's armchair dominated, surrounded by newspapers and magazines in haphazard piles. On the little rattan side-table, perched against a broken china mug in which Daphne kept biro pens, was a paperback copy of *The Chorister's Carbuncle,* by Millicent Fox. Corinna sat down on the only other chair, where she had to fold her long legs awkwardly. Through the glass panels she gazed at the large, low-walled terrace, and the sparkling bay beyond. The conservatory felt uncomfortably stuffy. Daphne fitted a strong Marlboro into a long ivory holder and lit it.

"It's a lovely day. Can't we sit out?"

"Oh, I think we're all right in here, aren't we, dear?"

"I just thought you might like the air…" Corinna did not object to cigarette smoke as a rule, but this was at very close quarters, and the heat of the morning was beginning to be overpowering through the glass.

"I took plenty of air this morning, dear, watering the plants. Now then. Drink up and tell me your news! First I want to know about poor Constanza."

"Moh! Constanza's fine really – complaining. I've taught Becky how to do the injections..."

"Well, I suppose, dear, if she's determined to be a veterinary nurse, she might as well have some human beings to practice on..."

"Honestly," said Corinna, "what with Constanza's insulin and Hedley's antibiotics, I seem to spend most of my time puncturing people. Yesterday was the last day of Hedley's course, thank God. Hedley's been such a baby! So's Cecy. She has to leave the room." Corinna rolled her eyes. "Moh!"

"Is that the sight of the needle or Hedley's bare bottom, I wonder..."

Corinna giggled. "Oh, Daph! Honestly! You're just *too* awful! But Cecy always plays the drama-queen, especially now that Hedley's getting all the attention if you ask *me*. It's only a tooth abscess after all, and his dentist is a marvellous man. I recommended him. I can't think why he complains all the time."

"Very painful, poor Hedley. And Cecy is squeamish. Some people are. But you're such an angel of mercy, dear...It must be such a relief that Becky will take over the care of her grandmother for a while. You won't be quite so indispensable. Now then. Tell me. I want to know about your friend."

"Which friend?" Corinna was a little on edge. She was making a number of preparations, and Daphne was inclined to interrogate. Daphne tapped her nose and poked Corinna's arm with a bony finger. Corinna noticed that Daphne was not wearing her usual ring. "Oh – what happened to the Palm Springs diamond?"

"It keeps falling off. I'm going to get it made smaller. Don't change the *subject*!" When Daphne became agitated, she would bounce in her chair. She bounced now, and Corinna wondered if she had been killing time before her arrival with a breakfast vodka. "What about your *friend*!"

"You mean Pietro?"

"*You* might mean Pietro, dear, or whatever his name is. *I* meant Cad. John Cadwallader Jones…"

"Oh, God, *Cad*! He's complaining about his arthritis. His knees. And his feet hurt. I've told him to get himself a good pair of trainers but he refuses. He's so vain, insisting on his ancient handmade brogues…"

"Cadwallader is quite a gentleman. I'm afraid, dear, he is also *utter* chloroform! The most boring man on the planet, and possibly the ugliest. But if you're treating him badly, I won't have it! I met him in the market on Monday, and he insisted on talking about knees. And feet. And your absences…"

"Moh! I've been quite fantastically busy, darling. I can't massage his feet the whole time…Daphne, listen, darling, *I* want to talk about a certain date in July…" 'A certain date in July' was Daphne's eightieth birthday, and the cause of a great deal of local agitation.

"Are you sleeping with him?"

"What? Who…?"

"Cad. Are you *fucking him*, dear?"

"Cad? Daphne! No, I'm not. You must be joking. Look, Daffy darling, please listen! About July the fourth. When I went to see Constanza yesterday Dennis was there and he said to talk to Silvana and they've apparently…"

"He thinks you want to, evidently."

"Who thinks *what*?" Corinna felt distinctly uncomfortable. Her legs were cramped, her drink was too strong, and she was being quizzed.

"Cad. Wallader. Jones. Thinks you want to sleep. With. *Him*." Daphne punctuated herself with bounces. "He didn't put it like that, naturally. But he evidently thinks of you as his *fidanzata. I* haven't given him that impression, dear! But you. Clearly. *Have*. And speaking of rings…" On the third finger of Corinna's elegant left hand was a large, ungainly antique emerald set in marcasite. Daphne was giving it a meaningful stare.

"It was a present. I can't *not* wear it…"

"On *that* finger, dear? No wonder the poor man thinks his boat's come in."

"Moh! It's true he's become a bit – well, attached. I've had to save his feelings a bit. I'm terribly fond of him as you know. And he's been – well, grateful, since all that hospital business last year. But it's all completely innocent – a nice, platonic friendship. I mean, honestly, Daphne, *you* can't possibly think that in a million years I'd…"

"What I think is neither here nor there. It's what people are *saying*, dear…"

"Moh! People say far too much," said Corinna with a spike of anger. "*What* people?"

"Minette and her daughter saw you kissing last week outside 'La Terrazzina'. Perhaps you didn't see them…being preoccupied…?"

"Kissing who?"

"Cad. Wallader. *Jones*! How many more times?"

"Damn! No they didn't. She might have seen Cad kissing me. And on the cheek, whatever Minette Marquis says. Fucking A!" Corinna took a larger mouthful of vodka than she meant to. "I hate the way everybody *gossips* so, Minette especially…she's nothing better to do, that's the trouble. Of course he kisses me goodnight when we've had supper…"

"Well, dear, I think it's a terrible pity to lead the poor man on. You've not told him about this Piero, of course…"

"Pietro… He's my *doctor*! Listen, Daph, about…"

"*Only* your doctor, dear?"

"Pietro is a specialist…" When certain thoughts occurred to Corinna, her expression became that of an errant schoolgirl. Now, she had to suppress a private giggle.

"Oh, I'm sure he's very *good*, dear," said Daphne meaningly. "Your shoulder hardly seems to trouble you at all these days. And really, anyone listening to Cadwallader would think that you're virtually disabled. But then, he's been helping you with this treatment, hasn't he?"

"He told you *that*?"

"No. I guessed. And if you're making a fool of poor Cad, it's not very nice, dear. I don't approve. It's just as well Dorinda is cheering him up. She rang early this morning. He had supper with her last night."

"With *Dorinda*?"

"Yes, dear. At her flat! She made him her special Irish stew with dumplings and a fruit pie! Perhaps he hasn't told you. I expect he likes his little secrets too. She's going to help him sell some of his stuff on the internet. All that fussy china, and some of his paintings. She knows *all* about these things of course."

"Of course…although anybody can look these things up, you know. I'd do it if I had time."

"I expect he'll be very grateful that someone is taking a proper interest, dear…"

"Yes…" Corinna frowned.

Daphne had emptied her glass in a gulp and got up to refresh it, holding her hand out for Corinna's.

"Just a very weak one, there's a darling. Moh! I'll have to sleep this afternoon if I'm not careful."

"You always do anyway, dear," shouted Daphne from the kitchen. "Don't try to talk. I'm too deaf!"

"Damn, damn and *damn!*" Corinna swore under her breath "Thank you, m'darling," she said, as Daphne returned with the fresh drinks. "Daph, listen. About your birthday dinner. I know you left it to us, but this is important. Silvana and Dennis have booked the 'Gazza'. *Again.* You must remember how frightful it all was at Christmas. *I* told them to book at 'La Terrazzina'. It's so lovely under that glassed-in pergola, and they said they'd think about it, but now Dennis thinks *they're* in charge. He as good as said so. I mean, as if *I* have a vested interest, which is more than you can say for *them*. It's *not* fair. They're trying to boost Federico and Donata because they've got some special deal going for their guests, but the food's just awful really *and* overpriced for something so ordinary. If they want to push the boat out, they might as well book Camillo's and take us all to San Gregorio in Dennis's bus! They're just setting it all up without asking *me*! It's really not *fair*...Moh!" Corinna sipped her new drink, which tasted stronger than ever.

"Well, as I'm supposed to be paying for it, I don't think the price needs to come into it, do you, dear?" Daphne fitted another cigarette into the ivory holder.

136

"Well, *exactly!* It's not fair, choosing somewhere so…well, so *unsuitable*. Actually, I think it's outrageous!"

"I don't know what I'm supposed to do about it, dear. Silvana and Dennis couldn't be kinder to me. I'm sure they know best."

"You mean better than me?"

"I mean you do keep dashing off to Rome these days, don't you? I expect you weren't here, dear, and they were. We'll all miss you on Saturday. Cad, especially – I imagine he had hoped to introduce you to Freddy's special guest. Such a pity to miss all *our* fun."

"Oh, yes, of course. Dear sweet Freddy. What guest?" Corinna's strongly-boned face could look almost ugly when startled out of its habitual smile.

"Such charming manners, Freddy. The dear boy pretends to like my egg and rocket rolls. He joked last week that he'd put me into his 'Epicure' column. What a hoot! You should have heard him!"

"I know, I did," said Corinna, exasperated. "I was *here*…honestly, Daph, really! What are you talking about? Who will I miss?"

"Ah! I thought you didn't know! Freddy is expecting a *friend*…" Daphne watched Corinna's face slyly. "From London."

"Oh…what friend? A young man, I suppose…"

"No! A *woman* friend. A writer. Journalist. She's going to interview Cadwallader."

"*Interview* Cadwallader?"

"Yes! There! I knew you didn't know! She's famous, according to Cecy. She's written a dreadful autobiography about drugs and being in prison, and something else about a courtier of Elizabeth the First's. And she's a *ladyship*! The Dearborns. Fitzrivers, I mean. Or perhaps it's Bullivants. Anyway, Dorinda knows the family. There! Cadwallader has been telling absolutely everybody. I'm surprised he's not said anything to you. She'll be staying with the Barkers, I gather, so you can get it all from Silvana."

"Oh…" said Corinna, at pains to keep the irritation out of her voice. "But what on earth? I mean, *why* interview Cad?"

"Millicent Fox, dear! The famous *Millicent*. She's being reprinted or something."

"Oh," said Corinna again, and muttered: "Of course. He did say something. Oh, damn!"

"I'm not liking this one much, I have to say." Daphne indicated the novel on the rattan table. "Silly plot. Of course I read them all once, but they're entirely forgettable, like Agatha Christie. I only read them for Cadwallader's sake, poor man. But I can't think why people have to write *about* books, can you?"

"No. You say *Dorinda* knows the family?"

"So I understand, dear. She is fairly well-connected, you know. All those antiques in Bond Street…"

"Moh! The antiques trade is hardly a *connection*, Daffy. When's she coming, this journalist critic or whatever she is?"

"Now, I think. Today. Or tomorrow. Or possibly she might have come yesterday. You'd better ask Silvana, hadn't you, if Cadwallader is being mysterious. She'll have the booking. What a pity you won't be here to meet her…which reminds me. Aren't you off to look at silly old George Helpston's spare barn at Castelambra?"

Corinna said airily, "Oh, yes. Tomorrow morning with Eduardo. It's not a barn, Daffy. It's a little *dipendenza* in those fabulous grounds. Have you seen it?"

"Well, of course, dear, but not for about twenty years. Marvellous place, I believe. But as he never invites me, I can't *quite* bring myself to join one of the FAI tours and pay my sixpence on the gate. Pride. He used to step out with poor Sophia, did you know?"

"Yes, you told me…"

"In my young days, he was notorious. Everyone called him NSIT – Not Safe In Taxis, you know, dear. That was just after the War. I don't suppose he's changed. There was that scandal over that actress that Hedley says he knows, when he was sacked from the Government. Fenella somebody. She did the rose garden. I gather they've turned into Darby and Joan. It must be quite an effort being a scandal when you're a certain age and losing your marbles. Good luck to him, I say." Daphne chuckled. "He must be broke if he's letting off bits of Castelambra. He gets charabancs in to look at the rose gardens, too…"

139

"Look…you won't tell Lorrie or Cy about Helpston's place, will you, darling? Not even by accident? This is my catch!"

"You think *I've* lost *my* marbles, don't you, dear?"

When Corinna tried to turn the subject back to the Birthday, Daphne obstinately told her to talk to the Barkers about the venue. "Now then, I'm not going to offer you another voddy, dear, " she said, definitively closing the issue. "Two's quite enough for a morning, I think…"

Knowing herself defeated, Corinna glanced at her expensive sporty wristwatch and rose, crying, "Moh! So much to *do…and* my hair! I haven't got a bean this week, either…the bastard's defaulting again, would you believe…"

"Dear me," said Daphne, unsympathetically. "I expect poor Alfredo's business is suffering from the recession like everyone else's. We're *all* so broke, dear…" She accompanied her friend down the narrow corridor to the door.

"Poor Alfredo my bloody foot!" Daphne's sympathetic attitude to her ex-husband annoyed Corinna for any number of reasons. "Moh! I shall have to get back on to Pollini, I suppose, but they're all in it together, the legal masonry. It's just not *fair*! Fucking A, Daffy! It's all been drawn up and agreed. I wonder how they imagine I'm supposed to *live*…eat, even! Sorry, m'darling…take no notice of me…" But she saw that Daphne was fishing in a compendious handbag.

140

"Now then, you won't forget to collect my corals from Sebastiano, will you? Pay for them out of this," said Daphne, pressing a crisp hundred-euro note into Corinna's hand. "And keep the change. It's not as if," she said innocently over Corinna's perfunctory protests, "you can ask Cadwallader Jones to sock you a hair-do in the circumstances..."

"Ooh! Daffy! Thank you, m'darling. You're far too kind. I say, why don't I take the ring to him as well? We might get it ready for the Big Day..."

"Well, all right, dear, but I hope it doesn't take as long as that. I love my ring. I must have got thinner..."

Corinna gazed at Daphne appraisingly. "Perhaps you have. What are you going to eat for lunch?"

"I've got tuna and eggs. And an avocado for this evening...nice bread, olive oil..."

"You ought to have more carbs. You *must* look after yourself, Daphne darling. We all worry about you so *much*..."

x: .Bush Telegraph

"Corrin-na...'ow kind of you to call. No, no, 'e's fine today really. A bit low still, but getting better, thank God. The antibiotic injections 'ave 'elped no end but they upset the stomach. Vairy boar-ing this pain was. I'm just making 'Edley his lunch...something vairy soft to not aggravate the teeth, and bland for the guts." Cecilia Porter spoke almost perfect idiomatic English in a gravelly baritone with a pronounced Roman accent which her uxorious husband claimed to adore. "What? Leetle Fraid-dy's friend? She's no- toarious, my dear. She was a junkie who wrote a book, an autobiography all about her addictions and her time in that preeson for weemin, 'Olloway...It is going to be made into a film, so I read. Then she wrote something not bad about someone in Queen Elizabeth's government. Good reviews in the *LRB* and *The Guardian*. I 'ave ordered it from Amazon, but it 'asn't come. 'Er name? Dear-born. Veronica...What's that? Yes, yes, so I believe. A ladyship, an aristo, anyway, but certainly...old English family. Per'aps you know them from your grand days? What's that? Oh, so you are off to'ob-nob with the Lordship...'Ow exciting. What? I don't know. Yes, I think so. 'Ang on, I will ask 'Edley."

Corinna held the line and heard a brief exchange in the background.

142

"'Er name's Fenella Fanthorpe, not Fanshaw, and she was in *The Price of Empire*, not *The Jewel in the Crown*. 'Edley says she isn't very bright, but she was good to work with. What? 'Ang on, *cara*."

Corinna sighed and hung on.

"No, just a *compagna*. 'E never married 'er, Edley thinks… What? Yes, we will both come on Saturday. Without doubt! I imagine, don't you, that nobody will stay away… Oh, really? More treatment for the bad shoulder? *Poverina*! Too bad. Well, *buon viaggio, carissima*…"

"That Corinna, she is the worst snob," Cecilia said to her husband as she dished up their modest tomato and onion pasta. "First she boasts that she's going to see this Lord Elpus tomorrow, but she's only an estate agent and what is all this about 'omework? And it's a laugh, the way she wants to meet Fraid-dy's friend, this writer. No small wonder that poor Alfredo could not stick her no more…*poverino*! I 'ope he don't owe her a bottom dollar…and as for that poor sap, Cadwallader…*che stupido*! I bet she don't even touch his dick for his money, yet 'e buys 'er rings and bags and dinners…and she *says* she's seeing a specialist for the shoulder, but this is just a blind. And as for Daphne! She told me in person that Corinna owes 'er *thousands*…yes, even now. Yet when she 'elped us we paid 'er back on the nail. I 'ope this new doctor boyfriend is rich as Croesus, that's all I can say, *tesoro mio*."

"This is delicious, my love," said Hedley Porter pacifically.

After their lunch in the mountains near San Gregorio, Freddy dropped Veronica at the Piazza Umberto, where she fully intended to have a long siesta in her room in the Albergo before the supper date with Freddy and his uncle. A small plump woman of about fifty-five stood behind the desk, poring over some papers through reading glasses. She was dressed in the smart Italian way – a black frock with a large ornate brooch at the shoulder, and her dark curly hair had evidently been recently coiffed with gold streaks. She removed the specs and looked up and smiled a professional welcome through a lot of mascara.

"*Buona sera, signora,*" said Veronica. "*Numero quattro, per favore...*"

The woman took a key from a rack and placed it on the counter. "Ahh! There we are, Lady Veronica...it *is* Lady Veronica, isn't it? I'm so sorry I wasn't here at breakfast to greet you. I do hope you've got everything you need. Just give me a shout if there's anything at all...I'm Silvana Barker..." Her voice was so like Sybil Fawlty's that Veronica, who had lunched very well, blinked and had to suppress a giggle. Mrs Barker proffered a hand.

Veronica took it, shook. "I'm fine, thanks. Very comfortable. But I'm afraid I'm not Lady Veronica..." Veronica was aware of making mild mischief and rather enjoying herself.

"Oh, but – I mean I was sure! Number four…Becky checked you in yesterday, didn't she? My daughter, Rebecca…"

"She did, Mrs Barker. I mean I'm not 'Lady' Veronica. I'm not 'Lady' anything."

"Oh!" Mrs Barker's face fell comically. "I thought – that is Freddy, Mr Partridge…"

"Is a good friend of mine, and he recommended your hotel…but I'm just plain Ms Dearborn, I'm afraid…" And I'll kick Freddy in the balls, she thought.

"Oh – of course, I *see*. But you're the *writer*, aren't you?" said Silvana Barker, as though that explained everything. "Well, fancy! Well, you have a nice rest after your lunch. 'Il Cacciatore'? Oh, it's just charming there, isn't it? So tranquil in the hills, and such lovely views, aren't they? We get out there every so often if we can, but you know, with a hotel to run and everything…You're tired, my dear. You go on up. We're here if you need us…"

Too tired and too full of lunch to do anything else, Veronica removed her shoes and collapsed onto the bed, cursing Freddy roundly as she fell into a deep and untroubled sleep.

"Hiya…Rinna? Sorry! Am I disturbing you?"

Corinna de Benedetto, interrupted in the middle of her afternoon nap, instantly recognized the squeaky, drawling, refined estuarian tones. She was slightly annoyed – she had wanted to pick her own moment to talk to Silvana about the

145

Birthday Dinner and slide in a casual question about the Guest. Nevertheless, she made her own voice sound as bright as possible.

"No, no, Silvana, m'darling. Not at all…" She suppressed a yawn. "I was just catching up with some chores. What's up m'darling? Not Constanza, I hope."

"Oh, no. She's fine. Having a little doze. I just thought you'd like to know! She's here! Freddy's friend!"

"Who? Oh, you mean the Dearborn woman. Yes, I know all about her. Daphne said. She's come to talk to Cadwallader. Er – what's she like?"

"Well, you know, quite *ordinary*, I'd say. I was quite disappointed. And she turns out not to be a ladyship after all…or so she *says*. Perhaps she's *incognita*…or little Freddy's been telling porkies. Well, you know, exaggerating, like he does…"

"Oh….Or Cad has…or Daphne. You know how she gets. She was practically legless this morning. Moh! Well, I expect I'll hear all about her soon enough. Cecilia says she's an ex-junkie. Does she look like one?"

"Oh, no – not a bit. Quite nicely dressed, casual but not especially, you know, *bohemian*. More academic. She seems very polite and pleasant, really… sort of poised, *you* know."

"Oh," said Corinna again. "Is she good-looking?"

"Well…" Silvana Barker paused, making up her mind that tormenting Corinna was worth sacrificing pulling Veronica to pieces. "Yes, she is fairly. She's what I'd call handsome, you

146

know, tall, striking…greying, hair in a bun. Elegant in a sort of off-hand, casual sort of a way…*very* understated jewellery…"

"Oh…"

"She'll be there Saturday, at Daph's. The charming Freddy promised to bring her. Oh, but you're off gallivanting, aren't you?"

"Hardly *gallivanting*, Silvana. It's a medical appointment…my shoulder."

"Oh, yes of *course*, you poor thing. Oh well – at least the weather's keeping fine. Staying with Letizia, are you?"

"Of course. Who else?"

"Well, give her my love, will you? Tell her to come and see us soon."

Corinna, completely unable to go back to sleep, decided to interrupt somebody else's.

"Dorinda m'darling!"

"Hello? Oh, it's Corinna! Sorry, sweetie – I was watching something and I didn't hear the phone. What can I doooo for yooou?" Dorinda had a 'manner', a Dublin accent that could sound almost well-bred, and a throaty, smoky voice to speak it in. She coughed noisily, and Corinna held the receiver well away from her ear.

Dorinda Daly and Corinna de Benedetto secretly loathed each other, partly because they had far more in common than either could perceive, let alone admit. Both were much of an age

147

and ladies of leisure, who pretended to have serious interests and involvements (Corinna's, houses; Dorinda's, furniture and china) and thus to be far 'busier' than they actually were. Each took a great deal of care over her appearance and owned – and wore – a great many pieces of ostentatiously expensive jewellery; and each had her beady, well-made-up eye on the main chance. Corinna, put out because a bargain had fallen into the adroitly grasping hands of Dorinda, would allude in passing to whoever happened to be listening to 'the tinker mentality', whilst Dorinda, learning of a successful property coup, would remark with exasperation, these days usually to Daphne, "And *this* is the woman who says she can't afford a pot to piss in, for the Lord's sakes!" Not for nothing had the late Hilary Blyth, a man of wit and not a little wickedness, dubbed them 'Motes & Beams Inc.', a piece of persiflage that neither lady had found remotely funny.

They were rivals in favour, and now, it would seem, also in love. Both – and this was a serious rub – were friends with Daphne Allerton. Here, Corinna felt she had the unquestionable edge: she and Daphne went back years and years, from the time when her ex-husband, Alfredo de Benedetto, had been the young Notary who had supervised Daphne's purchase of her apartment. Dorinda, a new arrival on the scene – a matter of less than a year – was naturally a diversion for Daphne, who liked 'new blood' as she put it, but distinctly a 'wannabe', surely, when it came to the Old Guard. But now, to Corinna's irritation, Dorinda and Daphne appeared to be as thick as thieves: Dorinda now had her regular slot in the Routine, which involved a stroll, shopping trips, drinks, and the exchange of a great deal of local gossip (and just how many of Corinna's own private affairs were confided during these weekly *tete-à--tetes* could only be guessed at.) More perturbing still, and becoming pressing, was the matter of the eligible if ancient J. Cadwallader Jones. Here again, Corinna found herself out of countenance. While without any doubt at all she was Cadwallader's serious 'fancy', Cad was a man who craved female company, and Corinna had been neglecting him. Visits to Rome had become longer of late, and had begun to occupy weekends, and their regular Friday dinner date had been postponed several times. So far, she had managed to soothe Cad's querulous demands with many a pained grimace and much sweet regret, and the incontestable problem of clinical logistics: that her shoulder required attention when the specialist was away from his public hospital duties and keeping private surgery on Saturday mornings. But how, she wondered, was she to stop Dorinda Daly from stealing a march whilst she was away? First, china and pictures, and now cosy home-cooked lunches – who knew where it might lead? Corinna had made up her mind to become allies with the enemy.

"I just thought you'd like to know! We have a visitor in our midst."

"Ooh, tell, tell! You don't mean Cad's nephew Freddy do you? Because he's been here for at least a week! No, well, you saw him last Saturday, didn't you?"

149

Corinna, scenting an edge, smiled to herself. "No, not Freddy," she said. "Someone else…"

"Oh – then you must mean Her Nibs. Cad's told me *all* about her. He came to supper last night, as a matter of fact. He's terribly excited, bless him."

"Oh…What did he say?"

"Well, you *know*, just thrilled to bits someone's coming to write about the marvellous Millicent. He's meeting her this evening. I suppose he *must* have told you. He was telling me all about what he's going to wear, bless his heart…you know what he's *like*…such a snob for a handle."

"Well he's about to be disappointed, poor old boy. She isn't a Ladyship, according to Silvana…"

"Well, I knew *that*! I *told* Cad she wasn't. I said she was just an 'Honourable'. That family's fairly crap anyway. The Dearborns. My ex knew them of old, sweetie."

"Oh! The antiques trade, I suppose…"

"Oh no! I mean, *of course* they did business together, and my ex-father-in-law arranged the auction when they sold the estate. They were old, *old* associates. But they *knew* each other. James Dearborn, her father, Lord Fitzrivers, he used to invite Oz to go over to stay all the time. He met *all* their friends, went shooting…" Dorinda lit a cigarette and coughed audibly down the line. "They became great mates."

"Oh, but *Hugh* was the father, surely. The brother's called James."

"Oh, perhaps it was Hugh. Anyway, it doesn't *matter*… Oz just called him Fitz, like all his friends…But so tell me, what's she *like*?" Dorinda coughed again.

"Silvana says *very* ordinary. She's supposed to be coming on Saturday. I take it you'll be there…?"

"I *think* so," said Dorinda, pretending to consider. "But I've still got this chest, and if Merrick rings, I mightn't bother. I mean I see Daphne most Fridays anyway. She'll understand."

"Hmm. She might *say* so, but you know Daphne. She gets very upset when people don't turn up."

"Oh, for heaven's sakes! I had enough of roll-call at school! I've *told* Daphne."

"Well, I think you should try to go, Dorinda. I can't be there this week because of my medical. It can't be helped."

"No, your shoulder! You *poor* thing! Are you still in lots of *pain*?"

"Up and down. Look, m'darling, are you doing anything this evening?"

"Hadn't really thought about it…why?"

"Oh, I just wondered if you fancied a cocktail at that new 'Allegro' place in the Piazza Garibaldi…just a chat, nothing dressy or anything."

"Okay…that sounds fun. But I can't afford much at the moment."

"Oh, tell me about it! Just a small *mojito* each and some of their free nibbles, okay? That'll do me for supper…On me, of course." Sometimes, an investment was necessary.

"Oh no, sweetheart, we'll go 'dutch'," said Dorinda, recognising a ploy when she heard one.

Dorinda rang her friend Lorrie as soon as Corinna had hung up. "You'll never guess who's just rung me!"

"Dorinda? Hang on. This isn't Lorrie. It's Cy. I'll pass you right over…" Cy Dillon covered the receiver with his hand. "It's your pet antiquarian…for chrissakes make it brief."

"Dorinda! How're you doing?"

"Lorrie? Well – you'll never *guess,* sweetie!"

"Try me, honey."

"Corinna's just rung me and actually invited me out!"

"Wow! And you're going?"

"Yes…I mean why not? Apparently, the Ladyship is here, and madam's in a bit of a doo-dah…"

"Uh-oh…"

"Are you coming to Daphne's on Saturday? She's going to be there, apparently, the so-called Ladyship, except she isn't – I did *tell* Daphne. *And* Corinna now admits I was right! I *knew* that family, or at least my ex-husband did and she's such a silly *snob*…she said…"

Lorrie broke in with difficulty. "Wouldn't miss it for the world, Dorinda. Look, honey, I have to keep this brief – Cy and I are just off out to meet some friends down from Milano…Yes, here in Monty. We're meeting them for drinks and dinner…they're fun. You must meet them sometime…" Lorrie could see Cy making faces and tried not to laugh. "No, nothing, Dorinda honey. Have a lovely evening now. Yeah, sure. Saturday. Take care now! Pass on every good wish to Corinna."

"That woman is poison. Pure poison," said Cy when Lorrie put the receiver down. "Dorinda?"

"Her too. I meant that Corinna nightmare. Jesus, Lorrie, how the fuck did we end up here in this backwater with all these fag-hags anyway?"

"Oh, my. You're not enjoying being here, are you? Cy…I do wonder if this move hasn't been a bit of a mistake… Hey, buddy-mine, don't have any more of that. We do have to meet Phil and Francesco, and you're not even changed yet. Hey, Cy, don't just close off on me. Cy, sometime I think we need to *talk*…"

xi: J. Cadwallader Jones

"You're right enough. It could almost be an island...mountains one side and sea on the other." Freddy was leaping lithely up a series of steep stone steps and waited for Veronica to catch him up. "We're heading for the southern wing of the butterfly, as it were...it's less populated than the northern wing where we had supper yesterday. That's the seaside. This is a cliff-top, more or less. Uncle Cad's artist's retreat, complete with twelfth century castle, lighthouse and view of dangerous rocks. Bloke I used to know vaguely drowned on them last summer...Don't ask old Cad what he's painting, by the way...he's done bugger all since he got here apart from little vignette miniatures to amuse his friends...far more interested in his paramour...But he's writing his memoirs...it's his new 'thing'..."

"I looked at some of his children's books. I thought they were rather delightful..."

The narrow street suddenly opened out onto a small square where before them stood the grand, gaunt castle ruin, with its famous jug-handle buttress framing the setting sun, rich as egg-yolk, descending into the water. "My God, how absolutely lovely!" The sea was calm, iridescent with golden light. They paused by the railings to stare out at the panorama of the little bay, where boats chugged merrily, and below them, the north 'wing' of Monte Farfalla, the seaside and the marina, was alive

154

and jaunting. "Good, isn't it? I say, come on, old thing." Freddy tugged at Veronica's sleeve. They walked past a corner restaurant where a white-coated waiter prepared tables under an awning.

"Oh, how inviting that looks!" exclaimed Veronica.

"Our venue for tonight, I fancy. *Salve,* Saro! Now then, dearie, about old Cad. He's a perfect petal, but he's very deaf and inclined to wander…you might have to be a bit patient."

Another narrow street led off the square. "Here we are – this double fisherman's cottage. Number 10's my abode when I'm here. Jane too. He lets it to summer visitors sometimes. Frankly, he must be the holiday landlord from hell…constant fuss and endless rigmarole. This is his. Number 12." Freddy pressed the bell, beside which was a post-box bearing an ornate notice: J.Cadwallader Jones, RA, FRSA, FRWS. "He won't hear – but he is expecting us. I hope."

They waited. It struck Veronica that Freddy was more than slightly nervous.

The door opened suddenly and an elderly man, tall and stooping, and with a long lock of pale hair falling over a high domed forehead peered out at them. "Oh!" he said. "It *is* you! I was expecting you, waiting by the bell. I don't hear too well, you see! Come in, come in! Everything's ready! Now – I've set us up at the back…I *think* it's still warm enough, don't you, Freddy, dear boy? Lovely day, today. Now then! Introductions! You must be Veronica, my dear! Cadwallader Jones." He shook hands

155

solemnly. "Everyone calls me 'Cad', but I assure you I'm not, only Cad by name and not by nature, eh? Hee, hee! Come in, come in – oh, and mind the bicycle!"

Veronica was standing in an extraordinary room – a ramshackle kitchen behind a sort of breakfast bar, cum dining room, cum artist's studio, with indeed a bicycle propped against a long and overflowing book case, a vast easel covered in a dust sheet. A great many more books sat in piles on the floor, and every available space on the high walls was filled with big oils in ornate frames, some of them portraying the same young man. Others were startling: Veronica thought she recognized a Canaletto. "Now then…we're going to have supper at 'La Taverna del Castello', they're very good there, not at all pricey, but I thought we'd like a little something beforehand… Now then, I've got some nice little crackers from Gaetano's, very edible, and not at all expensive…Olives, too…I think they'll still be all right after being in the *frigo*. I think we can make ourselves pleasantly comfortable… Come through, my dears! I hope you can drink prosecco, Veronica, my dear? So nice now the weather's getting so much better! So depressing when it's so dull, and the winds here have been a perfect nightmare…blew down my poor cockerel, can you imagine! Hee!" Cadwallader's laugh was a high-pitched squeak.

"He lost his cock," whispered Freddy, then explained loudly, "Uncle Cad has this wonderful weathervane. It blew down in a storm, but he's re-erected it, haven't you, Cad?"

156

"Indeed. In-*deed*. Now, Freddy, I did mean to tell you that Enzo – he's a local handyman, my dear – he quoted me no less than seventy-five euros! Can you believe that?"

"Well, I suppose if he had to get up on the roof…" Freddy said, watching Veronica's astonishment as she gazed at the walls. Above a doorway hung a Rembrandt self-portrait…and beside it, a Vermeer, the young woman at the virginals… "Take a closer look," Freddy whispered in Veronica's ear. The paintings were extraordinary – exceptionally well-executed copies, ones which to Veronica's inexpert eye could almost pass for originals, master forgeries…except that the faces had been subtly altered.

"Good grief!" Veronica cried, and saw that Freddy was chuckling.

Cadwallader was not listening. "I had *fearful* floods over the winter, you know, my dear, a drain pipe burst and everything was *sodden*, I can't tell you! My poor, poor carpet! And he was quite reasonable about those, Enzo was…nice man. His mother cleans for me. But then dear Corinna recommended her chap and he did it for almost half the price and fixed the leak in *il bagno* into the bargain – now, where was I? I do get a bit distracted…"

"Your cockerel, Uncle Cad," said Freddy.

"Hee, hee! Well, he's up again! Always a good omen. Hee! Now then, here we are. I've got the bottle all nicely chilled. Do come through…" J. Cadwallader Jones placed the bottle and some small dishes rather precariously on a small papier-machè

157

tray. "No, no, thank you," he said as Veronica offered to help. "I'm nicely balanced, you see…"

He led them through another extraordinary room: this time, a grand drawing-room on a tiny scale, with a Persian carpet, a gilded sofa in the Empire style, a deep Victorian armchair, several occasional tables, a Chinese lacquered screen, a rather wonderful eighteenth century square piano with a great many framed photographs on it, and the walls festooned with a huge gilt looking-glass and more pictures, watercolours of Venice, a number of Rome, and a huge depiction of the Duomo in Florence by night. More portraits, this time of an elderly woman who vaguely resembled the late Queen Elizabeth the Queen Mother, variously depicted playing piano, nursing spaniels, arranging flowers, formally seated on a sofa with a spaniel at her feet, and against a backdrop of the Swiss alps…And, in miniature, the Arnolfini portrait, perfectly detailed in oils. When she looked more closely, Veronica saw that the wife's face was a younger version of the woman's in the other portraits, and the husband was the image of the young man who hung in the kitchen…

"Good grief," murmured Veronica again.

"Oh, my dear! You're admiring my little conversation pieces, I see. Hee! They're my little joke. A sort of diversion, once upon a time."

"They're amazing,"said Veronica sincerely. "Extraordinarily clever."

"Cad should have been a master forger, shouldn't you, Uncle Cad?"

"Well, you know, my dear boy," said Cadwallader seriously, "someone once told me that, and that's when I had the idea of altering the faces so as not to leave anyone in any *doubt*...Hee! I think they're rather amusing..."

"Are these Millicent?"

"They are indeed. There! That's Milly at work..." He indicated a little oil in a plain frame, a rather clever piece, Veronica thought, capturing its subject looking up quizzically through half-moon spectacles over the top of an old-fashioned typewriter in the foreground.

"She looks quite a character," Veronica said.

"Marvellous, wasn't she? I sold that Olivetti to some Americans before I left Somerset... Fans, you know. I got quite a bit for it. Now then!" Cadwallader Jones opened a glass door that led out onto a tiny terrace entirely surrounded by the adjacent buildings, a little jungle oasis of palms and scented plants in terracotta pots, spilling over a stone staircase. On a wrought iron table candles flickered invitingly and three small antique lead-crystal glasses waited, with Coalport plates and napkins. "Come through, come through...Will you do the honours, dear boy? Freddy's a wine expert, you know, my dear. My fingers...arthritis, you know..."

Freddy prised the cork with a practised near-silent hiss, and poured the wine.

159

"How very lovely," Veronica said.

"It is quite nice, this one…one has to select a bit. I actually go to the local Co-op with Corinna. Hee!"

"I actually meant this lovely courtyard…and these wonderful old goblets. How nice to use them."

"Oh – the glasses! George the Fourth. Dorinda admires them so much. Yes, they were Milly's…my late wife, you know. Now do have a little nibble, my dear…now, we've got olives, of course…I hope you like olives…and these little things from Gaetano…woof! I feel quite exhausted…" Cadwallader Jones suddenly sat down and raised his glass. He was an odd-looking individual – he wore his lank straight hair rather long and somehow asymmetrically, Veronica noted, as if he cut it himself. His long, thin, rather mobile face had the look of an amiable camel: a large and bony nose with very large and flaring nostrils and a large-lipped mouth that contained rather too many prominent teeth. "Cheers, bottoms up and welcome, my dear. We should say '*Cin, cin*!' Welcome to Monte Far-falla…" He drew out the syllables. "Now sit, sit, do…I already have which is very rude, but I suffer with my back. Arthritis… I think you'll find these chairs fairly comfy…I have to bring the cushions in at *night* which is a bore, but *vale la pena*, I think…"

"*Cin, cin*! Thank you. It's so kind of you to invite me."

"The honour is mine, my dear. So now then – Freddy tells me you're writing something about Milly…"

"Well, actually I'm…"

"Now then, my dear. I shall say straight out that I'm not going to tell you anything *private*, that's understood. Darling Milly was a very private person. Hee! I take it it's her books…"

"Well, sort of. Actually, I'm writing something about a friend of hers…"

"What? Sorry, my dear – I don't hear very well. Do have an olive and do mind the stones…I do hope they're not too dry…" Veronica helped herself to something that resembled a very bitter raisin and decided to try Gaetano's 'nibbles' instead.

"Veronica wants to know something about Flora Forde, Cad. You were telling me about her the other evening, remember? Flora Forde, with an 'e'."

"Flora Forde? I don't think so, dear boy…Who's Flora Forde?"

Freddy raised his eyes discreetly heavenwards. "She was a writer, Uncle Cad. You said Milly used to know her. Before the War…"

"Oh! Now that's possible of course. Milly knew a great many people in the writing world. Now, I understand you're a writer, my dear, and I gather you're very famous…"

"Oh, no, not famous," said Veronica, glaring at Freddy. "Not famous at all. I've just published a history book."

"A mystery book…well, now, just like my dear Millicent! Her stories were immensely popular, although you know, when I met her in nineteen forty – or, wait, perhaps it was actually nineteen forty-one, because I remember there had been a watercolour exhibition at the Academy and I'd put in a little series of English canals, and it was cancelled because of the Blitz…anyway, it was all a very long time ago…Er, where was I?"

"Aunt Milly, Uncle Cad," said Freddy.

The subject of the late Millicent Fox ("*quite* a bit older than me, my dear, but a lovely lady, perfectly delightful, and so *free* of stuffy conventions") dominated the conversation erratically for the duration of prosecco ("I only got in the one, my dears, because of course we're dining out…"), followed by the elaborate process of bringing in the chair-cushions, locking Cadwallader Jones's back door, checking the thermostat ("the poor piano!") and trooping back through the kitchen gallery ("You're *so* clever, my dear – yes, these were me! I *was* quite a looker, wasn't I? Hee!") checking keys, and locking the front door and security grill ("One can't be too careful of one's little treasures, although I have to say that everyone round here seems entirely trustworthy, but of course we're entering the *tourist* season, and you never *know*, do you?") glancing back at Cadwallader's roof to admire the weathervane ("Up, out and proud," murmured Freddy) and the short walk ("So handy – I sort of use this place as my club…") and so to the little trattoria in the square. Here, Cadwallader Jones was warmly embraced by the smiling plump proprietor, introduced as 'Tony', with a great deal of deference and not a little irony. There was a stout-looking awning over the outside tables and tall pillar gas-heaters, and they had a small debate as to 'inside or outside'. They opted for outside under the awning, and Veronica was glad she had brought a shawl. Below them, boats with little lights scudded serenely on the black water. "Squid fishers," Freddy informed her. A young waiter came up and said in English, "Meester Cad, you are ready to order?"

"*A- llora*," intoned Cadwallader. "*Acqua frizzante, obbviamente, per fav-ore*, Rosario…and Freddy, do choose the wine, dear boy, but I have to say their house offering is good if not excellent…*Un at-timino, mentre noi dicidere, per fav-ore*, Rosario," he said to the waiter, who kept a politely straight face at the mangling of his native language. "They're utterly charming here," he said to Veronica. "Do choose just whatever you would like. It's not expensive, and this is my treat…"

"How kind," Veronica murmured, still feeling rather full of lunch, let alone the near-inedible snacks in Cadwallader's courtyard.

"I'll share a grilled spigola with you, if you like," hissed Freddy in her ear.

"Thanks."

"What?"

"Nothing, Uncle Cad. Just helping Veronica with the menu…"

"Ah. Freddy's Italian is just a *wee* bit better than mine. Hee! I'm spoilt. I tend to rely on dear Corinna and hers is perfect." Cadwallader frowned suddenly, as if at some

163

uncomfortable thought. Then he shook himself. "Just choose whatever you prefer – this is a special occasion! So as I was saying, *apropos* dear Milly…it was during the War. She had the house next door. She was a widow you know…lonely…as indeed was I myself…Mother could be *very* difficult by then."

The rigmarole was interrupted by the arrival of a starter of bruschetti and a selection of smoked fish, which Cadwallader Jones, who appeared to have an enormous appetite, tucked into with relish. They ordered the second course, but Cadwallader ("It's my lunch really, you see, my dears…I hardly *touch* anything in the daytime…") insisted on having a small pasta dish in between, which he ate greedily, urging them to share if they wished.

"Millicent must have already been a best seller when you met her," Veronica said, politely refusing the offer, and trying not to watch Cadwallader Jones sucking pasta up between his large lips from a spoon and fork.

"Oh certainly, certainly. That piano-tuner – you know, he was her brainchild. The hero detective…now what was his name? Dear me, my memory! Scott Burgess played him in the television series…"

"Aubrey Calder Watson…" Veronica was glad of her homework.

"Aubrey Watson! I say how *clever* of you my dear! I had entirely forgotten! Silly, because I owe him a fortune, really. Hee! Now tell me, what exactly *are* you writing about Milly?"

164

Veronica sighed, she hoped inaudibly. "Well, you see –
I'm not really writing about Millicent at all, in fact, Cadwallader.
I really was hoping that you might be able to tell me something
about Milly's friend Flora. She is quite a mystery. She only
wrote three books and then just sort of disappeared…"

"She had a beard? Well, now that's possible, I
suppose…but unlikely. Hee! Do pour again, Freddy, dear boy.
Milly was a good pourer, poor dear girl…" Freddy spluttered,
and Veronica kicked his ankle under the table.

It was towards the end of the main course that
Cadwallader Jones suddenly exclaimed messily through a
mouthful, "Flora Forde! Of course! Milly used to talk about her!
It might be in the chest! We'll have to have a look."

"The chest?"

"Uncle Cad has a chest full of Milly's old drafts and
working notes," Freddy explained. "Don't you, Cad?"

"Indeed I do. Followed me about ever since poor Milly
died…I always think they might be worth something – you
know, to a university library, somewhere like that. Er,
eventually…" he added hurriedly, glancing at Freddy. "I'm
writing my memoirs, you know, my dear. I was actually born in
Wales, in Snowdonia. The family is Welsh, you can tell from my
name perhaps, my dear…my mother's side was really quite
grand, Cadwallader is quite a *regal* name, but of course only
regal in *Wales*… But of course the Welsh were the *real* Britons,
did you know that? Once, they spelled it without the 'e' – just the

165

'r' – but long before my time the family moved over the border to Somerset…that's where I grew up, and then I went to London, to the Slade, you know, and I had a few little adventures…but then I looked after Mother in Nunney…tiny village, picturesque, a ruined castle, but only a very *local* life… If I remember rightly, there was an uncle of mine who was a church organist in a village very nearby. Just think of that! But Milly was far more musical than me…she played the piano and she sang…beautiful mezzo-soprano voice…Er, where was I?" He wiped his mouth and straightened his knife and fork and looked round for the waiter. "Now, now then – they know me well here, you know. I have my little routines. They'll give me a pudding and a whiskey. You two dear young people have just whatever you like…Coffee? Oh yes, they'll do *espressi*…"

Veronica was whispering to Freddy that she couldn't possibly eat a pudding, and Freddy, agreeing, was studying the dessert wines list when two middle-aged women, one tall, blonde, and dressed in trousers, jacket and smart trainers, the other short, with hair dyed black, large spectacles glinting, and wearing a shiny mac and high-heeled boots that clacked on the cobblestones, suddenly arrived at their table. "Well *hello!*"

"Goodness me!" Cadwallader Jones almost upset the table in his hurry to stand and Freddy, rising also, reached for Cad's elbow to steady him. "My dear! My *dears*! My goodness!"

"Oh, don't get up, Cad, darling. Please. We were just passing! I thought it was you! Isn't this just *marvy*?" the blonde one said, while the dark one stood behind and grinned rather inanely.

Cadwallader Jones kissed the blonde woman on both cheeks, kissed the hand of the smaller woman. "Now then! This really *is* a party! Sit down, do…but we need more chairs! How absolutely marvellous…Fancy! Hee! *Allor-a* – introductions. My nephew, Freddy Partridge, you both know of course…and this is his dear friend, Veronica Deardon…no, Dearborn. Sorry, my dear. She's down here on a research mission! Veronica – Co-rin-na de Benedet-to, and Dorinda Daly… Now, I think if we move these chairs about a bit…and there's a spare I spy over there! Freddy, dear boy, could you..?" Hands were shaken, chairs shuffled.

"We were only passing by…we wouldn't want to *disturb* you," the woman called Dorinda said to the table in general. Her voice was faintly Irish; she wore very red lipstick and her large red specs had 'DG' picked out in diamante.

"Nonsense! You must join us, join us! Now, then – how *clever* of you both! You must be psychic! Hee! You're both in the nick of time! Have a whiskey…or a brandy…or perhaps an averno, Dorinda my dear!" He gave the dark-haired woman a roguish smile, then became conscious of the fixed gaze of the blonde woman. The young waiter materialised, bearing an ashtray which he placed at Dorinda Daley's elbow. "*E una festa, verit-ah-bee-lay*!" exclaimed Cadwallader, as Corinna snuggled closely into his side. They ordered drinks. "Just a small one,"

Dorinda said. "*Solo un poco bicchieri…*" "*Piccolo*," murmured Corinna de Benedetto under her breath, smiling all the while. Both newcomers were assessing Veronica, not very discreetly. "And your poo-ding, Meester Cad?" inquired Rosario the waiter. "*Certamen-tay!*" cried Cadwallader Jones, now in the highest of spirits.

The blonde woman, who had picked up a table knife to examine her lipstick, put it down and fixed Veronica with a dazzling smile. "You'll have to forgive us, I'm afraid, Veronica. We're all completely potty here, aren't we, Cad? I do hope you enjoy your stay…And I *do* hope you're staying long enough to meet everybody."

"Well, of course, I…"

"She's met most of you now already," said Freddy. "Overwhelmed with welcomes, you might say."

"Oh, Freddy, really!" said Corinna with an intimate crinkle of the eyes. "Isn't he *marvellous*! But of *course*…you're staying with the Barkers! Such a lovely hotel, I always think…"

"It's very comfortable," agreed Veronica, resigned to shelving the topic of Flora Forde, and hoping very much that less welcome topics would not come up. Her hopes were dashed.

"So, *another* writer in our midst," cried Dorinda Daly. "I've not read your new book yet, but it's on order. I say, you won't mind if I smoke, will you?" Her cigarettes were already on the table.

"Not a bit. I'm a fellow traveller when I'm not trying to quit. I just always assume they won't let you these days, even in the semi-outdoors like this…"

"Well they *know* us here," Dorinda said cosily and offered Veronica a cigarette. "Now then, Veronica – I hope you don't mind being on first name terms but I can hardly call you Lady Dearborn, now can I? Or 'your Honour'?" She glanced pointedly at her companion, and Veronica decided Mrs Daly must be a little drunk.

"Well, *no!*" said Veronica, more vehemently than she had meant to. "I mean one wouldn't. Oh, dear. There seems to have been some sort of muddle, um, Dorinda…let's just stick to first names, shall we?" She glared in Freddy's direction, but his attention had been caught by the plump proprietor, Tony, greeting four tall, casually-dressed men who had come in from the street and who were debating loudly about 'inside or outside' in American accents.

"Oh look! It's Lorrie! And dear Cy!" cried Corinna. "Cy! Lorrie, m'darling!"

"Let's see – seven down, four or possibly five to go," murmured Freddy, giving Veronica a look of mischievous sympathy. One of the men, a boyishly good-looking person in his mid-forties wearing Buddy Holly spectacles, detached himself and hurried over. "Hi, there – wow! I'd no idea you-all would be here! Hi, Cadwallader, Freddy, ladies…Look, I'm afraid our friends from Milano have opted to dine indoors, if you'll forgive

169

us being unsociable. Don't get up, Cad, please. Wow! A small world, eh?" He grinned at the table in general showing a great many very well-tended teeth.

Corinna had decided to take over. "Lorrie, m'darling, Dorinda and I are gate-crashers too. We just spotted them and barged in, didn't we, Cad? Veronica, this is Lorrie – Lorenzo Lucifora. Freddy's friend Veronica Dearborn is over from London, isn't that right? Yes, London. I want to talk to her about lovely London very soon..." Corinna's eyes crinkled at the corners again. "I'm afraid Veronica's having to meet most of the Crew this evening, aren't you, m'dear? Don't worry, we're all just absolutely crazy here...it's all this sea air..."

When Lorrie Lucifora had bade them good evening and darted in to join his companions, Corinna said in a stage whisper to Veronica, "Americans! And fruitcakes – I mean *gays*, and no offence, Freddy, darling, but there's this network, you do have to admit. At least among the Americans. Lorrie's sweet, but *very* beady...they've been busy buying up Monty ever since they got here..."

"Oh dear," said Freddy as he walked Veronica towards the Albergo. "All the gargoyles in one go. Sorry, dear heart."

"I hope I wasn't too rude. Does that let me out of the Saturday bash?"

170

"Well, not exactly. I promised Daphne. She's absolutely the best of the bunch, and you know, old. Don't be too cross, dearie. Be a sport."

"Oh God. All right. I said I'd be a sport. You don't deserve it. That's *the* famous Corinna, I take it. And the side-kick who's the antiques expert…blimey…and both with their caps set at Uncle Cadwallader!"

"He eats it, dearie. It amuses him no end to have two aging glamour-pussies vying for his attention. They actually hate each other's guts, didn't you guess? Did you see how the fair Corinna practically pushed little Mrs Daly off on her merry way before seeing Cadwallader to his door? He's incredibly vain. But he's all right, isn't he? I mean I know he got a bit distracted this evening. He can't help it."

"He's rather a pet. I like him."

"I think he'll help with Flora if he thinks he can talk a lot about Milly…and himself. Silly old boy! He remembered about Flora Forde perfectly a few days ago…" They ambled slowly down the cobbled street, Freddy pointing out lamplit baroque masonry. "Better in daylight. We'll do a morning's explore tomorrow if you like. You are supposed to be on holiday."

"I can't. I've got a date. You were too busy amusing the ladies. Cad has invited me over for coffee and cakes tomorrow. He's promised me a squiz at Aunt Milly's notes."

The steep descent down uneven steps made them go silent. The street levelled and widened, and Veronica recognized

171

the Albergo Del Mare, suddenly on familiar ground, her hired car visible outside. "Strange to think I've only been here since yesterday. This place is a maze, Freddy. I'll have to make use of Mrs Barker's little map..." She yawned, suddenly tired to death. "I'm zonked, Freddy. I just must fall into bed..."

"Sweet dreams, then, *carissima mia*. Let's have lunch tomorrow after Cad's elevenses...Let's hope he remembers. I'll give him a nudge in the morning and then make myself scarce."

"Only for a moment, then, m'darling...I've actually got to work in the morning..." Cadwallader ushered Corinna inside.

"Oh, but just a drop of malvasia, my dear! Or do you prefer whiskey? There's something I can't *resist* giving you! Hee! Now then...I promised you a little present! I was going to wait until after you were back from your little travels, but..."

Corinna perched on the empire sofa as Cadwallader fussily poured malvasia at a dainty drinks tray. She smiled at him intimately as he handed her a tiny gilt glass. "You're being very mysterious, m'darling..."

"I'll be back in a trice!" he exclaimed, and disappeared. There was a fairly long interval, during which there was a tuneless whistling coming from the bathroom, which Corinna tried to ignore, suppressing a yawn. She sipped, and gazed at her reflection in the gilt-framed looking glass, absently tucking a stray strand of gilded hair behind her ear, and thinking idly about her plans, for the hairdresser's, for Castelambra, and for

Rome…her reflection smiled back at her, complicit. The whistling had stopped and she heard the lavatory flush. She composed herself. Cadwallader emerged, beaming, with something clasped behind his back, like a child.

"You are a darling old silly!" she exclaimed. "Whatever can it be?"

"Now then! Hee!" He produced a small flat package done up in brown paper and string. "This isn't your *real* one…I'm still working on that. But I thought you'd like this now as I've just varnished it…"

"Goodness!" Corinna was good at hiding disappointment, and smiled all the while as she pulled at the wrapping.

"I haven't had time to have it framed, my dear, but you shall choose one and I shall pay for it…"

"Oh!" A small painting, pastel on board, depicted an intricately drafted baroque building with a high balcony on which stood a blonde woman with a watering can, tending cascading plants. "Oh," said Corinna again, propping the painting on the sofa and standing back to look at it. "That's my house! And that's supposed to be me…"

"I so hoped you'd like it…"

"Oh, I *do*. So clever, my darling!" She kissed him on the cheek, but he rather insistently found her mouth. "How lovely," she said, breaking away with difficulty. "I say, I hope my bottom isn't quite as big as that…"

173

"Oh, no…that's simply perspective…And you – you have a marvellous bottom, my dear! Perhaps soon we can resume the other one…Hrmmph! Hee! This calls for a celebration! Whew!"

Corinna, who felt she had celebrated quite enough, reluctantly accepted another glass of malvasia, put the painting beside the arm of the sofa, and firmly sat down again. "So, our celebrity guest…I gather she's coming to see you tomorrow. What did you make of her?"

"Oh, utterly charming! Delightful, in fact. Very *unaffected*, I thought, didn't you? Do you know she isn't writing about Millicent at all? Just fancy! You see, when Freddy said…"

So much of the art of engaging with the interminably garrulous Cadwallader involved saying 'yes' and 'no' and nodding in the right places, that Corinna, after a full half hour of yessing, no-ing and nodding, found herself in danger of nodding off completely. Finally, she managed to extricate herself from a last, very affectionate embrace on the doorstep. It was only as she was almost at her own doorstep that she realised she had left her picture behind. She decided it did not matter.

xii: The Chest & The Chocolate Box

In Cadwallader Jones's cramped bedroom, Veronica knelt in considerable discomfort on the floor, sifting the contents of a rusting tin chest, ignoring as well as she could the dust, the powerful odour of frangipani and old shoes, and the fact that Cadwallader was hovering in the doorway. She willed herself not to sneeze.

In about thirty notebooks, the spiral bindings stiff with rust and age, and representing an almost annual output since 1940, Millicent had drafted each of her novels with, Veronica thought, an unusual clarity and definition. "It's so very kind of you to let me look at all this. It's fascinating..."   And it was: to a writer, the chance to view another's labours-in-progress was to glimpse not only the building blocks of a book, but an attitude, as it were, to the architecture. Essentially, Veronica realised, this was the literary equivalent of visiting a working museum: now, one would make notes on a word processor, jot ideas in pen only if one were not at one's desk. For Millicent, the pen and notebook had been the tools of her craft. To someone researching the work of Millicent Fox – Alison Truce, for instance – this material could be entirely useful, for Millicent had noted down her plot summaries, portion by portion, clearly and simply, complete with character studies and a startling amount of forensic detail of deaths, poisons, and autopsies. Where she had

175

made alterations, she had done so with a deft and reasoning hand. It was possible to see her mistaken routes and blind alleys, and how she had worked out alternative courses. Occasionally, a 'No!!' in the margin signalled the writer's frustration; an asterisk in red would lead to an amendment. Veronica had recognised the embryonic form of the novel she had read on the plane. She hardly knew Alison Truce, but it would be a kindly gesture, she felt, if she could put her in touch with Cadwallader Jones, if he agreed.

"Oh but that would be wonderful, my dear...it's perfectly marvellous that Milly's books are popular again, and of course – I'm sure you understand – the *royalties* are such a great *help* in these very *difficult* times...if this young lady would like to get in touch with me, I will show her these with the greatest pleasure!" Veronica smiled a little at Alison Truce being called 'this young lady'. Evidently Cadwallader Jones had never heard of this venerable novelist or read her work. He pottered off to make coffee.

If the late Millicent had been scientific in her approach to her fiction, leaving records as a laboratory technician might, there was a disappointing dearth of personal data. There were no personal diaries, no 'little moleskin' of jottings... A dog-eared address book, inscribed on the fly-leaf with Millicent's own address in Nunney, Somerset, and the year 1944, contained a great many entries – clues, doubtless, to Millicent's social and professional life, but nobody listed under the name of Forde. It

176

was as if Millicent had thoroughly harrowed her belongings and left as much – or as little – as she had calculated posterity deserved.

As she was replacing the notebooks carefully in the tin chest, a large spider scuttled out and over her arm. She gasped and dropped the notebook.

"All well, my dear?" inquired Cadwallader, who had reappeared.

"Yes – a spider startled me. I'm almost done here."

"Nothing of especial interest? About the mysterious Flora?"

"No...but never mind."

"Come and have your coffee while it's fresh, my dear. I'm just taking the pot outside to the cor-tee-lay!"

Feeling very much in need of refreshment, Veronica picked up the fallen notebook. It had come open at a random page towards the back, covered in Millicent's neat and by now familiar hand. She idly noticed the words, 'Madeleine & Eustace', and turned to the front cover. 1941. She opened the first page, and found the heading 'Granite Grange' – the embryo of a title she knew of but had not read – and skim-read the summary, noting, now by no means idly, that the story seemed to contain no characters called either Madeleine or Eustace... Suddenly excited, she flipped the pages...the notebook contained a brief design – mostly a cast-list and roles – for another work. Its working title was 'Staircase'...

"I thought you might enjoy some of these cinnamon biscuits with your coffee, my dear…"

"How nice. Thank you. Cad…could I possibly borrow this notebook, just to photocopy? I'll return it this evening or tomorrow, I promise."

"I don't see why not, my dear. I know I can trust you to treat it with care."

Over coffee, and very grateful to leave Cad's bedroom, Veronica urged Cadwallader to talk. She found that alone together in the quiet of the little enclosure, and pitching her naturally low tone into his 'good ear', he could hear her perfectly. The atmosphere became almost peaceful.

"Did you ever actually meet Flora Forde, Cadwallader?" she asked gently.

"Well, now, there's a thing! Do you know, I'm not sure I ever did. She might have come to our wedding, maybe. Milly knew so many people…"

"But she spoke of her…"

"Oh, yes…I mean, she must have, mustn't she?"

"You see, I've a suspicion that 'Flora' must have been somebody's pen-name. Perhaps you knew her as someone else. Freddy said Millicent had been a good friend…"

"Milly had a number of little secrets…I never pried, you know…" He sipped his coffee, all lamblike innocence.

"Tell me about her. Tell me about Millicent. How did you meet her?"

178

"Ahh. Well. Millicent owned the big house next door to us. Inherited it from husband *Numero Uno*. Her mother joined her there during the Blitz, and they turned it into a sort of sanctuary for refugees, or do I mean evacuees? Anyway, poor children from the East End. She had the money, you understand. I was just a poor artist, teaching – hee! just think! – art classes at the local WEA in Yeovil…and Frome…and illustrating children's books in my spare time. But I had Mother, you see. I always wanted to travel and paint properly…"

"You weren't called up?"

"No…I was too young for the beginning, and I'd had TB, you see…weak chest. I still have to be very careful of my health. Do smoke if you wish, my dear. Other people's cigarettes aren't a problem. Just damp…Yes, that was how I really met darling Milly. She was older than me, but still far too young to be a widow, poor girl. Mother fell ill, and I wasn't strong myself, and Milly used to send round one of the young people with soup, and then she came herself, in person. I used to watch her in her straw hat from my window, clipping the roses and seeing to the tomatoes and the beans. I fell in love! Even Mother liked her."

"How lovely…" She meant it sincerely.

"We both had mothers. She understood. Do you know, she cured my virginity…Hee! One afternoon after the soup. She made it herself, some for Mother and some for me, with chicken and onions and just a twist of curry…I can never smell curried chicken soup without thinking very – well, very *nostalgic*

179

thoughts…sorry if that's all a bit candid…I was very innocent…"

"Oh! How – um, sweet! Milly's husband…her first husband…was he killed?"

"Yes. In an air-raid. He was a Mr Seale, very wealthy man, a lot older than her, and manufactured parts for bombers, I believe. Or maybe it was runways. He left her really quite nicely off. Milly couldn't bear to talk about the Past, she could be very secretive, Milly, but I got the impression they hadn't been terribly happy together. We were. We travelled the world after the war, after Mother passed away…Milly's mother too. We waited, of course. She had always wanted to go to Athens….and we were nomads for almost a year…the Greek islands, and then Sicily…Palermo, Siracusa… Hee! I painted, Milly wrote…" He sighed. "I do miss her, you know. Milly."

"I'm sure you must. But it seems as if – well, that you have quite a social whirl here."

"It's very pleasant. Rather a new lease of life! Hee! You know, I've always had a bit of a *thing* for the ladies in my way, I'm afraid, my dear. And life goes on! I've met a wonderful woman here…Well, of course you met her too, last night. The lovely Corinna. I'm very fortunate…She saved my life! Think of that! Hee!"

"I'm sure she must have…"

"Oh, but I mean quite literally. She's a nurse, you know, by training. She spotted the trouble, and she got me to hospital

180

just in time! I thought it was just one of those problems – um, *down there*, you know. But I needed a serious operation, and I could have *died* if it had been left. She was in the nick of time! I'm rather hoping – hee! – that there might be a little announcement soon…"

"Oh! Goodness! How super…"

"You don't – um – think that dear Freddy will think I'm being disloyal?"

"Disloyal? No, I'm sure he won't, Cadwallader. Why should he?"

"I have yet to tell him. Meanwhile, mum's the word, my dear!"

Before she left, he wrapped Millicent's notebook carefully in a sheet of brown paper, and then he rummaged in the book heap in the kitchen and found a hardback copy of S.N. Doughty's *Agnes & Mr Bozo* which he signed with a flourish and gave to her. In the doorway, with a giggled apology, he embraced her just a little too warmly.

Corinna de Benedetto also stood in a doorway, being not embraced, exactly, but his Lordship stood very close behind her, pointing. She could feel his breath on her ear. "All of this is mine. Far as you can see."

"It's breath-taking, Lord Helpston. Fabulous," murmured Corinna, gazing at the sloping terraces of vines and olive trees. In the valley stood tall cypresses, imperious, mist-laden.

"Not bad, is it? I've made it very private from the main house. Farmers' servants' quarters, once. Late eighteenth-century. Not older." His Lordship wore an open-necked check shirt that poked through the holes in the elbows of his ancient cashmere sweater. His clothes rather hung on him, and he leaned on a stout stick with both his brown-spotted hands. He had one of those thin, lined faces that naturally falls into folds of something that could be melancholy. He was at least eighty. "Pretty, though. Come."

They entered the small brick and stone dwelling, where Corinna exclaimed with delight at every whitewashed room, at terracotta tiled ceilings with wooden beams, at frayed and faded Persian carpets on dully gleaming terracotta floors, at a kitchen with a long oaken table and a discreet modern cooker, at small, pretty sofas before a wood-burning stove in a book-lined sitting room, at old-fashioned iron beds and painted chests, at a bathroom with a claw-foot bath and brass taps, at a tiny private courtyard festooned in wisteria and shaded by parasol pines and mimosa, while her colleague, Eduardo, followed taking measurements and photographs. One of the bedrooms gave out onto a loggia, where his Lordship put his hand lightly on Corinna's shoulder, pointing to the distant mountains.

Now, wandering back through the rose garden, with Eduardo pausing and snapping his camera at a small distance behind them, they made their way slowly through a long pergola, where the scent of a luminous pink rose made Corinna pause. "Hmmm," she sighed snuffing a large silky bloom. "Heaven!"

He was watching her through slitted eyes. "'Madame Gregoire Staechelin'. Missus calls it 'Spanish Beauty'. Dare say she's entirely right." At a vantage at the end of the walk, he pointed with his stick. "That's San Gregorio in the distance. Handy. Doesn't bother us."

"You can see the Duomo! How marvy – I mean, completely thrilling!"

"So. Think you can let it?" He put his hand on her shoulder again and turned her with surprising firmness to look at the main house, and once again, she felt his breath on her earlobe. The house, a seventeenth century *casa colonica,* was a perfect rectangle of mellow reddish-blond brick, its green shutters and pillared doorway inviting. They had reached a lawn, hedged with bay and arbutus. When she turned to look for Eduardo, the *dipendenza* was now invisible. "Cleverly done, isn't it? Private. Don't want any riff-raff. Last lot who came stuck their laundry out on the loggia – drying smalls visible from the rose-garden. Not edifying. Lot before that had teenage boys with cars. Revving and rowdiness all night long. Upset the missus. Want someone quiet. Right people can have it on a regular basis. Think you can do it?"

"Oh, I'm sure I can, Lord Helpston. I can't imagine anyone not adoring this place! I think we should go for some very discreet advertisements and assess the response with great

183

care…We can place it in whichever publications you prefer, or I can give you a list of suggestions. We could go for English or American or both…"

"Sounds like you're offering me breakfast, m'dear! I shouldn't turn you down, either. Don't much like Americans, but they can pay. Don't care one way or the other. Quiet is the thing, and for a minimum of three months. Don't want the short-stay crowd. Bad enough having to have the bloody charabancs for the roses. Say, are you attached to the photographer feller or can I offer you lunch?"

"Oh, no…I mean, we came in separate cars. I'd love to join you for lunch. Eduardo!"

Eduardo Renzoni, a compact man in the mid-forties and shirtsleeves, with a complicated-looking camera arrangement slung over his torso, replaced a lens cap and walked over to join them, mopping his brow. The morning had turned warm. He and Corinna had a hurried conversation in Italian, and Eduardo shook hands with his Lordship, and made his way back down the gravel sweep to his car.

"What was he saying?"

"He was saying the property is lovely, Lord Helpston. *Un bomboniera*…he meant like a little chocolate box…"

"Hmmph."

"He was wondering if you wanted to sell it…I realise you couldn't possibly! Don't you speak Italian?"

184

"Don't see the point! Never did. I've been coming here on and off for the past thirty-five years and I've never had to learn a word of Wop. Call me George." They walked slowly towards the house.

"Your Italian's not bad, m'dear," he said over the cold collation laid out on one end of a splendid mahogany table in the large and magnificent hall. He waited while she put a discreet amount of bread salad and salmon mousse onto a piece of ancient Worcester, staring with unashamed greed at the vanishing point at Corinna's bosom, where a gold pendant nestled in her discreetly displayed cleavage before it disappeared beneath the crisp white cotton of her shirt. "Very good, in fact, s'far as I can judge. Bring your grub and sit down."

Corinna sat, trying not to stare too avidly at the walls, the paintings, the marble staircase with the heavy carved mahogany banisters and the Aubusson hangings, the stone busts, the extraordinary hand-painted pottery urns from which greenery overflowed; nor to assess the weight of the silver, and the age of the faded, wonderful carpets. Instead, she gleamed at her host, who turned out to be a messy eater who enthusiastically waved his fork about as he spoke. Only in this respect did he remind her remotely of Cadwallader Jones.

"How come? Have a spot more of this…this is ours." He poured with pride into large, intricately-cut lead-crystal goblets. "Last year's. A bit young, maybe." He waited while she sipped.

"It's lovely, George…Light, fruity. Oh dear! I must remember I'm driving back to Monty…"

"This stuff'll just give you a little glow, m'dear," he said, watching, apparently, for the glow to appear. "Ah, yes, Monte Far-la-la! Bloody enclave of suburbia. Avoid it all I can. You're not in any hurry, though, surely, m'dear? So, tell me…how'd your Italian get so competent, eh? Pillow method? The horizontal grammar book, eh?"

Corinna giggled. "I think you're a rogue, George! I suppose you could say it was. I married an Italian. It's as simple as that. We – um – we aren't married anymore."

"You married one? Good God! How come? Don't tell me this was a folly with a Wop waiter in your teens because I shan't believe you, m'dear. You'd have done better than that…" His Lordship's eyes were a shade of vivid violet blue, and they stared into Corinna's assessingly, with a mixture of ironic flirtation and something that could have been interpreted as a powerful sexual intelligence. "Tell me," he said, more softly. "I really am interested to know…"

"Oh! Well, he was my patient when I was nursing in Oxford. I was still training. He was a postgraduate student, reading Law. Fractured his skull on a motorbike. We fell in love. Silly, isn't it? In no time at all I was expecting Valeria, my elder daughter, and we married and came out here so he could join the family law firm. I've been here ever since." She sipped wine meditatively.

186

"Nursing, eh?" His Lordship's eyes slid once more to Corinna's chest.

"Yes...I was idealistic. I passionately wanted to do something useful, care for people...I was so young..."

"And hook a senior surgeon?"

"No!" But she was laughing. All of George Helpston's powerful personality was concentrated on her, and disconcertingly, Corinna suddenly felt a violent attraction to him, despite his age and the yellowish, almost tortoise-like appearance of his head and neck.

"Regrets?"

"Some, I suppose... Alfredo, my husband – he was so much more married to a very narrow world than he was to me, unfortunately..."

"And so you parted...and you never thought of going back home? To England?"

"I *thought* of it, of course...but my children are here, you see. They're half Italian. This is home now..."

"Here, m'dear. Have some more wine...and some more of this nice salmon thing that Marcella made...I've got Fenella to teach them all my favourite dishes. So! You're still roosting in little Monty. Must be very dull...no society..."

"Oh, we have a life, of sorts. We've got Hedley Porter, the actor. Retired now, of course. He's a very dear friend. He used to know your – er – *compagna*. He worked with her once, I believe..."

187

"Probably. Fenella met all sorts on the stage… And apart from the lapsed actor?"

"Well, I think you must know Daphne Allerton. I think she knows you."

"Little Daffy Duxbury? Married some Yank oil man. Whathisname? Alston, wasn't he?"

"Patrick Allerton."

"That's it. Allerton. Never see her! Went in for Americans, did Daffy. I used to fuck her sister. Sophia. Never see her either. Come to think of it, I think she's dead."

Corinna persisted. "We have a number of visitors, too. And at the moment, we've got Veronica Dearborn, visiting friends…they were from Leicestershire, I think, or perhaps it was Rutland…she has a house near Siena."

"Dearborn? Hugh Fitzrivers's girl? Junkie who wrote a memoir? Used to fuck her mother."

At that moment, a voice fluted something in very correct Italian in a very English accent, and with a sort of heavy, breathless rush, a very large woman in floating orange linen and green leather slippers descended the staircase followed by a small, neat, middle aged woman in trousers who hovered discreetly. George Helpston half got to his feet. "Fenella – this is Corinna di – what is it again, m'dear?"

"de Benedetto. Corinna." She held out her hand. Smiled brightly.

"Ah, yes. The agent. Hullo! I'm so glad George is giving you some lunch." Fenella Fanthorpe's voice was breathy, stage-school modulated, and powerful even when, as now, it was lowered and directed to a very small audience. She had a lot of greying dark hair flowing loose from an elaborate clip, and her face, despite her many chins, had once been beautiful. "You'll have to excuse me, I'm afraid. I'm just *madly* busy today – we have the Consorzio Dragonello coming from Rome at the weekend! I *adore* the concert season, but such a *headache*…now, I *know* I left the papers about the seating contractors on here somewhere…Marisa!" She turned to examine an ancient *madia* which was heaped with papers and leaflets. "We have to hire all this stuff to sit on and make the stage, and they *will* let us down if we aren't very careful…"

"I've been admiring your wonderful garden, Miss Fanthorpe," said Corinna.

Fenella Fanthorpe turned briefly. "Sweet isn't it? Everything's too early this year. We've had such strange weather. Now, where in *hell*…ah! Marisa – *ora dobbiamo cercare la roba per il concerto*…please don't feel you have to rush, Mrs de Benedetto…Do use the bathroom if you care to." She followed the factotum through a door into what was probably an office.

"You musical?" asked George.

"Oh yes!" breathed Corinna. "I've attended concerts here on several occasions. I just adore music!"

189

"Do you indeed? Can't stand it myself. Leaves me unmoved to the point of irritation. Tone-deaf. Fenella's thing. Likes to have her little shows…Now, m'dear, let me see you to your car. Bathroom's just through there, if you want it."

In the courtyard, Helpston opened the driver door of Corinna's aging sporty little yellow Fiat, and watched with unabashed enjoyment as she wriggled into the driving seat, admired the long trousered legs, the tanned feet in elegant flat loafers.

"I'll be in touch the moment we have the advertisement for you to look at, George," she said gaily. "It won't take long."

"Why don't you bring it over in person? We won't be disturbed next week. After this concert of viols thing, Fenella's going away for a few days…"

"So, how's the great Flora research getting on?" Clutching her package, Veronica had met Freddy in the bar in the Piazza.

"Oh, progressing… Uncle Cadwallader has lent me a notebook of Milly's. I need to think about it…"

"All right. Be mysterious. Don't mind me. Now, the big question of the day: where do you fancy for lunch? Did you know, by the way, that that is how you trace the process of evolution? Early man asked 'How can we eat?' The Classical Greeks asked 'Why do we eat?' and, with a little pause for the Dark Ages and several world wars, all we've been asking ever

190

since is 'Where shall we have lunch?' Survival, inquiry and sophistication in a nutshell…"

"You are wonderfully idiotic, Freddy. Did you make that up?"

"Alas, no…*Hitchhiker's Guide to the Galaxy* with a bit of embellishment…Good, isn't it? I've used it in the 'Epicure' column with due attribution. You look a bit happier, my sweet…Now then, the big question remains: meat in the hills or fish by the sea?"

Veronica realised that she did feel better. At a street table in a steep little alley festooned with bunting, with a vista of blue sea at the bottom, eating a very fresh prawn salad and watching Freddy slide oysters into his mouth with tidy, casual relish, for once she didn't wish with all her heart that Todd was there. "Tell me, Freddy. Which of them is actually related to you? Cadwallader Jones, or Millicent Fox?"

"Milly. Her father was my grandmother's eldest brother. My grandmamma was a Miss Fox who married a Partridge. Sounds like bad gamekeeping, doesn't it? Milly was actually a second – or perhaps it's a third – cousin and not an aunt at all. My God! Heaven forfend I'm actually genetically connected to Cadwallader!"

"Oh, he's a sweetie…" She frowned, remembering Cadwallader's overheated farewell… "He's lucky to have you. How did you come to be connected to him at all after Milly died? I mean, you and Jane seem to almost nurse him. Why all the love and care for a batty great-uncle or whatever that makes him by marriage who isn't really a relation?"

"You mean apart from venality? Well, as you point out, he is rather a sweetie. Jane lived near them in Somerset, and she did the angel of mercy bit when Milly died. He came to rely on her, I suppose, and I couldn't not muck in and help. Gay bachelor with no family ties and all that. Poor old Cad went off the rails a bit...made some very stupid investments and sold up and then kept moving house within the same five square miles...and of course there were the gold-diggers. He's a bit susceptible in the lady department..."

"Hmm..."

"Actually, Vee, and to be perfectly honest, I – that is, Jane and I – we both thought we'd better stand by and stop him from spending *all* of Aunt Milly's dosh. The literary estate will come to us, it's entailed, but he went through the TV royalties like a dose of salts, and it seemed a bit, well, *crude* to make a fuss. The main point was making sure he eked his income out. He's next to nothing of his own, and all of a sudden he was Mr Moneybags and then appealing to Jane when things got a bit tight. It was a relief when he seemed to settle here, and it was less of a burden on Jane, but now there are more harpies. I guess it doesn't matter if he's enjoying himself, bless him. Just a shame to see him – you know, preyed on... I say, I'm actually enjoying this, aren't you? I'm going to ask that splendid little waiter for a word with his boss...*fra poco*, as we say here..."

When Freddy returned he was beaming. "This place is a deffo, wouldn't you say? I'm afraid we're going to have to sample the puds in the interest of research…"

"Oh God, I'll get *huge*…"

"You're on hols, darling!"

"I give in. Can you tell me something?"

"You have the *fragoline al pepe stagione* and I'll have the chocolate mousse thingummy and then we'll do a swap. Ask away, darling!"

"Well – about Flora. You said Cadwallader had told you Milly had known Flora. Buddies. Do you remember what he actually said?"

"Yes. He said she was a friend of Milly's. Or something. Does it matter?"

"It might. I'd just like to know how – you know – how the subject came up. That's all."

"Lordy-lord. I can't remember. I said something about a friend of mine – you, sweetie – doing some mystery research…No, wait! I told him about Vixen Press re-doing Milly, and he got all excited, because of the royalties, you know…"

"Makes sense. And?"

"And then I told him about you doing Flora Forde. Who was too obscure for anyone to remember. Sorry, darling, but it's true, isn't it?"

"Absolutely. But what did he say to that?"

193

"He said something like, 'Flora Forde? Milly knew Flora Forde'and I asked when, and he went vague, like he does, and said something like 'in the old days'."

"Ah. Nothing else?"

"Don't think so. What's he said to you?"

"Not much. Either he's being cagey, or he's forgotten. He's sweetly said he's prepared to talk to Alison Truce about Milly – I'm planning to see her when I get home. Oh dear, Freddy – you'd better get a spoon into this before I polish off the lot!" Whole hours could go by when she did not give Andrew Todd a second thought.

It was later, reclining in her Albergo bedroom, that she examined the notebook in detail. Later still, she texted Miranda Hooper.

xiii: Village Gossip

"So our Corinna's swanning off to Rome again, I gather."
Hedley Porter was puffing – it had been a steep climb, but
puffing was good for him, so his doctor had said. "New
boyfriend, according to Cecy."

"Seeing a specialist, so I believe, dear, and she goes to
stay with Letizia. I say – look! A hoopoe! They're nesting at this
time of year…magnificent little bird the hoopoe…" Daphne, a
lot fitter than Hedley and puffing less, was stoically ignoring the
pain in her hip. Sometimes she wondered for how much longer
they could keep these walks up.

"Listen, Daphne, I know it's none of my business, but I
expect you've been helping her with this so-called specialist,
haven't you?"

"If I have then that's between Corinna and myself,
Hedley…Oh look, there's another! We must be very near a
nesting site. I hope we're not disturbing them, poor things."

Hedley Porter declared: "Oh, Daphne, Daphne…I despair
of you, I really do!"

"I'm sorry, Hedley, dear. I know you can't see properly –
such a shame. There he goes. 'Hoo-poo-poo…'You can hear
him. How delightful!"

"Quite. Lovely little chaps. About Corinna…" Hedley
Porter was a tall, well built man who did not stoop despite his

195

age, and whose once handsome face and abundant white hair were still striking. Recent surgery for cataracts had revealed something more serious, and his failing eyesight was a source of immense frustration to himself and provoked genuine dismay and sympathy in his friends. However, Hedley had some supremely irritating qualities, one of which was to have somehow subsumed his old dramatic roles into real life. The 60s radio series in which he had played a gentleman detective had provided him with the singular delusion that he personally was a great unraveller of mysteries, just as his role as the history schoolmaster in the TV series *Blessington Hall* had given him the notion of solid scholarship.

"I don't see why you should despair, Hedley. I know perfectly well what I'm doing, thank you."

"Frankly, Daphne… Damn it! I have to say it! That woman really *gets* me, Daphne. Annoys me. There she is, pleading poverty to anyone who'll listen, when she's got rents from about three properties, and probably gets ten percent a corpse from that seedy Neapolitan of Valeria's. Don't 'but' me, Daphne! And now this rich doctor in Rome and I'll bet she's setting her cap at Lord Helpus, too…"

"Hedley! These are vile things to say. Irresponsible, too. "

"Yesterday Cecy saw her in town wearing a brand-new jacket. Armani, Cecy said, and she should know. Knows about clothes, does Cecy. And now gallivanting off to Rome – specialist, my left foot!"

"Please, Hedley. Dear. You know perfectly well that Corinna looks after her clothes beautifully. If she was wearing a jacket Cecy's not seen before it's because it has probably been under mothballs in her wardrobe for the past five years."

"Humph. I still diagnose a gallivant, and new clothes are probably the wages of sin. I hope someone has the heart to put that poor idiot Cadwallader out of his misery."

"Hedley! Really, Hedley, if you're going to turn into a prig, I'm going to turn round and go home, and you can find your own way back to Monty. You can tell Cecy to keep her caustic opinions to herself as well. Cadwallader Jones knows what he's doing. "

"That is supremely unfair, Daphne. I happen to like Cadwallader. Don't like to see someone taken for a ride, that's all."

"You liar! You were only saying the other week how boring you both find him."

"Nonsense! I may have said that Cecy finds him hard work…but then Cecy too can be a little difficult. It's not priggishness, I assure you. I just – it just *gets* me that Corinna seems to have it all plain sailing.. Too poor to feed herself properly, so Cad told Cecy a few weeks ago, so why doesn't she sell some of her jewellery? She must wear a clerk's annual salary on her earlobes alone…and what about the new parquet floor?"

"Oh, Hedley! The apartment belongs to Valeria. Stop it at once."

"No, I shan't stop it, Daphne. I've been meaning to have my say for quite a while. We watch you being taken advantage of, and that is what has to stop. Cecy perfectly agrees with me. It's damn nigh unbearable, watching you being taken in, when it's perfectly obvious to everyone except Cadwallader that…I mean, Cad may be an idiot, but *you*…"

"Hedley! I meant what I said about going home. You are insulting my intelligence and behaving like a jealous little boy."

"Well at least we paid you back," said Hedley sulkily.

"And so will Corinna. You and Cecy have no idea how difficult things have been for Corinna, because I am probably the only person she confides her troubles to. For the rest of the world she keeps a smart shopfront for the sake of her own confidence."

"Humph. A jeweller's shop!"

"That family has treated her shamefully, and you don't know the half of it. Now, are we going to walk to the top of the hill, or shall we turn round?"

"Perhaps we'd better turn back. Cecy was wondering if you'd like to have lunch. Between you and me, she's all agog about this lady-writer."

"I can't. Not today. Thank Cecy, but Dennis is coming round to fix the video at twelve-thirty." They walked back grumpily towards Daphne's little car.

198

"There we are, Daffy. All fixed. Try it out?" Daphne pressed 'play' on the remote control and a familiar signature tune played.

"You are wonderful, Dennis, dear. I'm going to watch *Upstairs, Downstairs* all afternoon. Was it serious?"

"Just a loose wire. I've bound it up with some insulation tape. Should be okay for a bit. Really, the main problem is it's old, wearing out."

Daphne chuckled. "It's not the only one, dear! I don't want to replace it if I don't have to."

"No? Well, it should be good for a bit. But really you need a proper DVD player. I'd better run – I've left Silv coping with a party from Blackburn. I take it it's okay to have the 'Serena' next week?"

"Of course, Dennis. The poor boat needs to be used. Count it as yours on permanent loan, provided you see to the proper insurance if it's in public use. You know the rules. I might even join you one day if there's room."

"Always room for you, Daffy. Whenever you want. Thanks a million. This season looks like being a goody, we hope. About time, after all the chaos last year..." Dennis Barker was a short, stocky, ruddy-faced man in his early fifties, whose facial expressions wrought an extraordinary change in the way he might be perceived. When he smiled, as he was smiling at Daphne now, he resembled a genial, almost clownish sort of person; a man, you would think, of good humour and even temper. To Daphne Allerton he was like a cross between a favourite nephew and a trusted retainer. It was a position that Dennis appeared happy to maintain.

"Ah, yes…Silvana tells me the mysterious sponsors have rather disappeared. That is probably just as well, I should think."

"Well, you know. Favour returned." Dennis looked at the floor. "I never got involved with any of that, Daff. You know that."

"I have never suggested that you did, dear."

"Saturday, then!" he said. "I'll come if I can."

"Good. We have the Ladyship coming, you know. Freddy Partridge will bring her."

"Gawd, the Dearborn woman? We've got her already. Seems nice enough, but I don't see what the flamin' fuss is about. I'll try to get away. Silv'll come. She could do with a break… Look, Daff…" Dennis hovered a trifle awkwardly on the 'Welcome' threshold. "Silv told me not to say anything, but it's Corinna. Getting well above herself, she is, these days. Now she's kicking up the dust about the 'Gazza' – she and Silv were supposed to be arranging all this about the birthday between them but then Corinna went away, and Silv had to book something for such a big party on a Saturday in the middle of the season. For some reason, Corinna's taken against Federico and Donata, but we think they're okay. More than okay. I hope she's not been saying anything…"

"She mentioned it. I'm sure everything will turn out very nicely, dear, whatever it is. You go on to your Lancastrians…"

Dennis still hovered. "Thing is, the 'Gazza' – it's a bit important to us at the minute…"

"They're friends of yours, I gather. I'm sure it will be lovely." Daphne was only longing to put her feet up in front of her video.

"Thing is, now we've had the kitchens done, if we *could* open a restaurant at the Del Mare, they'll lend us Massimo part time. I think you'll be well pleased, Daff. The idea is that they'll keep a lunch menu, and we'll do dinners, and share the cost of Massimo…"

"We'll discuss the restaurant idea later, Dennis dear. I'm tired. I shall see you on Saturday, I hope…" It was a royal dismissal. Dennis went.

"I mean, I don't suppose she *meant* to…I just feel sorry for the poor old boy, you know. It meant so much to him, and she seems to have just dismissed it. If nothing else it was very careless of someone else's feelings…when he rang me this morning – Mrs Battaglia had found it behind the sofa, you know – he was terribly *upset*…"

Dorinda and Daphne were sitting on Daphne's terrace, enjoying the view and a second Friday elevenses vodka.

"She's very busy, dear…I expect it just slipped her mind. It's very nice for Cadwallader that you're keeping him company so often these days. I expect he appreciates it very much."

"I mean, I'd have thought unless she'd had a complete well, skinful, she *couldn't* have just forgotten. Why didn't she ring him when she realised she hadn't got it? It's been *two days*!"

"Corinna *never* gets drunk, dear. Not in all the time I've known her. More than twenty-five years, dear. That's a *very long time*!" It was a rebuke, but Dorinda began to grow exasperated. Why, oh why, did Daphne *always* make excuses for Corinna?

"So in other words, you're saying it *was* deliberate! Poor old Cad – he thinks she didn't like it, that he'd made her bottom look too big!"

"Well, dear, you have to admit that Corinna *is* a little broad in the beam, despite her height…and, it's true, just a little vain…"

"But, Daphne, this is his *work*! He's a professional, and he did this for her as a present, a gift, a special *gift*…she doesn't deserve him, that she doesn't…"

"Perhaps not, dear…Now! I want to hear all about your *son*! When is dear Merrick coming out to see us?"

xiv: Interlude: A Soiree

"I thought you said nobody takes wine, or I'd have brought some."

"They don't, as a rule. I'm the exception. Call it enlightened self-interest…your interest, too, my sweet. Don't worry! It's only a modest prosecco."

"I have a horrible feeling I'm going to hate this, Freddy…"

"We won't stay long, promise…"

Veronica buttoned a sigh.

"Think of it as a play, an interlude…"

Shrieks, guffaws, braying laughter and the clinking of glasses, becoming more audible as three people make their way through a slightly scruffy baroque courtyard with bicycles shoved against the walls, a decaying scooter, weeds growing through the ancient stones. They climb the uneven staircase towards an upper apartment. The trio comprises a tall, tanned, casually elegant man in jeans and a cream linen jacket with a rather ostentatious red silk handkerchief in the pocket who looks – at least from a distance – rather younger than his fifty-four years, and who bounds up the stairs lithely on espadrilled feet, bearing two wrapped bottles of prosecco in a carrier-bag, a little ahead of his companions. One of these is a woman of a similar age, also tall, also handsome in her way, slightly frizzy greying reddish hair not quite tidy in a tortoiseshell pin. She is dressed in a loose pale grey shirt over slim-fitting trousers and is unadorned apart from a large silver brooch of a Celtic design at the bosom of the shirt. On a close inspection it might be seen that she is wearing rather more make-up on her face than usual, and if one knew her at all well, one would realise that she has applied what she would call 'war-paint', and suspect that she has been suffering from nerves. As it is, she smiles bravely as she turns to the third member of the group, an elderly man with the countenance of an amiable camel, a pronounced stoop, and a silver-knobbed walking-cane on which he leans, pausing to regain his breath. He has evidently taken great care over his appearance: a pale green linen suit cut in the Armani fashion which flaps a little round his skinny legs, a flowing pink and grey silk cravat, and a panama hat which he has worn purely for the dramatic effect of being able to remove it with a flourish once he enters the room.

"Don't rush, Cadwallader," says the woman. "We'll go in together, shall we?"

"Thank you, Veronica, my dear. It's my knees, you see. Hee! Not so young or limber as once I was…anno domini…You go on. I'm slow. Coming, Freddy!"

"Take your time, Uncle Cad. No hurry."

The woman joins the younger man at the door, which is ajar. The mat says 'Welcome', and over the door is a framed sampler proclaiming 'Good Friends Gather Here'. "Oh blimey," says the woman, not quite under her breath. The party-noise from within has resolved into actual words and voices.

"She *is*!" cries a voice: female, English, patrician, insistent. "Corinna *said* so!"

"Oh well, if Corr-eena says so, it *'as* to be true!" Another female voice, considerably lower in pitch, a pronounced Italian accent, and a suspicion of sarcasm. "She knows all the aristocracy! This Lord Elpus, for instance."

"My dear..." Male voice: English, a modulated, well-pitched bass, interrupted by another male voice: tenor, American this time, tinged with a touch of petulance: "I just don't understand this crazy British class system...what in hell does it matter, anyway? Do you *know*, Hedley?"

"It matters to get it *right*, Cy," shrieks a voice of excruciatingly refined cockney which Veronica recognises at once: her landlady. "And I say she's *not*. Sorry, Daffy, but it was us who took her passport..."

"Protocol, I guess..." Another male American voice, softer.

"I *told* Corinna!" cries the Cockney. "And it's not as if she's the last word on everything. She was wrong about that ambassador chappie from Lithuania or wherever it was..."

"I think you'll find it was Ukraine, Silvana...but it's perfectly true. One would never, so far as I am aware, address him as 'Excellency' out of office...These things do matter to a degree, Cy…you see –" The elegant *basso profondo,* preparing to be profound.

"I think our Corr-eena found Is Excellency *very* excellent, if you ask me…and now she 'as another Lordship for 'er collection."

"Now then, Cecilia, dear. Best not to gossip. As far as we know that is simply business."

First American, losing patience: "I *still* don't know what to call this dame!"

"Well *I* call her Veronica…" Another female voice, trace of an Irish accent, which Veronica also recognizes. Dora? Doreen?

(On the threshold: "Oh *God,* Freddy…" "Don't worry, dear heart." "Fat chance!" "Here I am! Hee! Made it!" "Well, if we're all set, let's make our entrance, shall we?")

"Oh, for crying out *loud!*" Explosive male voice: estuarian vowels with a brutal edge. Her landlord. The trio make their way down a cluttered corridor towards the gathering. "Who effin' *cares*? She's just an 'otel guest…on 'oliday…she could be the Duchess of f…flippin' Kent for all I care…"

"Den!"

"She's also *my* guest, Dennis, and she will be here at any moment!" The first voice sounds more agitated than ever.

First American, exasperated: "Well, *do* I call her Your Ladyship or don't I?"

"Please…please just call me Veronica…" Introductions, handshakes, air-kisses; Freddy feted with loud, arch cries of welcome and gushing thanks for the prosecco; Cadwallader Jones (who has removed his hat with less of a flourish than a sudden desire to be less hot) placed in a comfortable armchair in which he sits with an audible 'whew!' where he is fussed over by Dorinda Daley who has embraced Veronica like an old friend…

"Have lots to drink – there's red *and* white…and dear Freddy's contribution! You know you don't have to, Freddy, dear…we're all *so* thrilled to have an historian in our midst…" The owner of the first voice: her hostess, Daphne Allerton, a tiny, leathery, elderly woman with curly grey hair wearing a silk shirt and red trousers and a great deal of very good jewellery. Her eyes are very blue and very bright. "Will someone please give our guests a *glass*!" she screams.

"No sooner said than done!" A loud 'pop' as Freddy opens a bottle theatrically.

"Ohmigawd," says Dennis Barker under his breath, not quite inaudibly, and merely nods to Veronica's cordial 'good evening'.

"Now then…Don't *you* worry, Daffy – I'll see to everybody. You sit there, Freddy, dear…and Miss Dearborn – sorry, Veronica, dear – you're the guest of honour! Why don't you sit next to Daphne…?" Silvana Barker: plump and dressed in a cotton Indian trouser-suit in swirling browns, is on her feet, evidently the mistress of ceremonies.

This gathering – squeezed as it is into a small, overcrowded and stuffy sitting room festooned with sentimental china ornaments and a great many framed pictures, one of them recognizably an original 'Cadwallader Jones' watercolour of the Bay, and with the guests arranged at the perimeter on sofas and chairs around a low table stacked with plates of filled bread rolls – has the look of a disorganized committee and is claustrophobic in the extreme. Perched on a long sofa between her hostess and a large elderly man in thick spectacles who has courteously got to his feet and introduced himself in his distinctive deep voice as Hedley Porter, Veronica feels a little like an 'aunt sally' at an old-fashioned country fair: bombarded by eyes and questions on all sides, mostly innocent inquiries as to whether she is enjoying her stay and if she has seen the Signorelli in the Chiesa or visted the Castello, to which she tries to respond in turn. She accepts a glass and a plate, and tries to concentrate on what Hedley is saying, or rather intoning, into her left ear, while at the same time trying to have a conversation on her right with Daphne and the florid, rather whining American introduced as 'Cy'. Everyone seems to talk at once, talk over each other, and the braying din is already colossal.

Hedley Porter explains: "My wife, Cecilia – there she is, in the purple jacket – she is reading your book, my dear. I gather it is a deserved triumph! I'm afraid I have not yet had the opportunity, and my eyes are not, unfortunately, what they were…I rely on Cecy these days to tell me about the world, alas. But, now, Sir Henry Cuthbert…was not he a certain *very dark character*?"

"Cuffe…"

"Cuffe?"

"Yes, Henry Cuffe. Not Cuthbert…he was someone else…I think…"

"Oh, I beg your pardon! I might mean Collingridge! Or *is* it Cuffe? Cecy? Darling?"

A diminutive woman who could be seventy, but who has the lissom figure of a girl, an elaborate elfin cut of dark-copper hair and dressed to kill in a purple Missoni jacket and jeans with high-heeled purple boots, looks up through vivid, much made-up brown eyes: "Of course it is Cuffe, daarrrling…we 'ave your books at 'ome, Veronica…I am coming to talk to you once I get a chance…" and looks away again, concentrating on something Freddy is saying about Roman cuisine. "But nobody, Fraid-dy, can do a prop-per *carbonara* except in Rome…" "Now when *I* cook," Dorinda interrupts, "I just go where my instincts tell me…I can't be fished with recipes unless it's a cake…" "Moh! In Ee-ngland, they put 'am and cream in it…" "And *I* say, what's wrong with ham and cream?" "Nothing, dear lady, but we couldn't *possibly* call it *carbonara*, could we, Cecilia?" "Oh, well, Freddy, of course you're the *expert*…" "Oh, but so is Dorinda! Hee! You should just taste her Irish stew!" Veronica

209

has heard the plural 'books' and braces herself, accepting another glass of wine from a cut glass decanter.

"It *is* Cuffe, it's Henry *Cuffe*! Why is everyone so *stupid*?" cries Daphne Allerton at her side and bouncing with fury. "We do have the author sitting here! Now then, dear, I can't pretend I've read it yet, because I haven't, but I enjoyed the *Literary Survey* review very much. Now then! Tell me! We all understand you're here to write about the wonderful Millicent *Fox*! Isn't that so, Cadwallader, dear? Oh dear, he can't hear, you know..."

"Well, I..."

"You've got it wrong this time, Hedley!" shrieks a voice from across the tiny room. Silvana Barker's antennae are sharp. "Of course it's Henry Cuffe – isn't that right, Veronica? Now, wouldn't you like another of these egg rolls? Or there's tuna and tomato. I do them specially for Daphne, don't I, Daffy? And how's your wine? Henry Cuffe was Essex's secretary, wasn't he?" She puts down a plate and squeezes her plump self beside Cy, who looks slightly alarmed.

"Yes, he was." Veronica, with fake brightness, tries to catch the eye of Freddy, but Freddy is still in the cookery huddle which the other American, Lorrie, has joined, apparently explaining the American culinary habits of ham and cream. Dorinda Daly, who is leaning forward agog into the conversation and waving a glass of wine, is stroking Cadwallader's sleeve absently and proprietarily with her other be-ringed hand, while that gentleman is speaking – apparently about the exorbitant prices of Venice hotels – to Dennis Barker.

"Now this is fascinating!" Silvana Barker, who evidently has done her homework and is anxious to prove it, holds forth on the topic of Henry Cuffe for some moments, and argues shrilly with Hedley about the Essex Rebellion across the laps of Veronica and Daphne.

"Don't tell Cadwallader this, dear," Daphne confides in a loud hiss in Veronica's ear, "But I can't think why anyone would want to write *about* Millicent's books…"

"Well – oh, dear – *I'm* not actually writing about Millicent at all… But someone is. Her books are all being reprinted and there's to be a special introduction to each writer in the series…I'm actually doing someone else."

"Well, I hope you've told poor Cadwallader, dear!" shrieks Daphne Allerton as if the sky has fallen in.

"Ooh! Who are you doing?" Silvana Barker leans towards Veronica cosily across Daphne's lap. "Anyone we know?"

"Probably not. She didn't write much. She's called Flora Forde…with an 'e'…"

"Flora Forde! Yes! *The Pearls of Wisdom*! How lovely! I've got that book somewhere! How nice! And you say it's all going to be re-published…"

"Yes…How nice you've even heard of her…she's almost disappeared. Did you ever read *The Well-Trodden Stair*? It was her third and last…"

"*I've* never heard of her! You don't mean *The Spiral Staircase*, do you? By Ethel White…I was in the radio production, you know, with Helen Hayes…marvellous woman, Helen…"

"No, Hedley. She doesn't mean *The Spiral Staircase*…and that was Elsa Lanchester, surely."

"You obviously have a passion, Silvana," says Veronica tactfully. She accepts another glass of decanted wine – red, this time, which is almost as foul as the white. She glances over and sees that Freddy's group is hugging the prosecco to themselves.

"Oh, I don't have time, not these days, dear…but I used to want to be an English teacher before…" She glanced at her husband.

"I imagine the hotel must leave you very little free time," Veronica murmurs.

"You can say that again!" chortles Mrs Barker.

"I don't *know*," Daphne Allerton says in a loud hiss to Cy, bouncing in her seat for emphasis. "My dear," she commands Veronica in decibels considerably louder than the general din. "Now then! Tell Cy all about the *Dearborn family*!"

"Recusants," whispers Silvana with authority to Cy. "Catholics who refused to go to Anglican services…"

"You don't say…"

"And her great, great, great-something grandfather was beheaded in the Tower! It's true! Isn't it, Veronica dear?"

"Are you serious? Wow, that's terrible!"

Suddenly a great many eyes are upon Veronica, and now a volley of questions. "Oh! Well, yes…He was. They – yes, I mean they were a recusant family during the Reformation, but not very devout, I don't think…yes, I suppose I am a direct ancestor…I mean, yes, I am…Write about them next? I don't know…I might…The interesting one was of course the late Elizabethan Sir Hugh…He allowed his friend to hide in his house. It didn't please Elizabeth very much. It was rather a sensitive time…"

"Ah, yes…Church and State, Church and State." Hedley Porter nods wisely.

"And his friend was Edward Campion!" cries Silvana Barker. "The poet!"

"Oh no, m'dear, excuse me, he was earlier," butts in Mrs Daly, suddenly all ears. "Who?" inquires Cadwallader Jones. "Search me, Uncle Cad," says Freddy. "It was Edward Pursuivant! Veronica has just SAID so!" yells Mrs Allerton, bouncing, in Veronica's ear.

"Percy? You mean the dukes of Northumberland?" "*Pursuivant*, Uncle Cad." "Oh, gawd! Who gives a flying *toss*?" asks Dennis Barker.

Someone asks an insistent question. "Sorry? Oh, Henry Cuffe…Yes, yes, Cuffe was executed along with his master, accused of sedition, inciting rebellion…" Again Veronica tries, and fails, to catch Freddy's eye.

"So do you think Elizabeth went mad towards the end? Megalomaniac?" Mrs Barker asks Veronica, but Mr Porter answers, "Not really, no. But she had to protect her throne. Essex was a serious contender, fomenting sedition. In terms of the day and age, she seems to have been fairly moderate. But she was the Lord's Anointed, you see, which gave her a sort of divine immunity. Is that not so, my dear Miss Dearborn?"

"The sheer barbarism!" cries Daphne passionately. "What a terrible world!"

"Yes...of course... Torture and death-sentences were the way rulers dealt with their enemies, and – well – democracy hadn't been invented. Everyone was trying to pit their version of God against everyone else's, which included extremist Catholics and extremist Puritans who all believed their choice of monarch to be the divinely appointed one. The Catholics wanted Mary Queen of Scots, of course... Oh dear – it's so difficult to picture it through a modern lens and not see it as just barbaric, but from Elizabeth's point of view, given that the ruling religion was also the political rule too, she didn't have much choice. I think Essex was just basically trying to create a power-base, creating knighthoods and so on, and he had to go..."

Murmurs of 'my, oh my,' from one of the Americans, 'fascinating' from the other, and Cecilia Porter's world-weary "Religious genocide. It 'appened. Umanity is foul. And the so-called Christians were just as bad as the extremist Muslims now...isn't that so?" "Still are, if you ask me." "Oh, come on,

214

Silvana. No one's as bad as the Muslims…" "But what about all the extremist Jews?" puts in Dorinda. "Oh, we can't talk about the Jews, dear," cries Daphne. "Not at all tactful…" "I wasn't being *tactless*! I was having a *debate*. I *like* Jews! But it's true, isn't it, surely? You can say exactly the same of the Marxists *and* the Fascists!" "The Zionists have a genuine cause, thank you, Dorinda! God, the sheer ignorance of some people…" Cy looks up to heaven. "You can't be suggesting…" "Cy, buddie…" "*I* think we ought to change the subject," says Silvana Barker. "Sorry, Veronica…"

"Oh, not at all…" Now, she sees Freddy's eyes on her with something that could be helpless sympathy.

"We heard that *you* were almost executed, milady," says the charmless Dennis Barker, standing up.

"What was that?"

"Nothing, Uncle Cad."

"You going back, Den? Don't forget to get the cheese out of the fridge and under the net…the butter can stay now it's turned warm."

"*Jawohl, mein fuhrer*. Daffy – I'm off. I've got a hotel to run." He pecks Daphne on the cheek, pats Cadwallader on the shoulder, nods curtly at the others and leaves.

"Don't mind my husband, Veronica dear," says Mrs Barker cosily. "It's the time of the month. *Accounts*!" She screams with raucous laughter, in which most of the others join…

"No thanks, Daphne…" The wine is next to undrinkable, and she wants to find the bathroom. With Dennis Barker's departure, the room has shifted and, Veronica is curious to note, quietened briefly, although Dennis has said almost nothing. Hedley Porter has lumbered over to talk to Cadwallader; Cy has gone to join his partner at the cookery symposium, and Silvana and Daphne are in a huddle of their own, conducted in fierce whispers. Now, Hedley's wife, the tiny glamorous Italian, is advancing to take her husband's place. "At last! We can talk about your book…"

"Your husband has been telling me you're reading it…how very kind…"

"I don't mean Enry Cuffe…I mean the earlier one…about your child'ood. Arrowing…"

"Cecilia …I'm sorry, but could you show me where to find the loo?"

"Of course. And do you want to smoke? I do…Why don't we go out on the terrace and 'ave a cigarette? We are not allowed in 'ere…" She gives a meaningful glance in the direction of Cy and Lorrie, and summons Veronica in the direction of the bathroom.

"Helloo-ooo! Do you mind if I join the naughty people?" Dorinda Daly, with a huge smile and a cigarette already at her carmine mouth, totters up to join the two smokers on the terrace.

She lights up, inhales deeply, and blows smoke out to sea. The interruption is welcome. "We can't in there because of the *Americans*...I mean, it's not as if Daphne doesn't smoke herself, and it's her *house*..."

"I imagine it would get horribly fuggy in there if people smoked..."

"Oh, but we do all the time unless *they* come...they don't always, do they, Cecy? I mean, they're not *regulars* ...*I* think they came out of plain *curiosity*!"

"Pr'aps..."

"What do you all do normally? Play bridge and things?"

"Oh, *no*! We just talk, don't we, Cecy...put the world to rights, *you* know...nothing strange or out of the ordinary..."

"When anyone can get a word in edgewise..." Cecilia looks put out. "We're talking about Veronica's autobiography. You 'ave read it, Dorinda?"

"Oh, yes! Of *course*! It's *brilliant*! Beautifully written! And you must be so excited about the *film*..."

"I'm sorry?"

"The film! I've been reading all about it in the papers...well, you know, on the internet. I get the *Observer* and the *Times*...And Radio Four...I'm an *Archers* addict." Dorinda puffs happily.

Veronica feels her guts sink and says faintly, "They've been talking about a film on Radio Four? Of my book? When?"

"I can't remember *exactly*. The day before yesterday. Yes, I *think* so…or maybe it was Wednesday. I can't remember exactly, sweetie. It must be so *exciting*."

"Oh my God! Look, I know there was a mention of it in some *Observer* piece a few weeks ago, but it's honestly all a mare's nest. There isn't going to be a film."

"*Really*? Oh, what a *shame*…I could have *sworn*…Perhaps you should talk to your agent. My daughter's a writer, children's books, and…"

"Films can never capture the essence of a book, in my op-eenion. I theenk you shouldn' make a film."

"Oh, but you don't understand. There's not going to be a film. I mean, it's true there's been talk of one…in the *Observer*. But it was just gossip, hearsay. There was an – an approach, but – well, I've forbidden it, in fact."

"Really? But *why*? I mean, I'd have thought, for a *newish* author…you'll be needing the publicity, surely?"

Veronica takes a deep breath and forces herself to say pleasantly, "Three reasons, Dorinda. One, I'm sick and tired of *Too Big To Cry*. I don't want it all dredged up again. Two, as Cecilia points out, I don't think it would translate at all well into a drama. And three, I don't actually need the publicity…" She smiles grimly.

"Oh, *well*…" Dorinda Daley throws her cigarette butt haphazardly over the terrace wall. "Woops! I've gone native, as you can see! Well, I'm sure you know best, my dear. Now, I'd better get back in and rescue poor Cadwallader. They're teasing him about Corinna…" She turns and totters off, leaving an impression of a 'huff'.

"Oh dear…"

"Take no notice of 'er. " Cecilia Porter makes a drinking gesture. "I think we go in now…it is not warm out here…and it's going to rain. We will speak again, I 'ope…"

"Well, go on, Cadwallader dear – *have* you asked her?"

"He can't go down on one knee!"

"Barkis is willin'!"

"Shh!"

"That's a preposterous suggestion!" Cadwallader Jones is in an obvious agitation as they enter, mopping his brow on his cravat and swallowing the bad red wine as if thirsty. Dorinda Daly is perched on a pouffe stool at his side. "I regard anything between Corinna and myself to be entirely private!"

"Don't worry, Cad," whispers Dorinda.

"No! Don't take it seriously, Cadwallader dear," Silvana Barker is saying. "We're only teasing. We don't mean it."

"Exactly! It's not at all the same thing as Brunero! Forget I ever mentioned Brunero, dear! Ah! Here is our star guest! Sit, dear! Have another drink!" Daphne has evidently taken quite a number herself.

"Thank you...er..." Veronica spots Freddy and sits down next to him. "Can we go soon?" she hisses into his ear. Cecilia Porter takes the place between Daphne and Hedley.

"Wow! Who's Brunero?" The American Lorrie is agog. "This is better than *Frazier*!"

Freddy hisses back: "Yes! As soon as we can prise Uncle Cad from the harpies!"

"Oh, nobody special. Just another of Corinna's bruised hearts...Don't worry, Cadwallader, dear. She'll be back on Monday, won't she, Daffy? After her *treatment*...at the doctor's." More giggles.

"What? What did she say?"

"That Corinna will be back soon, Cadwallader. After her *treatment*!" Daphne bounces. "He's so deaf!"

"Brunero. He was a local estate agent. Nice man. Had a bit of a thing for our absent friend-ess, poor fellow...she didn't give him any quarter, which didn't prevent a man from hoping... The latest one's only quite young and married."

"As if that makes a – "

"It'll be His Lordship next, I'll bet..."

"Shh!"

"But he's ga-ga!"

"Lovely house and grounds...jewel of a place. If he ever wants to sell it..."

"Have *you* ever been to the famous rose garden? You have a lovely rose garden, too, don't you, Veronica, dear? In your house near Siena?"

"Well, I…"

"She created it. Fenella Fanthorpe. In Castelambra. Lovely woman in her heyday…"

"Den's got a party booked to go there next week…people from Lancaster…"

"Now is he *married* to that actress? *I* think they're only living together…"

"Well, I 'ope this Roman doctor's rich," says the waspish Cecilia Porter, a remark which fortunately Cadwallader Jones does not hear, being in sudden urgent conversation with Dorinda at his side.

"Freddy…*please*…"

"My goodness! It's half past eleven! We'd all better leave Daffy in peace. Do you want to walk back with me, Veronica dear?"

"No – thanks all same, Silvana. I'll see Cadwallader home with Freddy…"

"Just as you like, dear. We don't bolt at this time of year…you've got your night-key?"

"Yes, yes, thank you…"

This seems to precipitate a general departure. Hugs, handshakes, thank yous and good nights, promises of another visit, another time, and a clattering, chattering down the stairs…

At the street door, Cadwallader announced his intention of seeing Dorinda home. "No, no…you young people go on. I shall be perfectly all right…" Dorinda bade her farewells, giving Veronica a smirk that was both complicit and derisive, and took Cad's arm proprietarily.

"Incorrigible old goat!" remarked Freddy out of earshot.

"Freddy? Can we scram? Now?" She was anxious not to arrive at the Albergo at the same time as her landlady, and they found a bar on a tiny side street and ordered grappa.

"Penny for them?"

"Don't ever, ever do that to me again, Freddy…" said Veronica quietly.

"Oh dear. You're furious. I'll give you a fabulous lunch tomorrow."

"Of course I'm furious!" Veronica suddenly exploded. "How the hell do you think I feel? Exposed to that ghastly crowd, shrieking their heads off and talking at once and nobody listening to anyone else and all that covert bitching. And that's without all the ladyship crap, their nasty insinuations, and all the nudging about the film. What a nest of vipers!"

"A pity," said Freddy mischievously, "that you don't write fiction, dear heart. Wonderful novel fodder, I'd say."

"Don't be so fucking frivolous. You just don't get it do you? Oh, hell! *Forget* it!"

"I really am sorry, Vee. I sort of can't take them remotely seriously. Forgive me?"

"Oh God, I suppose so…it's not your fault I've lost my sense of humour."

"What did you think of Daphne?"

"I might like her if I ever get to talk to her properly. But if that's her idea of fun, I'm not so sure. I mean, honestly, Freddy! And teasing poor Cadwallader so mercilessly."

"He'll survive. He loves attention, hadn't you noticed? He's as bad as the rest of them, really."

"Hmmph. I expect that's why he fits. It's my idea of absolute hell. And you really mean they do this every bloody week? They don't even play cards, someone told me! They – they're *appalling*! Oh God…" She laughed in spite of herself. Soothed by cool air and grappa, Veronica was recovering her temper.

Freddy yawned suddenly. "They're tiring, I'll give you that."

"I'm glad you're exhaustible after all. I was beginning to think you were Peter Pan. Freddy, can we go out somewhere away from here tomorrow? Back into the mountains, maybe? I'll drive."

"Claustrophobia?"

"Something like that."

"Good idea. Let's get an early start. I'll call for you after brekkers."

Veronica yawned too. "I expect the Barkers will be all tucked up by now. I'm going to risk going back."

"As your ladyship pleases." Veronica hit him.

xv: Gathering Storms

As Veronica and Freddy wound their way into the green and blossom-laden hills the next morning, they left more than the clangour of Sunday bells behind them.

The weather had turned humid by the sea, where an unpleasantly thick mist was gathering on the water, and the air was sticky, unrefreshing. Julian Blyth, after a frustrating morning trying to find Monte Farfalla and getting lost twice after he left the Rome autostrada in a hired car in which the air-conditioning as well as the sat-nav appeared to have failed, hovered hot and thirsty in the reception area of the Albergo Del Mare while a party of young people – Australians, by the sound of them – checked in with vast amounts of baggage. He waited. A surly-looking youth with slicked-back hair helped them load bags into the tiny elevator, while the human cargo slip-slopped up the marble staircase chattering. A woman emerged from an office and began checking names off a list against a pile of passports without noticing him. He coughed. "Oh!" she said, looking up. "I'm so sorry! Didn't see you in all this chaos. Can I help?" A London voice. Julian advanced with tentative confidence.

"I hope so…I wondered…" he mopped at his forehead with his sleeve.

"It has turned warm, hasn't it? We're in for a storm, I'd say! We get sciroccos here. What can I do for you, sir?" She had an elaborate hair-do and a bright professional smile, which became less rigid as she took in Julian's height, his crumpled blazer, his bandaged wrist, his lop-sided, diffident smile, his voice.

"I'm – er – not a guest. I'm just here on the off-chance. Sorry. I wondered, do you happen to know where I can find Via San Giovanni Battista? Perhaps you've got a little street map...I'm looking for number fifteen..."

"Number fifteen? Are you sure?"

"Yes. It's someone called – er – here we are. Yes. Mrs Daphne Appleton. No, sorry, Allerton. She's English. It's possible you know her..."

"Daphne? Well of course I know Daphne...everybody does. Is it anything special? I say, would you like a glass of water? You do look hot! Let's go through to the bar, shall we? Becky!" A thin, dark haired girl in jeans emerged from an inner office. "Mind the desk, there's a love. I'm going to give this gentleman a drink before he wilts!"

She led him through coloured glass doors to a dark, deserted bar-cum-breakfast room which smelled of stale sugared buns, and poured mineral water from the fridge into a glass full of ice.

"Thank you...very kind."

"Not at all! It's a bit cooler in here, isn't it? This room's north-facing. Now then, you said you were looking for Daphne, Mr – er...."

"Blyth. Julian Blyth."

"Blyth! Well, blow me down! I thought you reminded me of someone! You must be a relation of Hilary Blyth..." The woman had a voice that bordered on a screech as its natural pitch.

"I'm his brother. You knew him, I take it."

"Oh, *yes*! *Everybody* knew Hilary, bless him. I'm Silvana Barker. My husband Dennis should be in any moment....Well, I never! Just fancy. Can I offer you a proper drink, Mr Blyth? A campari or something? Beer? Of course! I'll join you if I may..." Mrs Barker poured light bottled lager and teetered round to his side of the bar on high heels. "Let's sit, shall we? So! You're on a pilgrimage!" she said, looking suitably serious..

"Not exactly. Well, sort of, I suppose. Actually, I've been selling his house."

"*Oh*...Well strike me pink! You mean it's gone?"

"Yes."

"Well, now, that *will* be a relief! A friend of ours does a bit in the property way, and she said it would be horribly difficult to shift, the state it was in...and poor Faye, she *would* stick out for something a bit – well, on the unrealistic side..." She eyed Julian quizzically, the unspoken question 'how much' hovering between them.

"Well it's all settled now, Mrs Barker."

"Oh, Silvana, please! Did you sell to a local? I mean, I do hope not, because the locals will never pay a fair price for anything…" Again the hovering question. Julian, whose natural inclination was to give away as little as possible, watched the woman's frustrated curiosity with a flicker of amusement.

"It was all done through lawyers. The buyer is some property developer from Rome, I believe."

"Oh…I see. You were lucky to find him, I should think."

"Yes. We were."

"You must have found one of those international agents…?"

"Something like that, I believe. I've just been signing papers."

Silvana tried another tack, her plump pleasant-looking face taking on a look of deep sympathy. "Now tell me," she said. "How *is* poor Faye? Has she decided to settle in England now? Much better, I should think, than here with all the memories, poor thing. Not that she didn't have good friends. We all tried to support her as much as we could after Hilary passed away. *Such* a tragedy, that. Poor Hilary! A lovely man! I felt so *sorry* for poor Faye…we all did."

There were people who could describe a sudden drowning as 'passing away'. Irritated, Julian said nothing of Faye's accident, and murmured that she was as well as could be expected. "She couldn't quite face coming herself, and so I – um..."

"Well of *course*! That's only natural." Silvana Barker seemed to be one of those supremely annoying people who would ask questions and simply run on, not waiting for the answer. *Everybody* had known poor old Hilary, *such* a charmer, old-fashioned manners, a real gent...such a shame... "If only he hadn't had a sudden mad impulse to go swimming in the middle of the night...a tragedy, truly! A rogue current, but there was a daily coastguard warning and the Bay can get very rough...ask Dennis...but you couldn't tell Hilary anything, could you? And he did like a drop, if you know what I mean, well didn't he? And going off into the night in a temper like that! It was an accident waiting to happen, that's what we all said at the time... But he was marvellous, wasn't he! A real one-off! And his stories would have you in stitches..."

"Yes..."

"Have you been to see his grave? Oh, not yet...well, I keep saying to Dennis someone ought to go up there, put some flowers, tidy up a bit...but when you run a hotel you have to give so many things the go-by... I've got my elderly mum poorly, now, so I've got my hands tied most of the time...We used to leave her holding the fort, but she's not up to that these days...I've got Becky at the moment, my daughter Rebecca, you know, but she's starting veterinary training in the autumn...And Dennis has his bus-tours. There's another party just arrived as

229

you came in. Aussie students this time. Sometimes it feels like we're running a youth hostel rather than a hotel! Still, mustn't complain, must we? And there's so much misery in the world. And tragedy….Nearly a year…Fancy! Seems yesterday *and* about ten years ago if you get my meaning… Now then, dear – you wanted to see Daphne…"

"Well – um – yes. I mean, whilst I'm here. I thought – that is, I – I should like to meet some of Hilary and Faye's old friends. I've still got a day or two in Italy, and there's someone I still need to see on business."

"Oh! Well, I'm sure Daphne'd love to meet you, Julian. Your voices really are amazingly similar! You sound just like him! I'll give you Daphne's number. Don't try it until early evening. She always has a little snooze in the afternoons…and she's a bit deaf, so you might need to leave it ringing for a bit…where did you say you were staying? Oh, well, in that case, if you wanted to, we've still got a couple of rooms free here…give you more time, won't it? Car in the square, is it? No problem! I'll get Gianni to collect your bags and we can put a notice in the windscreen. Looks like you've been in the wars," she added, indicating Julian's bandaged wrist.

"Just a sprain."

So it was that Julian Blyth checked into the Albergo Del Mare. As he descended the stone steps into the humid, deserted early afternoon accompanied by the surly Gianni, he almost

230

collided with a thick-set man wearing a bright Hawaiian shirt over a pronounced stomach and khaki shorts.

"Jesus Harry Christ!" exclaimed the man, blinking at Julian through dark spectacles.

"So sorry…" The man removed the sunglasses and continued to gaze at Julian. "No harm done, surely?"

"No – no, mate. For a second, I thought you were somebody else. Sorry. Stupid mistake…" The man shook his head as if he had a wasp and hurried into the Albergo.

"Silv!"

"Mum's upstairs with the new group. Anything up, Dad?"

"No!"

"All right. No need to shout."

Dennis Barker pulled the hotel's register towards him. "All present and correct," said Becky. "Nine, six doubling up in the twins. You sure you're okay? You look like you've seen a ghost."

"Did someone just check in? Tall, middle-aged bloke in a striped jacket?"

"Oh, yeah…him. He came to see Mum…he's gone to get his bags."

Silvana clacked down the marble steps on her high heels. "Oh, hello, Dennis. Everybody's settling in. I've got to ring the 'Gazza' and tell them to expect a party of ten. I take it you'll be going with them. Beck! Get Donata on the phone, will you?"

231

"Okay, Mum."

"Silv! A bloke was just here – a bloke who – "

"Looks just like Hilary Blyth…I *know*, Dennis! He's coming to stay for a couple of days. He wants to see Daphne. Thanks, Beck. Donata? *Sono Silvana…Allora, dieci minuti per dieci, va bene, cara? Si, dieci. Anche Dennis…*"

"Silv!"

"*Grazie, Donata, gioia.* It's his *brother*, Dennis, and he's not really like him. Thinner, and I'd say a bit taller. What? Oh for heaven's sakes! He's just down on a visit, seeing to the grave and selling Hilary's house. It's gone, so he says. Fancy! And of course Lorrie and Cy didn't say a word, but I bet they knew all right! Tell Gianni to fold the brollies in the garden, Beck! The weather's turning. Corinna won't half be pee'd off…"

Corinna, curled up in the back of a Roman taxi and a reverie on her way to see her younger daughter Letizia for lunch, was as yet untroubled by anything other than a rather delicious lack of sleep and some lubricious recollections as rain beat against the darkening windows and forks of lightning lit the sky, while back in Monte Farfalla, the bush telegraph clacked happily.

Over a jug of bloody mary on Dorinda's wide balcony, Cadwallader Jones sipped and lamented. "I can't stop thinking about it! It was a special *present*. Daphne's going to buy hers. These little vignettes, as I call them, of people's homes, are going down rather well. Hee! The idea is a snapshot, you see. Daphne's will have tiny figures of all her usual guests. I've drafted it, you know. I've put Daphne behind a barbecue, and yelling 'Sausages!' and I wondered if she'd like Hilary and Faye there, as a memento… I'll do yours soon, my dear…Oh dear…she can't have liked it, can she? I took a great deal of trouble over it. And I'm sure the – er – the posterior problem was merely a matter of perspectives. She's in trousers and a white shirt, watering plants…very elegant, I'd hoped. I took such care…"

"Have a griddle-cake," said Dorinda cosily. "My own recipe. I baked them just for you."

"So kind of you, my dear. *She* never so much as invites me to her home these days. She's never cooked me a proper meal, even. She brings round some prosciutto, olives, a pasta salad, maybe, but only bought, never *made*…these are delicious, my dear!" She watched him chew greedily. "So clever!" he said through a mouthful of crumbs, and she urged a napkin on him. Dorinda was inclined to be house-proud. "Oh dear. I do feel really very *upset*. And do you think it's *true*?"

"Is what true, sweetie? I must listen out for the timer on the oven."

"Do you – do you think…" It wasn't just his mouthful that caused him to stammer. He swallowed hard. "Is she just making a fool of me, Dorinda? I get the impression everybody is laughing at me. They all seem to know more than I do…This Brunero, now…the estate agent man!"

"Oh, come now, Cad. That was nothing. A mild flirtation, maybe. She was never *seeing* him. It was all professional, surely?

"I'm not so sure. We met him by chance at 'La Terrazzina' a couple of weeks or so ago. He came over to our table – so rude, just marched up and ignored me – and she was all over the man! Can you believe it? Hee! She kissed him, called him '*tesoro*'. It was as if I wasn't there. Completely *de trop*! I was – well, I was offended. Offended! Angry, even."

"It's very naughty of her, but I'm not *surprised*…Corinna is a bit of a compulsive flirt. And she's very Italian in her ways. You know what she's *like*…"

"The point is I'm not at all sure I do…I thought I did…This new one, Eduardo, the new colleague, you know, now he's a youngish family man, by all accounts… But now there's this doctor chap in Rome…I helped her with that. I shouldn't be telling you, but I did. And now she vanishes for whole weekends at a time, wearing her best clothes and sort of fired up, excited. Now they're all hinting things about this Lord Whatsisname. Notorious womaniser! Milly met him once, you know! Mixed in some serious *circles,* did Milly…" He finished his glass. "*She* must think I'm a bloody fool…and I'm *not* a fool, Dorinda!"

"Of *course* not, sweetie. Have a spot more?"

"Thank you, my dear. Very soothing. I think there's something she's not telling me. She wears my ring, you know that?"

"And it's a *beautiful* ring. Have another griddle-cake. There! Shall we finish the jug?"

"So kind, my dear," murmured Cadwallader. "She wears my ring, you see, but – may I be frank? – she's never – I mean, we've never... When we met, she made it perfectly plain she wanted to go back to her husband, you see, and I respected that..."

"*Really*? She told you *that*?"

"Oh yes. They're only separated, and they have daughters, you know. It's only fair and right. But then – I gather the husband has found someone else – and we became – well..."

"Closer, so to speak?"

"Exactly! But not – um – to the point of *complete intimacy*, if I may put it that way. She's always said she wants to wait for the *right moment*. I'm not sure the right moment will happen now..." He blew his nose. "But sometimes, she seems very *keen indeed*..."

Dorinda bit her lip and stared out at the Bay where it was beginning to cloud over ominously.

"You see...it's been really quite *serious*. I am *fidanzato a casa*...that is, I've been invited to Sunday lunch with them all, Valeria and Salvatore, and Salvatore's father, Mario, on several occasions. The Italians are very *formal* about this sort of thing.

235

Her daughters seem to have accepted me! It's *not* a matter for all that very unfunny teasing last night. I don't feel like going to Daphne's ever again! Oh dear..." He drained the last of the bloody mary and wiped a tomato moustache on his napkin. "I feel so – so thoroughly humiliated..."

"You don't *know*, Cad. And you know what the others are like. They will gossip and make trouble. Silvana. Even Daphne. She doesn't mean to, but..."

"I've had such plans! As a measure of my good faith, I've even been thinking of giving her my house!"

"Giving her your *house?"*

"Yes, my dear. Next door. Number Ten. A gift. To avoid inheritance taxes and so forth. I've thought it all out. I am planning to leave it to her in any case, but I thought this made more sense. Then she can live next door, and we can be nicely companionable, without being on top of each other, so to speak..."

"Goodness! Have you told her?"

"Not yet, no...I've been waiting for the right moment..."
Dorinda bit her lip again.

"I haven't really anything much to leave," pursued Cadwallader. "When I go, Millicent's literary estate belongs to Freddy and his sister Jane – did you meet Jane? Nice woman. Doctor's wife. I think of her as a niece. As Milly's closest surviving blood relations, that's their due, and it's entailed for them after I go. She had the money, you see...but the houses are

236

mine outright to do as I please with. Freddy and Jane don't need two! It – it pleased me to think of poor Corinna a little bit set up after I'm gone. Secure. She's very hard *up*, you know! Her ex-husband – I call him 'ex', hee! – has provided for her very *badly*. Some days she hardly gets enough to eat, can you believe that?"

"Are you *sure*?" Dorinda's mouth hardened.

"Oh yes, my dear. She lives in *very* straitened circumstances."

"Well! I call that very, very generous, Cadwallader. But are you *sure* she's as broke as you think? I mean, she has that lovely apartment in Via Tibaldi…and her little letting and selling business. I would have thought…"

"Oh, no, my dear! The apartment actually belongs to her daughter Valeria, didn't you know? When Valeria moved in with the boyfriend, Corinna moved in as Valeria's tenant. They make her pay her way…Corinna pays quite a large rent to Valeria, apparently, which has always struck me as a bit mean…and as for the letting and selling, that's only on a commission, my dear. It's this Eduardo's business, not Corinna's. She's hand to mouth, truly! It's always been my pleasure to help where I can. Hee! She saved my life, you know, last year. For that alone…" Cadwallader's eyes became misty.

"She's a very lucky woman, I'll say that…"

"I feel that I am the lucky one! Or I did… I think on the whole, I should prefer to give her the benefit of the doubt… I say, I am so grateful for being able to tell someone these things.

You're a very sympathetic, wise friend, Dorinda. Hee! But what shall I do? What do you advise?"

"I don't know, Cadwallader, I don't truly. It's a very big step. I think in your shoes, I'd stop at a Will. That way, you could still change your mind. Especially now…"

"If only I could be certain," Cadwallader said wistfully.

"You could try asking her."

"Challenge her, you mean. D'you think she'll tell me?"

"I would, if it was me. I'd rather be honest, because lying is so difficult, isn't that true? You'll be able to tell in an instant from her eyes, from her whole manner. It'll be obvious. It almost always is." Dorinda Daly's own eyes, large and light blue, were full of sympathetic Irish charm.

"Oh dear…I do wonder if there are some things I should rather not know! I'd better go and use the facilities, my dear."

"You know where it is. Oops! That was the pinger! Come through, m'dear, when you're ready."

Dorinda went to attend to the kitchen while Cadwallader used the bathroom, where he whistled under his breath as he tried to pee, and mused unhappily, a thoroughly unpleasant scenario playing itself over in his imagination…

"Ah, but you're a *tesoro*, my dear," murmured Cadwallader, seeing the table, the starched cloth, the steaming stewpot, the fresh napkins, the heavy silver, the twinkling crystal glasses, the open bottle of a local red wine. Over a plateful of mildly curried chicken and steamed rice slathered in butter,

Cadwallader said messily: "I'm almost beginning to think I chose the wrong woman. Hee!"

Freddy had a passenger's annoying habit of taking the driver for granted, and despite the sudden downpour insisted on needling Veronica with questions.

"Freddy, for God's sakes! I simply don't know why you're so agitated. This is incredibly silly! Now please, just let me concentrate, will you? This road's becoming a sodding nightmare. Stop being so neurotic before we drive into a ravine." Freddy was so seldom serious that it had taken her a while to realise that he was genuinely put out. Now she had, she was annoyed. "I was only sounding out an idea, for Christ's sakes."

"You practically accused Aunt Milly of living a double life!"

"But I didn't, Freddy! I said I thought she might have used a pseudonym. There's nothing morally reprehensible about that. It's like 'Epicure'. Now, shut up, do!" The windscreen wipers were at their most powerful setting but Veronica slowed to a crawl. "I can't see a bloody thing..."

"Used a pen-name to write about going on the game, you said!"

"I said nothing of the kind. I said she'd probably had a bit of a past. A venal interest in a rich boyfriend or two. And since when did you become so suburban all of a sudden?"

They did not speak for the rest of the journey.

He had cheered up by the time they reached Monte Farfalla. They parked the car and dashed into the Albergo out of the pelting rain. "I need a drink!" Freddy declared.

"So do I!" The hotel appeared deserted, but the 'Gazza Ladra' off the Piazza gave them coffee and large grappas.

"I'm sorry! I was being absurd. *Cin-cin...*"

"*Cin-cin...* Yes. You were." She realised she was quite relieved he was going away.

"I know, I know. I've said I'm sorry. You *will* be here when I get back, won't you? You won't just leave in a huff..."

"Yes, of course. I've arranged to see Cadwallader again. And unlike some people, I don't really do huffs."

"Sorry, sorry, sorry! It's just that when you start digging into things, you never quite know what's going to crawl out...this could be a can of worms."

"Do you always think in clichés, Freddy?"

"Phnar, phnar! Look, Vee...if something *did* turn up...I mean, if you found something out, you would tell me, wouldn't you?"

"You're actually bothered, aren't you? There's something you're not telling *me*. Stop being so mysterious."

"Cadwallader isn't always reliable...Look, I know! Come with me to Venice! I'm sure we can get you onto the plane on standby. Do! It would be fun!"

"Oh, balls, Freddy! You don't want me to come. You're only suggesting it because you don't want me to get into a merry huddle with Cadwallader anymore. Yet it was all your idea in the first place."

"That was before…"

"What *is* it, Freddy? For heaven's sake!"

"You'd better talk to Jane. She knew. I mean, talk to Jane after you talk to Cad. I mean, don't publish anything unless you talk to Jane…"

"Freddy, dear, you're blathering. What is all this?"

"It was just a funny old family story. Probably nothing. Now, my dear, as the rain seems to be stopping, I'd better get off if I'm to get to the airport by the crack of dawn tomorrow. Sure you don't want to accompany me?"

"Certainly not. I'd cramp your style. Isn't that so?" Veronica was amused. "Mudlarks from the Lagoon? *Nostalgie de la boue?*"

"Something like that…"

"Don't pretend to blush. Sweet how the French style ' a bit of rough stuff' as 'nostalgia'…"

"It is a spot of work *as well*…"

"Of course, darling. And you might even win your return flight back at the Casino…"

PART THREE: CAN OF WORMS

xvi: Encounters

After her lover had left early to open his Monday morning clinic, Corinna was alone in the apartment, having enjoyed a long warm shower. Now wrapped in a fluffy towel, she gazed about the bathroom with sublime satisfaction. It boasted a quiet luxury that was deeply pleasing: dark blue and grey tiles, angular, functional appointments in heavy chrome: masculine, refined, expensive…like its owner. She uncapped a bottle of Penhaligon's 'Endymion' aftershave and sniffed deeply, and then, feeling deliciously wicked, splashed a little on her collarbones and a little more behind her knees… There was a small radio-cum-CD player plugged into the wall beside the basin, and she pressed the play button out of curiosity, and recognized Sarah Vaughan's sexy contralto: 'Sweet Embracable You'. Did he shower, soap his brown hairy body, listening to this? As she hummed rather tunelessly along, she did not hear the near-silent swish of the elevator to the upper floor from Pietro's surgery, and did not hear the sound of the key turning the complicated latch as she peered critically at her face in the glass, plucked a stray hair from her neat left eyebrow…

She wandered, still humming softly, through to the bedroom, where the bed was still disordered, and sat on the edge

242

of it, examining her toes, planning a pedicure and imagining a future. 'You Go To My Head' snaked through the open door of the bathroom. *Hasn't the ghost of a chance...* She smoothed a rich lemon-scented unguent into her long, strong calves.

"Good morning!"

Corinna's towel dropped to her waist as she turned. She heard herself cry out.

"Who – ?"

"No. I ask who. Who are you in my house?" The voice was not English, but it was not Italian either.

Corinna grabbed at her towel, speechless.

"Well?" The woman, not very tall, very slim, and brisk-looking in a white medical coat with a pen and reading specs in the pocket, was about Corinna's own age. She wore her short blonde hair in a style that suited her small elfin face. She stared at Corinna without blinking.

"I might ask the same," said Corinna, recovering her composure and tucking the towel tightly under her arms. "I'm a – a friend of Doctor Borella's. I thought this was Pietro's house."

"Did you? In fact the whole premises belongs to both of us. I daresay not for much longer. The Italian *beni in comune* only holds good until there is a divorce settlement. In our case, there's a business to consider. I suppose you're the famous Susanna."

"I'm Corinna. Look this is awfully awkward, I know. You must be Signora Borella...I had no idea that..."

243

"That Pietro was still on 'key of the door' terms with me? Ach! I'm afraid he must have got careless and forgotten to tell you I have access to this apartment and to the medical records he keeps here. We still run a physical therapy business together in the clinic downstairs. I am Doctor Johannsen. Gisela. I am afraid I am always surprising Pietro's little friends. Most embarrassing. He will be absent-minded and entertain without telling me...I am sorry you have been disturbed. I heard sounds, and naturally..."

"Naturally..." Corinna had had a shock.

"You are older than most of them, I have to say. He normally goes for the distinctly pre-menopausal ones. Well, I have a patient waiting downstairs. I must check in the files and then I shall leave you to get dressed in peace. I am so sorry to have disturbed you. Good morning."

"Good morning," Corinna responded automatically, and then, realising that Sarah Vaughan was still warbling from the en-suite bathroom, she went and punched the 'stop' button on 'What A Difference A Day Makes' with more force than was strictly necessary.

Julian Blyth, balancing a brimming cup of cappuccino and *The Times* in his usable hand, escaped the scrum of the Australian students round the breakfast buffet and wandered outside to one of the little tables under the awning in the hotel garden. He saw he was not alone: a woman he thought he vaguely recognized had beaten him to it. She did not look up, being absorbed in writing in a notebook and staring at a laptop. He went to sit at the furthest table, and discovered the bench was still wet from the rain. He cursed.

Veronica looked up, and recognised him instantly. The rather rude stranger from the baggage carousel at the airport. Small world! She looked back at her notes hurriedly, and hoped he would ignore her. Miranda Hooper had written an email: 'Bingo!! Am looking up V. Gollancz's registration and copyright archives. Hope the sun's shining – foul here! Bestest, MH.'

"I'm sorry," Julian said. "I can see you're very busy. Yours appears to be the only dry spot. Do you mind if I join you? It's a bit of a zoo inside."

"Isn't it! Go ahead," she said. "Please." She smiled briefly, and firmly went back to her work. The man opened his newspaper. At least he didn't seem to want to *talk*.

Silvana Barker, however, did want to talk, volubly. She bustled out bearing a tray of croissants and jam, followed by Gianni, instructing him to wipe the tables and chairs. "Sorry we're a bit crowded this morning, dear," she said to Veronica. "Oh, Mr Blyth! So you've met! Sorry our garden's a bit soggy after all that rain! But it's a lovely morning for us now, isn't it? Would you like a croissant, Mr Blyth?"

"You could share these," said Veronica. "There are far too many for me. Thank you, Mrs Barker. Silvana…"

"Not at all! Now then, Mr Blyth – Julian! I can't really call you anything else, can I? I do hope you were comfortable.

245

And I hope you find Daphne. I did try to ring to tell her you were here, but she's always up and out very early on a Monday…"

"Thank you. Actually, I'm meeting her later this morning."

"*Oh*! So you've spoken to her!"

"Yes. Last evening. Do you think I could have some sugar?"

"Oh! Of course, yes! Would *you* like anything else, Veronica dear?"

"Just another cup of coffee, thanks." Silvana bustled back inside, and the morose Gianni continued to wipe.

"I'm sorry," said the man with the bandaged hand. "I'd better introduce myself."

"Perhaps you better had, if we're going to share breakfast. I'm Veronica Dearborn." She had rather wild sandy grey hair which was escaping from an Alice-band and her unmade-up face was freckled.

"Julian Blyth." He shook her hand, and then appeared not to know what to say next, and coughed. "I – um – think we've already met. At the airport last week. You rescued my bag. I fear I was – um – a bit surly."

"Don't worry! I hate them…doesn't everybody?" Her eyes were straying back to her work.

"You're not on holiday."

"No…not exactly."

"Neither am I…"

"Here we are! I've brought you a big pot you can share, and here's some hot milk and your sugar, Julian dear, and this fig jam is my mother's own. Freddy not calling for you this morning, dear? Oh, Venice! All right for some, isn't it! Well, now, I hope you have a nice time with Daphne, Julian. She was a great fan of Hilary's, loved him to bits! She'll enjoy the chance to talk about him...and Faye, of course...Now, *Veronica* has met Daphne...such a thrill for us, but I expect you found us all a bit full-on! How are you getting on with poor old Cadwallader, dear? Being helpful, is he?"

"He's being marvellous, thank you, Silvana. Very helpful."

"Deaf as a post sometimes. He refuses to have a hearing aid, the vain old poppet! We've all *told* him the better ones are practically invisible, but he won't have it!" Someone shouted from inside. "That's my wake-up call! I'd better run. Have a nice day, both of you!"

Julian Blyth and Veronica exchanged glances, and Veronica half smiled. "I say," Julian hesitated. "I'm sorry, but are you a writer?"

"Ye –es... Why?"

"I thought I recognized your name. I read your book about Henry Cuffe on my last tour. I gave it to my sister-in-law before I came out here. She's – um – been unwell, and I thought it might cheer her up. I enjoyed it."

"Oh! Thank you. Thank you very much. Um...on tour?"

247

"Musician. Orchestra. Fiddler....or I was. If this thing ever heals…"

"I'm sorry…what...?"

"Repetitive strain injury…I shan't know if going back to work is an option unless I try…All a bit up in the air at the moment. I'm here to give the wrist a rest and settle my brother's affairs. He – um – died, last year. Speaking of which, I'd better go and prepare for elevenses with one Mrs Daphne Allerton. Do I gather you know her?"

Veronica's face was a studied blank. "We met on Saturday evening. For the first and only time."

"Ah…and?"

"I think you'd better make up your own mind, Mr Blyth." Veronica smiled solemnly.

Unusually for a Monday, Daphne Allerton was expecting a guest. She therefore made a detour on her way back from the market and bought some crisps of a superior kind and a bottle of tonic from the little grocery in the Via degli Angeli. This brought her virtually next door to Sebastiano the jeweller's. The little novelty wristwatch she had seen in the window was still there, and on an impulse, she went in to buy it. Daphne, to her regret, as yet had no grandchildren and, in view of her only son Jonjo's domestic situation, none in the offing. Her numerous small great-nephews and nieces in England were therefore the recipients of many a small gift of this kind. It was little Amelia's birthday.

Daphne's Italian was atrociously bad by her own admission. Over twenty-five years and more, mistakes of grammar, pronunciation and vocabulary had worn themselves into grooves in her brain, quite beyond correction. Her Italian-speaking friends had given up correcting her – indeed, it had only been poor Hilary Blyth who had still teased her – and the locals merely indulged her politely, spoke slowly, listened attentively, and mostly understood her. Her conversation with Sebastiano Minitti (who in any event had enough English to get by in a crisis) as he wrapped the little watch was therefore very clear and comprehensible. La Signora Corinna had collected La Signora Daphne's lovely corals, and Sebastiano had fitted a nice new gold clasp. La Signora could wear them with confidence! No, *magari!* The work ordered on la Signora's beautiful ring had not yet commenced. Sebastiano was profoundly sorry for the delay. He would be taking it to his brother in Napoli this very week. The Signora would like to change her mind? But of course! The beautiful ring is here, as yet untouched. Work of this kind must be sent to an expert, the very best! The re-setting needs very careful workmanship, and of course the new stone must be chosen with great care... Sebastiano unlocked the safe.

"*La pietra nuova? Che cosa?*"

Sebastiano explained as best he could. A great many ladies, concerned about security, exchanged a valuable stone in a pretty ring for one less valuable. The ring was virtually the same, and the real stone could be stored safely in the bank. Ah! There had been a mistake? Only an adjustment in size! Perhaps Sebastiano had misunderstood la Signora Corinna. Ah! It was insecure simply because it did not fit la Signora Daphne's tiny hand. Now Sebastiano understood! This was simply a matter of melting the gold to a sufficient softness, and remoulding it to fit. If Signora Daphne would like to try these measures for size…

"I was very fond of poor Hilary, dear. I hope you can drink vodka and tonic water. I always buy Schweppes. These crisp things should be edible. Sit there, dear. I want to look at you. Yes, you're very like him to look at. Thinner. Very different body-language."

"Er…"

"And that injury will have been caused by overwork, not carelessness…"

"Good grief! I mean, you're quite right, but how…?"

"I'm observant, dear. You would always be careful of your skin."

"Er…oh." Julian and the curly-haired elderly woman, who wore elegant white slacks, a Breton jersey and bright lipstick on an otherwise unmade-up, weather-beaten face, sat in deckchairs facing the sea. The breeze was cool, but not uncomfortable, and the sky was very blue after the recent storms.

"Life is too short – far too short at my age – to entertain illusions. That was where poor Hilary died…" She indicated the distant jagged rocks. She spoke in carefully enunciated tones, old-fashioned English patrician, and had a very disconcerting stare, as if constantly seeking an horizon.

"Yes... It – um – it's hard to believe even now. It was a shock."

"A shock, of course. These things always are. But, I imagine, not a *surprise...*"

"I'm sorry?"

"Oh yes, dear! I know it isn't a nice thought, but as one gets older, one has so few nice thoughts, don't you find? Probably not yet. You're still young. But you look very intelligent. I'm sure you *know*. How's your glass? I can put some more tonic water in it, if you would like."

"A bit strong, perhaps. Please don't get up. I'll sip slowly. Know what, exactly, Mrs Allerton?"

"That this very sad fatality was almost certain to happen. It was in your poor brother's nature, dear. Recklessness. A disregard of risk. Some people are just made that way, bound to die young. Very sad waste, dear." She shook her head and drank. "It's as if part of them *courts* death...I believe it is known as hubris. Do have some crisps."

"Hil? But Hilary was full of life. He was happy, busy, full of plans..."

"Yes, dear. The life and soul of the party. I personally miss him greatly. But in part of himself he held life in contempt, and that is dangerous."

251

"Forgive me, Mrs Allerton. I honestly think that's absurd."

"As you wish, dear." She stared gnomically out to sea, reminding Julian of a tiny witch.

"You – you're not surely suggesting that my brother – that Hilary – killed himself deliberately?"

"Ah, that, no, dear. Not *exactly.* And of course there has been an inquest, hasn't there, and it was put down to a most unfortunate accident, wasn't it? That's official. But I think we can construe something rather more *telling*, can't we?"

"But why? Recklessness is one thing, I'll grant. But Hil was an excellent swimmer. Even experts can misjudge. There was nothing to indicate that he had the slightest reason to – um – court death, as you put it. And Faye would have known if he was unhappy. They were very close." Julian Blyth suddenly felt he was talking too much and put his glass down.

"Ah, Faye! Moh! That's as maybe, dear. Wives are not always the most reliable witnesses to husbands' thoughts and feelings, are they? Or their professional interests. And Faye, poor girl, did become *very* unreliable, almost preposterously so. I'm sure you realise that too. Grief and shock make the most reasonable of people say the most unreasonable things, including making completely unfounded accusations…and Faye…well, she can be fanciful, can she not? I expect there were things he was not telling her."

252

"Mrs Allerton – forgive me. I don't relish the turn this conversation is taking. Do you actually know something about Hilary's death?"

"In the sense of knowing something concrete, then the answer is no, or I should have spoken up at the time. However, Hilary was not careful of his skin, dear. Some risks are suicidal in themselves. He must have known about the potential *danger*... Will you join me in another drink?" She had risen and held her hand out for his glass.

"Just a very weak one, if I may," said Julian, a trifle weak himself, trying to collect his thoughts, gazing at the picturesque, treacherous rocks where Hilary must have gasped, gone under, struggled, fought against an invincible, pounding current, lost consciousness and been battered again and again...

His fresh drink was if anything stronger than the first, and he tried not to blench. "Mrs Allerton ..."

"You may call me Daphne if you wish, my dear. Such a pity our formalities are so much more *woolly* than those of the Italians. Your health, Julian! And so you have the unhappy task of settling poor Hilary's affairs, is that not so?"

"Yes. Look – um – Daphne. I'm sorry. You spoke of danger..."

"Hilary was blind to danger, dear! And he could get alarmingly drunk!"

"So people tell me..."

"He really was in quite a state on the night he drowned."

253

"So I gather. That was here, wasn't it? At your party…"

"Hardly a party, dear. Just a few of my friends. Hilary was normally very welcome, but I'm afraid on that occasion…well, he alienated a great many people, dear. People he shouldn't have upset. He got very aggressive, when really it was poor Dennis who should have been upset after that very unfortunate article."

"I'm sorry – I don't quite…"

"*The Bystander*, dear! So unpleasant and unnecessary, we all thought. He also owed a great deal of money, dear, one way and another, morally if not actually."

Julian frowned. "Did he owe you money, Mrs Allerton?"

"Daphne, dear. No, not to me. But I think you'll find that the Barkers are out of pocket. Cancellations at the hotel. And poor Corinna, of course…she did everything in her power to help Faye to sell that terrible house. It's none of my business, dear, and you must do as you feel fit, but I imagine that now the house is sold, you will be making it your concern to settle some of poor Hilary's debts…"

Julian's frown deepened. "Well, of course. I have a list of people to see. I'm seeing to the actual bills first, obviously. Builders and so forth. That's only fair."

"There's fair and fair, dear. I suppose Lorenzo Lucifora is on your list…"

Highly irritated, Julian said, "Well, yes he is, as a matter of fact, if that's how you pronounce him. He found the buyer. I want to thank him."

"You'll find him very plausible, dear. A very pleasant young man in many ways. But he is a thief."

"A thief?"

"He steals business, dear. Our little backwater has not been the same since they arrived. Poor Corinna has struggled and struggled to build up a little business for herself, and then these smart Americans wade in and of course they have the contacts and so forth. *Highly* fortunate for Faye…"

Julian was keeping his temper with difficulty. "I'm based at the hotel if anyone needs to see me. I've got a busy couple of days ahead…and I'm still trying to find a man called Innocenti…he's an architect."

"Innocenti? Why?"

"Because Hilary owed him money for work he did. I have a cheque for him. A bankers' draft."

"I see. Well, that's very nice for Mr Innocenti. He is a nice man, but in some ways he is as naïve as his name…"

"I gather he was a good friend of my brother's."

"I shouldn't listen to him, if I were you. He has some very silly ideas…he's a philanthropist. Now, dear Julian! Let's change the subject to *music*! I want to know what it was like to work under Sir John Barbirolli!" She bounced in her chair.

"My daughter is vegetarian, too," said Julian to the smiling American over a frugal pasta lunch at Trattoria Luigi. No meat, no fish. Excellent bruschetti topped with very fresh tomatoes and the local oil, and spinach and ricotta tortellini.

"Good for her! Nothing that once possessed a face, you know? It's not a crusade, just the way I happen to be." Having had a very strong liquid elevenses, Julian was rather pleased that the American did not appear to want wine either, although in the circumstances this constituted an embarrassment.

"Look, are you sure we don't owe you anything, Lorenzo?"

"Lorrie, please, Julian. Everyone calls me Lorrie. I was born in New York. Mom and Pop were from Naples, so I'm first generation, but I'm really American through and through." The man was probably older than he looked, and he chiefly looked extraordinarily well-kept, healthy, and possessed of a magnificent set of very even white teeth. His large spectacles suggested frivolity, but his eyes were serious. "I have to be honest with you here, Julian. I found your brother a tad on the difficult side. Don't get me wrong, now. A great guy! Liked him loads. But he was – oh, how shall I put this? Like he was an ironist. I think we Americans have a difficulty with irony. I kept thinking he must be laughing at us…"

"That was just Hilary's way. He – he could sound very world-weary, but it was just his way of joking. There was no harm in Hil."

"No, I guess there wasn't. I always found him straight. Which I guess is more than you can say of some…"

Julian wondered which 'some' and tentatively phrased a delicate question. "It's very generous of you to waive your finding fee, Lorrie…"

"No problem. A pleasure. I was just concerned for Faye not to get, you know, ripped and burned. I was only too happy to help a friend in a crisis."

"Well, help you certainly did. I – we – are very grateful to you. I was wondering – normally, would one owe a fee to someone who had looked but – um – hadn't found, so to speak? I'm not altogether sure of the protocols here."

"Ah…" The American's eyes glinted behind the Buddy Holly specs. "Normally, no. No find, no fee. That's how it goes in the States. I don't see any call to operate differently here. Not unless you're feeling especially generous, that is. I don't like to name names or be unduly unkind, but some of these *Inglesi* are operators. If you see what I mean."

"I see," said Julian, beginning to. "Well, God knows how long it would have gone on if you hadn't stepped in."

"Oh, that was just a question of being broad enough. The locals here, you know, they just sell houses. Real estate as dwellings. Faye could have waited forever with a property half restored like that. People tried to help, but they didn't necessarily know how. It just needed a bit of vision. That place is perfect for the Foundation. The HSFF. The Health and Spiritual Fitness Foundation. They needed a place, a base in Europe. I found them somewhere. I'm just so pleased we could be of use, you know? Happy ending…The Universe looks after its own…"

"Yes. Er – I suppose so…" Julian imagined that Lorrie's trouble had been amply compensated by this 'Foundation' and felt less ill at ease.

He paid the tiny bill, and Lorrie shook hands with a wince-making grip. "Give Faye great big hugs. We're here if she ever needs us, you tell her now! This was *good.*"

Wandering back to the Piazza in the sunny afternoon, Julian was assailed by the inescapable thought that his brother might have been horrified. Or perhaps, knowing Hilary, he might just have laughed. On an impulse, Julian decided to risk the dodgy sat-nav and drive to the cemetery in San Gregorio.

xvii: A Bit of Outdoor Theatre

"What?" Corinna de Benedetto, after a morning at the Agency chasing leads for the Castelambra property, was stretched out on her bed in her dressing-gown, holding the telephone a good two inches from her ear and trying to untangle Silvana's pronouns.

"I'm telling you!" screeched Silvana, excitedly. "Since Sunday. He saw Daphne yesterday. Why? *I* don't know! You'd better ask her. He's here settling Hilary's affairs. The house? Yes! He says he's sold it....yes. I know. I *know*! Oh, I don't know *that*...Daphne might." Her voice dropped suddenly. "Wait a sec, Rinna! No, just the Aussies – they've been having a trip to the Tombs....Sorry, Rinna. Hang on...(there we are dear – here's your key...and yours, dear...) Are you still there, Rinna? Sorry about that! Yes, I know, dear...I know. Oh, I *know*! Look – why don't you come and talk to him? Find out from the horse's mouth. He's got his feet up now, but I expect he'll be up and about for a beer in a couple of hours or so... He's quite dishy, as a matter of fact..." But I bet he's no push over, Silvana thought as she put the phone down.

"Damn, damn and damn!" cursed Corinna out loud and rang Daphne's number, letting it ring and ring. When Daphne did not answer, she rang again.

"He didn't tell me and I didn't ask. Too rude."

"Oh, *Daphne*... Was it Cy and Lorrie?"

"I'm watching *The Forsyte Saga*, dear. Then I'm expecting Jonjo to call. He's getting divorced. I don't like divorce, dear...what was that? No, I don't know who bought it. Some developers in Rome, I think. Or perhaps it was Milan. I really don't *know*, dear! How many more times? I *like* Soames...so misunderstood, I always think...He's off to see Innocenti with a bankers' draft..."

"What?"

"*Innocenti!* What's that? Well, I don't know, dear. You'd better go and find out, hadn't you?"

"Oh, God...see you tomorrow, m'darling. I'll bring your corals."

Corinna cursed again and set her alarm-clock for five, tried to read her magazine and fell into an uneasy doze, from which she was immediately re-awakened.

"*Pronto*? Oh, Cadwallader, m'darling! No, back yesterday and work all this morning. Oh, darling, not tonight. Do you mind terribly? I'm absolutely tired to death, darling...Oh! Goodness! No, of *course* I haven't forgotten my *beautiful* picture, darling! I know, I left it behind...honestly, I'm getting scatter-witted, aren't I? I know, it must have been because you were kissing me! Yes, you keep it for me, darling, and we'll have dinner on Friday...Yes, a bit of pain, still. I'm taking a horse's dose of ibuprofen. Ibuprofen! Painkillers...Yes, m'darling!

Easier now after the treatment…a bit sleepy. Yes, *Tesoro*, it's a date…Yes, you too, m'darling…"

Corinna gave up her siesta and went to bathe and dress with some care.

"Dorinda!"

"Cadwallader! Helloo, sweetie!"

"Dorinda, my dear. I'm ringing on a sudden *impulse*! Will you do me the honour of joining me this evening? As my guest?"

"Ooh! How *lovely*! Where?"

"Well, I'd like to thank you for such a marvellous lunch! I thought 'La Terrazzina'. I think I need cheering up…"

"The 'Terrazzina'! Cadwallader, how nice! Is Freddy coming? Oh, in Venice! But what about her ladyship? Oh, she's going to a concert. So just us! Well, how very, very nice! I'd love to, sweetie. I'll put on some glad rags right now…"

Dorinda watched the last quarter of an hour of her recorded *Antiques Roadshow*, and wandered into the shower, putting on her best scent and her own construct on 'cheering up'…

Veronica had taken a stroll. A pleasant, warmly glowing evening, still fresh after the recent heavy rain, in a delightful little town built, as the travel writer had said, of sunny blond stone, encased in what remained of the older, darker walls and what still stood of the pre-earthquake architecture. Without Freddy, and without, therefore, the compulsion to eat, to have the

261

'restaurant experience', she wandered, gazed, became simply a tourist on holiday, and revelled, quietly, in a sense of freedom. Fomenting in her mind was a problem concerning a certain late novelist, and unpicking J.Cadwallader Jones' reminiscences had taken up most of her day. Now, she was enjoying the experience of not having to actually talk to anyone, let alone shout to make herself heard. She gazed into shop windows, bought some postcards, a little guidebook, and a pack of cigarettes. There was something almost delicious about simply pleasing herself, and for the first time in a great many weeks, she discovered she was as carefree as she was able in her nature to be. It was as if her grief for her lover and her vexation about the film had receded to an outer edge of her mind: there, as always, but for once somehow not acute, not insistent.

An extraordinary gargoyle set in the ancient stones of what a little plaque informed her had been the medieval Pretura made her stop and stare. It had a double face: one side was a sweet if grotesque smile of complicity; the other was a grimace of what could have been pain. Justice? Or perhaps just the tragicomedy of trade... On a noticeboard, a poster, like the one she had seen in the Albergo foyer, advertised the little concert in the gardens of the *Comune* building. A young Japanese harpist...she would have a drink, a light supper and she would go to hear it. Why not?

As staged entrances go, it was perfect. Silvana had paved the way by pouring Julian a glass of beer while he was using the office to check his email.

"Anytime, dear! We've got great broadband connections here." Manners forbade him to refuse the beer, and sheer internal delicacy prevented his drinking it too quickly. Now she spread a map on the counter top, and indicated local restaurants with a red manicured fingernail. "How's it going? Have you found Giacomo Innocenti yet?"

"No…The stupid thing is I can't find the email which had the date he was leaving. He's off to Africa."

"Well, I suppose he might have gone already, knowing him. Between you and me, he smokes so much of the wacky-baccy, he doesn't know if it's Tuesday or August, if you follow me… Now, I hope you're not going to leave without seeing some of our sights, Julian. We're very proud of the Signorelli Madonna in the Chiesa, and there's the Castello, of course – they've turned it into a conference centre since the Army left, but they're open for visitors in the mornings during the week…and of course, there's the catacombs. The entrance is on the marina. Monty's built on a sort of honeycomb full of dead monks, just fancy! They used it to hide bombs and stuff during the War…and smuggle spies. Dennis is the expert on that. Our own cellar used to lead down to the sea…Dennis takes parties down there by arrangement – I'm sure he'll be happy to show you…He'll be in soon…"

"I only want to eat somewhere, thanks," Julian mumbled. "I might do some sight-seeing tomorrow."

"Well, okay…Let's see…I know! Yes, here we are! There's a little concert this evening in the *Palazzo del Comune* – a harpist. A Japanese. That might be up your street, as you're a musician…and you don't need to book or anything." She gave him a leaflet. "Then you could have your supper at Luigi's overlooking the Bay. Oh! Sorry. I don't suppose you want to look at the Bay, considering…"

"Not really, no. But thanks. In fact – if you'll excuse me, I think I'll just take a stroll round town…see what I can see." He picked up some more leaflets from a small table.

"Of course, dear, whatever you like. It's a lovely evening again. Why, hello! Here's Corinna! Hiya! What a lovely surprise!"

Julian turned and saw a tall, trim, good-looking woman with bright blonde bouffant hair, dressed in mustard-coloured trousers, a floral jacket that matched, delicate high-heeled shoes which exaggerated her height…she removed her sunglasses, glanced at him briefly, and went over and kissed Silvana extravagantly on both cheeks. "Hi Silvy, m'darling!"

"Rinna, dear – how nice! Welcome back! You must meet our new guest. This is Julian Blyth, Hilary's brother. This is Corinna de Benedetto, Julian. She knew Hilary and Faye *very* well, didn't you, Rinna? Corinna was helping Faye to sell the house."

"Oh?" Julian tried not to look put out. "Well – er – I'm happy to say it's sold. I'm just finalising my brother's affairs…"

"Oh, you poor *man*! How very, very sad for you. I'm *so* sorry," said the woman called Corinna. She shook hands formally with a radiantly sympathetic smile. "Wasn't it just ghastly? I tried to do *anything* I could to help…I'm only sorry I couldn't do more. Your brother was a very dear friend…both of them were…he talked of you very often…and we used to get blow by blow accounts of all your tours, didn't we, Silvy?"

"We certainly did!"

"I'm not a horn player," said Julian drily, which sent both women into fits of giggles. Australian youth began to clatter down the marble stairs and Silvana became occupied at the desk.

Corinna patted his arm. "How marvy to bump into you! May I call you Julian? I've just got back from Rome. Oh! You've been in Rome too! What a coincidence! I just wandered in off the street to say hello to Silvana and I meet you! It would be so nice to have a little chat… Look, I hope this doesn't sound too bold, but would you like to go and have a drink? No offence to Silvana, but perhaps we'd be a bit quieter at Mauro's by the Chiesa…."

Julian allowed himself to be borne off into the evening, unaware of the complicit wink that passed between his new companion and Mrs Barker as they left the hotel.

Veronica emerged from a small, attractively plain *chiesa* where the minor Signorelli Madonna was displayed behind glass in its white and gilded Lady Chapel, and where she had given into superstition, paid a euro and lit a candle. There was always that certain tug, almost an undertow, of old Catholic Italy that got to her in this way: in London, she would never have dreamed of lighting candles in a church…and she had found herself, if not praying, exactly, at least wondering about the soul of Andrew Todd…if he *was* really dead… She shook herself. The café across the little street looked tempting, and she chose a quiet table under the awning and ordered campari, the holiday drink, which came served with tiny squares of pizza and toasted almonds. She concentrated on the guidebook, which was in Italian, and became engrossed, reading with care, only dimly aware of the street, the café, and the strolling, chattering people around her.

A party of youngsters sat down noisily at the table in front of Veronica's and ordered beers in English, and she looked up briefly. She thought they might be some of the young Australians from the hotel. She looked up again when they left, scraping metal chairs, laughing and joshing each other, and saw that at a further table sat Mr Julian Blyth with the tall blonde woman she had met the previous week: Cadwallader Jones's lady-friend. They had their half-backs towards her, and appeared to be in earnest conversation; or at least the woman seemed to be conversing in earnest, doing most of the talking with a great many hand gestures. Veronica went back to the section on the history of the Castle, and determined to look round it before she left...

"*Poor* Faye! It was so ghastly! But I should think it's so much better for her to be back in England – even if she did leave quite a lot of loose ends..." Julian Blyth's companion shook her gilded head with an eloquent frown. They had both ordered beers, and she held her glass in a strong-looking, well-manicured hand that wore several rings. "It can't be easy for you, shouldering her burdens like this." She smiled into his eyes with an intimacy he found disconcerting.

.   "But I've not done anything, really," he said diffidently. "Just seen some lawyers and signed things and so on. Everyone has been very – um, helpful. I – er – understand you were a good friend. To Faye. It was very kind of you." He saw Corinna's light green eyes narrow and widen.

"Well, of *course*! Anyone would have done what they could, but trying to sell her house was a bit of a nightmare, I can tell you! A lovely property in itself, of course, but moh! *So* many problems and only half built! Well, of course, in the end I simply failed. Anybody would have. The price might have made sense a couple of years ago, but not now. Faye just insisted on sticking out for it. Completely unrealistic in the circumstances. I did try to warn her. Everyone's been hit by the recession. It's very, very fortunate for her to have sold it at all...and to have you to help

267

her, lucky woman…" She gazed at him with unalloyed and – Julian thought – very practiced admiration. He found it distinctly off-putting.

Rather stiffly, he replied, "I don't think anyone could call Faye lucky, I'm afraid, in the circumstances…"

"Well, no – *obviously*! Heavens! I just meant to have people to help, and *you* to drop everything and come out on her behalf…"

"But of course. She's family. It was the very least I could do for her, and for my late brother."

"Family duty! It takes precedence over everything, doesn't it? I *completely* understand. But darling Hilary was another matter altogether! Anyone would have gone out of their way for Hilary! He was such *fun*, wasn't he? Nothing's the same without him!" She sighed. "We all miss him *so* much!"

"All? My brother could be frightfully tactless. I gather he was unkind about the Barkers' hotel in print." Julian watched her face.

"Oh, I suppose you mean Dennis! He can be a bit cranky. Take no notice! I expect he's been complaining about that *Bystander* article. We've all told him to forget it. Water under the bridge. It was Hilary's job, for heaven's sakes. He was a *journalist*. International! Dennis doesn't really understand these things. If you see what I mean…" Another intimate smile.

"I gather they almost came to blows on the night Hilary drowned…"

"Oh, that's been blown up out of all proportion, believe me! I was there! Hilary was just a bit drunk and – well, you know what he was like! He could get carried away, argumentative – nobody took him seriously normally. Dennis over-reacted, and Hilary stormed out. It was probably just as well. Everybody was getting a bit hysterical. But even Dennis tried to help *her*, we all did! For Hilary's sake. I can't tell you how much! The funeral, all the papers, lawyers, everything. In spite of the terrible things she was saying before she left, blaming us all – well, I suppose she must have said things…?"

Julian smiled and shook his head.

"You're loyal, naturally. The kindest thing to think is that she went – well, just a bit off the rails. I wonder…well, if perhaps there might – well, always have been a problem of this sort?" Corinna dropped her voice. "*Psychological*? Sorry! I used to be a nurse. Sister at the John Radcliff in Oxford, until my handsome Italian bore me away… One's professional antennae sort of wave sometimes. It's not always easy to talk about, I know – but it can't have been easy for poor Hilary always, can it?" Her eyes, slyly sympathetic, crinkled again.

Julian said evenly, "She had had a very bad shock. She said you'd all tried to help. I'm afraid I haven't seen much of Faye since she got back to England. I'm always away on tour, you see – or at least I was…" He indicated the bandage. "This is partly why I volunteered to take a furlough. Fiddler's wrist."

Corinna pressed her hand to her mouth like a schoolgirl. "Oh dear! Moh! That sounds far too funny to be taken seriously, doesn't it? But it's actually horrible. Tendonitis," said Corinna the nurse, rearranging her face. "So painful, you poor man! What a *bore* for you! You'll need to give it a good long rest and not try to go back to playing the violin too soon...If you're here for a little while, I can put you in touch with an excellent physiotherapist..."

"Kind of you, but – um – as soon as I've seen everyone I need to see, I'm going back to my specialist in London. Thanks all the same."

"Not at all." Corinna sipped her beer. "I quite understand." She was growing a little restive. Men, and Corinna had a great deal of experience of the male of the species, normally responded with more enthusiasm, and this man's palpable resistance had begun to grate on her. She decided he must be either humourless or *very* married. Possibly, of course, he was gay. Or in love with Faye himself. "So who's on the list?" she asked, businesslike, her smile fixed, professional.

"Sorry?"

"The list – of people to see? Sorry! I'm absolutely incorrigibly nosy! It's being a Sagittarian..."

"Ah. Well, I've actually seen almost everyone now. I just have to find an architect called Innocenti. Perhaps you know him. He was a friend of my brother's."

"Moh! *Everybody* knows Innocenti! He's another nutcase if you ask me! I hear he charges a fortune in spite of all that unworldly stuff. But as far as I know, he's gone away. To Africa, I think. Someone said he left last week."

"Are you sure?"

"Almost certain."

"That's a blow. I have something for him."

"Oh?"

"A cheque. For work he did."

"Oh. Well, lucky Innocenti. I hope he's got his accounts straight is all I can say. I'd go through them rather carefully, if I were you, before you sign anything. I shouldn't say this, I suppose, but I wouldn't trust him an inch, personally. Especially anything he says about Faye. Between you and me, I think he was half in love with her. And – well, I shouldn't be saying this, either, but I think he's involved with some rather *unsavoury* people..."

The café tables were beginning to fill up. When a family of holidaymakers sat down nearby, Corinna hailed the waitress and asked for some more snacks. "Sorry, do you mind? Beer always makes me peckish." He thought she was angling for an invitation to supper.

"Look, I don't suppose – " her hand briefly touched his sleeve – "that it would be too cheeky of me to ask how much the house actually went for? I mean, did poor Faye actually get her asking price? I'm just curious, being in the biz these days... I spent weeks and weeks trying to find someone for her. I really pushed the boat out. I'm just so sorry I didn't see results for so much *work*..."

"I'm sure you must be. It was very kind of you. These cheesy things look rather good, don't they?" He paused as he bit into one. He realised he was almost enjoying thwarting her. "No. She didn't get her price, I'm afraid. And there were a hell of a lot of overheads, apart from anything else...Hilary left rather a muddle to say the least. Didn't expect to die, you see..."

"No, of *course*," Corinna cooed. "Poor Hilary! But I understand that Lorrie – that is, Lorenzo Lucifora found the buyer in the end?"

"Yes. At least, he put Faye in touch with some people in Rome. It rather saved the day. Sorry – I know you must have been very keen to – um – secure the sale. I was just grateful that someone sorted it out in the end."

Corinna's face had hardened. "Well, of course, Lorrie's *American*...a great many more contacts than we poor struggling locals! I don't suppose that will come cheap either..."

"I'm sorry?"

"Well, Lorenzo's *fee*. He's a very nice man in some ways, but I think you might be in for a bit of a nasty surprise. He wouldn't get out of bed for less than five percent, I should think..."

"Actually," Julian said, "Mr Lucifora hasn't charged Faye a sou."

272

When Corinna's jaw dropped, she could look positively unpleasant.

Cadwallader Jones and Dorinda Daly, strolling slowly and companionably arm in arm from the direction of the seafront up the steps towards the Piazza, were also in earnest conversation. "I simply don't *understand* all this newfangled stuff, Dorinda," Cadwallader complained, puffing. "In the old days, one had an exhibition, and there were catalogues circulated in the appropriate quarters…"

"Cad, sweetie, it's just essential these days. Believe me! Catalogues don't reach nearly enough people in the ordinary way. Look, there's this lovely friend of my son Merrick's in London who'll make you a super website for a very small outlay, and then I'll help you run it. Easy-peasy! Then we can look up all the china and so forth, and get an idea of prices."

"Shall I – shall I actually have to buy a *computer*…?" Cadwallader paused and leaned on his cane.

"Well…" Dorinda sighed. Dragging Cadwallader into the twenty-first century was uphill work in more ways than one. "Shall we have a little sit down? Here's this nice bar."

"Whew! Why not, my dear...I do find that little climb quite a feat these days! My knees, you know…"

There was quite a bit of business with adjusting chairs and the table, and the waitress came hurrying out to assist. Neither Dorinda nor Cadwallader had noticed Veronica, who buried herself once more in her guidebook, hoping for invisibility, keeping an eye on the time.

"You'll have to help me if I do, my dear…I shall want something very easy to *operate*…" Cadwallader was saying. "They're all very user-friendly these days, Cadwallader. We'll find you a little lap-top. Nothing strange or startling or at all expensive. Don't *worry*!" "Well, that's a relief, my dear. I do have to be a bit *careful* of expenditure at the moment…I did tell you about Enzo, didn't I…"

It was Dorinda who noticed the couple at the further table, and being of a curious disposition, could not help staring. Corinna's hand was on the man's sleeve, apparently caressing it, and her eyes, only half-hidden from Dorinda's view, were gazing up at him in crinkle-cornered appeal which Dorinda recognized very well. The waitress came out with camparis and the accompaniments, Cadwallader engaged her in some banter in his tortured Italian, Dorinda lit a cigarette and continued to stare. "Well, *cin-cin*, my dear," said Cadwallader. "I can't tell you how much I appreciate all your help. My dear? *Cin-cin*! Cheers! What *has* caught your attention? I think you must be a compulsive people-watcher! Confess!" He looked up. "Oh! My God!" For now he had seen what Dorinda had seen. He stared too, fractionally mesmerised. Then, his face twisting in anguish, he grabbed his cane. "I – I – I can't stay here a moment longer! I'm sorry, my dear! I have to leave! Now!" In his agitation, he upset his chair and both of the drinks. Dorinda cried out and rose, her smart black trousers drenched in campari. The waitress came running out, followed by a young man in an apron with a cloth.

From her backseat vantage, Veronica saw Mr Blyth and his companion turn and briefly stare, the woman Corinna's strongly-boned face a remarkable study of embarrassment and something that could have been fury. Blyth's face was a well-bred blank. Neither of them, she was relieved to note, seemed to have noticed her.

Veronica smartly went inside the café to pay the elderly woman at the till and hovered, and thus did not see Julian Blyth make his courteous apologies to Corinna de Benedetto for being unable to do anything unless he had seen her accounting: the figure she had mentioned had astonished him out of any pretence of social niceties. "It's not really up to me, you see…I'm only here on Faye's behalf…I would need to talk to her. I'm sure you understand. There were several other agencies involved who also – um – didn't produce a sale…" She did not see Corinna's smile strained to the limit, nor hear Julian's apologetic impromptu invitation to supper being turned down, nor see his evident relief when it was. Nor did she see Cadwallader being coaxed back towards the Castle and the familiar territory of the Taverna by an attentive and sympathetic Dorinda Daly. "It's all right, Cad. They're black. It won't show, and they can go to the cleaners…It's only a bit sticky…You don't *know* it was her doctor-chappie, Cadwallader…you simply don't know…"

"But you don't understand, my dear," said Cadwallader sadly. "She'd refused to have dinner with *me* this evening, and there she was! Large as life with another man! It's – it's just *blatant*!" If Dorinda felt that being a *faute de mieux* date was also a little 'blatant', she kept her thoughts to herself over a perfectly acceptable supper and a lot of wine.

When Veronica emerged, none of the protagonists was any longer in view. She went to her harp concerto in the scented gardens of the *Palazzo di Comune*, listened with rapt attention to the baroque renderings, got a little lost in the Japanese compositions, and watched with increasing delight and fascination the shadow-play of the harpist's nimble, slender hands reflected and hugely magnified by floodlight on the ancient wisteria-clad walls in the deepening twilight, wondering if it was accidental or deliberate, and wishing suddenly that she could write poetry…

xviii: Confidences

Making her way throught the courtyard to the street, she was startled from a reverie. "Hello...Ms Dearborn? Veronica?"

"Oh! It's you. Hello!" Veronica looked round for Corinna de Benedetto, but Julian Blyth appeared to be on his own. "Quite fun, wasn't it? Or is this a busman's holiday for you?"

"I just – um – wandered in. I don't normally go to concerts, it's true. Rather nice, though, these local festival things. The Italians are rather good at them, I understand. "

"Yes, they are. I've been a good tourist this evening. Architecture and music. I loved the Scarlatti and the Bach...unusual on a harp. He was pretty good, I thought." She suddenly wanted to say how much she had enjoyed the shadows, and felt silly. There was an awkward pause.

"Not bad at all. I find eastern music a bit alienating, I'm afraid. I'm not very adventurous. I suppose we're both wandering back to the hotel..."

"Yes."

"Do you mind if I walk with you?"

"Not in the least." They walked in silence up to the Piazza. Veronica paused by the two-faced gargoyle, which was now floodlit and casting strange shadows. "Sorry to stop, but what do you make of that? The guidebook says it was placed by a fourteenth century merchant from Florence named Giuliano

Freccia in honour of his brother Ilario, who worked here as a magistrate. It's got two completely different expressions…"

"So it has…rather unsettling." Julian gazed at the strange stone face for what seemed a long time. "Did you say Ilario? How extraordinary! I say, are you – um, hungry?" Julian, normally an unsociable creature who in the last couple of days had been forced into the company of some very strange strangers, found himself badly in need of someone sane and reasonable to talk to. Quite why he assumed Veronica to possess such qualities, he could not have articulated, even to himself.

"Yes, I am a bit." Veronica's supper had consisted of the nibbles at the café. They turned down a side street and wandered in the opposite direction from the Albergo, and found themselves at the seafront, where the only open trattoria appeared to be Luigi's, where she had dined with Freddy on the evening she had arrived and where, yesterday, Julian had lunched with Lorrie Lucifora. The waiter recognized him and greeted him like an old friend. Apart from the odd concert-goer with the same idea, the place was quiet and they chose an indoor table out of the sea-breeze.

Veronica found Julian restfully companionable, and she told him briefly about her Flora Forde project over an octopus salad starter. "Not for another couple of days or so," she said, when he asked when she was leaving. "Then I have to go up and see about my house near Siena. It's let, and I need to do some business with the agent…What about you?"

"I've – er – decided to leave that open for the moment. I'm on agent's business too, in a way. I've been settling my late brother's estate…"

"So you said, yesterday morning. That must be dreary…"

"Good to get things *done…*"

"Tick the boxes?" She had an agreeable, good-tempered smile and intelligent, serious eyes that did not attempt to flirt. This was a striking contrast to Mrs de Benedetto, and he began to relax.

"That sort of thing. There's – um – someone I need to see and he's proving a bit elusive. In fact, I hope it's not too rude, but I've left my mobile on. He might text. I hope to catch him before he leaves for Africa if he's not left already. Someone's just told me he's gone. He's an architect. There's a banker's draft burning a hole in my pocket. I'll be very happy to hand it over."

"You could post it, I suppose. They have all the usual registered post things here. Or leave it with his lawyer or the bank. But I expect you've already thought of that."

"Yes. I'd really prefer to see him personally. I just hope we can find enough language to communicate in. My Italian's virtually non existent, I'm afraid. He was a great friend of Hilary's, and Hil spoke Italian like a native."

"Hilary! Was that your brother's name? Ah, I see! That gargoyle – Giuliano and Ilario…"

"Yes…A bit of a weird coincidence, that, isn't it? Rather good to have seen it… could have missed it altogether. You see, apart from this architect guy, I didn't really need to come to Monte Farfalla at all. Letters and emails would have been sufficient...."

"But?"

"But I was curious. I regretted never coming to visit him here. I only knew his little place in Rome. He had a flat in the Trastevere district. He was a journalist, foreign correspondent... Then he and Faye – Hilary's wife – widow now, poor girl – they moved here, and somehow I was always dashing about on tour. Hil and I saw far too little of each other in recent years..."

"It happens like that sometimes." Veronica thought fleetingly of her own brother, James, unseen and unheard of for many years. "That's really rather sad...and then it's suddenly too late. I'm sorry."

"Yes..." He crumbled bread onto his plate. "I thought – that is, I hoped – it would be simple now the house is sold. Just be a matter of saying hello and goodbye, as it were..."

"*Ave atque vale...*" Veronica murmured.

"Yes... I say, that's rum too. Faye – Hil's wife – she had that put on the gravestone. I saw it yesterday afternoon. He – he's buried in San Gregorio. Strange places, Italian cemeteries. Worse than France, all those bad portraits and votive offerings. One is sort of forced to take death seriously, or revel in it, or something. The other graves all look so well tended...Hil's is a bit forlorn. Perhaps graves don't matter."

"They're just shop-fronts really, " Veronica said. "Especially here. How did Hilary die?"

"Drowned in a swimming accident last summer."

"How awful...I'm so sorry."

"I was on tour when it all happened. In Tokyo. I didn't even get out here for the funeral. They do them very quickly, even when there's been an inquest. The heat..."

"Yes, of course..."

"There was a memorial in London about three months later. There were all of his old journalist cronies, as well as all the family, friends..."

"A proper *addio*..."

"Yes. This is supposed to be the last bit." Julian Blyth frowned, still flaking bread. He had an intelligent, troubled frown. The pasta gamberetti arrived, and Veronica poured more wine.

"Thanks. This is very nice. I seem to have been drinking ever since I got here, one way and another. Still, it's not as if we've got to stagger very far, is it? Look, may I confide something to you? I'm probably going to sound fanciful. You'll just have to believe me that I – I'm normally the most rational of people..."

"I believe you. Go on..." Her eyes, tawny green, were quietly humorous.

"It's not easy to explain. My brother Hilary was always a bit of a tearaway, you see. The official version is that he went to a party and got smashed, had a row with almost everybody and left. He walked round the bay to his house. Then he went swimming. He was probably fairly pissed. He drowned near some notorious rocks. Faye was away – with a student group of hers. She taught at the International School in San Gregorio, and this was a summer trip to Florence. She – she got back next morning just in time to find the emergency services fishing him out of the water, apparently…"

"Oh, God – how ghastly! Poor woman…" He saw her rather nice, square brows knit as if she were visualising the scene.

"It – well, it affected her nerves very badly. She's in quite a bad way still, in hospital. That's why I've been dealing with the Rome lawyers on her behalf. I've got power of attorney. Everything more or less straightforward, or so you'd think…"

"But?"

"But – well, the thing is, she – Faye – always insisted there was something wrong about Hilary's death, and of course I dismissed it a bit. She – she rather hit the bottle afterwards, and she – well, according to my daughter who is studying psychology, it's not unusual for someone who is grieving to want to blame an accidental disaster on someone else… The thing is, I used to think Faye was raving. Now I'm simply – well, I'm simply not so sure…"

"I see. Why?" He saw she was serious.

"This is probably going to sound as crazy as poor Faye. I can't put my finger on it exactly. It's these people, partly. In the last couple of days, I've met several people who knew Hil and Faye, and …well, everyone seems very keen to stop me asking questions, and telling me a great many things at the same time."

"Daphne Allerton…"

"Her. And others. Everybody seems to know everybody – all the ex-pats, that is. They seem to be a sort of masonry. They're trying to be friendly, doubtless, but they've been very busy telling me Faye is mad and Hilary was a drunk. There's a grain of truth in both of these things." He smiled wryly up from the bread. "But I can't help feeling they're all hiding something, sort of protecting each other. The Allerton woman kept hinting at danger, and I don't think she was just talking about submerged rocks. But she was sort of – well, wanting to shock me, and enjoying herself in a way I found a bit…"

"Distasteful?"

"Yes. Or just plain odd. What do you make of them?"

"Me? I've only just met them too, you know. They might be all right individually. They invited me to a sort of party last Saturday…" She suppressed a shudder. "But I find those things fairly ghastly anyway. My friend Freddy Partridge thinks they're amusing. A sort of sideshow. I just think – well, I think that this is the sort of world I should really hate to exist in. Narrow, bitchy, snobby…ill-formed opinions based on soundbites from

283

the *Spectator*, and politics just fractionally to the left of Genghis Khan. You know?"

Julian laughed. "But you do have a house near Siena?"

"I inherited it. And I haven't made a home in it, as it happens, but that's not what I mean really. It's not that I object to ex-pats, as such, people living abroad. I just hate the enclaves, the little monoglot capsules, everyone reading the *Daily Mail* and re-creating Little England, fancying themselves superior. It's as if they just live on the surface of everything, you know? As though the climate and the art are just there for them to revel in, and the local issues don't matter at all as long as their taxes aren't affected… It's just a middle-class version of the sun and sangria stuff in Spain, or a European version of colonialism or something. And there's this rather vile Johnny Foreigner attitude whatever, even if it is just sweetly condescending. Oh!" Veronica realised she was probably being very tactless. "Sorry! I didn't mean to bang on…I just mean, really, that there would be people who would be horribly insular wherever they were…"

"You sound like my brother on one of his rants! I'm sure you're right, too…"

"Sorry! I get carried away. But what was Hilary doing here? It – um – you don't make it sound like his scene at all."

"Simple. He'd lived in Italy since he left school, on and off. First university in Florence and then he went to work in Rome. He wrote for the *Guardian* and the *Times*. He felt at home here. He often said he couldn't survive in Blighty. He was probably right. I'm not too keen on it myself."

"Okay – but I meant why *here*?"

"He and Faye fell in love with a house. They saw a ruin by the sea with a bit of land and they bought it. Hil was all up for a new project – renovation and writing about it. I can see the reasoning. Faye was the country-lover, and I think she thought it would do them both good to escape Rome. Foreign correspondents live rather a relentless high life… I – I was always so pleased for Hilary that he'd found Faye. I – that is, my ex-wife and I – introduced them. She was our daughter's school teacher. Nice woman. Good for him. He seemed to settle down so happily, poor old Hil! The only trouble was that Hil took his own weather with him, if you see what I mean."

"Yes, I think I do…"

"I partly mean he would never have stopped being a serious journalist. He would never have just retired, Hil… And he couldn't resist stirring things up, teasing. He might have not been able to resist – well, bating these people. And he could come across as pretty arrogant sometimes. He wrote something derogatory about the Barkers' hotel. Everybody keeps telling me how much they adored him, but I think they must have had pretty mixed feelings."

"But not mixed enough to have killed him, presumably. Sorry. I don't mean to be frivolous at all."

"No… My God! At least I don't think so!"

"But that is what you're suggesting, isn't it? That he was killed?"

"I don't know….No! That's ridiculous, isn't it?"

"One hopes so, yes… I suppose there's no doubt that he drowned?"

"None. I've seen the autopsy reports, everything. Water inhalation, and injuries consistent with being battered against rocks…No, it's the fact that he drowned at all that I find slightly incredible. In his day, Hil was a serious swimmer. He loved the sea. Ironic, you know, that it killed him. Before old Hil got fatter and out of shape, he was a champion marathon swimmer. It was a hobby, a passion. He was beginning a book about coastal swimming in Italy when he died. The idea that he just got into difficulties and drowned in a millpond Mediterranean bay is almost absurd…"

"But you say he was very drunk…and a bit overweight and unfit…"

"You didn't know Hilary! Honestly, Hil was unsinkable. I see you're looking sceptical…"

"Well…"

"Well, okay. Accidents happen. Expert drivers shoot off into ravines sober. Professional jockeys break their necks… But – until I'm satisfied, I find I can't just dismiss Faye's fears outright. That's partly why I want to see this man Innocenti. They were good friends. Hil might have confided something. The more these people try to put me off seeing him, the more

286

convinced I am that there's a reason, and that they know or guess what it is."

"I see." She frowned again. "I suppose he might have found something out. Something damaging. Journalists can be very – well, uncomfortable people. I've wanted to kill them myself. Sorry! That was tactless."

"Veronica – I did read your earlier book."

"You did?"

"Yes. And I can see that you must have had cause to feel that way. About journalists."

"I'm sorry. I get – well, over sensitive, I suppose. I'd never expected quite the amount of vitriol when that book came out. It's partly why I wrote it, to put the record straight…at least put my side of the story. It didn't stop the journalists. I thought I'd done their job for them, but oh, no…not a bit. Then it was all reactions and comments and…"

"Another glass?"

"Thanks. Sorry. It was pretty foul at the time, and I hadn't been remotely prepared for that. All I wanted to do when I came out of jail was hide, and I hid and wrote, and then suddenly everyone was accusing me of self-advertisement…which I suppose in a way it was. I feel very foolish now. They want to make it into a film, did you know that? Somehow this thing's going to be round my neck forever…"

"But you have to stop them!"

"I can't. Not if they're really determined." She explained what she had learned of the intricacies of the law. "All I can do is hope that they might be put off by the difficulties."

"But that's damnable," he said, and sounded as if he meant it.

"Perhaps. Sometimes people, once they start something, can't just give up… Film making might sound frivolous to you and me, and of course I think it's ghoulish and all the rest of it, but somebody might care enough to risk it. Even I find I can't give up the mysterious case of the Mystery Writer, and I know it's going to upset Freddy, and I actually care about his feelings. It's been a rather salutary lesson." She frowned. "Perhaps that's what happened to Hilary. He was onto something or someone, and he couldn't let well alone. 'Satiable curiosity, like the Elephant's Child."

"And now I can't just give up either."

"No. At least until you've seen this architect, you'll always have unanswered questions, won't you?"

"Yes. God – you don't know how relieved I am that you're not just telling me I'm being crazy."

"I think…" Veronica looked at his face and decided she trusted it. "I think that within certain limits, one should go with one's instincts. It's usually obvious if one is being lied to. Perhaps you should try to have a serious conversation with your sister-in-law."

"I emailed my daughter this afternoon. She'll see Faye…I think this story of hers deserves another hearing. Look, Veronica, thank you so much for listening. I don't know why I've been confiding all this to you."

"I do. I'm a stranger. And another pair of eyes."

"Very sympathetic and intelligent ones."

"Thank you. And you have a very nice smile when you let yourself." Suddenly very embarrassed, they both stared round for a waiter. They ordered coffee.

"I wish – "

"I wondered – "

"No, you go on!"

"Well, I wondered if you'd like to speak to my friend Freddy. He knows these people much better than I do, and they've probably told him things. He's completely unpartisan as far as I know. He's gone to Venice, but he'll be back tomorrow."

"Well – I – that's kind, but – er- well, I shouldn't want to impose. Oh God! Hang on, did you say Freddy Partridge? Doesn't he do a restaurant column in *The Bystander*?

"Yes. Do you know him?"

"No – but old Hilary must have. Hil wrote an occasional Italy column for them. That's where he published the famous Albergo thing. I suppose they might not have met, though. I – I was going to ask if you'd – um – like to come and see Hilary's house? I have a key still. It's – it's my last chance…"

xix: Dreams

"Why do we have to go over this again and again? And keep your voice down, Den. There's a full house tonight. Just cos you can't sleep..."

"Why did you have to tell that stupid cow Corinna? Now I bet we see nothing!"

"Hilary didn't actually owe us anything, Den. Surely it's enough that everything's in the past now? Just forget it and act natural. Nobody remembers the stupid article now. We lost one couple who refused to pay and a bit of a season's business. Stop making mountains out of molehills."

"We lost far more than that, Silv, come on!"

"We got the plumbing fixed didn't we? And a makeover. Let sleeping dogs lie, I say. For God's sake, Den."

"He's sniffing."

"There's nothing to sniff, Dennis. Not any more, and thank God if you ask me. Shut up and go to sleep, do." She turned her back to him in the big bed and yawned. She was genuinely tired.

"He's trouble. I knew it as soon as I saw him."

"He's not trouble! How many more times? He's not a journo. He's just a nice man, a musician, come to settle the affairs of his brother. He seems quite decent. I might ask him. He might sympathise if I put it to him in the right way..."

"That's the girl…put it to me in the right way, eh?" His hand was on her plump naked knee.

"Oh, lay off, Den…d'you *have* to?"

"Yeah…" The hand slid further up Silvana's nightdress.

"Oh, go on then. If it'll shut you up…and only if it's quick, okay? No upstairs stuff." She rolled over with a resigned sigh, hitching her cotton nightie to her waist.

"Reckon this is how old Corinna does it?"

"Den!" Silvana Barker gritted her teeth as he mounted her.

"P'rhaps she's doing it with that Julian Blyth like this, right now…"

Corinna was too furious to sleep without the drops, and she took all ten of the recommended dose in a small glass of water and waited for the familiar oblivion, propped up in her bed over her magazine. Sleep came down suddenly like a heavy curtain, and her neck was still craned up on too many pillows. She dreamed a thick, benzodiazepined dream, queasily erotic, in which she was luxuriantly pliant in the arms of Pietro, who turned into her husband, Alfredo, who turned, before she awoke at four o'clock with a banging headache, into Cadwallader Jones. Climbing from her bed, she weaved into the en suite bathroom where she was thoroughly and unpleasantly sick.

Veronica was driving on a road that twisted ever more steeply, and she was glad that at last Todd was by her side. The road was dark and she could scarcely see, and she was afraid. The pedals would not obey her commands. There was something wrong with the brake. She glanced at the passenger seat to find it empty. Then she swerved and fell…

Julian Blyth dreamed of his brother. They were boys, and they were consigned to practice in the music room. Someone, very soon, was coming to hear their efforts. Julian, anxious, could not play his violin properly because of his hand, but the jazz on the piano was off-putting. Julian told Hilary to shut up. "All right," Hilary said. "I'll just swim away." He jumped out of the sash window and into the sea…

Dennis Barker, peacefully sated, slept heavily and snored loudly and dreamed of lapping water, a boat out in the sun, fish…The scent of salt air. There was a big fish on the deck. Someone threw it back. Its black plastic casing and rectangular shape caused it to spin strangely in the air before it splashed into the still water. Dennis stared down, to make sure the thing had gone under, and saw the pale bloated shape of a man, naked apart from shorts, slide beneath the keel…

xx: A Girl's Best Friend

Corinna was a little later than usual for her Wednesday drinks with Daphne.

"Sorry, m'darling. This morning I have just *got* to sit outside in the air!" Corinna firmly took her drink onto the terrace and sat down.

"You do look put out, dear," said Daphne, joining her with some crisps in a Tupperware container. "A pity, on such a lovely day."

"Sorry. I'm a bit…"

"Tell me about Castelambra."

"Castelambra? Oh, that! Seems eons ago…It went all right. Lovely property. And I don't think Lord H is gaga in the least."

"No? He used to walk out with Sophia, did I tell you?"

"Several times. And with Veronica Dearborn's mother, so he was saying…"

"Did he? Well, that's more than likely. She was quite a looker, was Anabel Trent. But then, George had anything in a skirt in those days. Probably still does, if everything in the hydraulics department still works…" Daphne Allerton regarded her friend with a raised eyebrow. "I expect he appreciated *you*…"

293

"Oh, honestly, Daffy! That's absurd!" But Corinna smiled to herself all the same, and briefly gazed down at one of her slender ankles, wriggled it and frowned.

"Nonsense! Good for business…You're looking rather pale, dear. Your shoulder is painful, perhaps. Do I take it all is not so well in Rome?"

"Rome? Everything is fine in Rome. Why shouldn't it be? Letizia sends her love."

"How sweet of her. Dear Letty! She must enjoy spending so much time with you these days." Daphne gave Corinna a look, but Corinna was examining her bag.

"Oh damn and blast, Daffy! I've forgotten your corals. I left them at home in the hall. Should I go back and get them?"

"No need, dear. Another time. It seems as if you're being rather forgetful altogether recently…so tell me, how is our Mr Blyth? Tell me *all* about last night."

"How did you – oh, Silvana, I suppose. Moh! There's nothing to tell! *She's* got to him! Faye! It's – it's absolutely outrageous! They're in it together! I named a perfectly reasonable sum, and he just blanked on me! Told me it wasn't up to him, and that he would have to ask Faye, for God's sakes! Fucking *A!*"

"Well, dear, frankly, I thought there was something very obstinate about the man. I did tell him how very hard you had worked on his family's behalf. Have some of these nice crisps.

They're still fresh. I got them in on Monday for him, but he wasn't very hungry. They won't keep…" Daphne lit a cigarette.

"No thanks. He's got a cheque for bloody Innocenti, apparently. I told him he'd already left. I mean, he probably has. The Barkers will owe me a debt of gratitude for that. He should just bugger off back home to London and leave us all in peace…"

"I didn't get the impression he wanted to do anything else, dear."

"He also told me that bloody Lorrie hasn't charged him anything. Done it for love, if you please! For bloody *Faye*! Moh! Can you *believe* it!"

"It might be true, dear. After all, why would he lie about a thing like that?"

"But if it's true, *why*? He might be a little snake, but Lorrie could have charged a legitimate finding fee. It's just not credible!"

"Perhaps he was feeling charitable. Some people do. But then, he can probably afford to."

"Well bully for him! What was it – *is* it – about that woman? Does the poor little widow stunt, and everybody comes to the rescue on white chargers, including screaming queens like Lucifora! What about *me*? I worked my arse off trying to help that neurotic little bitch, lawyers here, offices there, and this is the thanks I get! Sorry, Daffy! I'm just too furious for words. And that Daly woman has her hooks well and truly into

295

Cadwallader Jones. They turned up at Mauro's last night. It was the last straw! He saw me with friend Blyth and went into meltdown – practically pushed the table over. It was incredibly embarrassing."

"Dear, dear! Did he say anything to you?"

"No! *She* led him off towards the Castello, clucking like a mother hen. They're as thick as thieves. He thinks he owns me!"

"Well, he might be forgiven for that impression, dear…"

"Oh, balls! If he hadn't had a major tantrum in the street, I'd have introduced them. I could have explained it was only work. It was seriously awkward, because I'd just turned him down for supper…I turned friend Blyth down too – I was too angry."

"Dear me. Yes, I see. This place is far too small for subterfuge. I have always said so."

"But it was all a complete misunderstanding! To make it worse, I saw her ladyship or whatever she is hovering, too. She probably saw the lot. Moh! How was Saturday? She was the star of the evening, I suppose. How did you find her?"

"Very pleasant, dear. Very intelligent, I should say. Quite shy. A bit overwhelmed by us all, I think. But you'd better ask Cadwallader, hadn't you? He was here. I gather *she* monopolizes him, too, at the moment. He is much in demand."

"Moh!"

"All very well for you to say 'moh', dear. When you next see Cadwallader, you'd better pick up your little painting, hadn't you? I gather you left it behind…"

"Oh, *that*! It's all sorted. Or it *was*…But how on *earth*?"

"We live in a very small place, dear."

"Dorinda, I suppose?" Daphne's face was a composed blank, staring out at the Bay. "Hell! I didn't *mean* to leave it behind, for heaven's sakes! What's she been saying? I suppose he's been telling her he's very offended…"

"With cause, I should say, dear. Insult to injury by the sound of things, poor fellow…"

"But he's *always* painting me! He's asked me to sit for him again. And *whatever* you've heard, Daffy, it's a head and shoulders and I'm wearing that watered silk thing and pearls…"

"Hmm. I do wonder, perhaps, dear, if Rome is going so well, you might let poor Cadwallader off the hook a little."

"He isn't on a bloody hook, for God's sakes! Fucking A!"

"Temper, temper, dear… By the way, dear, if you want to check your messages, the signal will be better if you put your telephone onto the table," said the disconcertingly observant Mrs Allerton. "It will save you from glancing constantly at your bag. I shan't mind."

"Oh! Sorry, Daffy…how silly! I'll turn it off. There! I'm so busy! George might ring about the house. I never know who might want to get hold of me…"

"He's married, isn't he?"

297

"Who? George Helpston? *I* don't know! He calls Fenella 'the missus'. *Is* he married to her?"

"I doubt it very much, as I believe Pippa Helpston is still alive and there was no divorce… I meant your Roman friend. You don't have to tell me if you don't want to."

"They live apart. The marriage as such hasn't existed for years."

"I see. Seems the order of the day. You should have hung onto poor Alfredo, dear, while you had the chance. Would you like another?"

"Yes! I mean, yes, thank you, m'darling. Take no notice of me. I'm all out of kilt this morning."

"You mean 'out of kilter', dear. Out of kilt would be a very rude Scotsman…"

"For God's sakes, Daffy! Do I need you to pick me up on every damn thing?"

"I was only making one of my silly jokes, dear." Daphne went back inside to refresh the glasses, and Corinna checked her mobile. *Still* no message.

"Have you met her?" she asked bluntly when Daphne returned. "This new woman of Alfredo's?"

"No dear. Not as such. I don't think that she's terribly new, either, is she? I once bumped into them in the street in San Gregorio and was briefly introduced. Pleasant little woman, I thought. Italian, of course. Laura somebody."

"That's it. Lao-oorra! So *common*. Moh! Letty's met her. More than met her. She accompanied Alfredo to Letty's prize-giving do before Christmas, no less. Big framed photo on Letty's desk. She looks like a little *contadina* – hennaed hair and a fur! God knows what Alfredo thinks he's doing with someone like that, introducing her into the family. *I* should have been there! That was *my* place! As the *mother*!"

"But you went to her senior graduation, dear, and Alfredo did not. I expect Letizia was trying to be tactful. Difficult position for the young with all these ramified family arrangements…and it's not as if you actually speak to Alfredo, is it? I expect she was trying to avoid an awkwardness. Now then, dear. Cheers!" Daphne raised her glass. The large stone on her finger twinkled in the bright sunlight.

"Cheers…oh!" Corinna stared.

"*Cin-cin*, dear."

"Your ring! The Palm Springs diamond! You – I mean – how...?"

"I found I missed it, dear. Sebastiano did a little work on the shank and made it fit. See? It doesn't tend to fall off my skinny finger anymore. Lovely, isn't it? I love my ring. A present from my poor darling Patrick when he was still making sense. I can't think why Sebastiano thought he had to send it away. It was a very simple job, apparently."

"Oh," said Corinna through a constricted smile. "Oh, well that's wonderful, isn't it? Sebastiano usually sends things away

299

to his cousin in Naples. He's very good, but things always take a while…"

"I just caught it in time, dear. He did it in the shop while I waited. Wasn't that fortunate?"

"Very," agreed Corinna faintly.

Dorinda Daly's day was a series of pauses punctuated by social activity. She enjoyed not only watching the world go by; if she got the opportunity, she greeted it warmly, and – as it were – shook it by the hand; and if the world tended to be living its busy life on the run with no time to pause at all, Dorinda thought nothing of putting out her small well-shod foot and tripping it over, as the late Hilary Blyth had been heard to remark.

The street outside the great Medici Gate where Dorinda Daly lived on the fourth floor of an adjacent *palazzo* teemed with activity most mornings. From the pavement tables of Bar Stefania, where she normally took her breakfast coffee, smoked her Marlboro, read her post and her *Daily Mail* (especially reserved for her by the newsagent next door), Dorinda could see the entrance to the market place and the fish stalls, the gift shop, the optician, the kiosks that sold cigarettes and coffee and icecream and cut-price DVDs. She watched the idling taxis and the wooden bench beside the rank, where the old boys gathered and sat with tiny plastic beakers of coffee – they contemplated the world with a phlegmatic insouciance which they were wont to spit onto the pavement – a sight and sound that Dorinda had learned to ignore. Her day thus began with a diet of cappuccino and sensational British news, accompanied by the chattering of local Italian housewives and the comings and goings of tradesmen, a number of whom she had designated 'friends'. She waved to the cheeky young man in the three-wheel truck who delivered gas bottles, and to the military-looking old gent in the cloth cap with his little black dog. Both now would wave cheerily back. She said 'buon giorno' merrily to the two girls who came by every week day in their smart little white uniforms to enter her own building to go to work at the dental surgery on the ground floor. She knew them by name – Isabella and Maria Grazia – and they too would hail her, sometimes stopping for a brief conversation. She knew enough Italian now to be able to talk about Isabella's mother, who was recovering from an operation. Young Daniele, the son of the proprietress of the little bar took her heavier shopping up the staircase, proud of his smattering of English and grateful for a small tip, and Stefania herself kept by a special foil-wrapped lasagne from her little *rosticceria* for Dorinda's lunch, which she would either eat or freeze if the day in question offered more sociable delights. Dorinda had accumulated quite a number of frozen parcels of lasagne...

On mornings like these – balmy, sunny, the starlings chattering in the great parasol pines, and the little town abuzz – Dorinda felt very much at home. This was how one could live happily abroad – a stranger in a strange land, certainly, but if one had to escape one's less fortunate associations at home (and thank the Lord that one had a son who could house a mother in such a lovely place!) then one could do a lot worse than hole up for a little while in dear Merrick's little buy-to-let in Monte Farfalla! Dorinda watched the outdoor tables fill up with elderly women with shopping bags full of bread , and vegetables, young women with small children in push-chairs, and toddlers in tow. She greeted them all.

Some mornings offered an opportunity for a thorough gossip, and on Wednesdays she was accustomed to see her friend Minette Marquis after her marketing. On this particular Wednesday Dorinda had to remind herself that Minette had gone on her annual sojourn in her native Scotland. Pity! Dorinda would have liked the excuse for a proper chat over a breakfast brandy, for now there was much to divulge. However, an article in the *Mail* had caught her particular attention – yet another politician caught out on an expenses scam – and she became engrossed. Something – a noise across the street – made her look up, and – what a lovely surprise! – there was a familiar figure emerging from a taxi that had drawn up at the rank. "Freddy! Hellooo!"

That gentleman looked a little agitated – he was fumbling for notes to pay the fare, and had made up the amount in loose coins. There was not enough for more than a derisory tip, and the disgruntled driver u-turned with a squeal of tyres and headed back to the station without a backward glance, despite Freddy's profuse apologies. As he picked up his holdall, he became aware of the black haired woman in large spectacles calling and waving from the café across the street. His heart sank a little. Ever polite, however, and realising that in any case he would have to walk past her, he waved back and made his way over to her table.

"Hellooo-o," Dorinda cooed. "You do look hot and bothered, m'dear! Sit you down! Come and have some coffee!"

He kissed her cheek. "Thank you, lovey. I'm financially embarrassed until I've been to the cash point…I've just mortally offended a cabbie. Can I dump my bag and go for essential supplies?"

"Don't be silly! This is on me. I want to hear *all* about Venice! Cappuccino okay?"

"Actually it's a bit late – I could murder a beer, though."

"Then I shall have a campari! I know it's naff, but I just love it! Don't report me in anything official!" She hailed Daniele and gave the order. In their day, she and her ex husband had been avid tourists and she began reminiscing about Venice with vigour.

"St Marks? Crawling, darling. Absolutely crawling! You can't move for French students at this time of year. Hell on earth, believe me! And just forget Florio's. It's become a ghastly side show, entirely déclassé now. And I'm no Mr Meanie, but I just *object* to nine euro a throw for a single gin and tonic…the restaurant? Oh, *that*'s a little peach. It's called *I Contrabandieri* – The Smugglers. Very amusing. One doesn't go to Venice for

303

the restaurants as a rule, but this is rather fun. Tucked down a backwater, tiny, no menu, old boy cooks, daughter serves…a deffo for the *Bystander*…yes, old 'Epicure' at the old stand…"

Freddy seemed a bit 'wired' as Dorinda put it to herself. The drinks arrived. "Ta, Dorinda, lovey! *Cin-i-cin-cin*! This looks *just* what the doctor ordered. I had coffee and a bad bun on the plane… You'll have to forgive my being so *travel-stained…*" Freddy looked as if he had not slept, his eyes were puffy and his hands shook slightly.

"So how was the Casino? Did you win?"

"*All* my naughty secrets waving in the breeze, eh?"

"Ho! You can't keep secrets here, dearie. Blame Cadwallader!"

"You're quite a friend of his, aren't you, Dorinda darling?"

"Well I *hope* so, dearie. He's quite a one, isn't he? Such a sweetie, but to be frank…" she lowered her voice to a smoky Irish whisper, "I do worry about him a bit. He's what I'd call a bit – well – naïve. If you get what I mean. I would think that you're a bit concerned too? I mean, he can be a bit what I'd call susceptible… Now, m'dear, the last thing I want to do is interfere and I deplore *gossip*, but…"

Soon, Freddy knew for certain what he had already suspected.

xxi: Damage Limitation

"*If* it's true – and I'm not saying it *is* – it's a secret! Milly's little secret! She never spoke of it. Her Past. I – I very strongly feel this ought to remain strictly between our two selves."

"But, Cadwallader, I don't see how I am to keep it a secret. I think I have to share this with Vixen Press at the very least. And if Alison Truce is going to do the Millicent books, this ought to be part of her history. I can't just not say anything, Cad. Is it really *that* serious?"

"It was something she would never have wanted to come out! Oh, I can't explain! I feel a traitor to her memory!"

"Cad, listen. Please. I truly don't want to bully you, but this can't harm Millicent now. Rather the reverse. The 'Flora' books are very good. Her reputation won't suffer, I promise. In fact – well, actually, I think this can only improve new sales…"

"Oh dear me," muttered Cadwallader. "Sales! Such a *dilemma*!"

Veronica stood by rather helplessly. "You see, if it isn't me, it will be someone else. I mean Vixen – the publishers – they'll just get someone else to do Flora, and they might reach the same conclusions…"

"Oh dear, oh dear, oh *dear*…I need a drink!"

"That's the telephone, Cadwallader."

"What?"

"The phone's ringing…"

"Singing? Who's singing?"

"Ringing! The telephone…Here." She passed him the cordless receiver.

"Please, Cad, darling! I can explain everything…" The voice, female, was entirely audible.

"What? I can't hear!"

"Oh, *darling* …"

Veronica tactfully disappeared to the bathroom.

Cadwallader, whose ears were famously faulty, heard the unmistakable sound of tears, and melted…

When Veronica emerged, she found him in a state of agitation, very haphazardly preparing a snack lunch in his untidy galley kitchen and fumbling rather badly. He dropped a knife which Veronica picked up, while he crouched at the fridge, muttering.

"Ouf! Thank you! Oh dear! I can't really *think* about all this now. I've lost some ham! I suppose I would rather it was you…I just can't bear to be involved in any kind of *scandal*…Milly, to be, I mean…Now, I did have some soft cheese…"

"There isn't a scandal, though, Cadwallader," said Veronica, feeling a little conscience-stricken. "I mean the fact that Millicent used another *nom de plume* is hardly…"

Cadwallader was arranging crackers onto a plate, and suddenly dropped a great many onto the floor. Veronica leapt to

306

help pick them up. "No, no – don't, my dear. So narrow in here...ouf! I can't stoop much. Will you take a glass of something?"

"Only if you're going to have one, Cadwallader. Do let me. Look, these are fine."

"A glass of wine?"

"I said these are *fine*...not dirty. No one will know."

"Oh, dear...thank you. Someone's coming round to lunch, and I'm not at all ready! I'd ask you to stay, Veronica my dear, but..."

"Don't worry, Cad. I'm off to meet Freddy. He's back today. From Venice."

"Playing tennis?"

"Venice!" Veronica raised her voice, beginning to feel desperate. Cadwallader's deafness was always much worse when he was feeling stressed.

"Ah. Of course. Venice. Milly and I went to Venice a great deal in the old days. Now I know I put some ham in the refrigerator...in *il frigo,* and – "

The doorbell rang, and Cadwallader did not hear it. Veronica heard voices, male and female, outside.

"I think that must be your guests, Cadwallader," she shouted.

"Guests? There's only one! And I can't find the *ham*!"

"Someone's here, Cad. Shall I answer the door?"

"Yes! No! Here, you say? I didn't hear anything. Oh dear! I'll go."

On the doorstep stood Freddy Partridge and Corinna de Benedetto, chatting merrily. Corinna wore a soft wrap over a sleeveless pale blue linen frock, and carried an exotically wrapped confection and a bottle of wine.

"Why, there he is!" cried Corinna, wrapping Cadwallader in a warm embrace. "Hullo, m'darling! Oh," she said, when she saw Veronica. "I didn't realise it was a party."

"Oh, it isn't," said Veronica, hurriedly. "Hullo, Corinna. I was just leaving to meet Freddy but he's beaten me to it. Hi, Freddy."

"Hi, Vee," said Freddy brightly. "I'm just back. Delayed. Having a late breakfast with a certain Mrs Daly." Freddy had changed his clothes and shaved.

"Oh – with Mrs Daly," Corinna murmured.

"She spotted me outside the Gate and gave me refreshment…"

"She is so very wonderfully hospitable, Dorinda, isn't she?" said Corinna, glancing at Cadwallader, who had dived back behind his kitchen bar, making clattering noises, whistling nervously through his teeth. "You must all have a drink," he muttered, and Veronica gave Freddy a look and a fractional shake of the head.

"We have a lunch date, Uncle Cad, don't we, Vee? Please don't go to any trouble for us."

"Very well, my dears…I haven't seen Corinna in so long…" He trotted round to bid them farewell, waving a bottle and a corkscrew precariously and resisting offers of help. "Now then – my dear. Keep in touch with me, and remember 'mum's the word'! Our little secret, yours, mine and Milly's!"

"Oh, the great work!" said Corinna, smiling gaily at Veronica. "Freddy was telling me you're leaving us on Friday?"

"Yes."

"What a pity! I do hope we shall see you here again soon."

"I'm sure you will," said Veronica, doubting this was true. She kissed Cad's cheek, and shook Corinna's hand, and she and Freddy stepped into the dazzling street.

"He's happy! Right, darling! I'm absolutely agog! Who is this man-friend you texted me about? And what's all this about a secret?"

"I'll tell you all," said Veronica with a sigh.

"But I left it here so you could have it framed! I thought that's what you wanted!"

"Oh…I see! Hee! What a dreadful misunderstanding! I thought – I thought maybe you didn't like it…"

"*Like* it? I absolutely *adore* it, and once it's framed, I'm going to put it in the hall way where everyone can see it! Oh Cad, you old silly…"

"Perhaps I am a little inclined to leap to conclusions…oh dear me! I thought – that chap last night – I mean…"

"You didn't seriously think that was my new boyfriend, did you? You darling old silly! New boyfriend! You are completely daft!" Corinna caressed Cad's cheek with a finger. "That was Hilary Blyth's brother, Julian. We were busy talking about selling Hilary's house. Remember? I was trying to sell it for Faye?"

"I don't know! I haven't met him!" Cadwallader's face clouded. He was still torn between anger and delight and sounded merely petulant.

Corinna sighed, prepared to be patient. "No, darling. I know you haven't. He's down here for a few days, settling Hilary's affairs. Remember Hilary Blyth? Oh, of course you do. Let's get some plates and things, shall we?" Efficiently, Corinna found plates, cutlery and even the missing ham, and they settled themselves in the tiny courtyard over glasses of prosecco.

"So you were trying to sell a house for this chap?"

"Yes, *Tesoro mio*…I have to make a living somehow. He's Hilary Blyth's brother. He suddenly called, and honestly the *last* thing I wanted was a social occasion. I'd planned an early night. But he's going back to England very soon, and he needed to see me urgently. It was only a quick drink to discuss business. You must remember Hilary! I couldn't just say no. Moh! I was absolutely exhausted!"

"Well of course I remember Hilary! And that delightful wife, poor girl…" Cadwallader, whose emotions had undergone a series of buffetings in the last forty-eight hours, began to come out of his sulk and did not see the downturn of Corinna's mouth. "Is he married, this brother?"

"Oh, yes, " said Corinna. "A daughter and a son. Come on, Cad, darling. Let me pour you another. I've brought you some very special chocolates.They're hand-made. From the shop next door to Letty's. It's famous. Now, tell me all about the great researches."

Cadwallader, cheering up considerably, told her at length and with a great deal of circumlocution. "Don't you see?" he said eventually. "It has to be tip-top secret, don't you agree?"

"I'm sorry, Cad, darling. What does?"

"Why, Flora Forde of course! Her identity!"

"Oh, absolutely! I agree entirely." Corinna suppressed a yawn, and gazed into his eyes. "Cad…I think it's turned very hot out here…" She slid her wrap from her shoulders. "Whew!" she said.

"Veronica wants me to talk to this woman – Alison somebody – about Milly. I've not made up my mind. On the whole, I think I probably shan't…although as the widower of such a famous writer, I suppose I have to expect these things…in a funny sort of way, it's fun. Hee! I can probably talk to her about my memoirs…she's terribly influential, apparently!"

"Cadwallader, dearest…I was wondering…about the other painting…"

"The painting? What painting?"

"My painting, Cad…the special one…"

"Oh! That! I gave it up! I can't go on doing it from memory. It's impossible!"

"I think you need the model…" She leaned and kissed his crumby mouth.

"My, my, you have been busy, darling. Seems we both have," Freddy said over a Taverna pasta, yawning dramtically and making Veronica unaccountably annoyed. "I mean, frankly, when I wasn't punting my shirt out at the blackjack table, I've spent the last forty-eight hours getting laid. There's this absolute peach of a trainee chef at Marcello's called Dante…I truly kid you not, Dante, as in Alighieri. Fabulous body, darling! Twenty-three, fit as a flea! And he – "

"Too much information, Freddy! I don't want to know. It's not like that at all. Julian wants to show me this house. He's walking there tomorrow from here...it's round the Bay. I said I'd meet him in the car. You don't have to come if you don't want to. I simply offered to introduce you, because you said you'd met him. The brother. Do you remember Hilary Blyth or don't you?"

"Slightly. He was the one that drowned here, wasn't he?" said Freddy. "Bad luck, poor guy. He was quite a big noise. We last met at some *Bystander* bash or other, I think. Big, hearty sort

312

of bloke, I recall. No, wait – I do remember perfectly. He picked my brains once about some Sicilian dish or other. Food, that is." He winked. Freddy was in one of his most tiresome moods.

"Freddy – try to be serious for *once*!"

"Nonsense! Absurdity is part of my fatal charm."

"Well, don't be too charming or absurd. Or fatal. This man has recently lost his brother. Can you be serious?"

"You underestimate me. We'll look at real estate if I'm invited too, and afterwards I'm taking you both to Cantina Valdambrini. It's work. I'm going to have to take notes, but you won't mind, will you, Veronikins? I thought as it's your last day, we'd have a bit of a flingette…In the meantime I need a serious zizz."

xxii: The Journalist's Widow's Tale

Hi, Phoebe...Beginning to think Faye might be right after all.
Can you go and find out? She's still in the Royal. Can pick up
emails every day. Tell her sale a-okay and I'll write properly v.
soon, but tell her I'm about to see G. Innocenti with a cheque.
Ask does she owe money to a female called Corinna? And ask
her about the row at the ex-pat party. And ask what H was
working on last year. This is a bit urgent. Love, Dad xx

Phoebe Blyth had been shown into an empty waiting
room where she had been sitting, standing, and pacing about for
half an hour. A notice told her in no uncertain terms that mobile
phones must be switched off. Regretting not having brought the
'Margins of Health' text book she should have been reading, she
turned guiltily to the magazines on a low table, and after the
irresistible problem pages in *Woman* and *Woman's Own* ('I think
my son might be gay'... 'I can't help being jealous of my best
friend...') she picked up a copy of *The Lady* and turned
automatically to the advertisement for her mother's catering
business. 'Willow Flower' – Delicious Homemade Vegetarian
Pies & Quiche to Your Door and Your Party...' She got up and
stared out of the window at the panorama of Bath's handsome
roof-scape, wondering if Robin had answered her text message.

Perhaps Robin was gay…Perhaps that was the whole problem…
Nervously, she sat down again.

"Phoebe!"

She started up, dropping the magazine. A large middle-aged woman with a bright helmet of chestnut hair wearing a light weight mac and a blue silk scarf stood in the doorway and seemed to fill the room with a vividly impressive presence.

"I've startled you! Sorry! I'm Clarissa, Faye's sister, perhaps you remember. They said her niece was here, and I knew it couldn't possibly be either of my two, so it had to be you. How are you, my love?"

"I – I'm fine," answered Phoebe. "They told me she was down in x-ray."

"That's right! I never would have recognised you, Phoebe. It's very sweet of you to bring flowers, I'm sure they'll cheer her up. And chocolates, too! She should be back up from the x-ray very soon…I'll take them in, shall I? You could write a little message."

"Oh…I hoped I could see her…"

"Well, perhaps not today, love. She's been having a lot of tests. She's bound to be very tired."

"Oh… It's just that, well, I need to ask her something about the house in Italy. Dad – Julian – sent an email. It sounds a bit urgent. I came over from Bristol this afternoon."

"Oh! I see. That's so kind of you. Oh my God! Did you gather there's a problem with the house? If so, I really think Julian should try to sort it on his own."

"No," said Phoebe firmly. "I'm sure there isn't a *problem* with the house. Just something Dad needs to know."

"Faye is still very fragile, Phoebe. She mustn't be tired or upset. I'm really not sure. Perhaps if you tell me what to ask her, I'll…"

"Hello? They told me there were visitors. Hello, Clarrie! And – why, it's Phoebe! How nice you managed to come." A very slight woman wearing a dressing-gown and slippers came into the room. A nurse hovered, murmured something about leaving them to it, and vanished. Faye's head was shaven and bandaged on one side. She was smiling.

"You're on your feet!" cried Clarissa. "That's the stuff!" She went and kissed Faye's cheek, huge beside the smaller figure.

"I'm walking wounded now," said Faye. "I have to keep moving so as not to seize up. Then I can go home."

"Well, we'll talk about that, love," said her sister briskly. "Can't have you overdoing it, can we? Now then, Phoebe's come with a message from Julian, Faye, but everything's okay, isn't it Phoebe?"

"Yes, absolutely," Phoebe said, feeling awkward. "The sale's gone through fine, Faye. Look, if this isn't a good time – "

"It's a perfect time, Phoebe," said Faye, taking the girl's hand impulsively. "Ahh, flowers. *And* chocolates! Ymm. So sweet of you... Clarrie, love, I want to talk to Phoebe. Why don't you go and do your Waitrose-ing now, and come back? She's come on the train from Bristol, Clarrie, just to see me."

"Well..."

"She won't tire me, I promise. The outside world is so important now."

Clarissa sighed, defeated. "All right, love. You're the boss. I'll see you in about an hour. Bye, Phoebe. Don't tire the patient!"

"No, Clarissa. Promise."

"It's this way," said Faye, beginning to walk down the corridor. "We have to use the lift."

"Don't *upset* her!" mouthed Clarissa before stomping towards the exit. Phoebe nodded and caught Faye up.

"This is okay, I suppose," said Phoebe, gazing round Faye's room. There was an armchair with a cushion and a little table as well as the bed, which had a side-cupboard arrangement and was strewn with books. A door led to a little private wash place, where Faye filled a vase and was making some instant coffee. They were in an older part of the hospital, and there was a long window with a view of handsome grounds. "If you have to be in hospital."

"Not too bad, is it? This is rather a *grande luxe* arrangement. They let you have this sort of thing if the trick-cycle department decides you're not actually 'at risk'. Clarrie insisted on this private room, bless her. But I'm sick of it. I'm just longing to get back to the flat now." She emerged with the flowers – roses and lilies – burying her nose in them. "These are so lovely. Thank you, Phoebe dear. I adore flowers. You know I can't really smell these? The head-injury's rather fucked up my sense of smell, I'm afraid. They won't say if it's going to be permanent…they never want to give you bad news."

"They probably don't actually know. I mean, head-injury cases are full of surprises, so they say. People can recover all sorts of things in time. Anyway, I thought they were pretty. No, no sugar, thanks."

Faye perched on the bed. "You're very, very kind, Phoebe. And so grown-up now. Sorry. That's a dreadful thing to say, but it cheers me. How's the course?"

"Hard going, if I'm honest. I'm not sure if I really have it in me, Faye. To be a proper child psychologist. I sometimes think I should have stuck to English. It was my best subject. Mostly because of you, probably."

"There's a lot more money in psychology, Phoebe. If I inspired a love of reading, then that's the main thing. Education shouldn't be just about training…"

"You always used to say that."

318

"Well, I still say it. And you'll need some other worlds to get absorbed in as an antidote to all those difficult cases. Some of them will be pretty sad, I should think…"

"Yes, some…They've been letting me loose on some field studies. Difficult kids with parents who're even worse. But what about you? When can you leave?"

"Once they're satisfied my head won't fall apart. Both senses. And I'm very determined to go back to the flat, whatever Clarissa says. She keeps saying I ought to go and stay with her, but one can't ever be *quiet* in Clarrie's house, and her sort of kindness is…well, I don't mean to be ungrateful. She means so well, and she's been a rock of support. It – it just does feel right to go back to somewhere I can call my own. I've sort of got to learn how to live again, if you see what I mean. And work. I feel as if I was about two years old and beginning from scratch…"

"Well – you are, in a way, aren't you? Starting from scratch…"

"Yes." Faye was unpicking cellophane from the chocolates. "You sound as if you understand. Choccy?"

"Ooh. Thank you. They're Belgian, very fattening. I love these white ones… I – I don't *really* understand, Faye. I mean I haven't been through anything like your – your troubles, and I don't know from experience what it feels like. But I'm sure that you need to feel empowered again. Independent. To function as yourself, I mean."

"Empowered! The times I've heard that word recently. And 'disempowered'..."

Phoebe coloured. "Sorry. I am doing a degree in psychobabble."

"I know. But it is the proper word. Nobody, including me, trusts me not to come to pieces again. That's disempowerment with a vengeance, Phoebe. If I'm ever going to convince anyone else I'm not an hysterical loony, I've first got to convince myself..."

"And I'm sure you will. One step at a time. It's a cliché but it's true."

"I know..." They fell briefly silent. "So – Julian has written to you. He's done the deed and the house is off my hands at last, that right?"

"Yes. He'll send you all the details very soon. Everything's okay, Faye. Moving forward."

"Dear Julian! He's been such a brick about all this. There'll be some money, too. I can begin to make a plan."

"Faye, I hope this isn't the wrong moment, but I do need to ask you some things..." Phoebe was very aware of being on fragile ground. She had a copy of Julian's email in her hand.

"Oh...okay. I'll try and answer if I can." Phoebe saw Faye bracing herself.

"Okay. Dad's in Monte Farfalla. You told Dad some things about Hil's death not being – well, not being an accident. Can you bear to talk about that?"

"Bear to? God help me, I've done little else since it all happened. I expect you know the drill. I am still in the 'denial stage' of grief, and looking for someone or something to blame. When this becomes logically untenable, I turn the blame inwards and throw myself off a balcony. Result – I am now officially unstable, in rehabilitation, under restraint, and my word on anything is suspect. I suppose you know what 'sectioning' means, yeah? Well, I'm de-sectioned now, I'm just in hospital with a sore head , but the little men in white coats can come back at any time. That's why Clarrie feels duty-bound to have me under her big white wing – she's like a swooping dove – and doubtless it's embarrassing to have one's own sister in the bin when you run a big social services department – but I really would prefer to live and die in my own surroundings than have that. Sorry. That came out a bit vehement, and I mustn't talk about dying or they'll lock me up again…Christ! They just don't get irony here. Irony-free zone! Big letters."

"God…" Phoebe shivered. *"One Flew Over The Cuckoo's Nest*? With a bit of Sylvia Plath thrown in?"

"Quite, and you probably should have stuck to literature, my child. Joke. Seriously, I'm just beginning to realise how much *credibility* I've lost. You have to put all this sort of thing on your CV if you ever want to do more than fill shelves in Waitrose, did you know? 'Can do simple tasks under appropriate supervision.' And the thing that will make the real difference now is going back to some sort of proper work. Eek." Faye buried her face in her hands and took a very deep breath. "Sorry...over-reaction. Sometimes it feels possible, and other times an impossibly tall order. Most of the time, we don't imagine abysses, even when things get vilely horrible... I don't understand how I got here, you know? In myself. Not quite. I don't even know if I fell or if I jumped. That's the God's honest truth. I was completely off my face, Phoebe. All I know is that it felt like a blessed relief to knock myself out and that I was bloody pissed off to wake up... I still am sometimes."

"Look, Faye..." Phoebe was feeling badly out of her depth. Barely adult herself, she was witnessing an intelligent adult who had come apart in a way that no text book could have prepared her for. "Faye...You mustn't talk about anything you don't want to."

Faye gulped and sat up. "Sorry. One can joke, but this isn't easy. It's actually hideously humiliating. You were my student when you were a child. And I suppose it's partly that I suspect that somewhere you've got a white coat hidden up your sleeve..."

"Faye, try not to see it like that. Please. I'm only a third-year psychology student. And I'm your niece, as well as your student. Hilary was my favourite uncle. I haven't got a white coat, Faye. Just Dad's messenger-girl."

Faye laughed softly. "Sorry. Very unfair. All right, no white coat. But everybody's been avoiding me, thinking I'm off my head, not to be trusted. All my ex-colleagues. Julian thinks I'm mad…"

"But that's just the point. He doesn't. At least not any more," Phoebe blurted out.

"What – what do you mean?"

"Dad's email's a bit cryptic, because Dad always is. But it sounds as if he thinks something's up too."

"You're not serious?"

"Yes, I am. Look." She waited while Faye read.

"Good God."

"Do those names make sense to you?"

"And how! Oh, God…he says 'Faye might be right after all'…" Faye was in silent tears. "So he's seen for himself! Oh, Phoebe! Sorry. You don't know…you can't possibly know…what this means…"

"Shall I make us some more coffee?"

Faye nodded with compressed lips, unable to speak.

"All right. I'm ready." Faye was blowing her nose and seemed suddenly charged with confidence when Phoebe emerged with steaming mugs. "Thanks, Phoebe. You'd better make a note or two, hadn't you?" Phoebe took a pad and pen from her bag. "Okay. First thing, you'll need to stress to Julian that I emphatically and absolutely do not owe the de Benedetto woman any money at all. Corinna. She'll doubtless try to persuade Julian that I do, and she'll be all over him if she knows there's a cheque in his pocket. I hope Julian isn't feeling susceptible. She'll lay it on with a trowel, big sympathetic eyes and a lot of leg. They're quite good legs, too. That's how she operates."

"Blimey! But why should she?"

"After Hilary died, she offered to help. In fact, she was sweetness itself to begin with, couldn't do enough. Helped me with the lawyers – poor Hilary didn't leave a will – and her Italian's a thousand times better than mine, and she knows everybody, and in Italy the whole inheritance thing is a hell of a process. I was pathetically grateful for any help I could get, and she was a real friend in need. Or so I thought. She offered to help me sell the house. She does this finding service for people – you know, when agents don't speak English but want to reach a foreign market? She liaises between agent and client, and takes a finding fee. Nothing official. Well, she had one of her pet agents look at the place, and he was all ready with his contract and the dotted line. But I insisted on a multiple agency deal – they don't like that – they want the bigger percentage, of course, but the place was a building site, Phoebe. Almost impossible to sell unless someone wanted a very large and expensive project. Hil and I had rather overstretched ourselves, but we planned to do it all very slowly. When he died so suddenly, I had this enormous white elephant, the – the dregs of a dream. And debts over my ears, builders, engineers, everyone. I wanted to put it with as many agents as possible, advertise it on the internet, Ebay, everything. I thought in the circumstances, this would have made perfect sense to her, but no. She sort of went strange on me, and was obviously pissed off that I'd decided to think for myself. In effect, I was doing her out of her cut. There's a phrase in Italian – *un pollo da spennare* – it means a chicken to pluck, literally. She saw a main chance and leapt at it. Now I expect she'll try to persuade Julian that her efforts should be rewarded."

"God…Well, Dad's pretty charm-proof, anyway…I *think*." Phoebe had visions of her father in the clutches of a seasoned seductress, and realised she knew absolutely nothing of his private life. The thought made her feel a little uncomfortable. "She does sounds pretty vile."

"Oh, it gets worse. Her very dopey daughter is engaged to the son of a local undertaker. I didn't have a clue about these things, and Corinna offered to bring in the mortician boyfriend's papa once the authorities released the body. I think she probably took ten percent there too, for poor Hilary's corpse. I'm not making this up. This is what her detractors said, and now I believe them. But they all say vile things about each other. They're pretty septic."

"How horrible. And – well, hurtful. Someone pretending to be a friend."

"Oh, they're all like that. They rip each other apart when they haven't anything better to do, but they close ranks the minute the hard core feels threatened. Acceptable newcomers get the 'treatment'. We did. Hil was grand enough for them to want

325

to lionise him and Hil rather liked playing the lion. I expect Julian's been getting it. They'll be all over him now, asking him about working with Simon Rattle and Howard Goodall. They're the most frightful snobs."

"God, poor Dad! He'll really hate that. He's really very shy in a funny way. What about this quarrel at the party? What was all that about?"

"The quarrel! That was the night he died... It was stupid but inevitable. Hil had just trashed the Albergo in his piece in *The Bystander* and naturally the Barkers, the owners, weren't very pleased. That evening there was a great big showdown. It was one of Daphne's regular get-togethers – she's the local queen bee hostess, very fond of Hil once – but she leapt to the Barkers' defence with everyone else, apparently. I wasn't there. I was on a field trip in Florence with a gang of young Americans. I – I arrived home next morning to find the lifeboat there, fishing him out of the water...the ambulance waiting..." She felt as well as heard the break in her voice, and stared ahead bleakly, willing herself not to cry. Phoebe kept very silent, staring at the floor. Poor Uncle Hil! And poor, poor Faye...

"Why had he trashed the Albergo, Faye?" she asked eventually.

"Sorry. Oh dear. I call them 'daymares'. It's all so horribly *vivid*. Worse now they've reduced my dose, but the only way I can get normal..." Faye gulped. "The Albergo. We'd had some friends staying there who hated it – shabby, overpriced and

326

Dennis Barker was rude to them, and they refused to pay the bill and Hil went and recorded it all for posterity. Not very tactful."

"The Albergo Del Mare? I think Dad's staying there."

"He probably is. It's the only proper hotel in town. Dennis Barker's a thug. A barbarian. His wife's not much better – shrill, spiteful, two-faced. But I can understand why they were annoyed. I *told* Hil he shouldn't write that piece. I heard all about the row – nobody could resist telling me all about it. Hil shouted a lot, apparently, and so did Barker, and everybody else joined in and then Hil left in a temper and apparently went home, and afterwards – well, it was rather revolting, nearly everybody trying to make out he was drunk enough for anything. He got drunker and drunker with each telling, if you see what I mean – everyone trying to convince me it was inevitable, that he was raving, that he could hardly stand, and implying that if he had been stupid enough to go swimming, and got into some sort of trouble, it would have been all his own fault. They'll be telling Julian that too – how crazy I am, poor paranoid Faye, demented with grief and claiming impossible, groundless things, and damned ungrateful to boot, I expect. But I *knew* something was wrong. The more I tried to find out, the more I just kept hitting brick walls. I began to feel very mad indeed – as if I probably *was* imagining it all."

"Imagining…but what, Faye? Tell me, if you can."

"I'll try. All I know, really, is that Hil just wouldn't have drowned like they said. Oh, I know what the inquest found, but it

327

just can't have been like that. It didn't make sense. Hil was a seriously good swimmer. It was a calm night, that night. A storm whipped up a bit later, but not until about four in the morning. I checked again and again, after, on the weather forecasts. And Hil knew our bit of the bay like he knew my fanny. That's what he used to say. Sorry. We had these private jokes…sorry. Very inappropriate."

"No…I think that's rather lovely…" Phoebe coloured a little and grinned.

"Honestly, Phoebe – you've never seen it, but our bit of water was a millpond most of the time. That's why he loved it so…my poor darling. I was never very brave about water…I hate the sea, now. It was such a blessed relief to leave the sound of water lapping against rocks, come inland…"

"Faye…Oh dear. I truly don't want to distress you."

"I'm all right, honestly…"

"So, go on, Faye. He knew the bay, and he swam in it often. Did he use to swim at night?"

"Often, in the summer and later, when the water was still warm. The real danger was jelly-fish. We both got stung, but you can see them better at night, actually. They get illuminated by the moon, and phosphorescence…"

"So this was normal. Okay. What happened? He walked home from the party, which was in town? Okay. Then he took a swim in warm, calm water that he knew well, and was found drowned the next morning…I agree it would be pretty unlikely, unless…Faye, look, Faye, there was a lot of alcohol in his system according to the – the tests they made, Dad said…and we both know that Hil could get a bit, well…sorry, I just mean accidents can happen. He could have lost consciousness in the water or something, couldn't he? I'm so sorry. This must be so awful for you."

"Don't be sorry! Hil was – let's face it – a famous piss-artist. Ask your father! But I believe he would have had to be virtually comatose to have drowned, yet he's supposed to have walked a kilometre or so home. They can't have it both ways. But nobody really bothered to investigate a death by drowning when the corpse involved had returned from a party where everyone could testify he was the worse for wear. His – his injuries were all consistent with someone being battered against rocks by heavy cross-currents. And yes, of course it's just possible that he drifted about until the storm got up and he got into difficulties…That's the inquest's finding. That's what happened, officially. Hil's death was an accident. He drowned. All very sad, all very likely, and all too bloody damned convenient." Faye glared and reminded Phoebe very much of the schoolmistress who had taken her to task for a sloppy essay. "Those rocks are notorious, of course. They call them the Dogs' Teeth – the 'Denti Dei Cani' – they were our local hazard to shipping, seriously dangerous to a boat. But they are nearly half a kilometre out. If he swam more or less at the time he was supposed to have got home, he'd have missed the storm by three hours or more. He'd just have had a dip and kept close to the shore. Then he'd have climbed out of the water, collected his clothes and his watch and keys and gone up to the house to bed. And that's another thing. The thing that convinced me, really. When they – they found him, he was wearing his shorts. His boxers. I mean, if he'd just gone swimming, in private, he'd have taken them off. He hated putting dry trousers on over wet pants so he took them off...does that sound ridiculous?"

"No...no it doesn't..." Phoebe frowned, jotting notes. "What do you think happened?"

"I've thought and thought about this. He can't have been killed, because he drowned and that means he was breathing, right? So I thought, I still think, that he was badly beaten up on the way home – that would account for the time. I suppose he could have come to, and gone home and swam, probably not realising he was injured. He might have been drunk enough to do that. Alcohol's a great painkiller. Either that, or someone was lying in wait for him close to the house, beat him up, undressed him and chucked him in the water...to look like an accident..."

"Jesus...but who? And *why*?"

"I don't know who, but I wonder if *they* do. The Daphne crew. Some involvement they wouldn't want made public. When I suggested he was – well – mugged or something, they all began to tell me I was being ridiculous. That's what really made me think they must know something, otherwise why not just agree it was possible? There had been burglaries, and there were some

330

gypsies, Albanians, camped out in the hills, begging in the local towns and stealing. The *Comune* wanted to get rid of them, but they were convenient, if you see what I mean. Scapegoats. So why not just at least agree with me that it could have happened like that? It was weird…"

"Yes. Yes, I guess it is. You'd think that if they knew, they'd want to shift the blame onto someone sort of anonymous."

"They're not really very bright. And they might have been scared, worried I was going to stir something up. They probably thought I knew far more than I did. I can only guess that Hil had been working on something dangerous. That's obviously occurred to Julian, too. He says 'what was Hil working on?' He never stopped being a journalist, you see, Phoebe. I don't mean just some retired hack blogging about tourism. I think it's possible he'd discovered something about someone that was potentially very damaging. I had no idea what it was, he was cagey, even with me. But I think he might have been less cagey with Giacomo – I think Jaco might have told him things – things he might have regretted or at least realised were unsafe to pass on…"

"Jaco being this Mr Innocenti? Sorry, I probably haven't pronounced him properly."

"Giacomo Innocenti. Hilary's friend. Our architect. Nice man. Decent. And we do owe him money. Several thousands. Julian's got his bill. It sounds as if the poor man is about to be paid. Giacomo loved Hil to bits. He went to identify his body.

They said – they said – it was – he was – in a dreadful state. Too bad for me to see. Oh God, sorry. I'll be okay in a moment or two..."

Phoebe looked at the other woman helplessly, not quite daring to touch her. "Oh, Faye, this is awful. I'm so sorry. We can stop..."

"No!" Faye blew her nose. "I have to go on now. Giacomo is one of the good guys, basically. *He* cried, he was in tears when he came out of the mortuary. He was Hil's closest friend nearby. They played chess together and Hil taught him backgammon. They used to sit out on our half-built terrace staring at the sea and get sloshed on red wine and talk about the philosophy of architecture. Jaco's a free spirit, intellectual, bit of an old hippie...almost unworldly. Very unlike the usual locals. Nice person. So kind to me...He's off to Africa soon on some third-world project..."

"So you trust him, this Inno – "

"Innocenti. Yes, I do."

"But you think he knows something – well, concrete."

"Yes. I think he must. When I confided my doubts to him, I expected him to tell me not to be so silly just like everyone else had..."

"But he didn't?"

"No. Not exactly. But he told me to shut up in so many words. He asked me if I had Hilary's notes, and if so to hide or preferably burn them. I didn't have any notes as such, Hil didn't

332

keep notes on paper. His pocket diary was just dates, meetings and things. I just had his laptop. He also told me to go home. He meant England. It was as if – well, as if he thought I'd be *safer*…"

"God…"

Faye swallowed coffee. "I couldn't just leave. I had a job and a house to sell. I locked up the laptop in Hil's desk and kept the key with me. I arranged to stay with a colleague and I was going to hide the laptop in the school safe. Someone – someone beat me to it. About a month after Hil died, while I was trying to sort everything, put the personal stuff into store, all that, the house was raided while I was at work. They mostly just took the telly, the sound-system and the microwave…but drawers had been turned out, cupboards emptied. They – they'd smashed drawers in Hil's desk…The laptop had gone. And his digital camera. It was pretty dreadful. Everybody blamed the Albanians for that, but they caught some locals who had been doing the rounds. One of them had been one of our builders, a casual labourer. It looked straightforward, just local opportunist jobs on empty houses, looking for stuff they could sell on, that kind of thing…but I can't help thinking someone was looking for something specific. I was a bit of a zombie by then…after everything else, this was almost not important…just a drag, all the police reports…"

"Oh, God! Poor, poor Faye…do you know what was on the laptop?"

"No. Hil hid all the real stuff under a battery of codes. And to be honest, I wasn't looking. After that raid, I took Giacomo seriously. Maybe, now he's going to Africa, Jaco will say what he knows. I think it must have been political. Perhaps not local at all. Perhaps he'll tell Julian. It's – it's so comforting to know Julian doesn't think I'm completely doo-lally, Phoebe."

"Yes." Phoebe shook her head. "God…it all sounds almost unbelievable… But look, good old Dad! He wouldn't have asked if he wasn't fairly certain. I mean it takes Dad ages to sort of wake up to things that aren't just in his own tiny orchestra world, but once he's convinced, well – I'm sure he'll do all in his power to help, if he can. He's not a complete wuss, my Dad, and he's not stupid either, really."

"No, I know. And I'm incredibly grateful. But, hell, look, tell Julian to take care, for God's sake…" Faye suddenly looked alarmed.

"Oh, Dad'll be okay."

"I hope so, Phoebe…"

"Jesus – oh, help, you mean?"

"Well…dear God, if I'm right, Phoebe, then Julian might be in terrible danger too.

xxiii: Idylls

On the loggia of the east wing of the first floor of the house that Hilary built, three people stood looking out to sea. The little pergola roof provided some shade from the blazing sunlight, but vines were brittle white skeletons, and lemons in vases were twisted brown wisps of cracking stems and fruit shrivelled to the size of puny walnuts. Paint on a once pretty iron table was blistered, lifting, showing raw red rusty weals. Three forlorn canvas chairs rotted in a corner. Veronica was relieved to see that Freddy and Julian – and how completely different they were! – appeared to be getting on, although Julian was understandably abstracted.

"It's amazing!" declared Freddy. "Absolutely bloody amazing...and sort of fantastical, like that guy whatsisname, all arches and stairs..."

"Escher?"

"No – much earlier. Eighteenth century. Piranesi, I think...anyway, it is a bit Escher-ish, I agree. Perhaps Piranesi influenced him. Are they original? The arches and loggias and things?"

"I don't know. It's the first time I've seen it. I'm meeting the guy who designed the renovations tomorrow. He'll tell me, no doubt." Julian was very glad to be outside once more. The interior was a vast series of connecting rooms, built on two-thirds

335

of a square, Arab fashion, and completely empty. Half of it was a building site still, with bare plaster walls and plumbing installed waiting for sinks, bath-tubs, showers and lavatories. Builders' rubble in a several tidy heaps. Cement bags full of broken tiles. The portion where Hilary and Faye had so briefly dwelt was now a place so utterly uninhabited, so eerily cold, that when he had tried to imagine Hilary and Faye here, their belongings, a bed in what had been obviously a bedroom, Hil's piano in the enormous sitting room, a fire in the pale marble grate in winter, pictures on the walls, a kitchen busy with cooking, the spicy aromas of food, friends chatting and quaffing wine round a table, he had failed utterly. As the trio trooped round the house, their feet had echoed in the high, empty spaces, and their voices had been reduced to whispers. The place had an air of utter desertion. No ghosts. Only an odour of damp despite the heat outside. Evidence of rats, and festoons of cobwebs. A large black scorpion had scuttled into a wainscot. Absently, Julian had picked up a ball of paper in the corner of a *mezzanine* room that might have been Hilary's office, and stuffed it in his pocket. Now they all stared down at the little shingle beach, at calm sparkling waters and at the savage teeth of the rocks where Hilary had died. In the distance a large ferry moved majestically across the horizon. Julian felt himself shiver in the heat.

"Great view – shame about what passes for social life across the water," said Freddy, and Julian, grateful to him, laughed. "That lot must have exasperated your brother."

"I don't think he cared much. He just loved being near the sea. And it's handy for Rome. They had some real friends there. His wife taught in San Gregorio. I take it this wouldn't be your – um – cup of tea?"

"Me? No fear! I get London-sick after about three weeks. I'm a fleshpots man. It's a dream, but not mine. Besides, it's the sort of thing you wouldn't do – take on – on your own, is it? I can see why Mrs Hilary might have felt lonely, after..."

"Yes...Shall we go down?" Julian glanced at Veronica, who had been very silent, and now, looking at her face, he thought she was near to tears.

On the beach, Veronica hung back, her sandals sinking uncomfortably into tiny pebbles, while Julian took off his loafers and rolled up his trousers. His thin calves were too white. Veronica looked away. "I'm sorry," he said. "I sort of must do this. Won't be long." Barefoot, he scrunched his way gingerly to the water.

"Sweet of him to invite us on his pilgrimage," commented Freddy, picking up a stone and hurling it with surprising force into the water where it landed with a small splash. "He's rather a honey, my dear. Congratulations."

"*Freddy...*"

"Sorry, dear heart. Previous." They watched Julian wade into the sea, his hands in his trouser pockets, and his linen jacket flapping. Veronica decided she liked his shoulders.

337

Freddy remarked, "Lovely house. Potentially. God, this is what we're all supposed to want, isn't it? The place in the sunshine, a climate that isn't British, an interesting history that isn't ours, not to mention cheap booze and food you can actually eat without having to spend a month's salary. But this is the Italian equivalent of living in Dorking or Surbiton."

"Surbiton on Sea, Freddy?"

"Frinton then. You know perfectly well what I mean."

"I'm not disagreeing with you." Julian was strolling towards them with his shoes in his good hand. Veronica noticed that his wrist seemed to be paining him less.

They wandered back to the house where Julian locked up carefully. He posted the keys in the box at the gate. "Not ours anymore, Hil," he murmured.

"Another ticked box?" Veronica said, and he nodded. "New owners taking possession as of Monday." They piled into Veronica's car, and Freddy gave directions to their lunch venue, a large cantina on a chuckling river in a mountain valley.

"This looks rather fun, sort of authentic…" Julian said as Freddy, being hugged and kissed by the large proprietor and his tiny smiling wife, introduced his guests, and they were seated with due ceremony. "Thanks for coming," he murmured to Veronica.

"Not a bit. I'm glad you didn't think we were – you know – *de trop*…"

338

Over a taster menu that involved a great many tiny courses and a different wine with each one, Freddy began by holding forth knowledgably on the subject of wine production, and Veronica tactfully drank water after the second glass.

"Here's to the tourist trade! May it forever keep me from starvation," said Freddy, raising his third. "God, sometimes I feel like a sort of whore-master..."

"Freddy! What on earth are you talking about?"

"Italy. Tourists. I'm not entirely joking. Take this place. I'm about to write it up, sell it. It's delightful, and authentic, as Julian observes, but people will come and turn it toxic. It's happened everywhere. Turned innocent locals into tourist prostitutes! Pizza at lunchtime! Pizza everywhere, not just in Naples and the south. It's depressing. The locals end up doing the jolly Italian bit whether they like it or not, poor buggers."

Julian laughed. "I don't see any pizza on the menu here." He wiped oily fingers.

"You do sound bitter, Freddy," said Veronica. "I'm not sure it's entirely fair, either. Places like this would scarcely keep going without the foreign interest. Most of central Italy relies on posh discerning diners and drinkers from abroad, surely...and exports. You turn interested Londoners onto this place, and they welcome you gladly for just that. Waitrose or something will buy the wine. It's simple economics from the local point of view, I'd have thought. I'd be interested to hear *their* comments about toxicity..."

"Always Mrs Contrary. But it's far too late! The regional identities have been airbrushed into tourist-guide post-Unification 'Italy' which almost no local takes seriously except to put on a circus for the grockles. Ask them! Sorry, darlings. Still getting the taste of Venice out of my mouth…"

"Oh balls, Freddy! The regions are alive and well. And I'd have thought you're doing your bit to put them into focus…"

"Perhaps nobody dares ask them," said Julian seriously. "I mean, about what they really think of us. Foreigners. They probably despise us all really. If they were to tell the truth."

Freddy said, "Which they wouldn't, because they're too polite, except in Venice, of course, where there's a palpable and *very* cynical resentment. Mostly, I think it's the reverse. We despise the Wops and sentimentalise them at the same time. As a race, the Italians in general are fairly forgiving and pragmatic, which doesn't stop them taking the odd foreigner for a mug occasionally as a kind of pay-back. Overpriced tourist menus, and so on. House prices that suddenly shoot up at the hint of an American accent. It's part of the deal… Ah! here's the next delicious morsel! *Pasta con ciliegini* and *fiori dei zucchini* with home-made ricotta…and now we have their special *bianco* to accompany it. You'll find this a bit like an Orvieto wine, Julian. Should be light as silk. Cheers! *Grazie, piccolo…*" The waiter, the son, a dark haired youth of sixteen with a ruddy, sunburnt face and bright brown eyes, gave them a blushing grin and departed.

340

"It's delicious!"

"Julian is curious about your Monty chums, Freddy," Veronica prompted.

"They're not *mine*! Blame Uncle Cadwallader, Julian. He seems to enjoy them, but then he would. He's nicer than they are, but not much. Life here is one big cop-out. Abroad, without really moving out of one's own sphere."

"Quite a lot like being in a touring orchestra," Julian said, munching.

"You tell me. But at least that's work. I mean, these people, they don't *do* anything. They're tourists who stayed. They gravitate to a place like Monty and find other people who have done the same and form a sort of elite club. People, mark you, with nothing much in common besides a mutual displacement and a common language, but they become bosom buddies on the strength of it, all ganging up together. The silly thing is, they'd hate each other to pieces if they were neighbours in dear old Blighty."

"You sound like Hil. My brother..."

"He was right, dear! Now, *they're* in the despising business! Darling Daphne's crowd despises everybody who isn't *them*. And then some. It's pure hypocrisy. Take those snazzy Americans, Lorrie and Cy, whom they all pretend to court, and then slag off behind their backs because they're a) gay, b) Yanks, and c) richer and more successful than they are. It's true! And let's face it, most of them are in the thrall of a rich old woman who can only buy the loyalty of her friends and more or less insists on a roll call for the vinegar plonk and fish paste-sandwich orgy every Saturday…But I love her!"

"You're the hypocrite, Freddy, darling. *And* you go on Saturdays! They all adore him, Julian. Take no notice."

"I'll be entirely frank. I absolutely can't resist. Every week a new row, a new scandal, a new bitch-fest. It's as good as a bad soap. But I'm a migratory bird. I can go back to London after my Monty fix whenever I like. I can't take any of that lot remotely seriously."

"I'm – um – not sure whether to take them seriously nor not…" Folded in the breast pocket of Julian's jacket was an email from Phoebe. He took another mouthful. "Oh, this *is* good. Zucchini flowers in ricotta and cherry tomatoes, did you say? It's amazing! My daughter turned me on to these flowers not long ago. In Bath last week, believe it or not. I feel as if I've been here forever. "

"So who've you met so far?" asked Freddy.

"I've met Mrs Allerton and – er – one or two of her friends. And the Barkers, of course."

"Oh dearie me, the Barkers! You'll never *guess* what someone told me recently. Apparently, they've been seeing some sort of marriage-guidance counsellor. It's true! When they were back in London last. Thing is, Mrs B don't care for it much, take it or leave it, and who can blame her? But Mr B – well he's like a rutting hippopotamus most of the time. So I'm told. But he's got his mother-in-law to think of not to mention his daughter, and in Monty everyone knows before you've even so much as tugged at your zipper, and he's not very spoilt for choice, let's face it…"

"Freddy…"

"Ooh, it gets better, darling. Apparently, this counsellor – *they* don't bear thinking about do they, when you think of what their qualifications must consist of – this counsellor suggested – at great expense, I imagine – that the pair of them get a bit – *enterprising* in the bedroom. As it were…"

"Freddy!"

"So the female Barker allows the male Barker to smother her nether regions in chocolate ice-cream – he's got a little weakness in that direction, too, I'm told, and…"

"Honestly, Freddy! We're eating!" But Veronica saw that Julian was convulsed in mirth.

"Now who's being suburban, lovey? But sorry, chocolate is a bit previous with the pasta…"

"It's very difficult to imagine…my God…" Julian looked at Veronica with twinkling, apologetic eyes. "Sorry. It really is quite funny… Do you think it's Haagen-Dasz, or Ben & Jerry, or some home-grown recipe?"

"Oh, the last without doubt. The gelateria on the Piazza has won awards."

Julian spluttered. "Perhaps they could get – you know, a whats'name – an endorsement. Quotes from satisfied customers…"

"Men are just absolutely all the same!" Suddenly Veronica was in helpless giggles too. "Regardless! And I wonder who has to do the laundry…"

"Thank the gods for the gift of laughter, eh?" Freddy's voice had an edge. Impulsively, Veronica patted his sleeve. For some reason she was very pleased that Julian was enjoying himself.

Julian cleared his plate. "So…we have the sexually enterprising Barkers – I'm never going to be able to look at them in the face now, you realise…but how do they fit in?"

"Fit in? Ah, I see what you mean. For that we have to thank the redoubtable Daphne. She has a rather *unsuburban* attitude to people in general, in fact. She's an elitist, but she's not precisely a snob. In fact I really am almost fond of her, but she lets some very silly sentiment get in the way of her better judgement. The Barkers look after her, and she sponsors them. Calls the unbeautiful Den her adopted nephew and doesn't seem to be able to acknowledge the man is a serious bruiser. He's an ex-pub landlord with previous from Stepney. Had an uncle who knew the Krays. His rapacious wife is half Italian, with a speaking voice that could shatter Perspex, but she's supposed to have a heart of gold. Her aging mother who used to sit on the desk but is now almost housebound with bad legs and diabetes and is probably a lot less batty than she pretends. They've quite a sweet daughter studying veterinary medicine, but I don't fancy her chances with that gene-pool, do you? Let's see. Who else have we got? A lapsed actor who still thinks he's the schoolmaster he played in the seventies. Going blind, poor man, so he relies on his wife, a failed Roman fashionista keeping up appearances with a pallet-knife. Read Art History in Florence in the 60s. Leftie sympathies, and pretends to be intellectual. Difficult to pin down, but rather fun. And then we've got the greedy aging beauty up to her diamond-studded ears in the property business and pretending to be a nurse...Met her yet, Julian? Mrs de Benedetto. The fair Corinna. I'd watch it there, if I were you, dear. Rapacious in every direction, I'd say. Family that makes the Borgias look like the Waltons...Ah! Here's the lovely *faraone*...and their own very superior vino rosso. And a 98, by *God*!" said Freddy, not entirely irreverently. "We're being seriously honoured." The young waiter placed the new course before them: roast slices of guinea-fowl in wine and red-currants, and his father poured wine with a flourish. "*Ottimo*!" cried Freddy, sipping. "*Un vino da Paradiso, Beppe, amico mio*!" The plump man beamed and explained some details to Freddy who scrawled some careful notes.

"Oh dear, it's impossible not to feel completely epicurean with all this, is it?" said Julian to Veronica. After a few silent mouthfuls, he said, "Freddy, did you say *pretends* to be nurse? This Corinna? I – um – I met her a couple of nights ago. She told me she'd been a hospital sister in Oxford."

"Sister-schmister. Her story changes with whoever's listening. I've always gathered she got swept off her feet by the

Italian lawyer in her first year of training at the age of nineteen. He's well rid of her! They've got two daughters: a pretty one on a career path in television in Rome, and a disastrous dopey one who breeds pugs and is about to join an undertaker in holy matrimony. Eugh! Imagine where *their* hands have been all day! But our Corinna likes being the one with the hypodermic and the latin terminology. Likes rich old folks with deep pockets and painful feet…seems to float on endless charity. Did she try to *vamp* you, my dear?"

"A bit…" Julian glanced at Veronica, who pulled a face. "Mostly, she just tried to extract money from my late brother's estate."

"Well, dearie, I hope you gave her the elbow. She's totel sham. An operator. She's after Uncle Cad's fortune, such as it is. But then, poor old Cad seems terribly anxious to give it all away…I met that loony Irish bankrupt antique dealer outside the Medici Gate yesterday morning, did I tell you, Vee? *She's* vying with the Fair Corinna for the attentions of Uncle Cad, did you know? He's a sitting duck. He only wants a spot of adventure in the departure lounge…*Si, si, complimenti, Beppe…salutami Glorana! Un' miracolo*! Do we want some sort of pud after this? They do this rather splendid lemon thing with soft pecorino. Gloriana invented it. Where was I?"

"The Monty Crew, Freddy…Oh, God, just a tiny sliver of cheese for me, if they've got it…" Beppe was hovering expectantly.

"Well I'm going for the lemon thing," said Julian. "Why not?"

"It's got cheese *in* it, Vee…and it's special."

"Oh dear…I suppose I must, then, mustn't I? Okay!"

Freddy gave the order.

"Do they – did they – ever talk about Hilary?"

"Oh yes. He crops up sometimes in conversation. Old Daffy gets sentimental. Cad rather adored them both. Everybody seems to have a fond word, except for Dennis Barker, who wasn't a fan, I gather. But then he hates me to pieces too. Chippy sort. I've got the wrong accent and the wrong attitudes. And I'm not too careful to hide the fact that I'm both gay and a diluted Jew…"

When Freddy's face fell out of its customary good-humoured life and soul grin, he could look comically melancholic. Perhaps, Veronica thought, Freddy's natural comic bent, his capacity for self-parody, was his secret tragedy.

Gloriana, still wearing an apron, a tiny woman with richly hennaed hair and as thin as her husband was plump, brought in the dessert in person, and some moments were taken up with sampling and compliments. The son, Niccolò, produced a liqueur of a delicate green in a decanter and three small glasses.

"Oh, go on, then," Veronica said. "Just a sip if you're really forcing me…"

"Attagirl! You sort of have to. They make it themselves from bay-leaves. I can walk in front of the car with a flag." They ate lemon pudding accompanied by the strange and rather wonderful bitter-sweet liqueur, and raised glasses solemnly.

"Thank you," said Julian with shining eyes. "Thank you both. I shan't forget today."

They clinked glasses. When Julian's eyes met hers, Veronica's smiled and dropped.

"A success," murmured Freddy.

"I understand it now," said Julian suddenly, waving a forkful of lemon pudding (and Veronica realised he was more than a little drunk) "and the thing is this. Everyone's so ashamed of being middle-class in England. Here, you can be as snobbish and as right-wing as you like, and find fellow-travellers even if you hate them personally. Better than having to apologise, and feel guilty. The – the economics of the place still mean you can live like a sort of gent, even if you're relatively broke. I mean, look at us, lemons, wine, tomatoes, game birds, it's the fat of the land...No thought-police, because no one understands what they're really saying. I can see why they do it...they can get away with it here. I mean can't they?"

"Quite," said Freddy, pulling a face. "Imagine a nice pastoral salad into which someone has drizzled a little napalm..."

xxiv: Ave atque vale

"Thank you, Freddy, darling," said Veronica later outside the Albergo. "I've had a lovely, lovely time. And it was so kind of you to be nice to my new friend. It did him good, I think…"

"Anything to oblige, lovey. I like him."

"Good. It's really not what you think."

"Bet you sixpence. Look – Vee – I was actually being serious. Before Venice. I wish you wouldn't go public with Aunt Milly."

"Oh, Freddy. I've promised I'll speak to Jane. But you know, I'm not sure I can stop it. Anybody – I mean any competent literary critic – is bound to reach the same conclusion I have, with or without the 'Staircase' notes. There are too many similarities of style. The musician motif. And those heroines in the Flora books who all have the initials 'MF'. It's not really a secret, you see, because Millicent left so many clues. This notebook just confirms what anyone could deduce…honestly, Freddy."

"So you're just going to hand over the – the leads and so on – to this Alison Whatsername, I suppose? I can't read her. All that cryptic moral philosophy…"

"I haven't decided. I can't *not* talk to her. In a way I've got the other half of her research. She is bound to pick up on it anyway, I'd have thought. If I don't say anything, or if I refuse to share what I know, I'm going to look at best like a complete wally, a dimwit, or worse, as if I'm being dog-in-the-manger about stuff that isn't *mine*. This is a – well, a professional thing, Freddy. "

"Oh, great! That's just wonderful! And bloody typical of successful amateurs! All of a sudden, we're a professional with a conscience. Terrific!"

"Freddy – "

"No, no, dearie. Go ahead. Talk to your ghastly lezzie novelist, hand it all over. Hang out the family laundry as much as you like! You'll be used to that!"

"Freddy!"

"Bye, dear! I'm off to charm the pants off another oyster fisher. Don't fall into any ravines on the way to Siena…"

"You absolute bitch!" said Veronica, but Freddy had turned on his heel and gone.

Early the next morning, Julian Blyth once again borrowed the office at the Albergo and sent Phoebe a reply. A familiar voice in the lobby made him hurry out, and he found Veronica with her bag, signing a receipt, and being bade a fond farewell by Mrs Barker. He waved the surly Gianni away when he came to help with Veronica's luggage. At her car parked in the square, he said, "It's been – well, so very, very pleasant to meet you, Veronica. Thank you so much for everything."

"But I didn't do anything!"

"Yes you did. You took me seriously for a start. And I enjoyed meeting the marvellous Mr Partridge! No, honestly. It was fun. I do hope we meet again."

"Oh, I'm sure you will. He'll be around for another week or so, I expect." She was still feeling angry and rather hurt.

"I meant you and I...if you would like." He sounded diffident, as if embarrassed. "In London, perhaps. Now I've tracked this architect bloke down, I'll probably be heading back myself very soon."

"Yes, all right. That would be very nice." She realised she sounded embarrassed too. She made her voice bright. "Besides, I really want to know how you get on. Do tell me what happens. You have my email address."

"Yes..."

"Well, good hunting – and – um – take care, Julian. Look...sorry. It's not any of my business. I just think that this could be a bit, well, dangerous. I don't mean to dramatise...it's just that if people – I mean if anyone – has tried to cover something up, they won't welcome anyone nosing in. It might be better to leave it alone." He regarded her solemnly with his lopsided smile. "But you won't, will you?"

"I can't, my dear Veronica. Not yet. But thank you for your concern." Very impulsively, he kissed her cheek, and she kissed both of his, Italian fashion, and they hugged, close enough for him to snuff the faint scent of her hair, and for her to feel the sinewy strength of his arm under the light linen sleeve. They both pulled away very quickly.

Veronica waved as she negotiated the narrow exit through the ancient gateway.

Julian waved back, having decided to stroll down to the *edicola* and purchase a paper.

"Damn," Veronica thought. "Damn and damn!" As she began her journey north, she realised she had begun to care for him. A little.

The evening Veronica left, Freddy Partridge wandered morosely down the the waterfront, bought a *Financial Times* and sat with a cold beer, reading, ignoring the *passeggiata,* and noting with dismay that his shares had gone down again. Dark thoughts obtruded: the necessity, at this rate, of having to sell his new little Highbury apartment; his recent fight with Veronica, which had upset him more than he realised; a certain beautiful Venetian boy chef who had not texted…was he turning into a Von Aschenbach? Fifty-four was *old…*

Merry cries from the water made him look up, and his attention turned to the fishing boats, where bronzed and fit-looking young men in shorts and gym-shoes did deft and dangerous things with rigging and ropes, calling to each other in the rough sing-song of the local dialect. He stared idly at them and felt soothed. Boys tended to believe he was rich, but then, most of these Italian boys were happy with a shirt, a meal that knocked their socks off, a donation to the *mammina*... Here in Monte Farfalla, however, Freddy had learned to operate with tact and discretion: he was almost welcomed as a *cumparo*. One cannot go picking up the neighbours...

Some of the boats were preparing to go out for a night's catch. Further up, at the 'posh' end of the marina, there were wooden jetties for mooring yachts and pleasure-craft – those with tinkly masts, rolled sails which flapped in the breeze, and made mostly of fibreglass. Here, however, it was serious wood, diesel engines and the reek of fish tossed in petrochemicals: sturdy, gay little vessels painted red, blue and yellow; some with the watchful gaudy 'eye' painted on the side of the prow, some with names, others with numbers. Freddy watched as a broad, sturdy-looking yellow and white *gozzo* chugged slowly up to the side, manoeuvred expertly into position, cut engine, and was eased smoothly into harbour by fishers on other craft who caught thrown ropes and pulled. She had an 'eye', and she was called 'Serena' in faded lettering on her side. He recognized Enzo, Cadwallader's neighbour, and Enzo's temptingly pert son, Tommaso, the backs of whose thin brown knees looked especially, almost tenderly, delicious. With him was Gianni, the boy from the Albergo.

Enzo jumped ashore with accustomed agility, leaving the boys tying up. His legs were wiry, muscled in the way of older men – hard, jutting, almost sculpted – and very bronzed, except for a livid scar that ran from ankle to knee and into the thigh, disappearing under his cut-off denim shorts. An accident with some fishing equipment? It explained his habitual limp. "Frai-dy! *Cumpà!*" Enzo cried, spotting him. "I stop work, and we have drink, *si*? I need a beer!" His teeshirt was sweat-stained and his brick-coloured face glowed with heat and recent effort. He ran a rough brown paw through his grizzled crew-cut, and took Freddy's hand in a wince-making grip.

"Cheers, Enzo. Good catch?" Freddy inquired. Enzo was proud of his English and liked to speak it whenever he could. He had been a trumpeter in a band on transatlantic liners when he was young, and spoke a rather extraordinary mixture of Italian, his local dialect, American English, and a smattering of German.

"Not fishing today," Enzo said. "*Turisti. Inglese.*" Enzo slurped with thirsty gusto. "Trip round the Bay. They make many photos. All good stuff. They give tip, not so good as *Giapponese*. They come next week." He patted the back pocket of his shorts. "No longer I go fish much…this leg, it is pain. And la barca, La Serena – she not mine no more. She belong to grand Signora Daphne, and the Albergo use her. Signor Dennis. Small parties. See the sights."

"Ah, I thought I recognised *il ragazzo…*"

"Si. Gianni, *è chiama*. He a bit fright of the sea. *Il capo, il signor* Dennis, he make him go with tourist party, but he no like. He have trouble in family. He live with me and Mammina and Tommasino…"

"Oh. Somehow, I'd thought he lived at the Albergo…"

354

"No. Just work." Enzo drained his glass and wiped his mouth on the back of his brawny arm. "I for another. You? It is get hot tonight. No wind nowhere."

"I'm okay with this, thanks. Too much gas…you go ahead." Freddy burped discreetly. He was watching the boys scramble lithely ashore. " 'Masino, *mio! Viene ka!*" Enzo hailed his son. The boy, a cheerful-looking youngster with his father's impish grin, left a small crowd of other youths and wandered over, swigging coke from an open bottle, and Freddy tried not to stare too hard at golden, flawless skin, narrow feet in dirty plimsolls, the tempting gap, brown with a faint bloom of pale fur, between teeshirt and hipster shorts. He shook hands with Freddy. Gianni hung back, giving the merest acknowledgement, scarcely looking up under scowling brows. Father and son had a rapid conversation that Freddy could not follow, and the boys sped off in the direction of home with a bare nod at Freddy, who stared after the perfectly articulated young muscles, and shook himself.

"La Mammina, she make dinner. They hungry…"

"I'm sure." Freddy was once more immersed in the *FT*.

"He worry me some, *il piccolo* Gianni. *Troppo nervoso, capisce?* Since cousin in trouble with police. He think he in trouble too. He think man in hotel after bust his ass. I say him nonsense, he ain't done nothing, see? He all right with me, I divorce, but Mammina, she make home like always. *I Piccione.* All in prison, now…bad family. But I say, the angels, *Il Signore*,

355

he make us to be kind to everyone. *Siamo poveri cristiani, tutti, capisce?*"

"*Ho capito*, Enzo," said Freddy wearily. "You're one of the good guys…"

They wandered down the Lungomare together, Enzo for his mother's supper, Freddy for a troubled night, trying to push aside thoughts that would not leave him.

PART FOUR: SLEEPING DOGS, LYING

xxv: Innocenti

Giacomo Innocenti lived above the Marina Grande. Julian Blyth
stood on the tiny rooftop terrace and from behind thin iron
railings he gazed out at the little lighted fishing boats, at the
lights on the strip of Monte Farfalla's other 'wing' where the
crag of the ruined castle loomed, casting its deep shadow, and at
the lighthouse which batted its great eye with a soft insistent
flood. Julian found himself timing it. Someone had told him that
each lighthouse had its own unique rhythm, and that this was
how seafarers of old and from afar had known where in the
world they were. Beside him were the roofs of other houses, the
murmur of TV sets through open windows, the aromas of
garlicky cooking, people settling to their suppers, the odd wail of
a child, a woman's voice commanding a family to sit, eat, shut
up. Below, a little bar did vigorous business with beers and
snacks, and young men on scooters, helmetless, some with their
girls clinging on tightly behind in sparkly tops and high-heeled
boots, yelled and whooped and snaked round the bollards against
which a loose dog or two peed, slowing gracefully to avoid
groups of people walking, chattering; and now, the plaintive
jangle of a very bad accordionist touting for custom at the bar
with a medley of Napolitan tunes... Julian, of the actutely

357

sensitive musical ear, was amused rather than annoyed. Beyond, across the Bay, the twinkling lights of distant houses and, beyond those, the little clusters of mountain villages. Above him, the moon was waning, but only by a day or two, and stars, almost impossibly vivid, filled a clear indigo sky. An opal brooch in a spangled lace mantilla, thought Julian, normally the least poetic of men; and laughed at himself, wondering if Veronica had reached Siena, imagined her competently dealing with agents, imagined her as he had first seen her, slightly fierce, at an airport…

"This is all very desirable in these parts, yes?" said the small, thin, ascetic-looking man who reminded Julian a little of Mr Gandhi, with his shaven head, his white Indian shirt and his wire-rimmed spectacles. He had brought bottles of beer and tankards on a tray from the tiny kitchen below. A pretty tortoiseshell cat followed him, and purred against Julian's legs.

"Very. I like it. It's fun." How little he had expected his mission to Monte Farfalla to be 'fun'!

"Fun. Yet this is just us. How we live. I was born in this house. My mother died in it. In January."

"Oh. I – I'm so sorry."

"She was age ninety years. A good long life and then death. It's just life going on here, like always. Not the life of the foreigners, so the foreigners think us exotic. It is irony, my dear Julian. *Cin, cin*, my friend. You say you go to the house yesterday…"

"Yes. It's extraordinary. It would have been magnificent…
an idyll. Poor Hilary."

"It is very beautiful, of course. An idyll, as you say.
Everybody think so. Too many now. So everything is second
homes and holidays. And *turismo*. They search for the 'real
Italy', but the 'real Italy' is a myth, my friend. In places like this,
the real Italy is become a showcase for tourists only. Painted
pottery and lemons on tea-cloths…" Innocenti sighed. "I used to
build houses in Mozambique, proper sanitary buildings in
villages with poison water. I come back here only for my mother
when she is old and need me. Now she is dead. So, I am going
back. To Africa. I have this – compulsion – perhaps that is not
the right word. My English is very crude sometimes. But I have
the need to be useful in the world. I am sick with building the
houses of rich men …"

"But you re-built my brother's."

"My last project here. And unfinished, *magari*. But your
brother – he was not especially rich. I never expect to get this…"
Giacomo Innocenti indicated the cheque with a wry twist of his
mouth. "Thank you." He put it into a leather purse he wore on
his belt. "Your brother Hilary was a good friend to me. He was
probably a little bit crazy, but it was a craziness I like. He was a
dreamer, a man with visions. He saw a lovely place, a – *rovina* –
a ruin, you would say, a place with a wonderful view of sea and
mountains, and a certain – atmosphere, a place where someone
had abandoned a farm with no living. He saw living there again.

359

We dreamed it together…Now, these men from Rome they make holiday villa for rich Americans with spiritual pretensions and a thousand dollar a day…" Giacomo Innocenti made a spitting noise but did not actually spit. "You know, I would have buyed it. Bought it, I should say. I did not have the sufficient money."

"I know…I'm very sorry. It – it must've been a wrench – I mean, to have to give it up, stop it…it was a huge project, wonderful. But I really did have to sell it to these people. We – that is, I mean Faye – well, she couldn't afford not to. He – Hilary – he left a lot of debt. He owed money. Didn't expect to die, of course, poor guy."

"I know. I was very sorry, and for her. It grieved me very much when he died. I think, somehow, that this place was bad for him. Monte Farfalla. There is a bad atmosphere here too, as well as good…" The cat stretched itself over its master's sandaled feet.

"You mean the incomers? The English? Americans?"

"Not only. The Italians too. Money is corrupting for everyone, my friend. I hope you do not dislike cats." He picked up the little animal and stroked it before setting it firmly down. "She is called Mimi…an *orfanella*, a stray, like the girl in the work of Puccini."

"Mimi. No, I like cats." He sipped his beer.

On the rooftop veranda, with the scent of the sea, faintly fishy, faintly oily, the calm water lapping gently at the marina and the almost musical clangour of the soft breeze in the masts of the yachts beneath them, it was hard to imagine a 'bad atmosphere'. Across the water, their lights dotted about in the hills, were other houses, other idylls; owned, doubtless, by 'rich men', or by men with dreams. At least one was in darkness. Julian gazed at the fragile, treacherous silhouette of the Denti dei Cani in the moonlight. "He died just over there," he murmured.

"In waters too deep and dangerous, my friend. Those rocks are three parts submerged. He should not have swimmed in the dark. I warned him." Innocenti wore a small straggly moustache over a mobile, ironic mouth, that half hid crooked, discoloured teeth. He sipped beer delicately, and wiped the moustache with the back of his thin hand, and then carefully rolled a tiny cigarette from a pouch of tobacco. "When is your flight in England?" he asked, inhaling.

"Soon. I haven't booked it yet. There's …there's still something I have to do. Here."

"More business?"

"I suppose you could call it that. When is yours? To Africa?"

"The day after tomorrow."

"So little time. I'm glad to have this chance to talk to you about – about what really happened to my brother."

"I see…"

"Do you?"

"Yes. It is natural. I too should want to know…"

"So. What – what can you tell me, Giacomo?"

Innocenti spread his hands. The fingers were oddly spatulate, and on one of them was a large silver ring, ornately worked, rather beautiful. "I know…truly almost nothing. Hilary was my friend and I mourn his death. He was too young and too good to die, and I miss him. But death does not choose. That is the best I can say."

"You see, I made a promise. I told Hilary's wife, I told Faye, I would see and talk to Hilary's friends. I have talked to some of them. The ex-pat crowd. The friends of Daphne Allerton. They – they – how can I put it? They seem to have liked him, they *enjoyed* him – he was a born entertainer, Hilary. And they all tell me how sorry they are. But none of them – oh, God, it's so hard to explain – none of them is quite telling me the truth. I just sense it. Faye said so too. They all seem to be protecting – someone. Maybe each other. You – you know these people…"

"For a long time. But not at all well or intimately. They live here. They have their own life. They are friends just with each other, I think, and always only with jealousy. They are not significant people. Faye – she go half crazy with the grief. She imagine – crazy things, maybe."

"Or maybe not. Faye is an intelligent woman, Giacomo. She said you were probably his only real friend here."

"Friend, yes. But not a witness. I was not there."

"No. But you are *here*…and he talked to you."

Both men stared out over the dark winking waters for some moments. A girl shrieked with laughter from a scooter. The cat Mimi washed herself insouciantly.

"What do you think I can tell you?"

"I don't know. I just think you know more than I know."

"Some knowledge is bad, my friend. Hilary drowned. It was an accident. The *inchiesta* was satisfactory. He is in the cemetery. Nothing can call him back. Do not dig. Go."

"You sound – you sound as if you're warning me away. You warned Faye too."

"You must do what you have to. My advice, as it was to her, is go home."

"Home...? I suppose you mean England. I don't think of England as home particularly. Home's a bag and a violin case...this wrist is almost healed. I need to get back into practice. Play music again."

"The wandering minstrel. We are similar, Julian, in some respects. I was born here, but it is not my home, not in my heart. It was my mother's home. Neither is Mozambique my home, but it is where I can work and be contented. Perhaps that is all that any of us can ask of the world, yes? Move on to where we can work in peace."

"Yes...but I feel I won't – how can I put it? I won't have any peace until I *know*. I didn't come out here wanting to know. I just wanted to settle Hilary's affairs, sell his house, pay his debts, tidy his grave a bit and leave him to rest. You have to

363

believe me, Giacomo. I am the last person to – to trouble the waters…"

"In Italy, when we speak of making the waters dirty – muddy, is that not right? We mean keeping everything obscure from the authorities…confuse the system. Sometimes it is very necessary." Another pause. Out to sea, a small wooden boat, illuminated by a powerful lantern, chugged into view, little runnels of foam in its wake. It was giving the Denti dei Cani a wide berth.

"Calamari," explained Innocenti. "They are attracted to the light, like insects on the land. Is squids in English, yes?"

"Squid. No final 's'. Your English is extremely good, I may say. How come?"

"A big London *progetto*, a project, in Covent Garden in the eighties years when I was a student. And the programme in Africa is English-speaking. I make mistakes all the time."

"That would account for it. You don't make many. Giacomo – I have to ask you this. Do you truly believe Hilary died by accident?"

"What I think I hold to myself," Innocenti replied. "I cannot help him now. You will have another beer? Is better than wine on a hot night like this. Italian beer…is fine, eh?" He opened bottles and poured.

"Very." Julian coughed. "Giacomo, I am asking you to help me. I think Hilary must have discovered something – something that someone did not want revealed. I think he told you what it was. Or perhaps you told him. I think someone tried to get him to stop. I think they beat him, injured him. And as a result of those injuries, my brother died. I realise you might feel threatened by these people, whoever they are. I can only try to reassure you that I don't want to involve the law. As you say, I can't bring him back. I just need to know. It's personal. He was my brother. I think he was as good as killed... And I think that as you and I are both going away, you should tell me. I do realise that whatever it is, it might be dangerous. I don't wish to put either of us in peril. I – I'm not a brave man. Not like Hilary. He *was* pursuing something, wasn't he?"

Innocenti sighed impatiently, concentrating on another tiny cigarette he was rolling. "You have to understand..." He lit the cigarette. "...that it is not simply a question of bravery, my friend..." He inhaled deeply. "Hilary was brave, but he was also reckless up to the point of stupidity – *malgrado*, in spite – of he was so clever. As if he could not see the danger. I myself, I am not coward, but I am not stupid and reckless either." He stood up and paced along the little railings, staring out at the bay, at distant lights on the further shore, smoking, apparently in the grip of some internal argument. He turned, sighed again, resigned. "And of course, it is only right to say you what I know. It is not much. Hilary, he liked to believe himself as conquering David, but Goliath is still a giant..."

Julian shook his head and laughed softly. "No. Hil would never have seen himself as a David! No...if he was onto

365

something, it was sheer base curiosity, if I knew my brother. Hilary was no reformer. He'd have just got the bit between his teeth – I mean, persisted and ignored the danger. Brave and reckless, as you say. But he wouldn't have wanted to change the world. He would just have wanted to bring it to public attention with his name on the by-line. The investigating journalist! Poor old Hil."

Innocenti sat. "Listen, my friend. I make my mind up to tell you what I know. And I will give you something. And then I will tell you again to go away and not to pursue this thing. Nothing can be resolved until we have another government, and that is our business, Italian business. Go back on a plane to England, and I will go to Africa. We will both be still alive to do the things we have to do. This is for you alone, you understand?" He stared at Julian, his eyes dark and fierce, the wire-rimmed spectacles glinting.

"I understand. It will go no further, I give you my word. I'm no journalist, Giacomo."

"No. You are a musician. And you are a brother. And this rightfully belongs to you." He fished in the belt purse and produced a tiny object.

"A memory-stick…"

"Your brother gave this to me for safety a week before he died. It is his back-up for whatever thing he was writing."

"For safety? You mean *he* thought he was in danger?"

"I tried to warn him. We were over there at his house, drinking wine. He laughed. But he gave me this, laughing, as if it was a joke. It was typical. I have kept it close ever after…"

"Do you – I mean have you opened it? Read it?"

"No. I can only request that you do not look at it until you are far from here. And never to speak of this to any person at all."

"So you know what is on it. What it contains…"

"No I don't! I can only make guess." Innocenti sat down. "I tell you now. With Hilary I was angry a little bit. You have to understand that, because it is like you say. I understand that he did not want to change anything, he just had a story, something for the papers and something for his own curiosity. I care about this thing very much, but it is subtle, you understand? And it is not something that can be changed because one bad man is caught. It has to come from government. True reform in the law concerning corruption, the blind eye. This government, it encourages these bad things. I have friends, journalists, reformers, working on this. We are arriving, we may succeed, but if you like, we are David, and the present government is Goliath. Or I should say, it is Mammon. People are too comfortable, but less so now, and so I have confidence that we will win. In the end. This history is very, very long, my friend, and it began long in the past with understandable motives, for survival. At no time has the state government been trusted, not since the Unification. So people in a small *comune* like this one

367

continue as they always have, the way they outwitted the big landowners long time past. They make laws for themselves, and avoid taxes that are squandered on stupid pointless things by the government, broken promises... People feel like *adulti*, in control. But because we are fallible humanity, we cannot resist the big chance, or the little chance for greed, and the desire for control it is everywhere. There is here, like almost everywhere in Italy, a – a societal cancer. It is like a disease, and in the south, it is worst. It was so very poor, so recent. You can understand a little, perhaps."

"Yes. I think so. I'm beginning to. My God...do you mean the Mafia, the Mob?" Even phrasing the question sounded absurd.

"Not locally no. Something much more little, how would you say? Petty. But it is still wrong. Big businesses, suppliers, they charge the small ones a *pizzo,* a sum of money, every month, not to get hurt, or only to favour them, or get materials cheap, and not record the sales to avoid the tax. It is corrupt. It is not fair and it is founded in violence because everyone compete, but it is – how can we say – endemic. Everywhere. Impossible to fight it on the ground." Innocenti spread his eloquent hands. He sipped more beer and went on: "But higher up there is a much more ferocious network established. Hilary, he knew this well because he had been a news reporter in Roma and Napoli. Then he come here, to retire, to write about holidays and renovating houses for his British reading public. But he has a nose for this

368

thing…and so I say him how it is. We speaked of many, many things. We play the backgammon game when Faye is with her students, or she cooks while we have the game, English food which I like, and we drink my grandfather's wine or Hilary opens a bottle of whiskey – and we simply talk. And me, I am lonely for intelligent conversation. Perhaps I say too much. It is not always easy for me! It is, in some way, a relief to speak these things. Often, I think I betray myself. My work involves the blind eyes. But I have to live, too. You understand me?"

"Of course. But that doesn't sound too – well, dangerous in itself. Hil always wrote pieces like that – no names, no obvious identities or locations. He was a professional. He knew how to keep his head down and he would have kept his sources of information a strict secret. There must have been something more to it than – well – a local racket – you know, a protection scheme."

"Racket. We use the same word. We say 'mob' too."

"How quaint! But am I right? Was there something else, Giacomo?"

"Is possible. One night last year we play the backgammon. He say me, I want to speak in Italian and I know from this he is wanting to be in secret. At normal times, we speak English. I want more English practice. He correct me." Innocenti drank deeply from his tankard. "Hilary, he wasn't like other *Inglesi*. His Italian was superb, my friend. He make – what? Two mistakes, tiny grammatical errors in a whole month! His

369

pronuncia – how do you say it? It was so good he pass for an Italian. If Italians thought he was *straniero* – a foreigner – it is because he has a little of the Fiorentino in the way he speak. Is where he studied first. Firenze. He understood Italy in a way very few foreigners can..."

"And...?"

"And – in Italian – he present me an *ipotesi* – a – I can never say it!"

"Hypothesis?"

"Si! Yes, heye-poth-ess-ees. A word so similar, but so difficult to say. Perhaps he want this not to be heard by Faye. Anyway, he say me, just suppose, there is a man on the run, fleeing from the law. A Mafioso. Important, but not so important, a man with a big boss in hiding, and another, lesser boss being interrogated by the police. This man, he need to establish a life, a base, elsewhere, somewhere quiet. So he go – say – to some quiet *paese* where he is not known, and he is there because he knows people who will protect him. But still he is unhappy. He feel too exposed, and he need to have his meetings with his gang in secret somewhere. So, his friends they have friends and they find him a place for meetings in *campagna*, in a place that is a place for holidays, and foreign people."

"Here, in other words...Monte Farfalla! Christ..."

"It was only *ipotesi*, my friend. Just a think Hilary had. An idea. And the place for meetings must be somewhere very in secret..."

370

"Such as a lonely house by the sea…My God! You don't mean *there*? In Hilary's own house? They were paying him to…?"

Innocenti laughed with genuine mirth. "You are seeing *con un occhio solo*, my friend. Think with your whole brain and see with both of your eyes! A house in the country by the sea, with neighbours not far from, as you see yesterday. One of the neighbours, he is retired *capitano*, of the *polizia*! Suddenly, there are big cars, and strange people, and someone recording what they see? No! Surely not!"

"Oh… then what…?"

"*Think*, my friend. Think about how you would hide, if you were this man, you and your colleagues, your associates. Think about *where…*"

"Good grief, I really don't know! But you think Hilary did…"

"My friend, I can say nothing more. Hilary, I warned him. He did not listen me. He had found something, a *storia*, and I say him to be very, very careful. Then he laugh. Hilary, he was foreign in just this one respect. He embrace Italy too much, and he has forget this danger from within. As if nothing else exist. Now he is dead…and I am truly so very sorry." Innocenti's cell-phone beeped, and he stood up, reading a text message. "Ah. Now I have to meet my *cuginetta* – my little cousin who will live in my house here with her boyfriend whilst I am in Africa and take care of Mimi. I have much organizing, and the packing of

371

the bags to do. I hope you understand I am not being unhospitable."

Julian stood also. "Not at all. I – I'm deeply grateful to you, Giacomo. Thank you." They stood facing each other, and Julian proffered his hand, towering above the smaller man, whose eyes glittered up at him from behind his spectacles. He realised he liked this intelligent oblique-thinking little architect as Hilary must have, and he knew he would probably never see him again. "Good luck," he said, feeling awkward. "In Africa."

"Good luck to you also, my friend. *In bocca al lupo*, as we say here." Innocenti shook Julian's hand firmly, and then embraced him with warmth, kissing him on both cheeks. "Only reach your conclusions later," he whispered into Julian's ear. "Please. Much later."

xxvi: Constanza

Julian was hungry as well as being full of beer. He found a small pizza restaurant by the Marina, and ordered a 'quattro stagioni' and a quarter-litre jug of red wine, and stared at the lapping sea, meditating on his meeting with Innocenti, turning the memory stick over in his pocket. He sent a text to Phoebe.

After his supper, he walked, feeling unable to face the confines of his small hotel room, glad of the rising breeze. He drank a whiskey in a bar, and his cell phone beeped. 'OK: RING FIRST THING MORNING. MUM'S. LOVE, P.'

Returning very late, letting himself in with the night-key, Julian crept into the hotel, suddenly feeling very unsure of the geography. A dim light illuminated the reception desk; otherwise the place was in darkness. Aware that the whole place must be asleep, he groped his way up the stairs, and was grateful to see a red night-light on the landing. .

At the top of the stairs on the first floor, to the right and left were the guest bedrooms. Up another flight were – he presumed – the private quarters of the Barker family. An old fashioned lift-shaft ran beside the staircase. He turned down the left-hand corridor, found the door of his room and inserted his room key into the lock.

He realised he must be a little drunk. Despite the tiny, red-glowing night light in the ceiling above him, it was too dark to see. The key slipped from his hand with a clatter loud enough to wake the whole place, or that is how it seemed, and he swore silently, and groped for it on the marble floor, putting unaccustomed pressure on his injured wrist, not quite crying out in pain, and nearly losing his balance. A shaft of bright light suddenly shone and he started up, turned, his heart hammering. The doors of the tiny elevator had swung open, eerily noiseless.

A tiny old lady stood before him. Her silver hair glowed oddly golden-red under the light. She was dressed in black from head to toe, as far as Julian could tell, and she was muching something. Over her arm was a small bag.

"*Allora*! You have come back. I count them all…in, and out…"

"Signora..?"

"Is so good to see you. I thought I see you dead, down below. *Grazie agli angeli*! They only hurt your arm, and you are here again, not killed. The angels, they see, and they atone. I see everything, once. Now, I not see too good. You remember! I am Constanza, the mother of Silvana. I come downstairs for the *dolci*, the sugar buns. I don't sleep. You don't give me away, no? No tell? They try – he try – to lock me in my rooms. He don't fool me nothing! I escape! I eat what I want, when I want, see?" The old crone took a croissant from the bag and crammed it into her toothless mouth and chumbled on it, spitting crumbs in every direction.

"Signora…I think there's some mistake…"

374

"No mistake. You come back. Gianni, he still here. Everyone else, they gone. *Il stormo dei piccione…Anche gli amici…*But you come! All will be well now. There will be justice! I go in my room now. You no tell nobody I here. Our secret. They think me mad. Good night. I hope the angels be good to you. *Buona notte, caro Signor Blyt'. Sogni d'oro…*"

After this rather extraordinary interview, Julian Blyth let himself into his room and sat on his bed for a long while, thinking, and his dreams, when he slept, were not golden at all.

"Mum?" Rebecca Barker found her mother in the office.

"What's up, love? Nonna okay, is she?"

"I'm not sure…she's in one of her states this morning. I think she's been at the buns in the night again."

"Oh Lord…I know she's my own mother, but that woman's becoming a bloody liability. We'll have to make sure it's all locked up in future, Beck. At least she can't get down to the cellars now her leg's so bad. Another bloody worry!"

"It might be best to put the sweet stuff away. It completely interferes with the insulin. She doesn't seem to realise it's so important to keep her sugar intake regulated…she was rambling on about something."

"So what's new? What is it this time?"

"She says that she saw Mr Blyth last night…"

"Mr Blyth? Well, I suppose she might have done, if she was wandering about. He comes in quite late. I hope she wasn't making a nuisance of herself."

"I think she's lost it a bit, Mum. She said that Mr Blyth had been killed, but now he's come back, and that there's a guardian angel with him..."

"Oh, take no notice, love. She's confusing Mr Blyth with his brother. They're twins. That's the explanation. Poor old Mum, it's a shame!"

"But the brother did die, didn't he? Drowned? Nonna just says to ask Dad..."

"She *has* lost it! Pay no attention, love. Nonna loves her little conspiracies. She's getting very confused. Just ignore her, I would. And we'd better make sure the door to the bar is locked every night now. God! This is *all* I need..."

"Mum...is it still okay if I go to Valeria's? She's got a litter being induced this morning..."

"A what? Oh, the pugs! No, off you go, love. Duties over for the day!"

When her daughter had gone, however, Silvana made up her mind and a tray, and went out with Julian Blyth's breakfast order with a certain determination.

In the Albergo's sunny garden, Julian Blyth was making a call from his mobile to England.

"Hullo...Angela?"

"Good grief! Julian? Where are you? Oh.. I see. Still there…Yes, she's here. No, no trouble. Yes, we're all fine…You?" Julian mumbled that he was. "Oh, good. No, she's by my elbow. Hang on, I'll pass you over…"

"Hi, Dad?"

"Feebs – did you get it?"

"Several. Have you got a pen? Okay. You should try any of these and see if they work." She repeated a number of passwords, which Julian wrote down. "If they don't work, I'll talk to Faye again. No, she's doing great, really. Much better. Coming out this week. Dad?

"Yes, darling?"

"You will be careful, won't you, Dad…"

Julian promised her that he would, and rang off, frowning. Mrs Barker bustled out with the tray of coffee and Julian's newspaper.

"Are you sure that's all you want, Julian, dear?"

"Yes, thank you. Honestly. I've been eating fit to burst these last few days."

"Well, it's very nice you're still here with us. I hope you've been comfortable."

Julian assured her that he was, and inquired whether the hotel provided a laundry service.

"Of course, dear! Just pop it all down to Reception in one of the laundry bags before ten. It'll be all ready tomorrow morning for you. Planning on stopping on in Monty are you?"

"It would be very useful to hang onto the room for a couple more days, if I may..."

"Well, I'd love to say yes, but the thing is I've got this big party expected the day after tomorrow. I think we might need your room...I'm really sorry. Stay tonight with pleasure, and then I can let you have the address of a really nice B&B in San Gregorio...or there's Loredana's by the Marina if she's not full up. We're all getting busy now...You found our friend Innocenti at last, didn't you?" Silvana Barker beamed, but Julian had the impression the smile was a little strained.

"Yes. Thank you. All done. I – um – I think I met your mother last night. Charming elderly lady. I'm afraid I came in very late..I think she was on watch, as it were..."

"My poor old Mum! Yes. We used to be able to leave her in charge, but not any more. She wanders, you know, bless her! Doesn't know quite where she is, sometimes, if I'm honest, not these days. Yes, it's very sad, really. Old age...She's diabetic. Likes to help herself to the croissants... I expect she thought you were Hilary, did she, dear?"

"She did seem a little confused, yes. I think she frightened me more than I frightened her..."

"People think she's a witch! She still thinks she's in charge, truth be known! Now then, Julian dear, you're most welcome to stop on another night, and let's get your laundry done, shall we? That's the least we can do, dear!"

"Thank you, Silvana. That's very kind."

Rather pleased that everything had gone so smoothly, Silvana went back into the hotel. Julian poured hot coffee and milk, thinking.

It was while gathering up some of his soiled clothes that Julian discovered what he supposed was a used handkerchief in the pocket of his spare jacket. It was the ball of paper he had picked up in Hilary's house. He smoothed it out. It was a standard sheet of A4, apparently discarded from a printer. Gobbledegook on the first inch or so and then some faded marks in pencil.

There was a diagram in the shape of a pyramid, with initials, or perhaps just codes, placed at strategic points on it. 'AB' was at the top with an encircled P next to it. Parallel, and further down to right and left, were the intials CD, and another circled P, and EF with a question mark. At the bottom of the pyramid, in one corner, were the initials LM, followed by GP and FP in brackets. Then DB, and the words 'dom sec. men' appeared next to these in what was undoubtedly Hilary's scrawl. Julian was the least fanciful of men – lacked imagination, according to his ex-wife – and certainly he was impatient with superstition and intolerant of what he thought of as woolly spirituality. However, he found himself unable to help imagining that this was somehow *meant*...he had found, on the last day he had access to Hilary's house, a cryptic note in Hilary's own hand. Impossible not to fancy it was in some way important, however much he balked at the idea of a *message*... He handed over his laundry to Silvana, and went out for more coffee in the square, where he studied the page more thoroughly. He checked the little memory-stick, still tucked into his wallet. Then he made a call.

"Freddy? Freddy Partridge? Hello…this is Julian Blyth…we met with Veronica the other day. Look, if this isn't convenient, just say, but I wonder if you could do me a favour…"

xxvii: Only A Movie…

Matthew Lucodin slammed the phone down. Now he and his lieutenant were arguing loudly in the Soho office.

"Well you heard him! Feltz wants *Cry*. Offered to buy the script. I'm not just going to abandon the whole goddamn thing, Roper. Shit!"

"So Cinéast Limited is serious about this benighted movie. Bugger! It was predictable, Matt." Roper ran his hands through his short curly hair.

"Fuck. I suppose I ought to be grateful he asked. For fuck's sakes, Roper, *we* saw it first! If Cinèast wants to play, and for the same stakes, then why not us?"

"Simple. Cinéast is bigger and uglier and a lot less 'limited' than we are. They could afford a punt to sink. We can't. Get real, Matthew, for Christ's sakes. Look, I've got hold of the agent for *The Hawk*. The estate would jump at a movie with some provisos. So would the biographer. Most of the action's in London, some Paris, some New York. Lots of archive stuff to play with, great part for the right actor – music, crime, tortured genius – Potter will love it. So will Logan. So will that lush Wardley-Hill if you still want him in. With everything nice and safe and legal, we'll get Porter-Maine and anyone else we ask. I suggest we arrange an options meeting with Potter right away, before he gets persuaded back to the US."

"And just throw this *Cry* thing away? I'm not letting that sonofacretin Feltz *have* this! This has got personal. We back out because we're too scared, and the next thing you know Cinéast will grab Potter and Pearce and have a bouquet of Oscars and a TV deal both sides of the Atlantic. No way! Shit, I want some decent coffee!" He hurled the plastic cup across the room and missed the bin.

"It's coming. Matt, look, at least let's pursue the *Hawk* idea. Have a plan 'B' and not waste all our energies."

"Always the voice of common sense. But *The Hawk* lacks... Look, I dunno. What does it lack, Russ? You tell me."

Roper sighed. "The scandal factor? Billybass Hawkins lived in louche-land. Apart from exposing the squeaky-clean doctor, nobody would be a bit surprised by all the sex and drugs, and the rock and roll's a given. That's what you want, isn't it? Scandal. Something to shock the poor Brits out of their complacency. But this *Cry* thing's history, Matthew. Nobody's going to be shocked. They'll just yawn, even if Mrs Penrose gets to be First Lady."

"My idea," said Lucodin, ignoring him, "is that we need to erase some of the rogue elements. Only three people can really object to this. The mother's dead. So's husband number one. Number two's next door to gaga. Number three is on our side. That leaves the brother and the sister and sister's porcine husband. If we knew it was only the fat honourable, we'd look a lot safer, right?"

Roper said, "She'd be as good as her best lawyer, Matt. I've told you this already. I've also told you that you're missing the point."

"I'm not missing it. I'm ignoring it. If we can be assured that the Penroses and his Nibs are out of the running, then we've got just one scared woman and scads of publicity she won't relish. True?"

"True…I suppose. But I really don't like the Penrose thing."

"Stop making objections, Roper. Why in hell not?"

"Why *not*? Blackmail's a crime. And whatever these people tell us, we won't get their written agreement *not* to sue for injunctions. And we have no idea what His Nibs thinks until we've talked to him. He might be right behind her. And first we have to find him. He could be anywhere. I'm not being funny, Matt. Let's let it alone now. It's got lawsuits and bankruptcy written all over it."

"I'm going to give it another week. So are you. Where the fuck's this coffee? That Minx kid has to be useful for something apart from decoration!"

"Come on, Matt. She can type, she can spell, she sounds good on the phone, and she's revolutionised your working breakfasts…"

"She's ambitious."

"That won't hurt. Keep her on her toes…and she's on the spot, remember? *Chez* Dearborn."

"Okay, Roper. She's hired. Go for it. But unless there's a movie this is for love and as much pocket money as you want to spare personally. And all this undergraduate journalism is strictly subject to review. Nothing about us unless we say. And – yeah. Keep it clean, huh? No emoting on the firm's time."

"Unworthy thoughts, Matthew."

There was a tap at the door, and Miranda Hooper entered bearing a large stainless steel flask and a paper carrier.

"Breakfast! Sorry I've been so long. There was a queue." She went into the little wash place for mugs and milk from the fridge.

"Get her onto His Nibs. If he's turned into a monk in the Himalayas, so much the better. You follow the Penrose angle. Okay? We need to step on the gas."

"A week, Matt. Seven days. I'm your partner, not a fucking gofer."

"Junior partner, Roper."

But the aroma of salt beef sandwiches instantly put Matthew Lucodin in a better mood. "This beats the hell out of crap plastic cups." He almost smiled as Miranda poured fragrant hot coffee into sturdy china.

"Doesn't it! I get Cohen's to just fill this up. Saves trips down to the Square and the coffee's better." She beamed.

"Told you," said Roper. "Smart as a whip!" Miranda grinned at him, and doled out the sandwiches and paper napkins.

"Minx – we have a little task for you," said Lucodin, munching.

"Oh! Does that mean I've passed the test?"

"Sure, kid. We want you to look after us. You can write about it, but you show the drafts to me personally before anything goes to press, and that includes your college mag, okay? And unless there's a movie, you do this in your own time."

"He means you don't get paid, honey, but you get a wealth of cutting-edge research. Suit you?"

"You bet your ass, boss," said Miranda to Lucodin.

"Don't get too lippy with me, babe. Tell her, Roper." His blue eyes, hugely magnified behind his thick lenses may have been ironic, maybe not.

"We want you to find a man called James Dearborn. He's got a handle – he's a Lord – but he probably doesn't use it. He's been out of circulation for at least ten years. As far as we know he isn't dead. But he could be in Australia or South Africa or somewhere. Try all the usual channels. He might be on Facebook, Twitter – but he's almost certainly using some sort of alias. There might even be a shortcut as you're on the spot with his sister…"

"You mean you thought I could raid my landlady's stuff while she's away?" When Miranda grinned, two dimples appeared in her smooth, round cheeks. Sometimes, Russell Roper felt positively faint with desire, and hurriedly he glanced out of the window at the busy Square.

"Well – um…"

She stared at his slim shoulders, biting delicately into a tuna salad roll. "I don't think that will go anywhere, Russell. She hasn't been in touch with him for literally years. Rory said."

Lucodin said through a mouthful, "All we want's an address. Or an email. Even a general whereabouts. If he's gone underground, he can stay there. What about this nephew? Is he still in contact?"

"Rory. My boyfriend. I don't think so. I get the impression that Uncle James has been off the air to the rest of the family for practically ever. I could ask. But it's much better if I don't. And maybe it's not necessary."

"It is necessary, sweetie," explained Roper patiently, mostly for the benefit of his colleague, "because we need his co-operation. Or at least to know where the non-co-operation might come from. Finish your sarnie and come and sit at this nice computer, there's a love."

"Whatever you say, boss. But I've already found him."

"What?" Both men cried in unison, Lucodin spattering crumbs.

"Well, I knew you were looking for him, so I looked too. Sorry – was I being ahead of myself?"

"Hell! Are you serious?"

"You mean you know where he is?"

"Well, Jesus Christ!"

"Yes." Miranda was enjoying herself watching their faces. She was especially glad to have impressed the grizzled man with the ponytail and the fishy magnified eyes. "It wasn't especially difficult. James Dearborn went out to Kenya, near Nairobi, and some revolutionaries burnt his farm down about twelve years ago. His wife had run off with someone else and taken his little daughter. That made news and it's all in the archives. There were hints that the wife's lover, another ex-pat farmer, had been involved with the raid, but nobody could prove anything, and James just seemed to disappear. Kenya was having a lot of political problems which took prominence, understandably. It still is, in case you hadn't noticed. These things about individuals just fall out of the news as soon as people lose interest. First year Media Studies, page one," she added, grinning at Russell.

"So what happened?"

"Where is he now?"

"Do you *know*?"

"Yep. He's at somewhere called Linfield House. It's just down the road, more or less. In E1. It's a shelter for the homeless."

"You mean he's in a London hobo home?"

"No, Matthew. He runs it."

"I don't like this much, Russell..."

"That wasn't the impression you've just given me…"

They were lying, naked, in Roper's bed, and Roper was making an effort to concentrate on business.

"You know what I mean… Here I am, two-timing Rory, and you're trying to get me to dig up dirt on his Dad. You've got no scruples whatsoever, have you?" But she was laughing, and there was a brief, hectic interlude with no articulate verbal conversation at all.

"You do," she murmured eventually, her voice thick, dreamy, "give a girl a hell of a good time in bed…this could get hopelessly addictive…"

"Mmm. I'm yours truly enslaved, oh admired Miranda… Okay. So according to Rory, his daddy's going to be up North in the constituency for the next week or so. You know what you're looking for?"

"Only up to a point. According to a dodgy source of yours in Whitehall, Papa Penrose has been massaging his expenses on a third home miles away from his constituency for which he's been claiming council tax and upkeep expenses. Naughty Mr Penrose. But I don't see that this is going to help much, Russell darling. If the object is to trade silence for his guarantee not to sue the *Cry* company, we're too late. There's a purge. Everything's coming out in the wash. You have been reading the *Telegraph*, I take it?"

"You really do take me for an idiot, don't you, honey-pie?"

"Not in every respect…okay, so there's something else. There has to be. Are you going to tell me what it is?"

"Not entirely. It's better you don't know for now. You are interested in renting a certain property north of Bath for yourself and – let's say, a couple of girlfriends – for a couple of weeks in the summer. It's on a website called Cotswold Holidays Direct. It's listed under a code number that I will give you. I'll also give you the address. There's an availability calendar, which you can study."

"But *why*, Russell? You've obviously looked all this up yourself already."

"Of course. But there needs to be verisimilitude. You then contact the website – they'll pass on your inquiry details to the owner, who will get back in touch with you in person – and you will then have an email address and a name. We need to verify that. You then express interest in one or two of the available dates and sound as plausible as possible. Needless to say, you do this on your own email, and not from Flix. Use an alias, maybe – probably your own initials are best. MH – call yourself Mandy Holland, say…"

"Sure you don't want me to be Mata Hari?"

"You little baggage! Listen - you're Mandy, and you're organizing a vacation. You'll need to talk to your holiday companions to fix dates. But, crucially, you will be in the Bath area very soon, and you'd love to look round if that's at all convenient. We need a bit of cyber-dialogue."

389

"Will I? Be near Bath?"

"You will. Expenses paid, of course. Okay so far?"

"I'm not sure…We want what? A name?"

"A name, a rental quote and some nice foties."

"The Penroses own this cottage, I take it?"

"That, my adorable girl, is what we need to find out. Or at least their involvement. Have you met them yet? The political parents?"

"Not yet, no…give me a chance! Rory and I have only been an item since just before Easter."

"And here you are cheating on the poor guy already…tsk, tsk…"

"I didn't *mean* to…" For a moment, Miranda felt almost ashamed, and hugged the sheet round her small body.

"It's all right, babes. I'm irresistible. And so's the film business…"

"Russell! That's not fair."

"No?" His intelligent brown eyes were amused. "If I were a humble bank clerk you wouldn't be here, babes…"

"I'm not so sure," she said, giving away more than she had meant. She said lightly, "I mean, for this afternoon, you could have been a pizza-boy or the man who reads the meter, you wickedly wonderful man…" She traced the line of his smooth light-biscuit-coloured bicep with her finger. "So, I still don't understand. And help, I mean the person who shows me round this cottage, she might be Rory's *mother*," she said, pulling herself together. "Then what?"

"Then nothing. You've not met her, have you?"

"But Russell, that means I can't *ever* meet her...I don't want to do this. It's too close to home!"

"Babes, Minx honey...I will bet my last cent that your guide to this desirable holiday home in Biford, or Barndon, or wherever it is, will not be your prospective mummy-in-law."

"So who will it be?"

"In all likelihood, it will be a nice little old pensioner biddy called Mrs Pemberton. She will adore to chat, and you will indulge her. Let her make you tea. Get her talking. Especially ask her about her family, her children, and ask her if she uses the cottage sometimes herself. Tell her it's delightful. Yatter on happily about London. Tell her you're training for the Civil Service. She won't be able to resist you...I can't..." He stroked the sheet, pulling it gently away, and then stroked her small, neat, naked breast. "Like a little brown berry," he said, kissing the nipple.

"Oh God... Who is this Mrs Pemberton? Is she the housekeeper, or something? Russell! Stop...please... oh...!" She grasped his springy dark hair in her fists, and halted his searching mouth which had begun to slide down her smooth stomach. "Russell! Beautiful Russell! *Please...* If I fuck up here – get caught – oh, shit! I mean it's not a question of in-laws. Rory and I haven't got past first base, as you know. But if I mess with the

391

Penroses, my career's on the line. My future. I'd never get my NUJ card. I might as well train to fill shelves in Waitrose…I can't do this. I don't understand why I need to meet this Pemberton person at all."

"You need to meet her, babes, because you can. You're anonymous. You work for Flix entirely unofficially. You're a holiday punter called Mandy, and you can take photos of a sweet cottage to show your chums. You take a particularly endearing photo of the Widow Pemberton outside the front door which will doubtless be all wreathed in roses. That's all you need to do…mmm…so, so, so lovely…"

His mouth slid past her navel, and Miranda groaned voluptuously and gave herself up…

xxviii: Home & Away

Veronica tipped the taxi driver, let herself in with her key, lugged
her bags into the hallway, and opened her own apartment,
assailed as always by that certain odour of a home unlived in for
a while and the uncomfortable thought that this smell, this
atmosphere, was the one that visitors were aware of when they
walked in the door. It was not unpleasant, but it was strange,
almost unfamiliar after ten days' absence, and she was very
aware of the stale smell of her own cigarette smoke in the soft
furnishings. She called her cat, who did not appear. Her post had
been piled onto her desk efficiently. She glanced through it, and
out of habit, turned on the computer and Radio Three.
Instinctive to re-establish one's little routines.

"Grim! Grimbles!"

She opened the French window into the courtyard. Most
of her plants looked happy and well-watered. She filled the kettle
and switched it on. Three in the afternoon – far too early for a
drink, but the flatness, the anticlimax, was a thing that required
smoothing over. She made tea rather firmly. Soon she would
need to unpack and sort her laundry, always a dreary task. In the
kitchen everything was clean, and fresh cat biscuits waited in a
bowl. Where was the cat? "Grimbles! Puss!"

She sat in front of the screen with a mug of tea, wearing a
cardigan – it was much colder suddenly in England. Among a

great many messages she could simply delete, there was one from Vixen Press, two from Lydia's office and another she did not recognize and put off opening. "Grim! Puss, puss, puss!" She was about to try the bell of the upstairs flat, when there was a soft knock at the door.

Rory stood on the threshold with the cat in his arms.

"Rory! And Greymalkin! Hello!" The cat bounded away from Rory, purred against Veronica's legs and ran into the kitchen.

"Hi, Vee…welcome back…"

"Hi! Come in, Rory… I wasn't expecting to see you so early. You're not in lectures…"

"Not today, no. I had an essay…old Grim's been keeping me company. He's been upstairs with me quite a bit. I hope that's okay. He's been quite happy…I mean he's obviously pleased to see you…I hope everything's all right."

"Sounds as if he's eating his head off…come and sit down, Rory…have a cup of tea…"

"What do you mean, you don't know? Are you saying Miranda isn't living here after all?"

"Yeah – she's living here. She's just out most of the time. With this new job, like I said…you know, gets back at all hours. Sort of work experience. It clocks up a lot of mileage on her course, apparently. She can write it all up for a project. She hasn't said all that much about it. It'd be great if…"

"Tell me, Rory. Just tell me. Try to be a bit more specific." Her nephew looked so chopfallen that she wanted to shake him. "You say there was this guy who came to the house...and you thought he was the press. From a newspaper...do you know which one?"

"I don't think it's a newspaper as such. Not now. I did at first, and I was frankly worried about Dad."

"About Peter?"

"Yeah...you know, all this expenses business. It's all been blown out of proportion. The Fallowdale house is legit. It's their constituency home. It's just that it was a bit – well, unnerving. They're implying that Dad's been as bad as the rest of them, claiming for stuff he shouldn't. Pool maintenance, that sort of stuff. Mum's been on the phone having hysterics. Frantic. You know what she's like. I haven't dared tell her my girlfriend's a journalist."

"I can imagine. And you say this guy just turned up here out of the blue and then offered Miranda some sort of job?"

"Yeah," said Rory miserably.

"Odd. And he really was a total stranger?"

"Yeah. At least to me. He was just here one morning, the day after you left. Just in the street, apparently. He rescued...I mean, Grimbles had run outside. It was an accident. Miranda had gone down for the post, and he – just sort of shot out into the road. This guy helped her get him back in the house...Grim scratched his hand and she did the first-aid bit. I thought they were strangers…I mean, that's how they seemed…"

"I see. Well, at least Grims is okay."

"Yeah. *He's* okay."

"Rory – do you know this guy's name? The name of the company? And how do you *know* it isn't a paper? Do you know *anything*?"

Rory heaved a very deep sigh and slurped tea. "A bit. He's called Russell somebody. The place is in Soho. It's some sort of publicity company, she says. I think they make adverts. But I just think…that is, I think she might be *seeing* him…you know."

"I see…that's rough, Rory. I'm sorry. Have you asked her? No, sorry. Silly question. You – um – don't really know anything much about her, do you?"

"Not much," Rory admitted. "We've not really had much time together. It's all a bit new. I'm sure she wouldn't be trying to shop my dad, though. Would she?"

"Probably not," said Veronica, who had her doubts. "She struck me as pretty ambitious. You know, determined to succeed. But what bothers me a bit is mysterious strangers on my doorstep. It might not have been just coincidence. Are you *sure* he's with some sort of advertising agency?"

"Sure-ish. I mean, that's partly why I think they're involved with each other. Miranda had got some sort of local borough gazette thing lined up for her project. A paper. Some real journalism. Unless it's a job with the *Sun* or the *Mail*, or something, she'd have been mad to just ditch it and opt for something else, wouldn't she?"

"Or not…I suppose this wasn't the *Mail* or the *Sun*? Masquerading? God, I'm sounding paranoid, but come on, love. This is probably quite serious for us all. *How* are you so sure?"

"Oh God, this is going to sound incredibly pathetic. I looked at her emails. I shouldn't have done that. Her business. She'd left her laptop behind one morning, and I just couldn't help myself…"

"Oh, Rory…" The boy was almost in tears and horribly embarrassed. She poured more tea.

"Anyhow, I'm sure it isn't a paper. It's something 'Publicity' – funny name, like Lucozade or something… PR, advertising, TV and cinema. She's been looking for locations, that kind of stuff… she's been in Bath or somewhere, looking at some estate or other. For an advert."

"I see…Are you expecting her back this evening?"

"Dunno. She didn't reply to my last text…"

It was one those mistakes that is easy to make in these troubled and ambiguous times.

"I'm afraid we're full right now," said the young woman to the man in the soup-stained suit and battered hat on the doorstep, "but we'll try to help if we can. I'm Sarah. Come on in

397

to the office." The man followed her into a tiled hallway that smelled of pine floorwash.

"We try not to turn anyone away," said the woman Sarah, showing him into a room with a desk, filing cabinets and two threadbare nylon easy-chairs. Stacks of *The Big Issue* occupied a battered coffee table. "Sit down. We're so busy right now, but I'll give you a list of places you could try for the night. Otherwise, if you need hot food, a shower or something, we can probably accommodate you. Coffee?" She had a wide, white smile in a very black face, and went over to the coffee machine in the corner and punched buttons. "Sugar?"

"Yes, please…lissen, I think there's some sort of mistake, actually…my dear." He breathed gales of wine fumes. "You're from the West Indies, I'll bet. Jamaica?"

"I'm from Stoke Newington, London, actually. Here's your coffee. I've put two sugars in it. Now, then, how can we help? Are you hungry?"

"Well, yes …but…."

The young woman sat down behind the desk. She had on a white shirt over dark trousers and looked businesslike, crisply efficient. She smiled. "We'll try and arrange some dinner for you, or at least a sandwich. If I may, I'll write down a few details. You don't have to tell me anything you don't want to. Do you mind telling me your name and where you are from? It's because we are an official charity. We have to make records."

"My name is Gilbert, and I…"

"Mr Gilbert...okay. And your first name, Mr Gilbert?"

The man enunciated carefully: "Gilbert is my Christian name. My second name – that is, my surname – is Wardley-Hill...I want to see James Dearborn."

"You mean Jim?"

"If that's what he calls himself. Is he here?"

"He's around somewhere. I'm sure he'll be along very soon. Now then, are you from Britain, Mr Wardley?"

"Wardley-*Hill*...of course I'm from Britain! England! Recently got back from the south of France...look, my dear, sorry and all that, but why are we doing this? I want to see James Dearborn. He lives here, I understand. We're related. He's my stepson, for God's sakes!".

"He's your – ? Oh, my God...I thought... Oh! Excuse me a minute." She got up hurriedly and left, shutting the door behind her. After a moment, Gilbert Wardley-Hill heard the sounds of an urgent whispered conference immediately outside.

"It's all right, Sarah...I'll deal with it..."

A large, balding, bearded man in jeans and a tee-shirt entered and stared hard at the visitor. "Gilbert Wardley-Hill. Well, well. What a surprise..." And it was, for both of them, since neither was at all how the other remembered. James Dearborn did not shake Wardley-Hill's proffered hand.

"Odd to see you in mufti. Only barely recognize you under all the face-fungus. You weren't at the funeral."

"What do you want, Gilbert? I don't mean to be rude, but I really am very busy."

"So am I. Your young woman, the enchanting Mooress, she seemed to think I need a bed for the night and a hot meal. I don't, thanks all the same. I came to talk to you in person. Can we talk here?"

"That depends. Will it take long? I can't monopolise the office for more than five minutes or so..."

"A drink, then. Let me buy you a beer."

"That's kind, but I've not got time. Can't you tell me what this is about?" Dearborn regarded the man in the chair with distaste.

"It concerns your sister."

"My sister? Which sister?"

"Both of them in a way...look, dear boy, I really do think this might go down better over a drink..."

Over pints of Fuller's Pride and a double whiskey chaser for Wardley-Hill, the two men occupied a corner table in the Golden Heart, which at this early hour was nearly deserted. Three middle-aged builders in overalls and stout boots stared at a football game on an overhead screen; a fat, unsmiling youth thumped buttons on an electronic game at a machine which whizzed and ka-powed with moronic insistence, and competed with equally moronic piped pop.

"I always looked after your mother, James," said Wardley-Hill earnestly.

"Oh, Christ, please spare me! I don't want to talk about my mother. She had rotten judgement. And I oughtn't to care a damn, but please don't take the liberty of calling me your stepson. I'm nothing to you, or you to me. I can't pretend I'm at all pleased to see you."

"Apologies, dear boy. Please don't let's get hasty. We're all on hard times. This is simply business, if you like."

"Business! You want to know if I have the time, money and energy to waste in initiating a lawsuit against a company that wants to make a film of my sister Veronica's book. That right?"

"More or less. In essence. I take it you don't. "

"You're barmy, Gilbert," said Dearborn frankly. "If my sister wants to have her rather pathetic attempt at setting the record straight dragged into the public eye again, that's her business. It's nothing to do with me. I rather hoped she'd moved on from all that, but there you go. Good luck to her, I say. I find it a bit odd that she sent you instead of asking me herself, but strange things happen…"

Gilbert Wardley-Hill allowed the misunderstanding to pass. "Probably couldn't find you. You have rather um – gone to earth with all these – um – good works. Personally, I'd just let the buggers rot on the pavement. Or shove em all in some labour camp to get em off the street. Bloody wasters. And half of them not even entitled to be here, free-loading shits."

Dearborn glanced deliberately at his wristwatch. "Is that all you came to ask me?"

"Well – um. I don't suppose you know – um – how the land lies in the other direction? Your other sister and your illustrious brother-in-law?"

"You mean Penrose? Do you really expect him to care all that much?"

"You tell me. He might. Embarrassing, y'know. Little Lucinda is his wife, and the – um – pantomime villain is his father-in-law."

"Look, Gilbert. I loathe, detest and renounce Peter Penrose and everything he stands for. He's next door to a fascist. If he suffers at the hustings because of his unfortunate connections, I shall rejoice. Good for Vee, if that's what it'll amount to."

"I see. No family solidarity, then? Spare little Lucie's feelings?"

"None. She married him, so she can lie with him. Lying is probably what she'll have to do. By all accounts, there'll be an expenses scandal that'll worry them far more than some stupid movie. I suppose you're backing this thing, hence all this subterfuge and finding me."

"I was thinking of doing so, yes. I'll be perfectly honest with you, James. I'm just doing some soundings."

"I see. Soundings. Defusing the mines before you put the show on the road. You don't change, do you, Gilbert? Well,

402

much as I don't give a damn one way or the other about your successes, you can rest assured there'll be no trouble from me. That is, unless – "

"Unless?"

Jim Dearborn got to his feet and drained his pint and looked steadily into the older man's bloodshot eyes. He was in his mid-fifties, a tall, thickset, fit-looking Henry VIII of a man who looked as if he could mean business. Gilbert Wardley-Hill felt intimidated instinctively. "If I get door-stepped by reporters, if you make my connection with the hostel public knowledge, I shall probably pull out the stops. Is that clear?"

"Crystal. And my dear boy – really, there's no need to be *aggressive!* You were not especially difficult to find. Anybody could if they tried."

"Very well. But you might make personally, doubly sure that they don't. I still have a number of stops to pull, if you get me. Now, if you'll excuse me, I have a show of my own to run. Goodnight."

"Russell?"

"Darling girl! How did it go?"

"I can't be too long. I was about to text. Not easy right now. But you wanted to know asap…"

"Fine. Just tell me."

"I took the location shots like you asked," said Miranda in a louder voice. "Lots of good ones, and of the street, and the number, and of the nice lady who showed me round. Not quite what you led me to expect...."

"Not the ma-in-law?"

"Not at all."

"Not a pensioner?"

"No way."

"Younger?"

"By quite a bit, I should say. You know, forties vintage. A bit whitewashed."

"Do we have a name?"

"Yes. It's just like you thought. I can text the details..."

"Bingo! Babes, you have all the makings of a secret agent. Should have said you were Mata Hari after all...send the pix over now?"

"Sure, boss. No problem."

"Angel girl...See you tomorrow, babes."

"Your secretary, I suppose," said Simon Drinkwater, making curly quotes with his fingers. "Jammy bastard." They were drinking a happy hour pint in an unpleasant chain pub close to Roper's tiny apartment near Angel, Islington at Drinkwater's insistence. For the purposes of this conversation, Drinkwater had wanted to put as much distance between himself and Whitehall as possible.

"Why is it," asked Russell Roper over the considerable din, "that everybody imagines I lead this wildly exciting life?

One long round of Hollywood parties, London parties and more girls than my tongue can cope with? It's not true!"

"Then stop smirking," said Drinkwater. "I don't like this one little bit."

"Neither do I, frankly, " admitted Roper. "In principle. In practice, it's almost watertight."

Drinkwater shuddered. "It's that *almost* that scares the pants off me."

"I'm a lawyer, Simon. So are you, come to that. There's enough here to scare the pants off Penrose, that's the point."

"Penrose! Bloody hell, Russell, he must be off his trolley to claim for another house. He's in enough deep shit as it is with this swimming pool. And the conservatory. Tried to make out it was drains. But they're all at it. But how come you got mixed up in all this other business?"

"Friends in low places. Well not, actually. Friend of a friend. And you do owe me one, Si..."

Drinkwater pulled a face and sighed. Being one of those young professional men who had become stuck in a well-paid but pedestrian job he was not especially enjoying, the chance of a little diversion was attractive. In theory. "Okay." He sighed again. "Press play."

"You get Puffer Penrose on his own. How you arrange it is up to you, but perhaps somewhere where there are no lurking secretarial staff. A pub, a lunch bar, say. Let him choose the venue, maybe. It shouldn't be hard to achieve – I imagine they'd all jump at the chance for a *sub-rosa* interview with the expenses office. You tell him that some journo has been trying to get you to leak information about a certain village property in Wiltshire and you thought he would like to know, given the current climate. A chance to withdraw the dodgy claims, all that. Except of course, you don't imply 'dodgy' – you're merely alerting him the possibility of a misinterpretation. As a friendly gesture."

"Christ, Russ, he'll think I'm trying to blackmail him. Bound to. They're all jumpy as hell."

"Well, you're not. Convince him. He's obviously made a mistake, and you're anti pushy journos, like most people are. If you want, you can emphasise that the journo in question wanted the info for free, in the public interest. That should satisfy the Puffer's cynical instincts. The crucial point is that it won't look remotely like a menace. It's not a menace. You're giving him a friendly warning. He has an opportunity to withdraw future claims, and you hint that you will try to delete it from the records…"

"You do know I can't actually do that?"

"Of course. But as far as the Puffer's concerned you'll try to limit the damage. He'll bluster at first and then be all smiles and gratitude…"

Drinkwater grunted. "Where I am, *nobody* is smiling at the moment. It was Thatcher's fault, you know that? Couldn't be seen to put up MPs' wages, and more or less agreed to look the other way when they all started claiming for the home improvements and all sorts of family concerns to make up the deficits. They all went for it. Duck ponds and tennis-courts as well as roof-jobs and damp-courses in the holiday homes…Can't blame em, really, can you?"

"So you genuinely sympathise. Better and better. You warn him that the shit's going to hit the fan, and establish yourself on his side. He's been watching his colleagues go down like ninepins, and this won't be a shock. Okay so far? Then you slide in a bit of insider journalism…"

"Oh Christ…"

"The journo in question hinted that the cottage is officially registered in the name of Pemberton. I have a feeling that might produce a reaction."

"You've lost me. Who in hell's Pemberton?"

"Only the mother of Puffer's ex Private Constituency Secretary…"

"Mother? I still don't get it."

"Penrose took over the lease of the Widow Pemberton's house when her daughter left his employ. It was a pay-off, of sorts. Or a sop to the Puffer's conscience. Mother and daughter now run the place as a small holiday letting. It still belongs to them, but Penrose has a vested interest which he's been defraying with some false accounting, mostly for philanthropic reasons, if you see what I mean. He doesn't get anything out of it, as such, but the taxpayer bears the expense of the building maintenance, et cetera, while the Pembertons pocket whatever they make on their lettings and effectively live for free. A touching story, as I'm sure any newspaper would agree…and as I'm sure that Mrs Puffer would not. I mean, it's one thing to claim expenses for a holiday house that doesn't fall into legit claims on the taxpayer, and quite another to be socking a third party a new roof and regular garden maintenance because you have to maintain your pristine image as a family man."

"Good God, Russell…How the fuck do you know all this?"

"Simple. The Land Registry. Completely transparent when you know where to look. I'm surprised you haven't looked for yourself…"

"It's not my job. I'm just a humble junior Civil Servant. It's the *claim* that isn't kosher, not the ownership. Mrs Penrose owns the Fallowdale place outright. The Puffer obviously thought that he was entitled to a house of his own, the stupid idiot. I've no professional interest in the details, for Christ's sake."

"You have now," said Roper.

"But – well, I mean anything could happen. This won't remain a secret for much longer. It can't. It sounds like a ticking bomb. I presume the ex PCS is also Penrose's bit of crackling…"

"In one, but she's ex-crackling. He ditched her more or less at the same time he got the shadow post as Minister for Social Affairs, the cold-hearted swine. The deal *in re* the cottage is her secret pension, and she's sitting pretty and very unlikely to blab. Mother ditto. But Puffer will be shitting bricks that someone knows the real deal. Far better for him to take the rap for the dodgy accounts on face value than have the whole thing go public. Wifey-kins would become rather a focus, I should think. Unpleasant all round…"

"Fair enough. But I still don't understand quite what's in it for you. Or me, come to that. That's if I agree. It all sounds totally out of order, Russell. I'm not sure that this is worth the price of you getting a dodgy tout off my case sometime back in the late eighteenth century."

"He was a very insistent tout, wasn't he, Si? And I seem to recall that when I was the only sucker among your acquaintance who was prepared to sock you the dosh and be an accessory, you were pathetically grateful that you wouldn't get sent down from Law School after all…"

"All right, all right. I'll do it. But I can't just lay my job on the line. Now *I* stand to look like an accessory, don't I?"

"For having a discreet conversation? No way. The claims are known to your office, which as far as I know has no vested interest in prosecutions as such. Play this right and you'll have gained a big buddy in high office for evermore. Fast track to Assistant PS at least, I should think. Promotion whatever. You won't have done anything more underhand than alert a man you like and admire to a potential problem, *ex gratia*. Nothing you can't square with your conscience or write in your memoirs…This can't hurt you personally, Si. Quite the reverse.

But look…" Roper swigged at his glass. "Actually, you know this isn't obligatory. If you don't want to play, I actually don't care much one way or the other. You can do me another favour another day."

"So now I *really* don't understand. What about you? What do you get out of it?"

"Personally, I don't stand to gain bugger all. Enough pressure on Penrose, and my crazy colleague thinks he gets to make a movie without the hindrance of a lawsuit on the part of an outraged MP defending the dubious honour of his wife's family name on the grounds that everything will crawl out of the woodwork if he tries. This is a species of blackmail, and much as I think Puffer Penrose fully deserves his grimy laundry waved for all to see, I don't much care for doing it this way. Nasty taste. I don't give a shit either way, to be honest. I'd far rather be making a movie that everybody wants to make and nobody's going to try to block from the start…" He drained his pint. "Are you married, Simon?"

"Eh? No – I mean not yet. Liz and I sort of well, hover…Er, why?"

"Nothing really. I've met someone. I've known her for about three weeks and I can't imagine being without her. How crazy is that? She's not in love with me. She just loves the film game. It makes you think…"

"You poor sod," said Drinkwater sincerely. "Another? This is my round."

410

xxix: Chez Penrose

"Peter?" Lucinda Penrose was busy ticking items off a list, putting some bread in the Aga, removing a pastry case and standing it to cool, and stirring a pan of rich bolognese sauce on the stove. A bowl of sponge mixture sat on the table, and a dish of hulled strawberries. The large kitchen was pungent with cooking. "Peter, darling. You haven't forgotten, have you?"

"Eh? Sorry…" Peter Penrose, dressed in jeans and a pullover, was studying the contents of an envelope with a deepening frown. "I'll get out of your way, dear. Something's come up. Now what's the matter, Lucie-mouse?" He gave her his 'full attention' look, which didn't, as she knew from long experience, mean anything.

"The *girls*! Oh, honestly, darling!"

"What? Sorry, Lucie darling…Am I supposed to be on duty?"

"Peter, I'm absolutely up to my eyes in everything, for heaven's sakes. Are you fetching the girls, or not? It's half past three! I suppose you want me to go and get them…"

"The girls! Oh God, I completely forgot! Sorry, darling. Too much stuff from surgery last night…when are they coming?"

Lucinda Penrose was exasperated. "Peter! Your daughters are arriving at the station at a quarter past four. With two friends.

411

Oh, forget it, darling! I'll have to go and this will be ruined. I hope you haven't actually forgotten it's Ellie's birthday tomorrow?"

"Ellie's? No, of course not," said Penrose with an attempt at heartiness, but he had. "You're cooking. I'll go and do my paternal duty."

"That makes a change," muttered his spouse under her breath, but only once he had left.

The telephone rang, and Lucinda, in the middle of the vital stage of a meringue, cursed and ignored it. It was almost certain to be for Peter in any case. She smoothed the foaming, sensuous mixture over the fresh strawberries, red and tempting in the crisp pastry case, with a certain satisfaction that amounted to joy. Very few people could make a fruit meringue to the perfection she could achieve, even Peter said so, and she pictured the girls' faces…except that one of them was bound to claim she was on a diet, silly child… Dimly, as if it were someone else's life, Lucinda could recall fashion and fads and diets…she herself was still almost slender, mostly because, like many serious cooks, she barely ate anything herself. She checked the temperature of the cool oven in the Aga. Just right. She popped the confection in. She glanced at the kitchen clock, and set the timer. Five minutes. The telephone shrilled again, and she picked it up.

"Hello?"

"Lucie?"

"Who's speaking, please?"

"You really don't know, Luce?"

"Good God, Jamie! Where on earth are you?"

"Oh…London. Listen, Luce…I know you're busy. Have you heard from the Wardley-Hill disaster?"

"From who? *Gilbert*? No, thank God. I've not seen him since Mummy's funeral and I don't care if I never see him again. Why?"

"He came to see me yesterday. He looks like the wreck of the Hesperus. Floating on an ocean of whiskey. Sarah thought he was one of our usual customers. He came to ask me sweetly if I'd butt my nose out of Veronica's film. Seems he's backing it. Obviously afraid of law suits. I thought I'd better warn you."

"Film?" Lucinda's hand clutched the rail on the Aga. "Oh God, Jamie! You don't *mean* it? A film? After all? But she *told* me! She said there wouldn't be a film. Oh no, oh *no*…"

"Sorry, Lucie. I think it's true. I think he might try to get some assurances from you and Peter too."

"Shit! Oh, *hell*! After all she *said*! I can't take it in! I can't take this *again*…Oh, God…so it's really true after all…" She paced the kitchen with the cordless at her ear, and then grabbed one of the rustic chairs at the long refectory table and sat down. "Why is everything so bloody *unfair*? I could *kill* bloody Veronica!"

413

When your life goes utterly pear-shaped, you either go under or you reinvent; and Lucinda Penrose, nèe Callington, had reinvented herself very thoroughly. Lucinda's life – her emergence from teenage wildchild with a circle of disreputable friends who were almost all, one way and another, grist to the daily mill of the *Daily Mail* and its ilk, and her own part in a tabloid-inflated tragedy involving her boyfriend's fatal drug-fuelled accident and her half-sister's criminal conviction into solid respectability – had taken years of effort, self-denial, and a species of courage. Now, her life as the busy political wife of a successful political husband, mother of a growing family, *chatelaine* of a large and comfortable house in a picturesque North Yorkshire village, an active presence in the local WI and the Constituency, speeches at luncheon events with presidents of children's charities, dinner parties with bishops and Cabinet Ministers, and a recipe for an orange chocolate cake that everyone begs for – was a fragile miracle of reinvention. She could love her obstinate, difficult husband for this alone. When Veronica's dreadful book had come out, Lucinda had disowned her sister and refused to talk to the press no matter how persistent. Most of Lucinda's troubles, historic and current, stemmed, it seemed, from Veronica...

"Sorry if this is a bombshell, Luce. I was a bit surprised myself. I thought it was only fair to warn you... Lucie?" There was the sound of sobbing on the other end of the line. "Lucie. Don't cry. I couldn't *not* tell you."

"I know! It's all *her* fault! The absolute lying *bitch*! She said she wasn't going to do it! She *swore*!" She grabbed the bottle of wine she had used for the sauce and poured a glass.

"Calm down, Lucie, please…Let's get this straight, if we can. You spoke to Vee? Yes?"

Lucinda took a deep gulp of wine. "Yes! After that article in the *Observer*. You must have read it! All those hints about making a film. I was appalled! She told me it was all a mistake and she wasn't going to sell the rights of that horrible book…she swore blind! She's trying to damage me! Trying to damage Peter! I – Oh God! Why can't you *do* something, Jamie?"

"She swore, did she? That she wasn't going to permit a film. She told you that?"

"Yes! It's all just so unbelievably vile! And *typical*! She's always despised me! And hated Daddy! She loathes Peter… Oh God…Jamie, hang on! I've got something in the oven…and the girls are coming home…it's Ellie's birthday…Oh God…" Crooking the telephone under her jaw, she opened the Aga and shrieked with dismay.

"Lucie. Luce, please. Look, if Vee said that she wasn't selling the rights, then I'd tend to believe her."

"Well that's just typical, too! You *would* believe her! She's your *real* sister!"

"That's not fair, Lucie…"

"Sorry! Oh God…" Sounds of clattering, and another shriek. "No, I've just caught my arm on the oven…Oh God! Sorry, Jamie. This couldn't be a worse time! Ow…"

"Luce…Look, do you have her number? I'll give her a ring, see what's up. Do try to calm down…"

"How can I? I've just ruined a *pudding*! It's all right for you, James! Now *you've* nothing to lose, you can afford to tell *me* to calm down! I haven't got it to hand. The sodding address book's in the hall, and I'm trying to organize your niece's *birthday*! I'm up to my eyes in *everything*!"

"Sorry, Lucie – I think I must try and get hold of Vee."

"She'll lie! How can Gilbert be involved otherwise? Tell me that! She must have sold it! Sold *us*! She doesn't give a damn about anything!"

"Not necessarily, Lucie. Look, Vee is still in Fulham, isn't she? That's the last address I had. What? Yes, Lucie, of course I'll keep you posted. Cheer up…of course. Promise…"

When a fruit meringue goes wrong, hardens into toffee, with the pastry base done to a crisp and the fruit beginning to roast, you let it cool a bit, then tip it out into a big bowl, break it into bits, stir in a lot of cream, and plonk it in the fridge with a scattering of Demerara sugar and wait. It becomes an Eton Mess…

416

"What do you mean, you *can't*, Peter? This could ruin us! Ruin *you*!"

"Darling – Lucie-mouse. Hush, please. The girls…try not to squeak. Please."

"I am not *squeaking*, Peter!" But she lowered her voice. "Why can't you just *do* something?"

Peter Penrose poured himself a whiskey and remained standing by the hearth. His receding hairline, prominent teeth and advancing paunch had been much caricatured in the press; in real life, however, he cut an almost impressive figure.

"Can I have one of those?"

"Oh – well, of course, darling. If you're sure…"

"Just give me a bloody whiskey, Peter! Stop treating me like a child. Why can't you just serve an injunction on her and stop her? For God's sakes, Peter!"

Penrose poured a small glass for his wife. "I hope this isn't the start of another habit, darling…"

"Peter!"

"Sorry. I can see you're upset. Understandably. Darling, Lucie-mouse – look. It isn't exactly simple. I – I'll confess. It – um – turns out I've blundered, darling. I've – um – made a rather unwise claim on expenses, Parliamentary expenses for the Constituency…" He coughed. "I – I'm rather afraid it could be a little embarrassing…" He sipped and coughed again.

"It's the bloody pool, isn't it! After all I said!"

417

"Lucie, please. The fact is, if I start making waves, all sorts of regrettable things could come out. In the press. I think we just have to keep our heads low for a while. An injunction would involve a lot of very unwelcome publicity…they always do."

"But what on earth have you *done*?"

"It was utterly stupid. I claimed for the swimming pool. And the new conservatory… Everybody else has. I thought I'd chance it. I said it was drains, but now it seems, I mean it looks as if…"

"So now you're admitting I was right! I *told* you!"

"You did, darling. You did. Um, it looks as if – well, it looks as if the pool's not within the code after all, and the conservatory could turn into an embarrassment…"

"Not within the *code*? What do you mean? You're talking riddles. And I don't understand how this makes a scrap of difference to bloody Veronica's bloody film! You have to stop her, Peter! Get Underwood onto it."

"Darling, Lucie – this isn't entirely straightforward. If we start rocking boats, this could be my Seat on the line. The process is extremely complicated. I don't expect you to understand. Just trust me on this one, please…"

"And just sit and watch while Veronica drags poor Daddy through the mud again? He can hardly defend himself now, can he? And poor Mummy's memory? And me! Oh, you don't care, except to save your precious Seat. It's your *arse* that's on the line! And what about *my* arse? Tell me that! As if you care!"

"Please, darling. Calm down. Try not to get hysterical. I care about your – your arse very much. I promise to find out how we stand. Ten to one, it's a mare's nest. James might be mistaken."

"He seemed very sure about Gilbert. And Gilbert wouldn't be involved unless there's something to get involved *with*, would he?"

"Then Gilbert might be mistaken. I'll talk to Gilbert myself. Get his story. Yes, that's the thing…get his story."

"Now?"

"He'll be out, I imagine. It's Friday night…"

"You have to *try*, Peter. Ring him *now*!"

"All right. I'll give his number a go. Look, we can't really tackle this while we've got a houseful of young visitors…" They were aware of shrieks of laughter from upstairs. "It's ten-thirty. Shouldn't you be doing a bit of motherly supervision?"

Lucinda frowned at her wristwatch. "Oh hell…The film should have finished by now. They ought to be getting to bed." She got up. "You'll try Gilbert *now*, Peter? You have to do something!"

"He might not make much sense, even if I do get him. Try not to worry, darling…I'll handle it. I always do, you know, my love…don't worry, please."

But Peter Penrose, remembering his recent interview with Simon Drinkwater, was a very worried man indeed. He poured another whiskey, went into his study, shut the door and picked up the telephone.

Lucinda, putting her ear to the door of Ellie's room, heard giggles and movie-dialogue, and decided to leave the children to it for another few moments. On impulse she went into her own bedroom, sat on her side of the big double bed, and picked up the extension with practiced stealth. She heard her husband's voice.

"...it's threatening to be a bloody mess, Mike. Lucinda naturally wants to stop this crazy film venture, I'm not too keen on it myself, obviously...but so much is at stake if we start rocking any boats now...Is it possible to put some sort of private block on it?"

"You mean, a block on the film?" Michael Underwood, Peter's lawyer. Thank God! At least Peter was doing *something*!

"I really mean the press coverage..."

"You mean, a press injunction on your injunction? That would be next door to impossible, Peter. And honestly, it doesn't work like that. You know how it goes. Big press announcement that the Right Hon X, MP, has acquired the right to prevent potentially damaging details being published...you might as well hire the town cryer...And that's only if you could prove that the press coverage is not in the public interest..." Michael Underwood yawned audibly.

"So what do you *suggest*, Michael? I wouldn't have disturbed you so late if this weren't a serious *crisis*." Peter sounded as if he were speaking through gritted teeth.

"Suggest? As far as this film's concerned, they can probably make it with impunity. It's basically a press story. Pretty old – I'm surprised they want to bother…You could try to sue for defamation on your wife's behalf, or your father-in-law's…show willing, you know. If they're determined, you can't stop them, I'm afraid, but you can make a noise. They'll be short of backing, if your sister-in-law hasn't sold the rights. Backers, insurance people – they get the wind up…If she has sold it, then frankly you can do bugger all."

"Damn! I don't *want* to make a noise!"

Lucinda made no noise at all and continued to listen.

"It's this other business that worries me…" Her husband's voice was a harsh hiss.

"If you mean the Bath cottage, that's going to come out anyway the way things are going…sorry, Peter. I did advise you at the time…"

"I might be able to cover that…I'm – um – told it can remain more or less private. I'm on the line over the bloody conservatory here in Fallowdale. But I haven't a snowball in hell's chance if there's a furore in the press about anything else…This is a very *significant* worry, obviously…" Lucinda often felt embarrassed when Peter sounded bombastic. "Apart from the domestic point of view…" Lucinda swallowed her whiskey with practised silence..

"Sounds like a rock and a hard place to me…" Underwood yawned again. "Sorry…long day. Still not over."

"I'm relying on you to *help*, Michael. Can I see you earliest next week? I'll be back in London on Monday."

"Of course. I don't know there's anything I can do, though, Peter. Look, my wife's got a dinner party in full swing and we've not even got the dessert…see me on Tuesday? After I've had time to check a few details? The office? Fine…I'll do what I can. Sorry not to be more consoling…"

Lucinda waited until both lines had blanked, and put down the extension.

xxx: Amateur Detection

Something about Freddy's cheerful scepticism was refreshing. Over a simple trattoria lunch by the sea, Julian found himself telling Freddy virtually everything: Faye's story, and his own doubts about Hilary's death; his meeting with Innocenti; and his oddly disturbing encounter with the ancient Constanza. "And now," he said, "The Barkers obviously want me gone. I can't help thinking the Barkers know quite a lot. But what? I can't just go ferreting. I've got a memory stick I can't open, and now this…" He produced Hilary's pyramid. "It may not have anything to do with anything, of course. I just couldn't help wondering."

"Let's see." Freddy frowned over the paper and said after an interval, "Some sort of game, maybe? I say, your brother wasn't into Mayanism, or anything equally loopy, was he? They go in for pyramids in a big way…cosmic messages in ancient geographical cross-points."

Julian shook his head, laughing. "Not Hil. At least I doubt it very much. He was an investigative journo, not a mystic."

"These letters…they could be some sort of mathematical code, I suppose. Algebra? Geometry?"

"Search me. It's gobbledegook, unless you know the key. I mean, whatever it is, it presumably meant something to Hil, and not to anyone else. And anyway, it probably isn't relevant. I'm

423

just clutching at straws, really. When I found it, it seemed like Fate…That old girl spooked me a bit."

"We won't know anything unless there's a clue in that memory stick, dear thing…"

"And we can't get at that unless one of these passwords works. Faye – Hil's wife – she could only guess. I left my laptop in London, and I can't ask the Barkers if I can monopolise the office again. And to be frank, I'm a bit technologically challenged…"

"I'm not, though. Tell you what. Come back and use mine. There's a sofa you could kip on too, if you like."

"That's extremely generous, Freddy."

"Not a bit. I could do with a bit of diverting. You're very welcome."

"I think I'm inclined to accept, but I think I might keep up the pretence with the Barkers that I've moved on from Monty…that okay by you?"

"More than! I adore a mystery! Me lips are sealed. You can park outside, too."

In Cadwallader Jones's little adjoining cottage, sitting at the tiny dining table in the comparative cool in what was currently Freddy's bolt hole, Julian sat poring over Freddy's laptop and tried 'HILARY', hilary, HILARITY, h1LARITY, HBLYTH, HGB123, Hgb xyz, and several other combinations and eventually gave up, exasperated and hot.

"Try anything else he wrote under," suggested Freddy, hovering, and pouring iced water from the fridge. "He wrote 'A Bit Off The Map' for the *Bystander*, didn't he? Try ABOTM. Sounds rather deliciously rude!"

"Might have appealed to Hil's sense of humour…okay. Here goes…No. No go…Shit!"

"Want me to have a go? Why don't you go and grab your car and your stuff and move in? I'll rack my brains in the meantime."

Julian walked back to the Albergo, lost in thought. Silvana handed over his laundry, and he thanked her profusely for such efficiency and told her he had decided to check out that afternoon. A B& B in San Gregorio would do nicely, and he could get to Rome easily from there to catch his plane. An unpractised liar, he left times and dates deliberately ambiguous, but Silvana, unremittingly garrulous, seemed not to notice.

"Okay, dear. Whatever suits. It's been *so* lovely to have you," she said after a long rigmarole about a party of Japanese who were off to see Herculaneum. "I do hope we see you again! But I expect now that your wrist's getting better, you'll be off on the concert tours again, won't you? Oh, Rome in the spring! Doesn't that sound romantic! I hope you have time to pop down and see us! Yes, indeed! Until next year then…Gianni!"

The surly Gianni waited outside Julian's room and helped him downstairs with his bags. In the foyer, Silvana gave him a final embrace, and Gianni loaded the bags into the boot of the hired car in the Piazza. Julian produced a generous ten euros, and Gianni looked startled.

"Thank you, but I cannot take this," he said, passing the note back, and looking at the ground..

"Oh, please," Julian said pleasantly. "For your help. Have a drink, or something."

"No! Thank you, sir, but no." Gianni wore very clean jeans and a short-sleeved white tee-shirt with 'Albergo del Mare' picked out in red embroidery on the left shoulder. Round his neck was a large gold cross, which he touched, still not looking up. His sallow face had gone white.

"Fair enough," said Julian cheerfully. "Thanks a lot anyway. Bye, now. Ciao."

"*Buona sera, signore,*" mumbled Gianni, as Julian started the engine and felt the blast of the air-conditioning which appeared to be working again.

'Scared,' thought Julian, frowning as he negotiated the narrow Medici Gate and twisted down onto the Lungomare. 'Scared stiff. But *why...?*'

When he reached the little house near the Castello, Freddy was outside waving him into a parking space with extravagant silent gestures.

"Come in, come in!" he whispered. "Mustn't wake Uncle Cad. He'll be having his little zizz. I think I've cracked it! Have

426

some tea. I haven't a clue what it all means, but you'll be able to interpret. I've also had a moment of illumination!" Freddy led him through the small, over-furnished sitting room to the tiny kitchen-diner, where the laptop remained set up on the table.

"I tried about a million combinations. Then I went back to ABOTM and tried it in lower case, and made the 'a' an 'at' sign, and the 'o' a zero. It worked! Pretty elementary, really, but it's a private memory stick. Now then, stick your gorgeous orbs on this…lemon okay in the Lapsang, my dear?"

"Please…Let's see. These just seem to be Hil's tourist files..." He scanned a short and very uncryptic list: 'Swims, 1-15'; 'Coast Road MF – R and MF –N', which turned out to be journeys, between Monte Farfalla and Rome and Naples respectively; 'Etruscan Stuff'; 'Medici Stuff'; 'Gardens & Villas'; 'Eats&Drinx'… he opened 'Eats&Drinx' and found the Cantina Valdambrini where he had eaten so recently with Veronica and Freddy. "These seem to be mostly connected with the *Bystander* pieces, Freddy. All good back-up for his current harmless tourist journalism. 'Music…Dancing, Diving. Spas…' Somewhere called Viticchia. 'Alberghi…' I don't see why he'd have wanted Innocenti to have this, do you?"

"It's pronounced 'vitikkia'. It's got hot springs where one can bathe in mud if one is prepared to stink like rotten eggs. Why don't you try the 'Alberghi' file? I expect there's a few places we know."

The notorious piece on the Albergo del Mare was easy to find. "I can see why the Barkers were annoyed," Julian commented. "Actually I found it all quite comfortable."

"That was before the great renovations. The place got a big makeover last winter…"

"Have you looked at any of this?"

"I confess. The teenziest, weenziest look-see. But I was waiting for you. Thing is, Jools, I've had an idea. Scroll down to the bottom of the del Mare article…see? There's a reference code: Dom/Sec/Men…"

"Like on Hilary's thrown-away paper…but what the hell does it mean?"

"Go back to the file menu. It's there. 'Dom/Sec/Men'."

"Okay…yes. Here it is…" He opened it and frowned. "Mmm. This is much more obscure. Hil talking to himself in initials again…Ah. We've got 'AB brackets P', and a date. 1999. And then 'R' 2008. And then 'CD, and a query. Then 'EF', 2004, and brackets 'dec. 2005'. December? These were all on that pyramid diagram thing. Then we've got 'DB/ LM' and 'GP & FP, and SP.'. Those 'P's aren't in brackets. It matches, by God! And there's – look! 'Fire at PP'. 20/04/09. That's a more specific date. But what in hell does it *mean*? Do you know?"

Freddy poured more tea and sat down, his face a comic study in not quite smirking. "I've been doing some guess-work, dear thing. I've also been doing a bit of internet homework. Makes a change from testing pasta and telling people to drink red with the tuna steak. I'll tell you my idea, if you like. First, I think these *are* initials, and that 'P' in brackets stands for 'prison'. And I'd bet a half-dollar that 'dom/sec/men' stands for *domenica, secondo, mensile*…in other words, the second Sunday in the month. You thought brother Hilary was onto something, and my guess is he was, big time. I also glanced at some historic Hilary Blyth – notably, his coverage from Rome of the trial of one Andrea Buoncompagni, the Mafia boss from Palermo who got caught on the mainland and who got sent down for about a hundred and ninety years in 1999. Note the ironic name."

"Er – good companions?"

"Yup! Not arf. He's out now, naturally, but he's doubtless under close watch. Your bro and a colleague covered his arrest and trial for the British press. I guess if Hilary's 'P' stands for prison, then 'R' stands for release, as in Buoncompagni's untimely one… According to the papers – your brother's among others – the anti-Mob officials tend to allow a bit of latitude so that old cohorts can get in touch with the bosses and then they can expose more of the network. It works, apparently…. Buoncompagni had a couple of lieutenants. Cristofero Daniele went on the run after his boss came to grief, and they failed to catch him…"

"'AB' and 'CD'…and there's that query after CD…"

"Quite. So far, Hilary's interest is public domain stuff, okay? Reporting trials. Explaining tortuous Italian legal processes for the benefit of the British chattering classes. But he moved to Monte Farfalla when? 2008?"

"2007...He more or less retired..."

"Sure. But San Gregorio is the nearest big town, and this was where another of Buoncompagni's lieuts was also caught and tried, but the trial was inconclusive. His name was Eduardo Fellini. As in *La Dolce Vita*. He's dead. Heart attack, so tis said, on remand...that 'dec' stands for 'deceased', I'd bet."

" 'EF'?"

"It's getting to look very possible, *n'est ce pas*? Now, we have to travel down to the basement of the pyramid...it's a hierarchy."

"Good God," said Julian again. "There must be a big San Gregorio connection. Innocenti wouldn't say outright, but he more than hinted that Hilary knew a great deal and didn't take the personal risks seriously enough." He smoothed out Hilary's pencilled pyramid once more. "We've got an 'LM' and a 'DB', a 'GP', an 'FP' and an 'SP '...Gang members, presumably? And what about 'fire at PP, GR'?"

"I can answer that one, too, I think. There's a rather smelly resort up the coast called Giardino Rosso. Big attraction for Italian locals, brash cheapie holidays. The kids converge on their *motorini* at the weekends and sunbathe, go to discos, have dancing competitions, that sort of joint. Snobby Monte Farfalla rather blesses its existence – you know – keeps the undesirables all in one place. It's pretty harmless, really, if your idea of fun is lying on a lounger about two inches from your neighbour and slathering yourself in Ambre Solaire all day and then eating pizza and dancing to bad 70s stuff and drinking German lager at night…nothing very awful, mostly innocent, and rather gorgeously ghastly…I sometimes go there for a spot of R & R…I have appalling taste…There was a big disco-cum-pizza joint there – part of the Pizze Panini chain which I think is now part of the Burger King conglomerate…anyway, they're all franchised. The manager was one silly sod. He was anti-Mob, and made no bones about it. When the local Men of Honour demanded their cut to stop the place being set on fire, he refused and informed the *Corriere della Sera*, and the place was razed to the ground the day after it went to press. Fortunately nobody was in it at the time. It's known as a gesture. You get the picture…"

"I think so…Jesus…"

"After the fire, this stupid cretin went round accusing people, naming names… not tactful…he's in a wheelchair…A rather bigger gesture…" Freddy shivered.

"Bloody hell. Are you saying that the Mob, these Buoncompagni people, were on to him?"

"No. Or not directly, necessarily. This was smaller potatoes. Local. Look, I hardly understand all this, to be honest. I just picked up gossip after the fire because I was staying here at the time. It made a lot of local news, mostly people complaining that there was a rotating 24/7 watch on a burnt out shell by at least five police departments using up their taxes…After all that

431

hoo-ha about those Palermitan judges who were assassinated, there had to be a lot of anti-Mob support on the part of the public services. Nobody would argue with that unless it was costing money…What about a drinkie?"

"Why not? God almighty, Freddy – it does sound as if poor old Hil had put himself in the way of some pretty unpleasant people…"

"Quite. Look – it's none of my business, dear thing, and I'd love to help, truly…but are you sure pursuing this is wise? One-man investigations tend to go wrong. I mean if your hunch about your brother is right… I thought we'd go for a spot of very light red and some cheese for supper…I bought some nice pecorino. See what you think of it. There's some olive patè. We can nibble, can't we?"

"Sounds fine to me…I keep thinking about Innocenti…"

"*He* told you to leave it all alone, didn't he? He ought to know. I would. But then, I'm a famous wuss, and Hilary wasn't my brother…"

"I suppose you're right. You've no idea about LM, DB, GP, FP and SP, I suppose?"

"One or two *ideas*…but I should hate you to get into any trouble. Veronica would never forgive me. She's cross enough with me as it is…we argued."

"Veronica?"

"Darling, isn't she? She's one of my oldest friends. I knew the bride when she used to rock and roll…as it were…"

Julian merely gazed at the screen while Freddy clattered plates and cutlery.

"She's a lot less fierce than she seems, Vee…despite the confrontational manner…"

Julian coughed. "I'm sure…I've only just met her…oh, thanks. Cheers! You must let me repay all this hospitality very soon."

"Understood, dear thing. This pecorino is *al punto, perfetto*…mmm! Listen, I can't throw much more light on the basement initials, but I wouldn't mind taking a punt that 'LM' is one Luigi Moretti. Small time local gangster, rumoured to be in with some very big cheeses. *Grandi formaggi*, you might say. It stuck in my mind, that name, because I associate it with one of the better Italian beers. Moretti is a fairly common name round here, even so. Other than that, I can't be much more help…Leave it alone, Jools, old thing. Jump on a plane and take old Vee to dinner…"

"I intend to," Julian murmured. "Oh God! Hang on….Hil's notes on the Albergo…look! He says 'The Albergo del Mare serves Dreher, Nastro Azzurro, and *Moretti*'…"

"Well, it would. It's got a well-stocked bar…"

"But he's put 'Moretti' in italics."

"Perhaps he liked the Moretti beverage…I do."

"No – no, wait, Freddy. It's something Innocenti said. It's all coming back. I didn't take notes and we were drinking a lot of beer. Probably 'Moretti', come to think of it. Listen. He told me obliquely about the Men of Honour infesting Monty for secret meetings, and suggested Hil knew more about it than was healthy. When I leapt to conclusions and suggested that Hil had allowed them to use his own house, he laughed and said I was being blind, only seeing with one eye. It's obvious, blindingly obvious! They used the Abergo! Don't you see? The place is a hotel – strange cars and strange people coming and going all the time… Christ! *The Albergo serves Moretti*… It fits, doesn't it?"

"Like a glove, I fear…" Freddy poured himself a liberal slug of wine. "Oh dearie me…"

"And the meetings took place – "

"On the second Sunday of each month. With Moretti playing local host to the Bosses, presumably Daniele and co, and the premises provided by one DB…"

"Dennis Barker, obviously. Who was in on it…"

"Up to his fat neck, I'd say…"

"No wonder they've been so jumpy to have me turn up. In return for… for what?"

"Money certainly. And a lot of perks including a refit and redecoration, employing their own foot-soldiers as brickies, probably…The place was closed for a full makeover for several weeks last year. The Crew put it about that the bill was footed by Daphne Allerton, but I bet it wasn't…"

"But I rather thought the Men of Honour only trusted their own…don't they?"

"You've seen too many movies, dear thing. They don't share their secrets, maybe, but they'd be happy to pay for favours from outsiders. You just said it yourself – a nice, respectable hotel in a historic resort run by Inglese…what could be more innocent-seeming? They were only a regular party of businessmen, after all. I don't suppose they brought their violin cases. Part of the pay-off would be the Barkers keeping schtum. But it's quite possible that the unappetising Dennis really didn't know any details. His Italian's crap…"

"But his wife's is native…And Hilary found out, or guessed. Maybe he recognised somebody. From the Rome days. Oh, shit, Freddy…It explains so much. About Hil…"

"All too much, I fear. And someone felt desperate enough to arrange that burglary at Hilary's house, after…It can't have been coincidence. They took the original of this, remember. The laptop."

"And the burglar that got sent down, Hil's builder, was called Fabio Pitch – Pick…Look! That's 'FP'…"

"Piccione? Soft 'c's. It translates as 'pigeons'. And Piccione is also the *cognome* of little Gianni at the Albergo…There's another brother or cousin, too. Enzo across the road knows them. He's little Gianni's landlord, did you know? Gianni stays there, or did."

"You mean Enzo is in it, too?"

"Probably not, as such. But they're all related, these fisherfolk…"

"But the laptop… it wouldn't have given them anything if they hadn't got the passwords. And it's all in English."

"So they probably just destroyed it and must have thought they were safe. They *still* think they're safe. The Albergo'll be clean as a whistle now. The Good Friends will have found another venue. Your poor bro was dead already. No one knows of the memory-stick's existence, apart from Innocenti, you and me. Or so we can only hope. Christ. I'm going cold all over. Another smidge of this cheesio? How's the wine? It's one of your better Lambruscos." Freddy was chattering.

"It's very nice. But I thought Lambrusco was white…hen-party fare."

"Only if it's bad and too sweet and probably a misnomer, courtesy of Tesco. There is a decent-ish white version, in fact, no skin contact, which sounds prudish of it, and I'm not a fan. This is the real Macoy. Pellucid red, short on alcohol, long on taste, with just a frisson of fizz. This one comes from Emilia-Romagna…"

"It's very pleasant indeed… Freddy, listen. I still don't understand *why*…" Julian turned from the computer and frowned, deep in thought. "It doesn't make sense…"

"Blimey Moses! It makes enough sense to me to be yours truly thoroughly alarmed. Moretti is still at large, as far as I know. Possibly Daniele too. Drop it, Jools, like a dear good fellow. I mean, how much *more* do you need?"

436

"I mean, why did Hil let the cat out of the bag? If I'm right, and he was beaten up even if not killed outright, then it was to shut him up like your disco owner. But how come they knew he knew? He'd gone to all this trouble of cryptograms et cetera, presumably to expose them in print when he felt the time was ripe. He was gathering information for an article. He didn't even tell Faye. The only person he probably told was Innocenti, and he's on the side of the angels. It really doesn't make sense, Freddy, unless Innocenti is an exceptionally good liar and turned informer. I – I'd rather not think that…"

"Well, he might have. Don't let's get sentimental. You're not going to like this, either, Jools, old thing. But have you thought about blackmail? A bit of the action? Sorry. I've got a nasty mind. I mean, perhaps Hilary was broke and thought he'd chance it. No offence meant."

Julian shook his head. "None taken. Hil was frequently broke, and he was capable of all sorts of things, but he wouldn't have done that. He'd have been far more interested in a story, and he'd have hugged it tight until he was ready. It sounds like the grossest piece of stupidity to me, and Hil wasn't stupid at all…Something must have happened."

"You really are determined to get to the bottom of this, I suppose…"

"I can't just leave it, Freddy. I don't want to involve you in anything, though. I'm incredibly grateful for all your help already. I can always really go to San Gregorio or Rome, and try

437

to turn up something from there…I think I might go and see the Consul again. Doc Holliday. He's got to be able to help."

"Great plan. But don't go just yet. I think we have to consult a rather unreliable oracle, but he'll be better than nothing, because he was a witness of sorts."

"A witness? Who?"

"Uncle Cadwallader Jones. He was there. If we can prise him from the arms of one or other of his wrinkled paramours, we need to quiz him."

"Yes. Okay. But why, especially?"

"Because, my dear Julian, the answer to your burning question rests on Hilary's last night. Well, doesn't it?"

xxxi: Tribulations of a Landlady

Sometimes, it seemed to Silvana Barker as though the weight of the world was on her shoulders. Her many burdens – the hotel, of course, first and foremost; her mother, who now seemed to need watching all the time; Daphne (who, despite her protests, also needed watching – too often lately, there had been too much of the sauce and a nasty little fall, and it was bruising, blood everywhere and a visit to the surgery) and where was Corinna these days when she was needed? Little Beck was turning into a better nurse than Corinna, and she only wanted to treat dogs and cats! And of course, there was Dennis, who wasn't so much a burden as a bloody pain in the arse… But at least they could put all of last year's little trouble behind them now, Silvana fervently hoped; secretly she was as relieved as Dennis that Hilary Blyth's brother had finally left. Somehow, he had made her feel increasingly uncomfortable – something inscrutable about his whole manner – the sort of man who would not let you know what he was thinking – and God alone knew what Innocenti had been saying. Or her mother.

Now, to cap it all, just when she wanted the fridges cleaned, the garden watered and weeded and some laundry hampers moved, Gianni seemed to have disappeared. He'd better be on parade in time for these Japs. Bugger the little toe-rag!

But she had another matter on her mind now, one which made her fairly bristle with unspent fury. Quite accidentally, that very morning, and apropos something else altogether, she had spoken to her friend Donata at the 'Gazza Ladra' and had learned that Corinna had taken it upon herself to cancel the arrangements for Daphne's 80th birthday dinner. And not said a bloody word! Of all the outrageous, bloody-minded cheek! The sheer nerve of it! Not trusting herself to speak to Corinna at the moment – Silvana wanted to calm down first – she was biding her time. Every time she thought about it, however, she seethed with rage and felt hot all over, and it took a considerable effort of will before she was able to concentrate on the task of ticking difficult names off a list.

"Where's that bleedin' Gianni?" said Dennis without preamble. "He was supposed to meet me to park the bleedin' bus!"

"Oh, hello, Den. Haven't seen him all afternoon…"

Her husband, red in the face and hot, fetched himself a tankard of beer from the tap behind the bar, and now dumped his bag in the office. It was getting dark. Silvana sighed. "Not where we'll all trip over it, Dennis, there's a dear."

"Sarky bitch. You'll never guess what I've just seen."

"Not unless you tell me, Dennis, I shan't. I'm not a mind-reader. Don't get in the way, Den. I'm rushed off my feet."

440

"Only the Bombshell in the garden at Lord Elpus's … all over him like a rash, she was. And he was slobbering over her like love's young dream. Nearly fell off his walking stick."

"Oh, you mean Corinna. Well, she's letting his little cottage, isn't she, Dennis? She'll have been measuring up or something. Now I put down that form on the desk, and my pen…"

"Reckon he was measuring up all right…" He leered.

"Oh, Den! Don't be so crude. And don't put that mug down on these – I've not photocopied them yet. How are the Pearsons and the Warners? Enjoying themselves?"

"Yeah. They liked the catacombs okay. Mrs P thought the cave paintings were like modern art. They all treated me to lunch. Not bad. Then we went to look at the roses. Mr W fancies himself as a rose expert. Mr P's all right. Quiet. Mrs P does enough talking for the both of them. Reminds me of someone, eh?"

"Thank you, Dennis. Look – why don't you watch telly or something while I finish up here? Beck's back. She'll make you something to eat."

"You don't believe me, do you? Them specs suit you. Make you look quite sexy."

"What?"

"I said, you don't believe me, do you?"

"Sorry. I don't believe what?"

"Silv! Honest to God, you're on another planet sometimes."

"I'm on planet Albergo, Dennis. For God's sakes, just tell me and get it over with."

"Gordon Bennett! Corinna de bleedin' Benedetto and his Lordship were as large as life in the flippin garden behind the hedge. Practically having it off. That snooty old secretary, Signora Bordoli or whatever her name is, she couldn't hurry us away fast enough."

"Oh, don't be so ridiculous, Den. I've told you – Corinna's letting his *dipendenza* for him. How many more times? He's famous for pawing women. He'll have been showing her the garden or something."

"All right, Mrs Clever. Since when does a landlord wear his dressing-gown to show the agent round at three in the afternoon? And since when did an agent wear a bathrobe?"

"Swimming? There's a pool, and it's been very hot today. Perhaps they'd had a little dip. Please, Den – I've got to finish this lot this evening. I expect there's an innocent explanation."

"Do you now?" Dennis Barker stood close behind his wife as she adjusted paper into the photocopier, and slid his hand adroitly into the neck of her blouse and grasped a handful of her plump left breast. "How innocent's that?"

"Ow! Dennis! Stop being so *gross*! You know I can't bear it."

"Only demonstrating," he said sulkily, removing the hand. "That's where his Lordship's hand was. Inside the Bombshell's robe having a right old feel. Plain as day."

"You're joking! Are you sure? Did they see you?"

"There! Knew that would get you. Of course I'm sure. And unlike you, Mrs Barker, my lawful wedded spouse, she weren't trying to push him away, neither. And no, they didn't see us. Too engrossed and we was all in the public part. But you didn't need binoculars. The randy old sod! Do you – um – fancy an early night tonight, babe?"

"I'm busy, Dennis. And if that's your idea of wooing, forget it!"

Hunger got the better of Dennis, and he departed for their quarters upstairs. After a busy and trying day, Silvana was tired to the point of aching. Nevertheless, when she had finished her office work, and had settled her mother comfortably in her room and half-listened to another rigmarole about ghostly journalists, and seen Dennis comfortably dozing in front of Sky Sport, Silvana Barker retreated back to the office. The bush telegraph was busy once again...

There is a certain grim satisfaction in revenge. Silvana locked up for the night, paying especial attention to the bar and the buns, put on the night-lights, and went up to her own quarters feeling better than she had all day. If she had heard Cadwallader Jones happily prattling to Dorinda Daly that Freddy had a new guest – a famous violinist, my dear, hee! – she might have felt

443

less happy, but she was spared this knowledge for the time being. As it was, she shared the sofa with Dennis in front of *Sex and the City*, and did not pull away when his arm slid round her ample waist.

"Now *that's* more like it," Dennis said.

xxxii: Bones of Contention

"I keep telling you it won't happen all at once, Mother. They just want to look at it..."

"But you've agreed to sell..."

"Yes, Mother...I'm sorry, darling, but that was always the arrangement...we're all having to tighten our belts..."

"Of course, of course, sweetheart...I'm not *blaming* you..."

"I just wanted to give you as much notice as possible...Look, Mum...I wondered, Tessa wondered, if this makes a difficulty, perhaps you'd like to come and stay with us in London for a bit?"

"*Tessa* said?"

"Just as an interim, while you're looking...we'll all help, rally round..."

"Well, I'd have to think about it, Merry...yes, of course, you just let me know when they want to come and view it, and I'll have everything ship-shape and shiny...no, of course not, dear. All in the way of things...and you always *said*..."

When her son Merrick had rung off, Dorinda's stoicism deserted her. She looked around the little apartment – at her pretty china on shelves, her pictures, the Japanese silk prints, the sunshine through her own fancy lace curtains at the French windows to the terrace (Tessa's choice of beige calico had struck her as singularly drab and she had folded them away in the wardrobe drawer under her winter woollies) and felt like weeping. An alarmingly bleak vista opened before her: all her capital had vanished with the failed antique shop. Now, she faced endless dot and carry round her children's homes in Britain (and Dymphna only had a studio flat in Bayswater, and Còlm was travelling in the East and had filled his Brighton house with lodgers) which left her daughter-in-law Tessa, who would be dutifully hospitable and frostily disapproving. She imagined being sent outside to smoke... And what did it *matter* if one fancied a glass or two in the morning? Dorinda poured herself one now, and, after gazing ruefully round the kitchen – where she had made all kinds of little homely improvements – not being one to let herself be daunted by circumstances, however dire (and the Lord alone knew she had faced plenty of those in her time) – she dried her tears and sat down to think.

"Oh, darling! How absolutely marvy and wonderful! Do you really mean it?"

"I do. Hee! I thought you'd be pleased!"

"I'm thrilled to bits, *Tesoro*! I can find lots of people who'd be just delighted with it! I'll start advertising it at once, and we'll go for only the very nicest people – you know, ultra-responsible and quiet..."

"But..."

"There's a very sweet couple I met in the Agency the other morning. They're Canadians. She's a painter. They want to spend at least three months in Italy. They might be ideal…"

"But – oh dear me! Hee! I'm afraid there's a little bit of a misunderstanding, my dear. I'd hoped you'd want to come and live in it yourself…"

"*Myself?* Oh! Oh, goodness…gosh! I thought you were giving it to me to *let*…"

"No, no, my dear. That wouldn't do at all… I'd hoped – you know – that you might like to come and make your home in it…beside me…"

"Oh, Cadwallader…you are *such* a darling. Oh dear! I – I simply *can't* at the moment. I'm all settled…and I've promised Valeria I'll remain in Via Tibaldi for – for another *year*, you see…"

"Oh…I see." Cadwallader, very crestfallen, pushed his spoon aside. "Valeria. Yes, I do see that's a little problem. I'm going to have a whiskey, my dear. One for you? I suppose you really can't let Valeria down, if you've promised…"

"Well, no…I can't. But, look! I tell you what, *Tesoro*. I'll let it for you for a year, and *then* I can move in! What about that? *Then* we can be next-door neighbours!"

"I always hope…my dearest…" He took her hand and brought it to his lips. "…that we can be a great deal more than that…"

"Oh, *Tesoro*…"

"One day…"

"I'll come to you, Cadwallader. Truly, I will…"

"Oh, my darling! I'm prepared to wait!"

"Oh, *Tesoro mio…*"

When young Rosario came out with glasses and the whiskey bottle, he coughed discreetly before interrupting his customers' passionate embrace over the table.

Saturday. Daphne and Corinna sat on the terrace in the setting sun. The barbecue was set up, waiting.

"Poor Dorinda! It was a great shock for her," said Daphne. "She was very *upset.*"

"Well she's had a free apartment for eighteen months…I wonder who Merrick's selling it to… I suppose this means she'll be going back to England…"

"She wants to stay, dear. She likes it here."

"Moh! For her it's little more than a tax and credit haven."

"Don't let's be catty, dear. I've suggested that she have a little word in the ear of a certain friend of hers…"

"Oh? Who?"

"Why, Cadwallader *Jones*, of course! Once Freddy leaves, his little guest house will be free. I don't believe he has any other lettings lined up. It would be ideal for her, I should have thought. Until she finds something else…"

"You can't be serious!"

"I'm very serious, dear. Why ever not?"

"Hiya! I'm late, Daffy. That bloody little toad Gianni didn't turn up this morning, Den's been in the Bay of Naples and I've had a stinker of a day. I've brought the rolls...Oh! Only just us?"

"So far, Silvy, dear... We'll be a bit thin this evening, I'm afraid. The American boys are in Milan, Cecilia's got one of her headaches but Hedley may come later, Freddy's going home, and Dorinda's having a telephone session with her family..."

"What a shame! What about our Mr Barkis?"

"I wish you'd stop calling him that, Silv. It's not very funny." Corinna was willing herself not to think about her last meeting with that gentleman.

"Oh, he'll be along, dear. He's part of the fixtures and fittings..."

"Like the elephant in the corner, eh, Rinna? Has Dorinda told you? Merrick's selling the apartment! She's going to be homeless!"

"We've just been talking about it, dear. I've suggested to Dorinda that she ask our friend Cadwallader to let her use his guest house *pro tem...*"

"And I think it's a terrible idea! I mean, it won't work – they'd be on top of each other!"

Silvana chortled and sat down. "Randy old goat! Listen, I'm not trying to make any trouble, but while it's just the three of us, can we *please* settle this birthday issue once and for all?"

Shortly, the menfolk, represented this evening solely by Hedley and Cadwallader, arrived to the inevitable shrieking of the ensuing catfight.

xxxiii: Cadwallader Recalls

"Come in, come in! And *do* mind the bicycle! I can't ride it these days, you know. My knees, I'm afraid! Hee! This is an honour, an honour!"

"*Déjà vu*," murmured Freddy under his breath, as he and Julian were ushered with due ceremony through Cadwallader Jones's extraordinary kitchen to the sitting room, where Beethoven's Fifth played loudly on an ancient gramophone.

"Andre Previn and the London Symphony Orchestra! Were you not first violin?"

"A little before my time, I'm afraid, Mr Jones," said Julian.

"Oh, Cadwallader, please. People call me Cad…by name, but not by nature, hee!"

Freddy sniffed. There was a powerful scent of turps. "You've been painting again, Cad," he said.

"Oh…this and that…I'm doing this little thing for Daphne…"

After Julian had been introduced to several of Cadwallader's ingenious 'forgeries', Cadwallader ushered them through to the tiny courtyard. "Dear me, yes. Poor Hilary Blyth! It's true you do look like him, very like him. And you say you were twins! Fancy! But I should never mistake you, except maybe at a distance, and even then…I still have a very good *eye*, you see! Hee! Now then, Freddy, dear boy, please do the honours…this is elevenses, but we might pretend it's later…I've already had my coffee, you see…"

A bottle of prosecco stood, still just chilled, on the little table in the courtyard, and Cadwallader had produced some aging gorgonzola and some rather bitter cinnamon biscuits which were strangely pleasant. Cadwallader dilated at some length on their merits…

It took some time and effort on Freddy's part to steer the conversation round to a certain night last year. "Julian's just trying to get a better picture of his brother's last evening, Uncle Cad…"

"Naturally. Dear me, " said Cadwallader. "*Such* a long time ago, and so much has happened in the intervening period…your poor brother! I was very saddened by his death. It was a terrible shock for us all. For the whole community! I thought him charming. A real one-off, if I may put it like that. And that lovely wife of his. Faye. Poor girl…poor girl. I have so much to thank them for! They introduced me to Corinna, who helped me to find this place, you know…perfect, isn't it? Hee*! Capri-ci-os-o*! That's how the agent described it, and I said that it must have my name on it, so to speak, because I'm just a tiny bit *capricioso* myself! Hee!"

"Cad…do you remember anything about that evening?"

"Yes…I'd be so grateful, Cadwallader. There was a party, wasn't there?"

"A party? No, I don't think so, dear boy."

"Julian means the regular Saturday at Daphne's, Uncle Cad…"

"Oh! I see! Now I never think of that as a *party*…oh yes, I was there, certainly…I was sitting with Corinna…" Cadwallader's ugly, eloquent face became sentimental.. "She had on a particularly becoming blouse, I remember…"

"Cad – there was a frightful row, wasn't there? A big argument, between Hilary Blyth and Dennis Barker. About the hotel. Do you remember that?"

"I certainly remember something of the kind…it was frightfully hot. Everybody was in a bit of a temper, I think. Daphne burnt the sausages. I do remember that! Nearly burnt the place down! Swore like a trooper. Hee! Shall we have more of this fizz? This is Dorinda's favourite. She's coming round later. I've bought in an extra bottle! Lovely woman. She's helping me sell some of my paintings. She has a contact at Bonhams in Knightsbridge! And Sotheby's! Isn't that clever of her?"

"That's great, Cad…Listen, about that night. Last summer. Do you remember what the row was about?"

"Row? Oh no, dear boy! Sorry. Is it important? I do remember the sausages catching fire. Such a drama! We managed to avoid calling the *vee-gee-lay del fuo-co…* the Fire Brigade, you know, my dear!"

453

Freddy sighed impatiently.

Julian spoke. "Mr Jones…sorry, Cadwallader. Can you remember what else you did that evening? Before the sausages burnt? You sat next to Corinna and she wore a pretty top. Then what? Who else did you talk to? After Corinna?"

"Now then, this is amusing, isn't it? I'm trying to cast my mind *back*, you see! Yes, I was with Corinna, and she went over and spoke to someone else, probably Cecilia, because I remember watching her standing by the railings and thinking how charming a picture it was. Their relative heights, you know. Cecilia is petite, and Corinna is – well, statuesque, a Venus…there was a moon…"

"Do you recall where everyone else was?"

Cadwallader closed his eyes. "I think *so*! I say, this is like one of those memory games! Pelmanism with people! Hee! Let's see. Daphne was cooking sausages on the barbecue grill, and the Americans were there, Lorrie and Cy, that is to say – they're property developers, my dear, and very beady with it, as Corinna would say…dear me. Sorry! I'm trying to concentrate! Let's see…there were some people Daphne had met from a yacht, they were American too, I seem to recall, and – yes! Hedley came and sat down beside me, and we reminisced about a television series he had been in, and an actor he knew who had played a villain in Millicent's series – my late wife, Millicent Fox, you know. Mystery novelist. Famous! Marvellous woman!"

"I'm an admirer, Cadwallader. So the Barkers weren't there?"

"Oh, yes. Silvana was. She was helping Daphne with trays and things. She always does. She gave plates of sausages to the new Americans. A couple with a daughter. A young girl, anyway. She gave me some sausages too. And Hedley. We were sitting down, you see...I always find it just a *little* difficult to eat from a plate perched on my lap...have some more of these, do! And Freddy, do pour, dear boy...Milly was *such* a good pourer! Um – where was I?"

"Eating sausages, Cadwallader."

"Sausages! Daphne always screams out 'sausages' when they're ready...it's a sort of rallying cry..."

"But these weren't burnt..."

"Burnt? No...no, that was later..."

Freddy's interest had revived, and he passed Cadwallader a fresh glass. "Do you remember when, Cad? When did the sausages burn?"

"That was during the row...Everybody's attention was turned, you see...Hee! Cheers! I'm recalling it all quite well now, you see!"

"You're doing wonderfully. Did Dennis Barker come in, Cadwallader? Did Hilary?"

"Wait! Don't interrupt! I can't *think* if you interrupt!" There was a pause while Cadwallader sat with his eyes closed and large lips pouted, and Freddy and Julian exchanged tacit glances and remained silent, waiting.

Then Cadwallader cried, "It's coming! It's coming! Dennis arrived. He was in one of his tempers. He can be very *tricky* on occasion. He was very bothered about something to do with the hotel. He shouted a lot, and swore, and the new Americans, the ones with the child, didn't like it. Corinna went over to placate them. She's an extraordinary diplomat, is Corinna. Silvana said shush, but she was busy with more sausages. She went to the kitchen to fetch them. Dennis was talking to Daphne. I couldn't really hear what they were saying, but then Daphne shouted something about Hilary being a journalist. I do remember that, because Hedley Porter joined in, defending journalists, and Dennis was very rude to him too. He often is, I'm afraid. Hilary had published something or other, I think…"

Freddy and Julian exchanged glances again.

"What did Dennis do then, Cadwallader?"

"Dennis? I can't remember. Perhaps he was doing something to Daphne's barbecue. It must have been about then that Hilary Blyth came in and Daphne screamed at him."

"Daphne screamed at him, Uncle Cad?"

"Yes. She told him he wasn't popular and to be quiet and have a drink and sit down. It's just Daphne's manner."

"And did he? My brother? Did he sit down?"

456

"He sat down next to me…Hedley must have got up. We were talking about something or other. Can't recall what. Oh, I know! Faye. Faye – Hilary's wife, you know. She was in Florence. We talked about Florence. The Medici tombs. Michelangelo's female figures were modelled by men, you know! Hee! Hilary knew a great deal about Florence…"

"He'd studied there," murmured Julian. "Did he seem drunk, Cadwallader? Hilary?"

"Oh no…I mean, he might have been a bit *partified*, so to speak, but not at all drunk. Making perfect sense. Everything went fairly peaceful…and then…oh, dear me! Hee!"

"And then?"

"Well, it was all most unfortunate. Silvana said something like, 'don't, Dennis, it's not worth it', but – hee! It's all coming back to me now! Dennis was suddenly in front of us. I mean, I looked up and there he was. He's rather a *bully*, is Dennis…hee! I felt quite *intimidated*, if that is the right word…he wanted to know what the hell Hilary had meant by printing some article or other and called him a name…and Hilary used a name, and then suddenly everyone was shouting at once…a lot of *language*…very disconcerting!"

"I'm sure it was…"

"Hilary stood up. He was taller than Dennis. Frankly, I thought there was going to be a *fight*… Someone, Daphne, maybe, said 'come away, Cadwallader, dear' and I did, rather gladly…there were a lot of words. Corinna and I sort of watched

457

from the sidelines, while Cecilia showed the Americans out, and I think one of *our* Americans, Cy Dillon, I think he went too…and Cecilia Porter defended Hilary and her husband, and Silvana burst into tears and accused Hilary of wrecking a decent innocent business, and Hilary told her to wake up and called her a hypocritical cow, I'm afraid…Dennis went for him, and Lorrie and Hedley tried to stop Dennis from hitting Hilary…and then Hilary said something to him in Italian, and Silvana screamed, Corinna gasped, and Lorrie, the American in the big specs, he said, 'Oh Jesus'…Everybody looked a bit stricken. I asked Corinna later, but she wouldn't tell me…it sounded something like 'buon amici' which only means 'good friends', I believe, so I expect Hilary was trying to make it up…"

"*Buon amici…*"

"Something like that, yes. But Dennis stormed out, saying something rude about Daphne's choice of friends. Daphne told Hilary to go too. Said he'd done quite enough damage for one evening."

"And did he? Did Hilary leave?"

"Well, no, not all at once, because suddenly there was this awful smell of burning, and we realised the barbecue was on fire…flames and smoke, and everybody flapped about trying to put it out. Lorrie grabbed a watering can but it was empty, and Hedley told everyone to stand back and Corinna fetched a wet towel and Daphne told her it was one of her best ones and to get another, but there were quite *tall* flames, and Lorrie went to look for a fire-extinguisher and Silvana screamed that there was one under the sink…and then Hilary called everybody cretins and tipped one of Daphne's decanters on it – she puts red from supermarket cartons into decanters, you see – and everything went fizz! Horribly dramatic! Hee! But the fire was out. The evening was ruined, of course…so were the poor sausages! I think, you know, that Hilary might have been the slightest bit the worse for wear, because he just laughed. Stood and laughed and laughed. And then he left. I can see his face now….And how amazing! I haven't recalled this in detail properly before…hee!"

Freddy glanced at Julian and poured more prosecco. "Have another glass, Uncle Cad…Jools?"

"Thanks…"

"Thank you, dear boy! I'm sure it was all rather a storm in a teacup, so to speak…"

"Except that a few hours later, Hil was dead…"

"Well, Jools…"

Freddy and Julian were back in the next-door cottage, drinking strong coffee in the sitting room. "Do you know, you're the only person to call me 'Jools' since Hilary…"

"Sorry. I'm a compulsive abbreviator. And I never had a brother. Do you mind?"

"No…are you thinking what I'm thinking?"

"I think so. Your bro was a bit tight. Too sloshed to resist having what's usually called a 'go'. He taunted them, and they

459

knew he was onto them for more than bad plumbing and worse manners. And '*buon' amici*' sounds far too like Buoncompagni to dismiss...even 'good friends' might have had a significance. He seems to have blabbed himself into a trap..."

"Yes, but what? Dennis didn't beat him up. Hil walked a mile or so home."

"A phone call is all it would have taken, Jools. Rally the troops, you know..."

"Who lay in wait for poor old Hil when he got there..."

"And that old crone heard the call or whatever it was, hence all the mysterious sybil stuff the other evening..."

"And young Gianni must have known. Or even been part of the gang of thugs that beat him up. He's scared shitless. It begins to make a ghastly sort of sense...poor fucking idiot Hil. And yet..."

"Drop it now, Jools, for God's sakes. You've got your answer, surely? Hilary got tight and blew it. End of. Don't be obstinate, there's a dear man."

"And just let them get away with it?"

"*Yes*! You've no choice. Honestly. What would you do? Confront Dennis in person?"

"I thought perhaps the police..."

"Huh! The local boys in blue are either in on it or won't care a monkey's. Drop it!"

"But that's damnable!"

"Damnable, but practical. And far healthier. Oh strewth, duck!"

"Eh?"

"Duck! Get down!" Freddy was grinning like an ape, and waving through the window at someone on the other side with one hand, and waving Julian away with the other. Julian darted into the kitchen. He saw Freddy open the front door. "Hello, *darling*! Fancy seeing you! *And* as *soignee* as ever…what a perfectly *fabby* frock…"

"Ooh, you flatterer, you! This is *old*…" Dorinda smoothed the navy silk self-consciously.

"It's utterly charming…and your *hat*! I'd invite you in, dear heart, but I'm in the very *middle* of a telephone confab on Skype…my editor wants me to do some *work*, would you believe? Are you off to see my lucky old uncle?"

"Yes – he's expecting me, bless him. I can't stop, either, sweetie, or I would. He'll be watching the clock. You know what he's *like*… Are you all on your owny-own, sweetie?"

"Fear so, petal…Not so fortunate as dear old Cadwallader…we'll have to go and paint the town as red as your charming bonnet very soon – just me and thee, shall we? Make Cadwallader jealous and get the tongues wagging?"

"Ooh, you kidder! But a little bird told me you had a *friend* to stay…"

"*Magari*," quipped Freddy, making a *moue.* "*Buon pranzo*, now! Where's it to be? The excellent Taverna?"

"Ooh, I expect so. Nothing strange or startling."

"Try the orata – they've got a seriously sooper-dooper fresh herb sauce with capers…I'm giving it a write-up."

"I would, darling, but I just can't bear fish bones…wimpy of me, I know…" Dorinda's eyes peered into the dark sitting room from under the hat and failed to see anything. Julian, from behind the kitchen door, saw her vividly.

"*Buon pranzo!*" said Freddy again, and closed the door with another wave of fluttery fingers. Then he charged into the kitchen, where Julian half hid behind the door, and fanned his face dramatically. "There are times," he said, "when it positively helps that everyone thinks you're as camp as a row of tents and not to be taken remotely seriously…".

"God! What was all that about?"

"Jools.This is serious. We wait for about twenty minutes until Uncle Curmudgeon and his aging Molly Bloom have tottered off to the Taverna. They'll pass the window, and they won't be able to resist peering in. We would draw the blinds in the interests of cool and decency, but we want to see that they've gone. Until they have, you will remain in here. Or go upstairs. Then, you really have to go,old thing."

"Oh dear…yes, I'm sure it's horribly awkward for you, all this…Sorry, Freddy…Listen, I've been thinking. It still doesn't add up. Hil was talking, laughing and putting out fires. The autopsy report suggested he was legless. Old Constanza…I

462

got the distinct impression she *saw* something…which means it must have been at the hotel…"

"Jools, please! These are mere details. Perhaps he stopped in a bar on the way back. And Constanza's batty. Silly as a wheel. She's had a year to fantasise about murders and angels. Even so…Oh, God, this is all my fault!"

"Your fault? I don't understand…"

"Oh, *think,* my dear man, please do! Any moment now, Uncle Cad is going to confide to his pet antiquarian-essa our conversation of this morning. She's a bosom friend of both Daphne and La Barker. The fat will be in the fire by four o'clock this afternoon. Everyone will know you're on the trail… My fault, getting him to talk like that. He won't be able to resist boasting now. Shh! Here they come. Darby and Joan…."

They both watched in silence as Cadwallader and Dorinda, who indeed cast a glance under the brim of her hat in the direction of the window, passed leisurely by, arm in arm.

"Whew. Look, Jools, you're not *safe*, dearie! You have to fly away. Preferably to Tasmania or Siberia…"

"This is *so* kind, my dear!" Cadwallader tucked into his orata, apparently intent on extracting every last atom of flesh from the skeleton "Very jolly and generous of you!"

"Nonsense, sweetie, it was my *turn*!" Dorinda had ignored Freddy's advice and had firmly ordered lamb cutlets and a green salad. She had also orderered one of the Taverna's more

463

expensive white wines for Cadwallader's fish, and drank the house red herself. She tried not to watch Cadwallader eating. "*Cin-cin*, sweetie!"

"*Cin-cin*! And may I say again how absolutely charming you look in that splendid hat!" He had told her at length about his visitors, but she had scarcely listened. "I remembered everything! How about that? Hee! About Hilary Blyth! He was what used to be known as a bit of a card..."

"Sorry, sweetheart...I'm in a bit of a tizzy today, I don't mind telling you. Such a shock..."

"Ah yes, of course, Merrick. Now, tell me all about it again. You say he's selling up?"

"Yes...He's found a buyer. It's all so sudden! It isn't poor Merrick's fault – we'd always agreed I'd only have the apartment until he found someone. But I don't know what to *do*, I don't truly...I don't want to leave dear Monty and all my lovely friends..." Her blue eyes, big and limpid, gazed at him from under the red brim. "I shall have to do a round of all the house agents when everything's open tomorrow..."

"Well, first and foremost, my dear, you must ask Corinna! I'm sure she'll have something on her books...marvellous, is Corinna! Hee!" He wiped his mouth and dropped the napkin onto the plate. Dorinda lit a cigarette.

"I'll certainly ask her, of course," said Dorinda, determined to do nothing of the kind, "but I must look at everything...I don't have any idea how *soon*, you see...oh dear…" She dabbed at her mascara with a hanky. "Sorry, sweetie…it's just the thought of having to go back to London…I'll so miss my dear little kitchen and my little lunch parties… Oh dear, I didn't mean to get emotional…"

"Oh, my dear! Don't cry, please!"

"Sorry!" She poured a glass of white wine for him, and helped herself to the carafe. "I'm trying not to…I just can't help feeling a bit…at a *loss*. Merrick and Tessa have invited me to go to them…but they're in Battersea, lovely big house by the Park, and plenty of space, but miles from *anywhere*…I've always had a bit of a *thing* about being south of the River…and they're *very* anti-smoking. And they've got a *dog*! It's not that I don't *like* Tessa…or dogs, as such. Oh, Lord, I just don't know *what* to do! I love it here. All I want is a couple of rooms, just to mark time…"

"*I* know what you'll do! You'll have an averno! On me! I shall have a little brandy with my pudding. I'm going for the tiramisu today. It's Sunday!"

Dorinda very nearly burst into real tears. "That's very, very kind, sweetie…no pudding, just coffee for me, thanks…"

Cadwallader hailed the waiter, and ordered.

"*Cin-cin*, my dear!" he cried, clinking glasses rather ineptly. "Now! Hee! I have just had *the* most splendid idea…It can only be a strictly *interim* arrangement, but listen…"

Dorinda's big eyes widened with surprise and pleasure as he told her. They were far too engrossed to notice the car drive by, with Julian grimly at the wheel, setting off for Rome...

xxxiv: The Handyman's Tale

Freddy was looking up Rome-London flights when a knock on the door made him start. Since Julian's departure, he had felt jumpy to the point of paranoia.

"*Chi è?*" he asked from inside.

"*Permesso, amico mio*? I come in? I have invite for you from *la mamma* to eat good pasta, and drink some wine. First, we drink good American bourbon whisky." Enzo Battaglia stood on the doorstep, flourishing a bottle of Jim Beam, almost full. "You like?"

"Oh, Enzo…That's very kind. I'm a bit busy…" He loathed bourbon.

"We drink in *cortile*, maybe. Private there. Cool. I need talk…Signor Cadwallader, he go out on date.. not interrupt."

"I'd honestly prefer beer…" Reluctantly, Freddy fetched glasses, and bottles of Moretti from the fridge, and led Enzo through to the back. Freddy's suitcase was open on the sofa, half packed.

"You go?

"Soon, yes, Enzo…I have to go back to London. Work…"

"Everyone go. Your friend, he go?"

"Yes."

"Home? In London?"

"So I believe…"

"You have bourbon whiskey with me, okay? Is good. Remember me much of America."

Freddy accepted a small one. "Cheers. *Salute*."

"Cheers. Bottoms up! I speak American!"

"You've been to America?"

"Sure. New York, on big ships. I play trumpet in band. I have long history…Frai-dy…listen, *scoltami*… Is true your friend, he brother of *giornalista, chi è morto un' anno fa*?"

"Yes…"

"And he gone to fetch police?"

"Police? No, I don't think so, Enzo. Why?" Freddy masked his sudden frisson of acute consternation behind his glass.

"Gianni, *il ragazzo*, he go…he uppanleave Albergo, he leave town."

"He's gone? What do you mean?"

"He not sleep in my house last night. He think your friend follow him from hotel. First he think he see ghost. Of *giornalista*."

"Ghost? Oh, I see. They're twins. *Gemmelli*."

"He know that now. Then he freak out when he see him here. He think *fratello* only here for *vendetta*. Bust his ass. *Capisce*? He have big fear. I say him better he not here if police come…"

"I see…but why? What's he so scared of?"

"Boss," said Enzo succinctly.

"Afraid of Barker?"

"Him too. He here earlier. He ask Mamma, where Gianni? Mamma, she say nothing, she don't know. But La Mamma, she worry. *Molto preoccupata, la povera.* Gianni he is like *nipote,* like Tommaso. She no like Barker. She say nothing…So." Enzo drank deeply, draining half his beer at a go, and burped loudly. "I like Ilary," he added. "Not like other Inglese. Very sad he die."

"Many people liked him, I understand," Freddy said, and Enzo looked at him with curiously pale brown eyes, unfathomable in the brick red face, and did not smile.

"You keep secret good, my friend?"

"I can try…but look, I say, Enzo, old thing, I'd far prefer it if you don't tell me anything at all…" Freddy thought suddenly of Julian and felt slightly ashamed of his cowardice. "I mean…"

"Listen, Frai-dy. I tell you something. But first you promise…you must promise you say *nulla, niente,* nix, nothing we talk…but if the *fratello* is a good friend, maybe is good he know too…" Again the hard unfathomable stare. Enzo, who drank beer like a drench, sipped at the whiskey, savouring it. "I have long history…I no have a boss. I am boss for myself. I work at many things. I catch the fish, I make the music, I mend the broken tables, I put the shelfs in houses, I mend the broken tubes, and for your *zio,* for others too. I clean and mend the boats. I

469

clean and mend the engine of 'La Serena'…*la piccola barchetta* of Signora Daphne, which once was mine and I know that engine like my own heart. She Saab, Swedish. Once, *quella barchetta,* she catch fish, *comè una donna onesta*! Now, she just trail round the Bay with the *Giapponese*, the *Tedesche*…My boss is who I work for, *capisce*? Who pay. I am *independente*…But once I work for a man. In Napoli. I was very young, and I marry beautiful girl...she have baby, we have so much no money…"

For a moment, it seemed to Freddy as if Enzo were about to weep, but he took another sip of bourbon. "But I don't like work for him no more. There is too much secret, too much – how you say? *Roba sotto la tavola*…and once I am nearly in prison for him. He boss of many people, and he have friends, *contatti*, in New York. One big bad guy. I do one big job for him, I fight with man and my leg nearly amputate. He grateful, but me, I *non posso lavoro* no more. I say me, that is enough. *Basta*! But I have little boy, I have wife, I have *la mammina, sempre da sola, poverina*… He find me work. I play trumpet, not good but not so bad. So I go to America, I travel in big ship with big band, in the tuxedo, very smart…I see world. I make money is impossible to spend on boat, and I come home back to the family with loadsa cash, *un sacco di soldi*! But this man I work for, he steal my wife. When I come home, there is just sad boy and Mamma…"

"How absolutely ghastly for you…*che terribile*!"

"*Si*! She is no good whore and he is shit. *Stronzo! Che cazzo! Che putana!* I see them in hell! He fix me to go away, so he steal my Maria. And he owe me money, and I am too much proud…" He poured more whiskey. "I am tell you true, Frai-dy. I am proud, but I am fright. Once, I see man die. They beat him up, then boss sit on him and they pinch his nose, *così* – make his mouth open, and they put a bottle of gin in him, he try puke up, then he nearly die, and then they take him out to water like dead fish in basket, tip him over. He drown, he die proper, and they say is accident. I very young and I scared to shit my pants…They make me witness, and they say, that what happen when not obey boss, when see too much.. I uppanleave, go with Mamma and Tommaso in Monte Farfalla. Mamma, she born here. It home. When I see boss again, it is many years more. I not know him, he not know me. But I *know*! So I say to Gianni, no, go, it not worth risk. I give him money…he go. He afraid…I understand this fear."

Enzo finished his bourbon at a gulp and poured another. The night was almost airless; clouds gathered above the little courtyard where Cadwallader's jasmines emitted an almost overpowering scent.

"I'm not sure I understand," said Freddy, helping himself to the bottle. His stomach seemed to have tied itself into a knot. "This boss…did he come here? To Monte Farfalla?"

"*Si…si*. I working for Albergo, sometimes. I fix bar, I fix kitchen. I see him, and I keep my head low, *capisce*? Dennis Barker, the Inglese, he pay me. He boss now. I just man on job. But I see, and I think of my Maria, and my blood boil over. And

471

I not *stupido*, see?" Enzo tapped his bulbous nose. "I know about Albergo. That too have *una storia…La Guerra*, the War, there is prisoners down there in the *cantina*, to the *catacombe*, there is join-on door and they hide, *scappano*, go, get away to the sea…and there is explosives. Bombs. *Catacombe*, they full of them once. *Granate*, stuff like that. Then, there is the drugs. Bad stuff. *Eroina*, how to say? Hard stuff. From *Turchia*, from the East. The *polizia*, they follow the big trucks from Messina on the road to France, so now the trucks, they go into mountains, and the – the *carico – è trasferito, capisce?* Come here with wine, *dentro le botte*, and go on the sea to *la Francia, Ventimiglia, Nizze…*"

"Bloody hell…No, thanks, Enzo…I'll fetch another beer…" Freddy realised he was a little drunk and decidedly hungry. He fetched more bottles from the fridge, and a packet of crisps as an afterthought. "Go on, please…"

"Okay. But you say nothing, nix, that I talk with you, okay?"

"Promise, Enzo. Look, how did you know about all this? *Comè avesti saputo?*"

"Ah…there are friends…I *know*. I am also work for Signor Ilary. In house over the water. I fix stuff for him. One day, I say him too much. I tell Ilary about my wife and my boss. My ex-boss. He – Ilary – he ask many questions. I answer, because I am still mad with the jealous. I go crazy, huh? Crazy! I think if ex-boss he get in big trouble, I no care. I tell him he

472

have meetings with bad men in Albergo. *Puo darsi*, I think, Ilary, he nail him good! *Bastardo*! And not just him. This shitface, *il quello stronzo*, he have a boss, *capsisce*? Big boss. In jail. And Ilary, this is his big business. He write about it all in big newspapers, in England, America. I say hell with it! Bad men, when me and Mamma, we pay taxes and Mamma, she clean houses, and we have nothing in hiding…we just small people, and maybe, Ilary, he get justice, tell the world."

"But mostly, you just wanted to get even with the bastard your wife ran off with…?"

Enzo nodded. Freddy saw there were tears in his eyes. "*Non ho il rammarico*! No regrets, *rien*! *Non per lui!* No way! *Non per il stronzo!* I tell Ilary all I know. I am – *sleale* – how you say? I must not say this thing to a *straniero*. But I do. I break the – the *codice*, the – "

"*Omertà*?"

"*Si…qualcosa così…*Is not a joke for the movies, *cumpà*. But I should kill him with a knife like a man, but I don't. *Sono vigliacco. Coniglio!* I talk instead…O, *mio Dio*…I say a name…"

"This one?" Freddy turned one of the Moretti bottles.

"Him! Not only. He and the Piccione, they just local gang. Small potatoes. Gigi Moretti, he big here, but just small time bruiser gangman…"

"And what about the Picciones…isn't that Gianni's name?"

473

"Si… He has *cugini*, cousins. Hard guys. Fabio. He in jail now. *Ma ladro, solo…*"

"*Solo*, Enzo?"

"*No' l'ho saccio…* Perhaps he involve with the drugs, I don't know. Now all in past. But *il piccolo* Gianni…he not bad guy, he just *un po'*…he not got much, you know…" Enzo tapped his forehead. "He see things. He work in Albergo, and he see big bosses come for meeting, *reunione…* He scared bad. He think if he talk to *polizia*, they kill him first. Moretti, he much to lose…"

Freddy poured beer. He had forgotten his hunger. "I take it they moved the operation…I mean, no more drugs and no more meetings…"

"Not no more, no...not there. Maybe in Viticchia…I know nothing no more…"

"And Moretti…he was the one who ran off with your wife?"

"No way! He just fat pig shit. I kill him no problem!" He made a graphic gesture at his throat.

"So it was Daniele. Cristofero Daniele…."

"*Sssss! Stai zitto, Frai-dy, ti prego, per carità! Non posso dirti…o, mio Dio!*"

"What happened, Enzo? *Che successo?* You told Hilary Blyth about the gang, the drug running from the Albergo…"

"*Si*…I tell Ilary. Is my fault. I go and pray in the Chiesa, and *Il Signore*, He don't forgive me." Enzo crossed himself. "*O,*

474

mio Dio…I am shame! I am shame! *Il povero* Signor Ilary, he die. Now, I have much afraid…"

They sat for some moments in silence, and Freddy now helped himself to the bottle of bourbon.. "I think…" he began, and his voice sounded strangely thin in his throat. "I think that Hilary knew a lot about the goings on at the Albergo anyway, Enzo. It wasn't just you…"

xxxv: The Reek Of Burning Boats

It is notorious that towards the hour of four in the morning, our troubles magnify like grotesque monsters that threaten to seize and crush us with panic, regret, shame or embarrassment, and sometimes all four. Freddy Partridge awoke, parched and hungover, from a pounding nightmare he could not shake off. He groped for his wristwatch, checked the time, drank a glass of water which tasted unpleasantly warm, swallowed a strong painkiller for his head, turned his pillows and lay for some moments, trying to collect his thoughts, which rioted. Each time he tried to push away one demon – his overdraught, his stretched credit, and his still unresolved intent to request an emergency bail-out from Uncle Cadwallader – another – his altercation with Veronica, and her all-too-likely lack of sympathy in regard to the Millicent Fox mystery – took its place. Rather shame-making to be relying on an inheritance in any case…Why could he never just stop when he was ahead? Perhaps a discreet visit to Gamblers Anonymous…he was addicted. Face it. He could tick all the boxes. Now, on top of everything, he had Julian's gangsters, and something important. And the fact that he could no longer recall in precise detail his recent troubling conversation with Enzo. He had gone to eat Mamma Battaglia's pasta and had consumed a skinful of red wine on top of the bourbon…There was something that, in his semi-consciousness, he had realised was crucial... Now all he had was the receding taste of a bad dream, and the stifling heat in his tiny bedroom, where Cadwallader had installed neither air-conditioning nor mosquito screens. Insects had begun their annual attack, and 'deet' made him sneeze. One could keep the window open in the hope of a blessed waft of sea breeze and get bitten to bits, or one could close them and asphyxiate. It is a complete myth that there are no mosquitoes by the sea. He gave up. Pulling on a teeshirt over his shorts, trying not to scratch, and slipping into espadrilles, Freddy decided to get up and go for a walk.

The night, still dark, was eerily silent, and scarcely cooler than indoors: still, almost stagnant air, laden with salt, and a thinning pall of cloud below the stars. A scirrocco, no doubt, which accounted for the cloying discomfort. What a hell-hole! He thought of his neat little flat in Highgate and felt a pang of longing that almost reduced him to tears. He wandered disconsolately on noiseless feet towards the Castello, past the silent Taverna, past little dwellings where the inhabitants were doubtless sound asleep, and the thought of so many sleeping people just feet and inches away vaguely troubled him, as if he were an intruder. He turned into the pedestrian-only part of the Lungomare. More restaurants, utterly silent. From inside one of them, a dog growled half-heartedly as he padded by. He leaned on the iron railings and gazed west out to sea, staring dimly into the blackness, his head thumping. Nothing illuminated the

477

further shore; the crags of the Denti Dei Cani were invisible. The squid fishers were in their beds; the sardine fishers would not be hauling their ropes and casting out for another hour. Freddy gazed down into the inky water and felt suspended in time. He glanced up and saw a faint glow on the horizon. The straggly beginnings of sunrise? He was aware of the faintest breeze, at long last. 'I'll go home,' Freddy thought. 'Get the fucking hell out of here…' He watched the distant glow grow brighter. Freddy yawned. Perhaps he might try to get another couple of hours' sleep. Then he rubbed his head, frowned. Through the fug of his hangover, he was dimly troubled by something. The sky was brightening, the shadows altering, but from behind him: sunrise, and from the proper direction…he stared at the glow out to sea. He was not wearing his contact lenses, but he could almost make out flames…and a small, dark, billowing vapour immediately above… It looked as if something were on *fire*… A sudden, violent explosion eradicated all doubt…

Illumination was swift and total. Back in the tiny kitchen of Cadwallader Jones's guest house, fuelled by a quart of strong coffee and hot milk, Freddy collected his racing thoughts and texted Julian. 'I know how, who and why… See email asap!' and then set down his deductions with the lucidness of the practised journalist.

xxvi: The Mouse That Roared

Lucinda Penrose was making telephone calls and maintaining an icy calm. Now, she rang a number in the Bath area.

"Who? Oh! Mrs Penrose...why, this is a surprise! I'm afraid that my daughter isn't here..."

"That doesn't matter, Mrs Pemberton. I think perhaps you might be able to help me, if this isn't an inconvenient moment..."

"Oh, not at *all*, Mrs Penrose! Any time. What can I do for you?" The elderly voice had a soft southwestern burr.

"Well, I'm going through some accounts on my husband's behalf, Mrs Pemberton. I need to know the position regarding the cottage in Biddendon....Do you mind confirming for me when my husband actually took over the lease...?"

Mrs Pemberton excused herself while she went to look at the books. Lucinda waited.

"Here we are, Mrs Penrose. Sorry to keep you waiting. Yes – it was in 2008, in November. We're very grateful for all his help, Mrs Penrose. Yours, I should say, both of you. Janet? Oh yes, she's fine. Still very much involved with the Party. And she works part-time for a little law-firm in Swindon. Oh, yes...the holiday business is doing very well, thank you. I think people are stopping more in England now, aren't they, now we've got a recession…not at all, Mrs Penrose. I'll tell Janet you called, shall I?"

Grimly, Lucinda made notes, and then called Mrs Bainbridge to tell her she was going away for a day or two and to ask her to take care of the dogs, and then drove to the station.

In the empty Hampstead flat, Lucinda sat in the deepening dark, nursing a very small whiskey. She was keeping her breathing even, as her yoga instructor had shown her. Eventually, she heard Peter's key in the latch. She waited.

Peter put down something heavy in the hallway – his boxes, she guessed – and called goodnight to someone. Ellis, or was it Khan? The driver, anyway, who would have helped him indoors with the burden of parliamentary paperwork. Poor Peter! How on earth did he ever get time for… She heard his footsteps – she couldn't help a frisson of panic now – the scup, scup, of well-made city shoes down the passage; she heard him visit the bathroom and heard the lavatory flushing, and then a clattering in the kitchen. The apartment was small – just a bedroom and a box-room, which Peter used for an office – and the acoustics permitted little privacy. The sitting room cum dining room was large, open-plan – any moment now, he would come in. The lights suddenly glared, and Peter Penrose threw a file onto the dining table. He had poured himself a gin and tonic, and was muttering something under his breath.

"Good evening, Peter…"

"Good God!" His hand clutched the dining table as he spun round. His face was a study of shocked disbelief..

"Don't worry, dear. It's only me…"

"Lucie! Dear God, Lucie, you frightened the life out of me! For God's sakes, what are you doing here? I mean, sitting here? In the dark?"

Lucinda had rehearsed what she was going to say. "I'm not staying long. I have a return ticket back to Fallowdale. I want you to tell me exactly why you won't sue this film of Veronica's."

"Lucie, darling…" Peter Penrose was recovering himself with difficulty. "Oh dear…you've been brooding. There really wasn't any need to come charging all the way from Yorkshire. You should have telephoned. Not that it isn't a lovely surprise to see you…" His voice sounded slightly strangled.

"You didn't see Michael Underwood this morning, did you?"

"Not so as to say actually saw him, as such, no…But Michael's going to help. He's advising me as to what best to do… "

"Advising you to do nothing, I suppose."

"I've got everything in hand, so do try not to get hysterical, darling, please."

"I'm not in the least hysterical, Peter. I know all about you and Janet Pemberton, and about that little house near Bath she runs as a holiday business. It makes perfect sense to me that

481

you don't want any of this to come out… If you start making a storm about Veronica's film, there will be a media fest and everyone will know everything, won't they? I quite understand, Peter. It might of course come out anyway. I mean, if I could find out, anybody could. As you often remind me, I'm not really very bright, am I?"

"Lucie, dearest. Please. I – "

"You're not going to deny it, Peter, please…I've got all the proof I need. It was common knowledge, apparently."

"Oh God, I suppose the Carsdales blabbed."

"Rhona Carsdale didn't have much choice when I asked her outright. I shall probably never speak to her again, although I can see she was put in a hell of an awkward spot. I've been very conveniently blind and deaf, haven't I?"

"Oh, darling…Oh, God…It was…I mean it wasn't *serious*…she'd just lost her father…Janet. She was upset. One thing led to another. I was a fool, I know…Oh, God, darling…"

"Peter, don't insult me even more than you have already. You don't think I can *think*, do you, darling? But believe me, I've been thinking a great deal…"

"Wh-what are you going to do?" Peter Penrose, defeated, sat in an armchair with his head in his hands. Lucinda could see his bald patch vividly, and thought how pathetic he was. She tried, as she had been trying for the past forty-eight hours, to imagine his erotic transports with the anaemic Janet Pemberton, and failed.

"Well, I could do one of two things, couldn't I? I could forget I know anything at all, and just sit like a lemon while Veronica's film gets reviews, and rebuff the interviewers when they mob me outside the house or the school. I'm used to that. And then when the press gets hold of your involvement with the Pemberton woman, I can pretend I knew nothing. All a rivetingly unpleasant surprise. And when they ask me if I knew about your dodgy accounting, I can stand up in court and claim I am as innocent as the day, which happens to be true. I'll get a lot of sympathy, if you remember Mrs Cook, and the fragrant Mary Archer. Or I can file for divorce right now, name the washed-out Pemberton female as co-respondent, and make an unseemly stink, for which I'd doubtless get another sort of sympathy. Either way I don't seem to be able to avoid a hideous amount of publicity...I might as well toss a coin, mightn't I?"

"And my career hits the skids whatever...Oh, Jesus Christ..."

"Of *course*! Your *career*! Do you know what, Peter? I don't give a flying *fuck* about your career. Neither did you, it seems, when you embraced the Pemberton woman and then decided to make it up to her after you dropped her! Did you truly imagine you could keep all this quiet? What the hell were you thinking, Peter? Eh? Were you thinking about me? Were you thinking about Rory, about Ellie, about Dinah? Thank you, Peter, for wrecking our lives!"

"If it's any consolation to you, I've been shitting bricks for the past several months, ever since the papers got hold of Thompson's duck-pond...I didn't want to worry you..."

"Your anxieties don't console me in the slightest, Peter. You've been a complete dickhead, haven't you? And a coward."

He watched her get up and help herself to another whisky. He scarcely recognized her. This was not his Lucie-mouse! This woman was firm of tread, with teeth, and a voice like icicles.

"I *know*...I've been such an utter, utter fool, Lucie...Oh, God, I'm so sorry..." His voice trembled. "Lucie...what are we going to do?"

"We! God, you're pathetic, Peter."

"It – it rather depends on you...oh, darling...!"

"Will doing anything make any difference? Like you said, your precious career's on the line anyway. You'd better talk to the Whip before he talks to you...but that's your affair. I don't want to know about these ghastly hypocritical party politics. They stink of the rotten corruption they are." She sipped whiskey, still standing, and regarded him with dispassion. "I've had enough."

"Will – will you tell Rory? The girls?"

She laughed, a harsh, brittle sound. "You mean, will I let them learn the story from the papers? You really are alarmingly dim, Peter."

"Oh God...what can I do...?"

484

"Talk to your children? Be a man, for a change, instead of a blustering hypocrite? As for what I shall do, I haven't made up my mind. Yet. You'll have to wait and see, won't you?"

"Oh God…I can't bear to – to lose you, Lucie…" Tears were dripping unchecked down his face. "Tell me it's not too late…"

But she drained her whiskey, turned firmly on her heel, and left. She did not even slam the door.

PART FIVE: HOME TO HAVEN

xxxvii: Alison Truce

After a brief exchange of emails, Veronica drove over to a picturesque village at the foot of the Chilterns for tea with the novelist Alison Truce.

At the wisteria-wreathed door of a thatched, whitewashed cottage, she was greeted by a small, plump, self-effacing woman in a denim gardening smock who introduced herself merely as 'Poll'. Poll's light blue eyes slid away from Veronica's in an apparent agony of shyness, and she led Veronica through a dark, narrow hallway and a powerful aroma of recent baking into a walled garden to meet her hostess. Alison Truce, almost as tall as herself, a grey, slender, handsome woman in her mid-seventies, wearing jeans and a brown linen shirt with a pair of reading spectacles on a chain resting on her thin chest, stood up and shook hands with brisk formality. Poll vanished, to return almost immediately with tea-things and scones on a tray which she set down on a wrought iron table.

In a bower of roses, honeysuckle and lavender, the near-silent Poll poured Earl Grey tea into antique china cups, adjusted the felt teacosy and promptly vanished again.

"Kind of you to come," said Alison Truce. "You know I only got involved in all this because Penny Crewe at Vixen is a

486

personal friend who just happens to know my bedtime reading habits. One should help friends and never be too proud to turn down honest work, I feel. Even so… Help yourself to more tea when you like, Ms Dearborn. And have a scone. Poll makes them, and the jam from her own strawberries. The cream is from a local organic herd. Please eat it even if you're on a diet. We can't offend Poll."

Veronica spread cream and jam onto a crumbly scone. "They're delicious…thank you."

"They're the very best. So, then," said Alison Truce, in a manner that took her straight back to school. "You have been assigned to Flora Forde, and you believe that 'Flora Forde' was the alter-ego of Millicent Fox… I gather you've met the widower. You'd better tell me all about it."

She told her about Cadwallader Jones and the stash of notebooks. "Mr Jones says he would be very happy to let you see them. I thought that in any event you might like to know of their existence…"

"Hmm. I realise I'm going to have to take my task seriously. I might get Poll to write to him. Poll is indispensable."

"As for the double identity, I think this will explain better than I can." She handed Ms Truce a large manilla envelope.

"Good Lord! Is this *War and Peace*?"

"I'm sorry it's so bulky. It's the photocopies of Millicent's working notes for two books plotted in 1941. One became *Mystery at Granite Grange*."

487

"And something is special about the *Granite Grange* thing?"

"Not in itself, no. But it's proof. I copied the whole of the 1941 notebook, because in it she wrote the summary and brief working notes of another book. The workng title is 'Staircase', but I recognized it instantly as the draft of *The Well-Trodden Stair*, by Flora Forde, which actually came out some years later. It was – well, a rather exciting find."

"So I can imagine. I take it you had already made a literary deduction, as it were. I mean, you seem to have known what you were looking for."

"Up to a point… I'd been frankly intrigued by the complete absence of biographical data on Flora, you see. And the fact that she seems to have stopped writing at a point in her career when it would have been logical to continue. The last book was a failure, commercially, but not enough, I'd have thought, to deter someone young and determined with two relative successes behind her. It seemed reasonable to guess 'Flora' was a pen-name, and that she had continued, using another name…"

"I see." Ms Truce had penetrating dark eyes, rather small, ferociously intelligent. "Unless, of course, she had died…"

"Or married," said Veronica, and was amused to see her hostess's mouth twitch. "But then we're back with the data problem, aren't we? When an old friend of mine turned out to have been Millicent's relation, that led to an introduction to

Millicent's widower in Italy, who claimed that Millicent and Flora had known each other. It was my first real personal lead, if you see what I mean. I boned up a bit on Millicent because I was about to meet him. As I read more of Millicent's work, I realised how similar the two styles actually are. As if Millicent is the grown up version of Flora. And there's the musician connection. And the familiarity with certain kinds of world – office routines, being broke, that sort of thing. And partly – I know this will sound silly, I'm afraid – but all of Flora's heroines have names with the initials 'MF'…as if 'Flora' were being deliberately cryptic…"

"Well, that's not at all impossible," said Ms Truce. "People do encrypt things. They abandon pen-names, too, especially if the pen-persona was unsuccessful. I abandoned one myself. In the Sixties, a young man called Elliot Makepeace wrote a lot of bad verse, published in various bad or at least very brave and amateurish magazines of which you have doubtless never heard. Elliot Makepeace was me. I wrote my first novel in 1972, and my agent convinced me to publish under my own name. I am an untidy poet, and a rather precise novelist. The rest, as they say, is history. Sooner or later, I shall have to make a decision as to whether to 'go public' about Mr Makepeace. Someone will doubtless dig it all out and write it up for Wikipedia, or a biography, possibly only after I'm dead. I'm past caring about juvenilia, and so I am telling you. But at the time, I was only too glad to shed Makepeace, and take on a more realistic Truce…if you see what I mean."

Ms Truce, Veronica noted, spoke in whole sentences. Veronica laughed a little, and began to relax.

"Does this Mr Jones corroborate this double identity?"

"No…Not exactly. He's being a bit mysterious…but actually, I think he knows perfectly well. He's quite a character, and very protective of Millicent's secrecy. But once I'd found the notes for the *Well-Trodden Stair*, I realised I'd got all the proof I needed. Now, there seems to be more evidence in the Gollancz archives. Flora Forde's copyright was registered to one M.F.Seale… 'Seale' was Millicent's first married name. It hangs together rather wonderfully…"

"This is intriguing, I admit. I say, what fun!" When Ms Truce smiled, she could seem actually jolly.

"Yes, it is, rather… I'm just not at all certain where to go from here…"

"My dear woman, you surely publish your findings! More tea?"

"Thank you. Oh dear. It's rather a relief to talk to you about this. You see, something troubles me a bit. *The Well-Trodden Stair* was Floras's third and last book. It came out in 1944, five years after the last, and while Millicent's early career was flourishing. I just wonder – well – *why?* She abandoned a pen-name, and then suddenly decided to revive it, and for a book drafted much earlier. There's only one explanation I can think of to disinter Flora Forde…."

"And what is that? Now isn't this strawberry jam just out of this world?" Alison Truce spread butter, jam and cream with gusto. "But do go on, Ms Dearborn."

"Ms Truce…I'm afraid this *is* going to sound fanciful…"

"Alison, please, and I shall call you Veronica. After tea, in about twenty minutes, I shall resume work on my book. I adhere to a very strict routine. Until then, I am all ears. Tell me, Veronica." The penetrating gaze stared unblinking.

"Okay. I think it might be that Millicent wanted to have a – a forum – to publish something that would have been completely out of keeping with the wholesome Millicent Fox stuff. You haven't read *The Well-Trodden Stair*, I suppose…"

"No. And nor would I ever have. Life is far too short to waste on fripperies, let's be clear about that! I have always been rather a fan of Fox, however, mostly because she is an excellent plotter and I can read her fiction last thing without polluting my own work…Still, if Flora and Millicent are one and the same, I shall be obliged to do some homework. Tell me about it."

"I've brought a copy for you – just in case you wanted to look at it. It…it concerns a talented young woman musician in a dead end job who turns to genteel prostitution to support a widowed mother and a sick sister."

"Eugh! Charlie Chaplin plot."

"I know. But it's an odd book. Far more realistic and gritty than the two previous ones, and rather ambitiously written. The heroine is left a sum of money by a grateful client, but just as she is seeing a way to achieving her dream of a place at the Guildhall, she falls victim to a blackmailer, and because she is in love with a very nice-minded young man, she has a brief moral agony in her diary and then sets out very deliberately to put the blackmailer out of the way. She invites her for supper, poisons her with something untraceable, and the victim dies of an ostensible heart attack on the way home. The murder remains undiscovered, the heroine gets away with the crime, and to cap it all, she ditches the young man on the grounds that he's too woolly and sentimental by half, and she has a career to consider..."

"Good grief! Sounds rather ahead of its time. *And* a she-blackmailer, to boot."

"Yes. The senior secretary at the firm where she works...bitter, twisted and jealous. A nasty piece of work the reader can't really regret. But the book was a complete failure...you can't let heroines get away with murder, or at least you couldn't then. Not in wartime England."

"Well, now I am thoroughly intrigued. I shall read it tonight. Do please eat these scones, Veronica, or Poll will sulk."

"Thank you, Alison. The thing is, I – I can't quite get it out of my head that this is not just a novel," said Veronica through a mouthful. "I mean, that it's a sort of record of things, of something real that actually happened. To Millicent…"

"I see. Why?"

"Because it's so…plausible. There's Millicent's own life, about which there is quite a lot of available information. The novel has so many parallels. Like the heroine of *The Well-Trodden Stair*, Millicent was a clever, musical girl who grew up in straitened circumstances with a widowed mother and a brother who was a polio victim and she had to leave school and abandon a scholarship in order to work to help support the family. She went to work in the typing pool of a hosiery manufacturers in the Midlands and she was struggling to get her first novel published. It's possible she was a lousy copy typist. Anyway, she was sacked, or she left, and her history gets a bit fudged for a while – according to Wikipedia and the rest, she went to London to sort of seek her fortune, worked as a typist for a publicity agency and gave piano lessons in her spare time. Cadwallader Jones corroborates this. Her relatively humble beginnings. God knows how she found time to write… Then she was offered a copywriter's post, where her talents were presumably put to better use. Then she married this Mr Seale, who was one of the agency clients, a man a great deal older than herself. According to Cadwallader, the marriage wasn't happy, but he's not necessarily reliable. Eric Seale was rich and he had connections, and he seems to have supported her work. Then he died in an air-raid in 1941. It sounds as if she married him not so much for

493

venality as security. He left her well set up with a large house in a country village in Somerset, where she met Cadwallader, who was her neighbour. By this time, of course, she was seeing some success with the first 'Aubrey Calder Watson' books, and was leading a busy and blameless life writing and helping the war-effort by taking in evacuees. I'm just wondering if the third 'Flora' novel wasn't a sort of confession of her early life. Not to murder, of course, but of her life in general. She seems to have had a strong commitment to her family. I think it's just possible that she fell in love with someone broke and a bit wet, and very possibly she was overweeningly ambitious. She was also remarkably pretty, to judge from photographs. People, women, might well have been jealous of her. Perhaps slightly in love with her..." Veronica coughed. "And maybe she did have clients other than piano pupils. Perhaps she got pregnant. It's possible she didn't have much choice about accepting an offer of marriage she didn't want, and for reasons that would have been scandalous at the time. There's something about the – the distaste. And the rebellion. And the ditching of the wet boyfriend. It comes across as real..."

"I see," said Alison Truce at length. "You don't write fiction, do you, Veronica?

"No...I'm not inventive in that way."

"Do you read it?"

"Well, of course."

"And have you considered, seriously, the relationship between fact, fancy and the imagination?"

"God! Not since I read Coleridge at Cambridge...I wasn't there for long."

"Ah. Yes, Coleridge. But I think you might consider the question again, and in a more practical context. I 'invent' my novels. I write fiction. But I don't necessarily write lies. A persistent and rather annoying interviewer recently badgered me about the biographical content of my books. Where, she wanted to know, did I draw my characters from. From life? And I could only answer, from wherever *else*? Doubtless I sounded sarcastic. But that doesn't mean I draw life-portraits, as I tried and probably failed to make clear. My characters share many characteristics of people I have met, perhaps, but they are inventions nevertheless, especially the complex ones, the ones that get the 3-D treatment, as it were. A much more interesting question would have been just how much of my own thought and consideration – moral attitudes, very particularly – end up being mouthed or thought or worked through in my fiction. Does that make sense to you? I have to say it did not to the interviewer. She is supposed to be a very intelligent literary journalist, but I frankly found her lacking. *Dim*, even, in certain respects, despite the fact that she goes in for a certain coloratura in print...No matter..."

Veronica thought suddenly of Marina Lavender.

Alison Truce went on, "The wonderful thing about fiction is the way one has so much control. The machinations, the details, these can be altered to fit, backwards and forwards. One of my characters, for instance, is a fine-art fraud. The fraudulence, all the moral mindset that goes with *being* a fraud, the ingenuity, the self-congratulation, the triumph over the experts, the justification, the amoral disrespect for the genuine, and of course the inner sense of *sham* which cannot be allowed to obtrude as *shame* – these were the vital things, when I was creating him. But then an art expert friend of mine suggests that my idea of having him re-create the work of a certain painter is absurd, impractical for my purposes, implausible in the real world of art reduplication. So – hey presto – my character, who *has* to be plausible if I am to hang all these weighty moral matters on him – he forges some drawings by a different artist instead. All that needs to be altered are a few of my earlier paragraphs in a previous chapter. It's mine, you see. *He's* mine. I can make this character do whatever I like, because I created him. I can delete, alter, re-work to my heart's content until it all fits satisfactorily…I'm not recording somebody's real history. Fiction is freedom. To all intents and purposes, one plays God. But always harmlessly, provided one bears in mind the need to tell a wider truth. If that makes sense…"

"Yes…Yes, it does."

"You see, the truth and truthfulness – they are not necessarily the same thing. Are they? I thoroughly enjoyed your autobiography, Veronica. You tell a very good story."

"Oh!" said Veronica, suddenly jolted. " Thank you. I do rather regret it, you know."

"Perhaps because you were trying to tell the plain truth. That must have been painful. Was it?"

"Not at the time. Not much, anyway. And not for me so much as for others. I was rather pleased with it then. It – well, it expiated something. Now they – someone – wants to make a film of it, and I'm trying to stop them. I may be too late…"

"Possibly. I'm sorry if so. That will doubtless be troubling for you."

"Yes. Very."

"But you will survive! And you should consider writing fiction. In its unplainness, fiction has a truthfully ambiguous nature that is really very liberating. Now then!" Alison Truce finished her tea and stood up. "What are we to do about Flora Forde?"

"I don't know. I'm just planning an introduction to the three novels on their own merits, and well – I thought I might leave the double identity hints out altogether. I don't see what else to do."

"Oh, don't do that. I wonder if we ought not to work together on this, at least up to a point. I shall read the 'Flora' *opera* and consider. Obviously, you must undertake the scholarship – this is your work, after all, not mine. We are only hired to write brief introductions, but it only makes sense to cross refer. I suggest you prepare a small essay on the identity question for publication with one of the better literary magazines and present it to Vixen as a separate matter and we take it from there. I should be most interested to see it." Poll had reappeared, and stood hovering. "Ah, Poll – we've finished this excellent tea, and Ms Dearborn must leave us." Poll was looking abashed. "This has been very pleasant, Veronica. Thank you once again for this Mr – er – Cadwallader Jones's number. Poll will get in touch with him."

Shaking hands and thanking them both again for the tea, Veronica got up and left, feeling both reassured and unsettled. Poll saw her to her car in the drive. "Thank you for such a delicious tea," said Veronica again, and the enigmatic Poll merely nodded.

xxxviii: Councils of War and Peace

"Hullo? Is that Veronica?" The voice was vaguely familiar.

"Speaking. Is that Julian?" She realised she had never heard him on the telephone.

The voice coughed. "No, Vee…this is James. Jamie. This is a bit awkward…I don't want to startle you…"

"*Jamie*? Jamie! My God!" She sat down suddenly and realised she was trembling. "Are – are you calling from Africa?"

"No, Vee. I'm in London. I wondered if we could meet…"

"God…sorry, Jamie. This is a bit of a shock. Are you okay?"

"I'm fine. Listen, Vee – I'd love to see you. And I need to ask you a very important question."

"Oh God…I can scarcely believe this! It really is *you*!" She knew how idiotic she was sounding.

"It's been far too long, Vee…you still there?"

"Yes." Veronica was wiping her tears very firmly. "Say on, bro…"

"God, that's a blast from the past, sis…"

Veronica gulped and reached for a cigarette. "Why – why did you ring?"

"In two hyphenated words, Wardley-Hill. Can I take it for solid that you haven't given your permission for this benighted drunken toad to make your memoir into a film?"

"Gilbert? Oh God, I might have known he was up to something! Of course I haven't! Not in a million years! I – it's – oh God…" Her tears were flowing unchecked now, and she knew she could be heard down the line.

"Vee…look, try not to cry. I've just heard from Lucie."

"She doesn't believe a word I say, Jamie. I tried to convince her…The thing is, I think it might be too late. I think they can make a film no matter what I say…"

"Lucie's got problems of her own now. And I think it might be about time we had a council of war. The three of us…"

In the oak-panelled waiting room of Carr & Overbury's august Mayfair offices, James Dearborn and his sister Veronica talked and talked. "I was just so proud of you, Vee. That Henry Cuffe book. So many times I nearly called you…I really didn't have a bloody clue what to say, apart from you know, well done…it's difficult, you know, after so many years…so much stuff…"

"You're here now, Jamie, and that's all that matters…Oh, dear… " her emotions were threatening to get the better of her again. "Jamie... did you send me some flowers? After the Cuffe book?"

"Um…well yes, actually. I didn't know what else to do…Never been much of a one for letters…and you might have just put the phone down…"

"You might at least have signed them!"

"You might have chucked them in the bin…"

"Oh, Jamie! You darling old idiot! You all along!" She hugged him very tightly. "You don't – don't know, just how nice it is to have my big brother back…"

"Here's our little sister…"

Lucinda came in, a little timorously, accompanied by Rory. James got up and hugged her, shook hands with his nephew and clapped him on the back.

Lucinda rushed into Veronica's arms. "Vee! Oh Vee, I'm so, so sorry! Please forgive me?"

"There's nothing to forgive, Lucie. It was a very understandable mistake…are you okay? I mean really?"

Lucinda's eyes were a little hollow, but there was a grim determination about her mouth. She glanced at Rory and nodded. "I'm – I'm going to be fine. I haven't made any radical decisions yet…I just want to try to get this business sorted first. I'd love to have a – you know – private gossip sometime…a sister thing? Soon?"

"Very soon, Lucie. Oh God, I'm horribly nervous about all this…Bright of Jamie to think of the old family firm…"

"Actually, it was my idea…sometimes a bit of the old feudal spirit can't hurt, I thought…"

An elderly clerk appeared from one of the panelled doors. "Lord Fitzrivers? Good morning, sir. Good morning, Miss Dearborn, Mrs Penrose…and, um, young Mr Penrose. Mr Overbury can see you now, if you will all come this way…"

Later, after Thomas Overbury, a young man who had inherited his father's sharp legal mind and who enjoyed a challenge, had shown them out, it was a convivial family party that lunched on steaks at the Guinea.

"So we've got em! Er, haven't we?" Rory, who had had ample cause for embarrassment in recent days, was hugely relieved. His mother, who had forgiven him – as she said later to Veronica, you can't blame the poor child for falling in love! – patted his hand.

"We can only hope so, darling."

"We mustn't be too confident," said James soberly. "Basically, all we've done is presented this Flix outfit with our written, signed disagreement, as it were. If they're really determined to go ahead, they can. You heard Tom. This is scare-tactics, which we can only hope will work. It more or less guarantees that we'll sue, but if they've got money to burn…"

"Oh, *Jamie*! Don't be pessimistic, *please*…"

"Sorry, Luce. But it's always as well to be prepared for the worst." He glanced at Veronica.

"It's not actually worth the paper it's written on, is it?" she murmured.

"As a legal block on them, no. But we hope it's going to pre-empt them. They'd have to be crazy to start it after this. Most people object after the event, when it's too late."

"It was clever of you to find Flix, Jamie. I suppose my unlovely agent, Marcus Frayle, spilled the beans, did he? He just blanked on me when I asked. I've decided to ditch him."

"Not Frayle, no. Call it a collaborative effort…" He glanced at Rory, who grinned, blushed and concentrated on his steak. "Then I just sat on the even more repellent Wardley-Hill…it wasn't difficult. He thought I wanted to talk turkey."

"Wardley-Hill? Wasn't he Granny's…? God, he's revolting! He called me 'young sprig' at Granny's funeral. How on earth did she come to marry a disaster like that? It makes him my step-grandfather! Gross!"

"I think that might be enough wine, darling…I mean, don't you have a class this afternoon?"

"Mum! I still want to know how he fits in. This Wardley-Hill."

"He's actually a total shit," said Lucinda, who had had several glasses of wine herself, and her son looked at her and smiled.

"Way to go, Mum – but I'm still in the dark. Who is he really, Uncle Jim?"

"Uncle *Jim*?"

James winked at his nephew. He said, "He's a backer, Rory. He puts up money for plays and films. They call them

503

'angels', believe it or not. He's got a stake in this Flix company...Lucodin and Partners..."

"Ah..." Rory looked abashed. "I'm afraid this was all partly my fault..."

"No, it *wasn't*, darling. We've talked about this. Rory's girlfriend – "

"Ex-girlfriend!"

"She works for this Flix, apparently. You met her, didn't you, Vee?"

"Yes. I really don't suppose she did anything very damaging. To us, I mean. The damage was done already." Rory looked at her gratefully.

"Wardley-bloody-Hill!" said Lucinda. "Ghastly Gilbert! God, do you remember when Mummy announced she had actually married him? I nearly died. Didn't you, Jamie?"

"It was a bit of a shock, yes...she had fairly rotten judgement. I mean – "

"I suppose you mean poor Daddy, too..." She looked at Veronica and shook her head sadly. "I've been meaning to say this for a long time, Vee. Well, since a few days ago. Jamie knows, don't you, Jamie? The thing is, there's more than one kind of bullying. Daddy bullied me, too. In his own way. He was sweet to me always, but he treated me as if I had no brains at all, all that teasing – and I believed him. It's – it's taken – well..."

"Mum...would it be all right if I skip coffee and stuff? It's just I ought to go and find something in the Library..."

"Of course, darling! That's all right, isn't it, everybody? You are such a lovely, tactful boy, Ro-ro…"

"Don't treat him like a kid, Luce." James stood up. "Keep in touch, eh, Rory? You know where I am." They shook hands, and Veronica noted the extraordinary family resemblance: the young man, tall, slender, not quite formed, fair, diffident, inclined to blush; the older man, her brother, solid, robust, balding, flushed with wine…but they bent their bodies in the same way, and the smile that passed between them used the same tilt of the mouth, the same slant of the brow…

"Sure thing, Uncle Jim…" He kissed his mother. "Bye, Vee – see you at home, yeah?"

"Sure thing, Rory…" They watched him leave, and Lucinda crumbled bread onto her side-plate.

"I'm so glad he's with you at the moment, Vee…this is going to be so bloody awful."

"Does Rory know?"

"Oh, yes! I had to tell him! And the girls. An edited version. Any time now, it's all going to break in the papers…"

"Not necessarily, Luce. You said yourself, don't let's be pessimistic. If we've muzzled the film, at least that's something…"

"Everything might hit the papers if I decide to give Peter the elbow, Jamie…the problem is that they love him."

"Do you, Lucie? Love him?"

"Love *Peter*? I hate him like poison…at the moment…"

505

*

"So! We start. Contract meet tomorrow, right?" Matthew Lucodin, who had consumed more wine than his usual frugal ration, was beaming round the table, where remained the remnants of an expensive Soho lunch. A waiter brought coffee and brandy. "No final objections, questions, suggestions?"

"Raring to go, Matt…" said Eddie Potter. He tucked the copy of his contract into his briefcase. "We can start casting as of next week. Locations sooner. Take some notes, Beaver. Get Catto onto extras, and ring about the Hokington Hall place. See if we can do a location reccy first thing Monday."

His assistant director, Walter Beaver, scribbled. "You know it's a spa, now. Country house hotel. We might need a plan B if they can't shelve some of their bookings…"

"Just get onto it, Beaver. And get Bunney. Fifties interiors. Find plans B *and* C. We'll need a production meet with Pearce tomorrow if we can."

Mr Beaver, a young man who prided himself on keeping his head when all around him were losing theirs, merely nodded, casting a glance in the direction of Miranda Hooper, who was also scribbling.

"Find someone good f'Annie…" Wardley-Hill, afloat on brandy, grasped Potter's sleeve.

"Of course he will, Gil…" said Lucodin.

"I thought Francesca Annis…"

"We'll try, Gilbert…"

506

"Whole thing's got to be very English...no phoney accents..."

"Point taken, Gilbert. We have to ensure that this thing sticks rigidly within budget, okay?"

"I thought we might go for some unknowns," Potter said. "Relative unknowns..." He glanced at Gilbert and felt glad he need not meet him again for some time.

"I'm happy," said a fat man in a silk shirt called Logan. "I'll always punt on Potter..."

"Me too," said a thin bald man, US publicity executive for Cosmix Cosmetics. "I smell a winner."

"Thanks, Rattray. That's just what we're going to make..."

Russell Roper, who had said nothing for some time, merely looked at his wristwatch.

"What about you, my pretty? You'll have a proper film company to work for, eh? What do you say?"

"I say please take your hand off my leg, Mr Wardley-Hill."

"Minx..."

Yes, Gil, my staff is out of bounds...Why don't you go and open up the office, Miranda? Check the mails? And draft a letter to Billings. Set them up."

"The caterers?"

"You got it, babe...Beaver will liaise closely re numbers."

"Sure," said Beaver.

"No problem...Thanks for lunch, Matthew." She grinned at Mr Beaver and left.

"Smart kid, that, eh, Lucodin? And you say she's actually involved with the family?" The man Logan, whose silk shirt looked about to burst at the buttons, firmly took the brandy bottle from Gilbert's grasp.

"Do you have to be so goddamn morose, Roper?" inquired Lucodin later as they crossed the Square. "We've got a movie, for Chrissakes! Lighten up!"

"I'm afraid Mr Holliday has gone on a short vacation, Mr Blyth. He's on holiday, so to speak." Mr Sheldrake's thin little mouth pursed in what might have been enjoyment of his dry little joke. "But we all work for the same firm. I'm certain his response would be exactly the same."

"You're saying you can't do anything."

The official coughed. "We can only advise, Mr Blyth. The thing is, your brother's death is a closed case. You say you have a strong suspicion that a serious crime was committed. I'm not suggesting I disbelieve you, or even that you are mistaken, but to set about proving it, you would need to open a police investigation, that is to say, to re-open a case that they have closed to their satisfaction. Which effectively means hiring an Italian lawyer and bringing a private suit against your – um – suspect. Sorry, suspects. And one of them is a British national, I

508

believe? To be frank, Mr Blyth, unless you could go to the police with some real evidence – something more than – um – private deduction and suspicion, something which could actually constitute a case for the prosecution that could be argued in a court of law… I don't think a decent lawyer would touch it. As for the police, well…you are rather implying they fell down on the job, aren't you? I don't think you'd get a very sympathetic response, to be honest. I'm sorry to be so negative, but it's only my duty to inform you of the potential pitfalls. I seriously advise you either to drop this altogether or try to interest a lawyer who will be able to guide you further. We have a list of the ones who speak English…" Sheldrake shuffled papers and sighed. "I have to stress that we – the Consulate – cannot offer legal representation or even, strictly speaking, any legal advice…"

"But I'm not asking for legal advice! I'm asking you for some support! Look, damn it, I mean, everything seems to point to my brother having been deliberately silenced. There's the fact that one of the key witnesses has gone missing, and now this boat has been destroyed. Someone was obviously afraid of a forensic test…bloodstains on the deck or something…"

"I fear if this boat is material to any accusation, it is now too late," said Mr Sheldrake. Julian, keeping his temper, resisted an urge to grasp his lapels and shake him.

"I see. And you think these notes of my brother's, given his profession, don't count for anything?"

"They might count for all sorts of things, Mr Blyth. But they don't prove that someone killed him, do they? They merely offer a slender suggestion he had knowledge that someone might have preferred him not to publish. That's two lots of suspicions, Mr Blyth, his and now yours. So far, I don't see anything that looks like a particle of proof that someone beat him, let alone killed him."

"What about the witnesses?" said Julian, beginning to lose heart.

"Witnesses to what, Mr Blyth? People came forward at the time to testify that they had seen the late Hilary Blyth very drunk and get into an unseemly argument at a party. He later went swimming, apparently in a state of considerable intoxication and very unfortunately drowned. All the autopsy findings were consistent with all that they said, including a blood-alcohol level of three hundred on a retrospective test during the – um – post mortem. That is very high, Mr Blyth. Very high indeed, I understand." Sheldrake pulled a face of prim disapproval.

"Richard Holliday explained all this…but according to someone else who was there, my brother was not nearly so drunk as some reports made him appear…I think this is highly significant. I believe the whole thing was confected, made to appear like an accident, and that his injuries occurred on land and not in the water…"

"Mr Blyth. A grieving widow convinces herself that her husband acted out of character. An elderly lady, wandering in her mind, may or may not have seen or heard something, and a young man in the employ of a hotel seems scared…"

"Scared enough to run! Who was scared that a brother – me – might have come back for revenge. There must have been a reason, God damn it! A young man whose cousin is in prison for burglary and who has a known connection with organized crime. Surely these Pick – Pitch…this family could be required by law to tell what they know?"

"Mr Blyth…a man is in prison for theft. Yes, very well. A series of house breakings, possibly, but he has only been actually charged with one incident, and this was not the larceny perpetrated on the Blyth property. He is due for release in two years. You would surely not expect him to gladly cooperate with a private investigation that could increase his sentence fourfold? To question him at all would require police sanction."

"We're going round in circles, Mr Sheldrake. I'm telling you I think my brother, an international journalist of some repute was onto a serious crime – drug running to be precise – and had evidence that a premises in Monte Farfalla was used as a base for the organizers. Even if the police don't care a damn about how my brother died, they might be interested in that!"

"I'm sorry, Mr Blyth. I have to tell you I think this is a fruitless pursuit."

"But surely…"

"I am very certain the police will be watching whoever it is they need to watch. If they need to see your brother's notes and so on, they will know where to find you. Yes, of course. Here or in London. Mr Blyth…this is strictly off the record, but as a fellow countryman I suggest very strongly that you leave this severely alone. I'm sincerely sorry for your bereavement, Mr Blyth."

Julian, with a flight to London booked for the next day, suddenly made up his mind, cancelled it and rang the car-hire company to extend his lease, and drove angrily back in the direction of Monte Farfalla. If he had heard the telephone conversation that took place between Sheldrake and Holliday later that morning, along the lines of what the blue blazes had Sheldrake been thinking of, to allow a key witness to the Turkish-French cocaine run to just disappear, and if the ROS got to hear of it they would have egg all over their faces, and Sheldrake's response that Holliday had no right to speak to him in such a fashion, he might have felt slightly comforted. He was drinking coffee in an Autogrill pit-stop when his mobile rang. It was Richard Holliday in person, apologetically requesting Julian's immediate return to Rome to talk to one Vice-Comandante Cèsare Baglioni of the Special Operatons unit…

xxxix: Onwards and Upwards

"What would *you* do, Aunt Vee? I know Dad's been a prat, but Mum…well, Mum isn't all that easy herself always…she talks more than he does for a start. Dad just goes off into a sort of private stratosphere…but I think this must be really difficult for him… It's doing my head in, a bit, having to take sides. I sort of want to help them both, you know…"

Veronica had made supper for Rory and herself, and they sat in the courtyard, Veronica smoking, aunt and nephew peacefully domestic. Rory stroked the cat Greymalkin absently.

Veronica considered. "I think you can only help by being very firm that you're not going to allow them to make you take sides, Rory. They're your parents, and I know you love them. But basically, they're both grown up people who have to sort it out for themselves. Get on with your studies, do you exams and live your own life. Believe me, it's the only way…"

"But should I tell Mum about tomorrow?"

"Well, that's up to you, but I wouldn't. Not as anything special. Just meet your Dad for lunch and see what he has to say. God, Rory…I'm no expert on this, you know. Families. Mine was about as dysfunctional as they get…"

"I'm going to hear stuff I don't want to hear…Mum's been saying…well, she's pretty pissed off…and she sort of needs me…when everything hits the headlines…"

"Rory – actually, since you have asked for my advice, I think the very best idea is that you go off and do this vac job in New Zealand. It sounds fun and useful. Good on the CV. Lucie can call you if she needs you. Show her how to use Skype before you go. I'm not being horrid, but you really mustn't get sucked in to all this. Do your own stuff, Rory…"

"Miranda and I were going to spend the summer in London…"

"Face it, Rory. She's buggered off. Get out of all this for a few weeks. I would."

Rory sighed heavily. "Yeah. You're right. I'll ask Dad…"

'Of course you will, you poor little idiot,' Veronica thought, after Rory had padded off upstairs. In herself, Veronica was considerably lighter of heart. She even emailed a brief businesslike note to Miranda, passing the piece Miranda had written on Flora Forde for the course magazine.

Miranda and Russell Roper were drinking coffee in Soho Square. "You know I can't do anything, Russell! I don't want Matthew to think I'm being obstructive, but it's impossible. I don't even live there anymore. Rory and I had a bit of a spat…well, more than a bit of…"

"Ah…"

"I've – um – broken with him. He sort of twigged I was seeing someone…" Her cheeks dimpled.

"I see."

"And she wouldn't listen to me anyway."

"I thought you'd done some research for her. She might feel grateful. No, sorry. Stupid thought…"

"I'm so sorry! You think this really is curtains, do you? On the *Cry* company? I wish you'd explain properly…the legal side…"

Roper explained, and Miranda scribbled notes.

"But they can't actually stop it, can they? You just said this isn't an actual block…"

"This could halt it. Indefinitely, potentially. We'd have to be crazy to begin after this. Think about it, honey. All those schedules suddenly in suspension…the cost…Matthew knows this perfectly well. He's just – you know – clutching at straws…and having fun with the temper-tantrum while he's at it. Sensible of us to escape for a spell."

"I thought he was about to break a window! No, I do see. Truly. Oh God, *poor* Russell…poor Matthew, too…"

"Actually, my love, I hardly care. I knew this was doomed from the beginning. I just wish it hadn't taken this to make Matthew see the light."

"So do I. I was *really* looking forward to it."

"Working with the great Director?"

"That as well. And working with you. And Matthew. It's just wonderful *experience*…"

"There will be another movie, Minx, rest assured. Give Luco a couple of days for it to sink in, and he'll start again. He's like mercury in a thermometer."

"With Mr Potter?"

"We can always hope…"

"I'm thinking very seriously of working in films when I finish. Do you think it would be appropriate to contact Mr Potter – I mean, if he doesn't do something with us next?"

"Why not? You know you could stay with us. See what pans out. A lot of advertising is mini-films…"

"I have to go back to school in September…"

"I've told you you can have time off for lectures. Do it as a special project…"

"Am I *your* special project, Russell?"

"You're…I think any man would be crazy to call you his at all, my beautiful Miranda." He kissed her sadly and shook himself. "Now then, do you suppose our fearless leader has stopped throwing things?"

Matthew Lucodin had his head in his hands when they returned to the office. "So! We're fucked," he said morosely. "Everyone wants time to digest…but they're out of *Cry*, Roper. Potter won't touch it now. Potter's out, everyone's out. Get me some coffee, babe…Only one who wasn't daunted was our friend Gilbert. He wants one last try to convince the dame…"

"I hope you told him it was useless, Matt."

"Sure, but he doesn't listen. Ah, coffee. Now! Mourning over! Damage limitation time! As I see it, everyone's been brought up to the line. We've formed a company. We have to offer an alternative, Roper, and fast. Where's that Billybass Hawkins stuff? Take notes, babe…"

Veronica had settled to composing her piece for Vixen Press when the telephone rang.

"Vee?"

"*Freddy?*"

"Yes, it's me…Oh God…"

"Freddy? What the hell's the matter? You sound terrible…"

"Vee…Oh, God, Vee…It's Uncle Cad. He…" A pause that could have been a choked sob. "It's ghastly. He – he's dead."

"Oh, no! God, Freddy! I'm so sorry…How?"

"Signora Battaglia found him…the neighbour who cleans for him…this morning. He was in his armchair…at home. They – they – took him to hospital, but I saw him…La Battaglia fetched me."

"Oh, my God. Where are you, darling?"

"I'm here – in Monty. I'd just booked a flight back home. Due to leave today. I've had to cancel. I'm trying to deal with everything…it's a nightmare, Vee…"

"Oh God, Freddy…how dreadful. What was it?"

517

"A heart-attack, they're saying…It's turned horribly hot…Or maybe a stroke. They'll do a post-mortem…Vee? You still there?"

"Yes, darling…The line's rotten. I'm really sorry. Poor old boy."

"Vee? Can you get in touch with Jane? I can't find her. Please can you let her know and ask her to come? Like asap?"

"I'll try my best, Freddy…leave it with me…"

"Thanks, Vee… Everyone's hysterical…including me, I fear…Shit – I'm waving this thing over the sea trying to get a proper signal…"

"Freddy – dear – calm down. I'll do what I can. Promise. Stay on this number and I'll text you. Freddy – just hang on in there... What? Of course I forgive you! Don't be so stupid. I'll get help."

Rory Penrose, in the middle of his revision, a TV programme, and several texts and emails to the friends with whom he was arranging to travel, did not hear the doorbell all at once. When he finally opened the front door, he found Gilbert Wardley-Hill on the step, looking much dishevelled, as if the effort of ringing and waiting had half killed him.

"Is Veronica at home, young man?" asked Gilbert without preamble.

"No…sorry. Can I help?" Rory realised he recognized him.

"Know when she'll be back? It's bloody important."

"She's had to go away…"

"Away? Where?"

"She…um…Look, could you tell me what this is all about, Mr Wardley-Hill?"

"Know who I am, do you? Ah! You must be Lucinda's young sprog…staying with Aunt Veronica, eh?"

"I'm really sorry," said Rory politely, "but I can't help you…" He tried to close the door firmly, but Mr Wardley-Hill's toe was in the way. "Please, Mr Wardley-Hill…"

"Now then, let's not be hasty…you remind me of Annie – Anabel, your grandmother. Same smile. Now then, back in Italy, is she?"

"I really don't know where she is," said Rory awkwardly. But he was a poor liar, and his reddening face gave him away.

xl: Obsequies: a Late Interlude

"*Povera Mammina!*" cries Valeria, rushing in and disturbing her mother's careful coiffeur with her brawny arms. Corinna shakes her daughter off.

"*Non ancora, carissima mia...Sono distrutta...*"

Valeria plumps herself down on the uncomfortable sofa. They both gaze at the coffin. Tears drip unchecked down Valeria's plain face. Corinna dabs carefully at her own with a hankie. Her makeup is smeared, but only just a little. John Cadwallader Jones lies peacefully in state in the refrigerated coffin in the cramped centre of the ornate little *salone*. His face is almost handsome in its repose.

"*Papa Lonero ha fatto lavoro meraviglioso..*"

"*Si...sss!*"

Valeria begins to pray, splashily.

A knock. Someone enters through the open front door. "*Posso? Permesso?*"

Corinna gets up. It is Signora Battaglia, the elderly neighbour who cleaned for Cadwallader, dressed in her discreet 'best', including wrinkled dark stockings up to her bony knees. She places a foil tray of edibles on the kitchen counter and two bottles of her own home-made limoncello. She enters the inner sanctum, crossing herself and muttering. Corinna helps herself

520

to a small glass and joins the others in a silence punctuated only by Valeria's sobs.

"*Forse una goccina per la figliola?*" suggests Corinna in a whisper, and Signora Battaglia helps Valeria up and leads her through to the kitchen.

A crash and a curse. "Damn! Why the hell hasn't someone shifted that bloody bike? Is...? Oh! My God...sorry!"

"*Signor Fraid-y! Poverino! Sss! Lui è arrivato ora...*"

"Mamma is in there, Freddy...with him. Salvatore has just brought him. *Povero* Freddy!" Valeria kisses Freddy's cheek wetly. She is dressed, as ever, in jeans and a polo-shirt stretched over her large, flapping bosom, and she smells strongly of dogs. Freddy holds her away from himself rather firmly.

"Thanks, Valeria... *Grazie, cara*. I'll go in..."

Corinna rises. She looks quite incredibly glamorous, Freddy cannot help noticing, in a black knee-length frock and high heeled sandals, a stark contrast to her daughter. The frock is sleeveless, but her long arms are covered in a black lace shawl like an outsize mantilla...she kisses his cheeks with decorous sadness. He catches a whiff of Chanel. She takes his hand lightly and leads him to the coffin. Someone has lit candles. The room, with the glinting mirrors and the paintings in the gilt frames, looks like a dressed stage-set. Cadwallader's mortal remains are like a waxwork. The refrigeration unit beneath the coffin hums discreetly.

"I still can't believe this..." she whispers.

521

"Nor can I…Poor old Cad… He looks – well, rather beautiful…" Feddy shudders. He remembers the stiffening waxwork in the armchair, the khaki shorts and a vest with paint on it. The lumpy, bony knees had looked especially pathetic, somehow. Now, looking at the grey-yellow face in its rigid composure, the knobbly folded hands over the the Armani suit, the best shoes, the silk tie, the quilted lining of the coffin, he is not sure which is worse, and feels a little faint.

"We got Lonero to do it. Well, Valeria did…" Her eyes crinkle in an intimation of maternal pride. "I chose the suit and tie, as you asked me…Poor darling…"

"I see. Thanks Corinna. You're a star…"

Corinna crosses herself and bobs a genuflection before turning her back on the coffin. "His poor old heart just…gave up…"

"It was so horribly sudden…" Freddy follows her out. "I've just got back from the Anagrafe…"

In the kitchen, Signora Battaglia is arranging food onto plates. Corinna says, "I think we should open up next door, you know…There are going to be a lot of people, and this kitchen is so cramped…we could take some of this food through…"

"Good idea. And we'll move the blasted bike into the courtyard…Do you think it's worth trying to move the easel?"

"It's awfully heavy…and God knows where we'd put it…Perhaps it can stay…" Corinna murmurs in an undertone to Signora Battaglia, who goes to the door and bellows.

522

"Enzo! Ora vieni ka!...Subito..."

Enzo shambles over, tucking a clean shirt over his vest, and wiping shaving soap from his face on the sleeve. He shakes hands with Corinna solemnly, mumbling *"Condolenze, gioia."* He greets Freddy, whose eyes are a little red, and Enzo hugs him extravagantly, his breath reeking of wine.

Corinna pats Freddy's arm. "Let's go outside, shall we? The others will all be here in a moment...and I think Father Bianca is planning to come. He'll want to talk to you about the funeral... *L'altri arriveranno presto, gioia...anche il prete..."* She kisses the old woman's face.

They walk into into the street and Freddy unlocks the door of number ten. "Here we are, Enzo – we can pull out the kitchen table...Get glasses and things..."

"Si...va bene. I bring wine?" Freddy gives Enzo a banknote.

"We can leave them to it," Corinna says. "Shall we wander down to the Taverna? This is going to be a long day..."

On the wall is the *necrologia* – the black-edged notice announcing Cadwallader's death, freshly pasted by Lonero's bucket team, who have indeed been announcing the news all over the town. "Oh, Lord...All the letters after his name. Poor Uncle Cad! Poor old boy. I'm actually sadder than I can say. And the funeral tomorrow! Everything seems so – well – rapid..."

"It always is here," Corinna murmurs.

523

"Cad wasn't Roman Catholic. Will that matter?" They sit at a table, and Tony brings a quarter carafe of red wine and a plate of bruschetti. He shakes hands with them both in a reverent hush. The waiter Rosario hovers, and Freddy thinks he spies the suspicion of tears.

"Not a bit…Father Bianca will keep the service simple…It's the Chiesa di Santa Croce. It's tiny, intimate. I was married there…Cad came with me once or twice, you know. To hear Mass. He was very – spiritual – in his own way. It was one of so many things we had in common…Bless him."

"Well, I'm blowed…glass of wine, Corinna?"

"Thanks…I'm just, you know…doing things. Helps me not to think…" She shakes her head.

"I take it you've told everyone. Daphne, everybody…"

"Of course. They'll be here any moment…So will all the neighbours…then Signor Lonero will take him down to the Chiesa. After the service tomorrow, they'll take him to the Cimitero in San Gregorio. Did you get hold of Jane?"

"I'm on to it. She's only just back from Sydney. I might have to hold the fort without her… make a start on all the – er – the legal side…clearing up. I haven't a clue where poor old Cad kept his will or anything…"

"I do. He left it with Stefano de Benedetto, the local Notary here…"

"de Benedetto? A relation of yours?"

524

"Cousin-in-law...my ex-husband's cousin. It's funny – I speak to Stefano but not to my husband. He's very good, very competent. I recommended him when Cad first moved here...he did the *contratto* for the sale...I was there as official translator. It was one of my houses, in fact..." Her eyes crinkle in a sad smile. "I mean, it was on my books. I'll gladly come with you both, if you like. Stefano speaks a bit of English, but you know – two heads and all that. You'll both need *codice fiscale*, and to sign inheritance things, of course, but there won't be any hurry for that."

"No, I suppose not..." Freddy wonders very much if Corinna knows Cad's latest testamentary position, and decides he cannot possibly ask."Thanks, Corinna. I'm frightfully grateful to you, dear thing..." he says, and realises he means it. "Oh, God. Silly, isn't it? I suppose it's always been at the back of my mind that this could happen any time really, and you know how it is – I sort of didn't like to think about it. And poor old Cad seemed so *well*. I suppose I ought to be glad I was more or less on the spot... Um, Corinna? You were a nurse...you don't think he – well – suffered, do you?"

"No. No, I'm sure not. It would have been very, very quick. You've only got to look at his face to see he didn't suffer... Poor darling Cad. I'm going to miss him so *terribly*...Oh, dear..." She dabs her eyes. "Let's go back, shall we?"

On the doorstep stands Valeria with a small, sinewy, sharply-dressed man who could be in his forties and whose arm is slung round Valeria's ample waist. This is Salvatore Lonero, Valeria's intended, the son of the undertaker. He shakes hands with professional solemnity, giving Freddy an assessing look. Freddy dislikes him on sight. There are papers to sign. Round the corner, puffing slightly in the heat, comes the priest, a diffident, rather burly young man in full clerical regalia who might look more at ease in football kit, and who introduces himself as Ignazio, Don Bianca's deputy. Corinna speaks to him in rapid Italian, and translates for Freddy's benefit.

"You need to sign some papers for the church, too, Freddy. And Don Bianca wants to know whether you want Cadwallader's English priest to attend…"

"Oh, God…I don't think he had one. I'm sure not. Tell him I'm happy with anything he cares to do…the simpler the better, I think." Corinna leads the priest's deputy inside, explaining.

The late afternoon has become almost unbearably hot and airless, with that unpleasantly sticky quality that stagnant salt-laden air is apt to produce. There is more space in the kitchen area now the bicycle has departed, and Enzo and Valeria have made a tidier stack of the books, but the legs of the easel are a trap for the unwary… As more people pour in, the kitchen begins to resemble a party held in whispers. Neighbours, including Tony

526

who has changed out of his white apron and has brought yet more food, troop silently in to pay their respects to the coffin, greeting with a strict formality first Freddy, with handshakes, then Signora Battaglia, with kisses and murmured greetings, and then Corinna, who has resumed her seat at the head of the coffin, looking queenly and dignified. Some of the neighbours look a little surprised to see her.

Someone has arranged chairs – every available chair, as far as Freddy can see – in a circle and trimmed the candles. The mourners sit in silence, making space for others as they arrive, and then quietly exit through the courtyard to the guest house, where a slightly less laden atmosphere prevails, and where they eat a mere morsel of the mountain of food, and take tiny glasses – Cadwallader's ornate little green ones, and others, which presumably have been supplied by La Taverna – of the revoltingly sticky limoncello, or rather larger glasses of Enzo's wine. Freddy is glad that his own stash of better stuff is discreetly hidden. The silence is oppressive with breathing.

A little stir. Daphne Allerton arrives with a phalanx of the Porters.

"I'm very, very *sad*, dear!" Daphne exclaims to Freddy in a loud stage-whisper. "You've lost a wonderful uncle, and I have lost a very, very dear friend! And so has poor *Dorinda*..." she adds, dropping her voice to a hiss. "Give me a ring, dear. Very soon. We need to *talk*..."

"Oh, m'darling," says Corinna, emerging from the inner sanctum, giving Daphne a sad, theatrical embrace. "When you've seen him, the priest will give a blessing and then they'll take the coffin up to the Chiesa…"

"All right, dear. Shouldn't we wait for the others?" asks Daphne.

"We can't keep the Don Ignazio waiting too long…please, just go through and see Cadwallader…"

"This chief mourner business is a bit thick if you ask me," murmurs Hedley who has hung behind.

Freddy offers Hedley a drink. "There used to be some whiskey," he said apologetically, pouring limoncello. There's some better booze next door…"

"This'll do…*salute* and all that, and I'm very sorry, my boy. He was only older than me by a year or so. Terrible intimation of all mortality. Heart failure?"

"That's what it said on the certificate…"

"I suppose Lonero is doing the funeral. Personally I'd have gone to Micelli…"

"Corinna arranged it. "

"Oh well, of course. Family connection, you know. Frankly always struck me as a bit common and *contadini*…All the paperwork done? They don't like it when an ex-pat dies in his own house…"

"More or less. Everything was pretty straightforward. Doctor's certificate, all Cad's papers in order…it all seems frightfully rapid, somehow…"

"Always is, compared with England. Heat, you know. Can't – um – spend too long above ground. Worse in Singapore. I was there during the War…"

"Lord…this is all pretty frightful…"

"A strain, naturally. Don't worry too much, dear boy. Corinna's in charge, of course. She nearly always is. Enjoys this sort of thing. Suppose I shouldn't say that."

"She's been rather an angel, actually…"
Hedley Porter gives him a look through his good eye that Freddy is not sure how to interpret. "Hullo…here's the competition…"

Cy and Lorrie are at the open door. Dorinda clings to Lorrie's arm. Her mourning is even deeper than Corinna's. She hugs Freddy effusively, nearly losing her balance.

"Steady, sweetie…"

"Ello, Dorinda. Ello, Cy, Lorrie. Come! The priest, 'e is giving a little blessing…now…" Cecilia Porter is at their elbows, tugging at Hedley's sleeve. "I'm an atheist, and 'Edley is a lapsed Protestant," she tells Freddy, "but this is an important tradition."

"Shouldn't we wait for Silvana and Dennis?" asks Hedley.

"No. They'll come when they can." They follow her.

"Poor boy, oh poor, poor old boy!" Dorinda exclaims, gazing into the coffin, and Daphne goes to stand at her side.

"Hush, now, dear…"

Corinna glares. "*Prego, padre…*" She bows her head.

"*Nel nome del Padre, del Figlio, e dello Spirito Santo…*" The young priest waves his censer over the coffin. Freddy tries not to sneeze. Very quietly, Veronica Dearborn enters with Jane Hardcastle and stands at the back.

Corinna exclaims, "Good Lord!" under her breath, and promptly claps her hand to her mouth. The others look round.

"*Amen…*"

"Thank God you're here," says Freddy, hugging his sister and Veronica. "Thanks a million, Vee. This is all a bit *macabre*, I'm afraid…"

"So you made it," says Corinna to Jane brightly, and kisses the air by her cheeks. "That's marvy! I mean – and Veronica! How very kind of you to come…"

"I came with Jane," Veronica murmurs. "I'm dreadfully sorry…" But Corinna has turned to talk to the priest. The little ceremony is over, and Valeria and Salvatore stand by, waiting to remove the coffin. The hearse has parked outside the door, where a short, stubby man, Salvatore's father, in a short-sleeved shirt and much adorned with gold round his neck and on his fingers, waits with a wheeled trolley and an assistant.

"Don Ignazio is going back to the Chiesa now," Corinna announces. "Anyone who wants to can go and see Cadwallader again this evening. There will be a vigil…"

"How nice to see you again, but you've come back at a very, very sad time, dear!" says Daphne to Veronica, her vivid blue eyes glistening. "Very, very, very *sad*!" They have mostly wandered into the kitchen, where Freddy pours drinks. Red and white wine have materialised. The gathering has divided somewhat: the local neighbours, tactfully leaving the family and friends to themselves, have mostly congregated in the house next door before gradually moving off to their suppers and the more convivial atmospheres of their own homes. Even so, Cadwallader's tiny quarters are crowded to the point of toe-treading claustrophobia.

"Signora Cor-eena, Signor Fraid-y – *c'è più*, more eat other house…" Signora Battaglia bustles past them with plates.

"I liked Cadwallader very much. I knew him all too briefly…" Veronica says to Daphne. Through the doorway, she can see Jane and Dorinda introducing themselves over Cadwallader's corpse.

"Come and have a drink, Jinx, darling," suggests Freddy when they emerge. "You too, Dorinda, sweetie." Dorinda is mopping tears and tottering more than a little, clutching Jane's arm with her little red talons. Jane looks at her brother rather helplessly. "Find her a chair, someone?"

531

"There's no room," says Corinna, but Lorrie fetches one from the *salone*. Dorinda sits, suddenly the focus of attention.

"Thanks, sweetheart…Sorry to be so emotional…it's just so *sad*…I still can't believe it…*Poor* boy! He was my *friend*!" Lorrie and Freddy stand in attendance, and Dorinda fishes for a cigarette.

"Of course iss sad. All death is sad. But for Cadwallader, death was quick…" Cecilia Porter glances at her husband, who nods sagely.

"Quite so. A shock for everyone else, but it's how we would all want to go when the time comes…"

"True, Hedley dear. Very true," says Daphne.

"And 'e 'ad a long and 'ealthy life…"

"Not long enough!" says Corinna with a tiny sob. "Oh, I'm sorry…excuse me!" She exits to the bathroom.

"She's very upset," remarks Daphne.

"She's been upstaged," murmurs Hedley Porter to no one in particular, *sotto voce*.

"How soon can we leave?" complains Cy Dillon in an undertone to his partner. "This is beginning to get to me…" He glares at Dorinda's cigarette.

"Depends on who's seeing Dorinda home," whispers Lorrie. "Just be patient, buddy…have a limoncello…"

"Huh."

Jane Hardcastle whispers, "Have you met all these people, Vee?"

"Some. Not most of the locals." The two women have retreated to the doorway where there is some air.

"Everyone seems to have been genuinely fond of him, poor old thing. This last move wasn't such a disaster after all. We'd both been terribly worried about him, Fred and I, just heading out into the middle of nowhere. He was like that. Sudden impulse, and he was packing his bags. But he'd seemed so happy here…"

"It must be like the end of an era…"

"Yes, poor old Uncle Curmudgeon. I'm really quite sad he's gone. You know he was having quite a little love affair…"

"At least one, so I gather…"

"I'd not met the little Irish one before. But I rather wonder if there might be a case of great expectations…".

Veronica glances at Freddy, who seems to have recovered his poise and is pouring wine and offering edibles, the gracious host. Daphne accepts a glass.

There is a loud altercation, and suddenly Silvana Barker barges past them, evidently in great distress. She grasps Daphne blindly, spilling Daphne's wine, sobbing. "Oh, Daffy, *Daffy*…"

"Silvy! My dear girl…please! Hush this noise at once!"

"*Si! Stai calma, carissima!*" says Cecilia. "*Era anziano,* he went very peacefully, *il poverino* Cadwallader Jones. An aving 'ysterics won'd elp."

Silvana looks up from Daphne's arms as if bewildered, her eyes bleary with mascara. "It's not *Cadwallader*! It's Dennis! Oh my God! I don't know what to do! They've taken him!"

"Taken *Dennis*?"

"Dennis? Where? Who?" Hedley Porter turns in the direction of the noise and blunders into the enormous easel. His brass blazer button has caught in the grey army blanket covering it.

"The *police*! The Carries! He's been *arrested...*"

"You're kidding!" Lorrie Lucifora is at Silvana's side.

"What has happened, Silvana? You must try to tell us calmly." Hedley tries to shake his sleeve free.

"Yes, calm down, dear, for heaven's sake..."

"How *can* I calm down? Oh *Daffy*!"

"Ang on, darrr-ling, you're all caught up...your button. Ere, I got it..." Cecilia tries to extricate her husband from the easel. "Don't move, Edley! Tell us, Silvy!"

"I'm sorry about that, everyone...I feel a bit better now. I just sat with him for a few moments...you know, alone, in peace..." Corinna has emerged with a brave, newly lipsticked face, but no one acknowledges her. "Oh! Silvy? What on earth's going on?"

"It's his fault! Yours!" cries Silvana passionately to Freddy. "All because of you! You kept him here, that snooping, spying, busybodying *bastard...*"

"*Freddy's* fault?"

534

"Edley! Stay still, for 'eaven's sake! You'll ave it all down!"

"Will someone get her a *drink!* I don't understand, dear. Take a deep breath and tell us *quietly!*"

The blanket, still attached by a thread to Hedley Porter's sleeve, falls away with a heavy flop.

"What the…?"

"Oh, fucking A…"

"Oh, *my!*"

"Jesus Christ!"

"Blimey…"

"*O Mio Signore!*"

"Isn't that the Rokeby Venus? I can't see!"

"Well, good old Cad, I say! It's a work of art, darling! A bloody work of art!"

And it is. On the easel is a near-perfect copy of Velàsquez's famous work depicting the goddess's 'toilette'. The luscious curves and extraordinary posterior face the viewer, and a chubby knowing Cupid holds a looking-glass to her face. Except that it is not the face of the Roman deity, but that of Corinna de Benedetto, in itself a remarkable essay of observation; even, one might suspect, of irony, gazing as it is with practised satisfaction at its reflection.

Jane Hardcastle nudges her brother. "Fred – we need a glass of water…No, raise her feet…Quick, Fred!"

For Corinna de Benedetto has fainted to the floor.

xli: Post Mortem

In the air-conditioned temple to gastronomy provided by the award-winning 'Da Camillo' in San Gregorio, four somberly clad people were ushered respectfully to a table.

"Well!" said Jane Hardcastle as the waiter tucked the chair under her slim behind, "That was about as nasty a a public spectacle as I have ever witnessed. So over the *top!*"

"To be fair, I thought Daphne looked embarrassed."

"You'd have thought they'd had enough drama after yesterday..."

"I honestly thought one of them was going to land up in the grave on top of the coffin. A sort of whatsitsname...when the bride burns on the pyre. That Corinna woman was determined to throw her orchid in first..."

"Yes...did you see her push little Mrs Daly out of the way?"

"She missed her footing," said Veronica. "She almost fell in. If I hadn't caught her shoulder..."

"Her gardenia got crushed..."

"And she was crying..."

"She was pissed, darlings, as the proverbial fart."

"Don't be so bitchy, Freddy," said Veronica. "She was genuinely distressed."

"Which is probably more than you could say of Mrs de Benedetto...tears of purest crocodile..."

"You were all gratitude to her yesterday..."

Jane said, "I couldn't forget that *bottom*! I mean, one shouldn't laugh. She was in front of me in church...stand up, sit down, in figure-hugging black...difficult not to, well, speculate..."

"Sorry, Jools, you missed the fine display of the *gluteus maximus* of the fragrant Corinna..."

"So I gather..."

"Do you think it was from life?"

"Darlings, please! The mind absolutely boggles."

"I thought it was just the Rokeby thing with her head substituted..."

"Well, that's very sad, if so, because I rather like the idea of poor old Cad having a bit of fun over the canvas..."

"Now then, I can't vouch for this place, having not been here since I did them the year before last, but Mr Michelin still seems to approve, I see..." A boy brought a bottle of prosecco and glasses, a senior waiter hovered with a wine list, and he and Freddy went into a serious huddle. "I was always promising to bring Vee here, wasn't I, Vee? Better late than ever, eh?" Freddy was still unsure whether Veronica had forgiven him.

"Yes...oh dear. The others all went back to Monty and 'La Taverna' as a sort of pilgrimage. I suppose they'll think us horribly stand-offish."

"Let 'em! It's *much* nicer here. The owner's Italian, but his chef's a little French genius called Henri…"

Jane said, "I don't think they'd want us. Not after yesterday."

"They wouldn't have wanted me, certainly, I gather," said Julian Blyth.

"It's brilliant you could join us, Jools," said Freddy.

"I still don't know what you're doing here," whispered Veronica to Julian.

"Tell you later…"

"Yup. Julian's the villain! Now, forget it, sweeties, do! Let's be a bit luxurious in our baked meats. Here come some delicious little morsels while we decide… You do realise we probably don't have to see them ever again. Cheers, dears!"

"Well that's something," said Jane. "But there'll be the houses to tackle, remember, Fred…"

"I've a feeling there might be a nasty little surprise waiting for us there, Jinx… Well, cheers, everyone. Welcome back, Jools. He's been fighting bureaucratic ogres…"

"And rounding up a gang, so I've heard! Is it true that the awful Barker man helped to kill your brother?"

"Er…" Veronica glanced at him with sympathy.

"Unfortunately, Italy's illustrious force is more interested in what the enterprising Barker used to keep in his cellarage, eh, Jools?"

"Something like that…"

538

"Shall I do the honours? Unless anyone's got a particular request?"

"Of course, Fred. You always do it better than anyone else," said Freddy's sister.

"Okay! We're having their special little *amuse gueules*, then some little crab and mango *torte*, followed by a very light asparagus soup, followed by the duckling, duckies, with a sage and myrtle *compote*. Okay? I don't know about you, but funerals always make me fearfully peckish. All that *memento mori*, I suppose...you hungry, Jools?"

"Yes, actually..." He smiled, lopsided, at Veronica. "Oh dear...Perhaps it's not very respectful." A plate of buttered quails' eggs arrived.

"Nonsense-constance! Cad was a great trencherman. We'll eat and drink handsomely in his honour. To John Cadwallader Jones. A life..."

"Poor old poppet. A long life well lived..." said Jane. They raised their glasses solemnly and drank..

"Well, *lived*, anyway. A life...someone ought to write it. Any takers, Vee, petal?"

"Don't kid, Freddy...not now."

"I'm *not* kidding. I'm serious. And these are seriously delicious!"

"Scrumptious," said Jane.

"Jane and Freddy and I knew each other practically from the egg," Veronica explained over the soup to Julian, who had begun to relax. Jane Hardcastle grinned at him. Despite a stentorian voice and a manner which suggested a great many terrified junior nurses and possibly a seat on the local Bench, she had eyes that twinkled like her brother's.

"Yes indeed, Julian. I've never forgiven Veronica for pushing me off a swing when I was six. I grazed my knee."

"And blabbed to Nanny, you cry-baby!" said Freddy.

"But Jane *had* just put nettles down my vest…"

Jane said, "Pax! Look, I'm still relying on you people to fill me in. What is all this about the arrests at the Albergo, for heaven's sake? Is it serious?"

Julian began to explain. "It was Freddy who got it all worked out, actually, Jane. Couldn't have done it without him."

"*Fred* worked it out?"

"Oh, just put two and two together…nothing special…"

"He's not quite the idiot he looks sometimes." Jane gazed at her brother with exasperated affection. "But what *happened*? *Has* Barker been arrested for murder?"

"He bloody ought to be," said Freddy.

"I think he's just helping the police with their inquiries. I got the distinct impression the brass hats were far more interested in their drug bust than in poor old Hil," said Julian. "I really don't know what will happen…he'll be let off with a caution if he agrees to finger the mob element, probably…one dead journalist more or less doesn't count for much…"

"Basically, Barker was allowing his premises to be used for meetings between a wanted Man of Honour on the run and a number of cohorts, including a very unlovely local godfather. He was also hiding a lot of class A substances among the wines and spirits. Julian's brother rumbled them…it wasn't a very healthy knowledge. Ah…ducklings!"

"So go on. There was this argument at Daphne's to all intents and purposes about a *Bystander* piece, and Dennis stormed out…?"

"Yes. And Hil's normal route home would take him past the Albergo…I walked it, just to see…"

"And I think our Dirty Den called someone, and they waited, and then Dennis must have invited him in – a drink, kiss and make up, perhaps a bit of insider information…"

"And knowing Hil, he wouldn't have resisted the opportunity…"

"Makes sense, doesn't it? Come into my parlour. The parlour being the cellars in this case. No noise, you see…Ugh…"

"God! And then?"

"This is the ghastly bit, I'm afraid. It seems that Dennis, having lulled Julian's brother into a state of false security over a couple of jars, either stood by or joined in while the gang beat him up. Probably with a good deal of skill…"

"Someone broke his ribs…"

"Probably sitting on him. Dennis's weight would have done it. Then – this is surmise – they forced a good half bottle of spirits down his throat, probably through a funnel…it's an old Mafia custom, so I'm told…more wine, anyone?"

"God…I can hardly believe this…your poor brother…"

"Sorry, Jools. Shall we stop?"

"No, no, it's okay. It all makes sense, because the autopsy report showed levels of alcohol in poor old Hil's bloodstream that would have made it virtually impossible for him to have walked home. And there was a witness, of sorts. It seems that Dennis's mother-in-law must have crept down…"

"To the crypt…"

"To steal buns. She's diabetic. And hid, probably scared out of her wits, poor old girl…I think she saw everything, Freddy…"

"But he's supposed to have drowned," said Veronica. "What did they do?"

"Well – let's hope Hil was unconscious. They'd have more or less undressed him, and then bundled him up and taken him through the catacombs to the Marina…they join up…"

"…and then loaded him onto a boat, probably in a fish-basket, and took him out to sea…"

"…where they dumped him near to the Denti dei Cane…"

"And the whole thing looked like a swimming accident…with all the appearances of Hil having drunk a skinful and deserving everything he got…"

"It was when I saw that boat on fire that I twigged that last bit. Your presence had put the wind up somebody. Probably afraid of – you know – um, forensics. I – um – had a bit of help from a certain ex-gangster…"

"Fred!"

The party fell silent.

"It's…it's damnable." Veronica said eventually. "Well, isn't it?"

"I can't bring him back, my dear…"

"And you're saying that Daphne Allerton must have known…This is making me shiver…"

"Yes, dearie. And she's *English*…"

"Or she simply guessed…"

"And cared enough about Barker's skin to maintain a 'see no evil, hear no evil' front after Hilary's very convenient death…"

Julian coughed. "Actually, I think, you know, that Hil must have thought the Barkers were more or less unsuspecting, or wilfully ignorant about the cellar part. It's the only thing that can account for the way he was that last Saturday. It was as if he were trying to wake them up. It makes sense of something Innocenti said, too. About the danger from within…"

"So you were right all along," murmured Veronica.

"Faye was too…"

"We just came to see how you are, m'darling!" said Corinna, kissing Silvana. Daphne Allerton was on an errand of mercy, and Corinna had insisted on accompanying her. "And if there's anything at *all* we can do…"

The Albergo was quiet, apart from a man drinking alone in the bar, and Silvana Barker and Becky sat at the desk, nursing a bottle of vinsanto.

"Thanks…we're just awaiting developments, aren't we, Beck?"

"Yeah. We think Dad might be allowed to come home…shall I leave you to it, Mum? I'll go and look in on Nonna before I go out, if you're sure it's okay."

"Yes, love. I'm okay now…Time you had a bit of a break…" Silvana dabbed at her nose. "This girl's been an absolute trouper…took the Germans off to the Signorelli while the forensic team was doing the cellars…"

"Brava, Rebecca, m'darling." Corinna's eyes crinkled.

"Can you just see if our friend wants another before you go? And get a couple of glasses." The girl sped off, and Silvana dropped her voice. "Inglese...quite the gent. Asking after *Veronica*…"

"After Veronica Dearborn, dear?"

"Some relative, apparently…I told him he must have just missed her…"

"How strange…You know that lot all stayed in San Gregorio…didn't think to invite *me* to their lunch! After everything I've done! Moh!"

544

"Freddy didn't invite me either, dear," said Daphne. "I expect they just wanted to be by themselves."

"Just as well," said Silvana. "I really can't face the idea of Freddy at the moment."

"Far better!" said Daphne. "Now," she commanded, "I need to talk to Silvana. Business. If Rebecca wants to go out for a while, perhaps you could mind the desk for her, Corinna dear…"

"Oh, I thought…Oh, all right. Why not?"

"D'you mind, Rinna? Just for half an hour or so? It's very quiet tonight…buzz through to upstairs if there's anything urgent…"

"No…of course. It'll help take my mind off – everything. You just go ahead, m'darlings…" She smiled bravely. Corinna was actually considerably put out: not only had her starring role as Cadwallader Jones's chief mourner been dimmed by more dramatic developments, but now Daphne was determined to exclude her from this private discussion with Silvana. She went to sit behind the desk, sipped vinsanto and idly leafed through the guest register. Wardley-Hill, G, and yesterday's date… Corinna fished in her handbag and began examining her face in her compact.

"I told Dennis not to get involved with those people! *Everybody* knows Moretti's dodgy! I told him and told him and told him…he never *listens* to me…sorry, I'll be okay in a minute,

545

I just can't stop turning it all over in my head…" Silvana's voice had risen and Daphne shushed her.

"Silvy, he didn't actually know, did he, dear? When a respectable business man asks if he can use someone's cellar for some goods he wishes to transport, Dennis is hardly going to start opening up packages, is he?"

"Wine vats, apparently…strapped under the lids."

"Even more reason. Nobody would go undoing those. Dennis was innocent! He was also stupidly naïve in his choice of friends, but that is water under the bridge, I'm afraid. You have to believe this, dear, or you will be no help to him at all, especially if they want to question you."

"Oh God, I feel so sick!"

"Pull yourself together at once, dear! Now, about this Avvocato Motta. I'm sure he's very good, dear, but I strongly recommend you go rather higher up. Avvocato Lombardi is half American, and I think you'll find he will provide a better defence…Lorrie recommends him too. I think we'd better get him at once, don't you?"

"If you think so. I can't stop *thinking*, Daffy…your poor boat…"

"Someone stole it, dear. Possibly a coincidence. Vandals, I should say. Cut it loose, and it drifted, and then it crashed into the rocks and the engine exploded…I've contacted the insurance people…"

"But – just suppose – it wasn't coincidence? I mean, perhaps it was *them*..."

"You mean trying to obliterate traces of cocaine, or whatever it is...well, that's possible, I suppose. In which case, it was very naughty of them to have involved the poor *Serena*! I think you have to forget it, dear. The insurers will be able to tell if it was deliberate, perhaps, but really I think speculation is ... very unhelpful. Yes, dear, thank you – another small one would be very nice. Now, dear, you really do have to pull yourself together..."

"But what about the Blyths? That brother started all this...the violinist!"

"Silvana! You must forget. All. About. The Blyths!" Daphne bounced in agitation. "We need to be *sensible*. I believe this Lombardi is fairly expensive...Now, I'm going to tell you my idea..."

"Always as moribund as this, is it?" inquired Mr Wardley-Hill. "Hullo! Your're a different one!"

"Good evening," said Corinna, tucking a stray strand of hair behind her ear, and folding her compact away. "Can I help you?" She smiled, assessing him discreetly.

Wardley-Hill's bloodshot eyes took in Corinna with a practiced gaze.

"I was hoping to catch a – um, a friend. Getting a bit peckish now, tell the truth. Your – um colleague said she thinks I've missed the boat…"

"She's not my colleague, actually. I'm just holding the fort for Mrs Barker while she's busy. I'm just a – a neighbour…"

"Neighbour, eh? Live close by, do you…?"

"Yes…I'm Corinna de Benedetto…"

"Charming name! Er – Mrs?"

"Only officially…"

"Widower myself…" Gilbert Wardley-Hill introduced himself and produced an engraved card. She gave him one of her own.

"Property, eh? What can you tell me about this place? Seems rather pretty, what I've seen of it…"

By the time Daphne and Silvana came downstairs, Corinna had accepted an invitation to dinner.

"Why does it seem as if we're always saying hullo and goodbye?"

"*Ave atque vale*?"

"Yes… It was so sweet of you to get up especially to see me off…" In the foyer of the busy hotel, they were an island in a sea of arrivals and departures.

"Oh…not a bit…I mean…Don't overdo the rehearsals…I mean, good luck…with the wrist…" She felt her face grow hot.

"Veronica, may I call you when you're back in London?"

"I – um – I should be very sorry if you don't…"

"We could have dinner…"

"That sounds lovely…very nice…Oh! I think that's your taxi…"

"So it is. Blast. Damn it, I'm going to kiss you…"

Over breakfast, Jane said, "I think we should give you Aunt Millicent's notes. I think it's rather wonderful that she was Flora Forde. And then I think you should write her life story."

Veronica sighed. "It's a bone of contention, I'm afraid. You'd better ask Freddy. He thinks there's a mystery and rather blames me for delving…"

"Fred's being a complete ass!" said his sister. "There isn't a mystery. Or at least not one that could possibly affect my little brother's material interests…or mine, for that matter. Here he is. Leave it with me." They watched Freddy, very dapper in a cream linen jacket and trousers with a hint of a pale stripe, help himself to orange juice, ham and mozzarella at the buffet.

"Morning, ladies! Lovely morning!"

"Fred. Just sit down and pour yourself some coffee. Vee's been telling me about her project. Flora Forde."

"Oh? Oh…well, um…"

"And I've told her I think she should take charge of all the Milly archive for her researches, and then if she wants to, she can write the Life."

"Jinx…I'm not sure this is wise, old thing…all sorts of things crawling out of the woodwork…"

Jane Hardcastle sighed. "Fred's convinced that we're not Millicent's heirs after all, right, Fred? Milly's mystery baby, hidden among the evacuees in Somerset, and now all grown up – a pensioner by now – and about to swoop down and scoop the lot. That so, Fred?"

"Well, you know…Granny Partridge…"

"Granny Partridge was an old witch. She didn't approve of Milly. She'd tried to help her, you see, Vee. Help the whole family once poor old Uncle Roger died. She was his younger sister. It was pretty cold charity, I think, but Aunt Marion, Milly's mother, was grateful for all the hand-me-downs, and so forth. Milly had a sick brother – polio – who needed constant medical attention. Even so, Granny P wasn't all that rich, Grandpa P was only a country vicar, and Milly was forced to abandon her dreams of studying music. Granny P found her a job in the offices of some philanthropic-minded elastic stocking firm in Nottingham…"

"Dear, dear, how thoroughly sordid and D H Lawrence…"

"Shut up, Fred…which she hated…"

"And left to seek her fortune in London…I've done a bit of homework."

"Yes. A move that offended Granny P, who thought girls alone in London came to No Good…"

"Vee thinks Milly had quite a time in London, don't you, Vee? And all confessed under the name of Flora Forde…"

"Shh, Freddy…Go on, Jane…"

"Well, Fred knows all this perfectly well. It's no big secret, or at least not now. Milly almost certainly had a wartime romance, probably more than one, and Granny P obviously thought there was a baby. She was ninety-something and in a nursing home, Fred, by the time she told me all this. Rambling a bit, but all her marbles more or less in place. Then Milly married Mr Seale, who was…"

"A rich client of the London advertising agency where she worked as a copywriting assistant."

"Quite. And poor Mr Seale died in an air-raid, and left Milly with two books to her credit which he'd helped her publish, and a small mansion in Somerset, and Granny P muttering about the wages of sin…"

"But what about the *baby*?"

"There wasn't any baby, Fred. Milly had an abortion."

"An abortion? How can you be so sure?"

"Simple. Dad."

"Dad?"

"Yes. He was doing his medical training and went to see Milly in a convalescent home where she was recovering from a hysterectomy, aged twenty-six, from complications arising from a botched abortion. Aka unmentionable female problems *down there*. Actually, the really unmentionable bit was the fact that

551

abortion was a prisonable offence. They tended to hide it under all sorts of euphemisms, even on medical records. Dad told me all this when I was doing gynae as a midwifery first year…"

"No one told me!"

"I did tell you, Fred. You just didn't listen."

"Poor Milly…"

"Yes…although I never got the impression she regretted it much. She never talked about that of course, but it was understood she could never bear children. I think she was happy writing books…"

"And with poor old Cad…he must have been child enough all on his own…"

"She adored him! She was terribly fond of Dad, too, you know. That's why she left everything to us…"

"She actually *left* everything to you? I mean, there's a will?"

"Of course. Milly was meticulous. She left the literary estate to Cadwallader for his lifetime, entailed to us. He could have as much of the profit as he liked, the royalties et cetera, but the estate comes to us. It's ours as of now, Fred…"

"And I don't believe there's anyone who could contest it, even a living offspring," Veronica said. "It's when there isn't a will that things get really complicated, but we can check…"

In the foyer that evening, another goodbye. It was Veronica's turn to wait for an airport taxi.

"All right, all right! I've been a berk…pax?"

"Pax! Don't worry, Freddy…"

"I won't now. Look…Vee…I've actually been quite exceptionally stupid. I can't seem to stop even when I know it's ruinous. I've even been wondering about getting cured…you know, Gam-anon, or whatever they call themselves. Trouble is, I've got to find a way of giving up the fix without thinking life's a bit – well, pointless…"

"Pointless?"

"Well, colourless, anyway. I do suffer from a singular lack of motivation…and cash. I think I just want someone to hug…"

"Oh, *Freddy*…" She hugged him. "Stay in touch, won't you?"

"Of course…and give my love to Julian when you see him…I know you'll both be very happy…"

For some reason, Veronica was rather glad to see Jane appear.

"Vee! Safe journey, darling! Expect a big parcel once we're back. We're off to Monty for the day first thing tomorrow."

"To examine the spoils and keep a hot date with Mrs de Benedetto and a Notary Public…"

xlii: The Old Routine

"Moh! Don't even *ask* how I am, Daffy! I've had the most dreadful shock!"

"Quoddy voddy, dear? As poor dear Hilary used to say…I still don't see why we can't mention him, at least just between ourselves, do you? So, how was your mercy errand to the Notary? I take it was mercy, dear, for the translation…"

"I'm frankly speechless!"

"I expect you'll tell me, dear, all the same. Cheers!"

"Cheers, m'darling… He'd changed it! After all he *said*…I never wanted him to die, poor darling, but once he had, I *was* rather counting…I mean, after *everything*…Freddy and Jane found a new one in his bureau…Stefano says it's legit, written in his own hand and signed by the Battaglias, and dated less than a month ago…I can't *believe* it! Fucking A!"

"Dear me, dear. But I suspect poor Cadwallader Jones was quite traditional in his own way…"

"But both houses! Jane and Freddy! They're not even a proper nephew and niece, only second or is it third cousins! And you know they're partly Jewish on the mother's side! Moh!"

"Really, dear…"

"Well, forget I said that, but I mean, it's *typical*! *And* they've got Millicent's estate anyway!"

"Well, blood *is* thicker than water, dear…I'm changing mine, you know. It's only fair to tell you. After a few little bequests, and I shall make sure poor Silvana can cope, of course, I'm going to leave everything to poor Jonjo, now that Felicity is trying to drag him through the courts for her cut. I think it must be true he's treated her very badly, but he is my son. It's only right, don't you think…?"

"Oh! Well, of course, m'darling. Only fair…If *I* had anything to leave, it would go to the girls, naturally…" She sipped at the strong vodka and gazed out to sea.

"I thought I might leave the Palm Springs diamond to you, dear…I've never had a daughter, you see…and Jonjo hasn't produced any heirs, although there is this new girl, apparently…"

"Oh, Daffy…darling…*I* don't want to talk about your will…"

"But the thing is, in Italy they don't actually like one leaving things away from one's family…the substance, anyway. Did Cadwallader not leave you *anything*?"

"Five thousand…"

"Well, that's better than nothing, dear. Very nice in these straitened times. You can buy yourself a nice little present. What about poor Dorinda?"

"Poor Dorinda! There's a letter of instruction in which he left her his paintings and his china. He's left me the big gilt mirror and that dreadful parody of me…"

"Well, you can always burn it, dear. On the whole, I'd hang onto it. I'm no expert, but I imagine those little National Gallery joke-pieces might be worth something. I think they're frightfully good. He undoubtedly had a talent. But I'd ask Dorinda, dear, because she *is* an expert, and she'll have the rest of them, won't she? The collection. She might even offer to buy it if she decides to sell it on. Are Jane and Freddy planning to sell up?"

"The guest house. *And* they're going to let Dorinda use poor Cad's house while they sell it. They've very kindly put it on my books at the agency. I suppose I ought to be grateful…Moh!" When Corinna's face fell out of its habitual smile, it could look positively aggressive.

"Well at least that's something, dear." Daphne lit a cigarette. "Poor *dear* Cadwallader! I'm going to miss him very much…At my age, one sees so many old friends drop away…depressing. Anyone would have thought Cadwallader was as fit as a flea…Would you be an angel and pour us both another? I have to confess to being a little tired this morning after all the recent excitements…"

Corinna got up, and poured weak ones in Daphne's messy kitchen.

"Thank you, dear. Now, let's be more cheerful! Oh, have you actually put any vodka in this? Oh, you have…I can't taste it. So! Tell me about your new *friend*!"

"Which new friend?"

556

"Mr Wardley-*Hill*. Is that not his name?"

"Oh...Gilbert...well, he's still here, staying at the Albergo. He's rather interested in buying a local property as it happens...he has a little capital he wants to invest, and he's rather enchanted with Monty...I've been showing him round..."

"How very nice for him. I'm sure you'll find him something, dear. Is it true he's some relative of Veronica Dearborn's?"

"He was married to her mother..."

"Oh, *that* Wardley-Hill. Of course. I remember reading. Lloyd's, wasn't he? And old cars, I believe..."

"Classic cars, yes." Corinna's eyes crinkled. "He's mainly a theatre backer. He puts up money for plays and films, you know."

"They call them 'angels', dear. He sounds quite rich..."

"He's got a little to play with, he says. We've been discussing his budget..."

"I see. I do hope he's not making a nuisance of himself..."

"Oh no...he's being a very...courteous escort..." When certain things occurred to Corinna, she could barely suppress a giggle. "He drinks a bit too much – well, like a fish, actually...but I think that's mostly because he's lonely..."

"I see...I expect you're cheering him up. I trust you'll bring him to meet us all on Saturday..."

"Yes. All right, why not? I expect Hedley will adore to meet him…Listen, Daffy? About your birthday dinner…I'm *so* worried about poor Silvana. And Dennis, of course. We thought we might go to the Gazza after all…if they can still have us…would you be happy with that?"

"I'll be happy with whatever you all arrange… I can't discuss it now, dear. I really am very tired today…too much excitement lately, I'm afraid. I plan to be very quiet this afternoon, and read the papers and watch *The Barchester Chronicles* with my feet up. They're puffed up and they ache."

Corinna regarded Daphne's feet. "Poor Daffy! You need a proper pedicure, m'darling. Shall I come round later and give you a foot bath? Paint your toes?"

"You're so good at feet, dear. But not tonight, I think. I'll let you know when I'd like a nice pedicure. Poor Cadwallader always so enjoyed your attentions to his feet, didn't he?"

"Poor Cad…I still feel so – "

"Speaking of feet, I've been reading a terrible story, dear…terrible! I was talking to Jonjo about it only last night. A care assistant in Massachusetts who polished off her elderly clients with a swift injection of insulin. Did you know it's not traceable? It's a body-product, you see. And entirely painless, unless you count the little sting between the toes…The pathologist people don't look there, apparently…I expect it's really a rather good way to go out… Oh, yes, that's how she did it, dear. She was only caught because someone actually saw

558

her…yes, of course you can have another drink, dear, and I should like one as well, but please do put some proper vodka in mine this time…"

2366901R00298

Printed in Great Britain
by Amazon.co.uk, Ltd.,
Marston Gate.